A

JASON ELAM
AND STEVE YOHN

NOVEL

PRESENTED BY

TYNDALE HOUSE
PUBLISHERS, INC.

CAROL STREAM, ILLINOIS

A

RILEY COVINGTON

THRILLER

INSIDE TH

Visit Tyndale online at www.tyndale.com.

TYNDALE and Tyndale's quill logo are registered trademarks of Tyndale House Publishers, Inc.

Inside Threat

Designed by Dean H. Renninger

Published in association with the literary agency of Yates & Yates, LLP, Attorneys and Counselors, Orange, California.

Scripture taken from the Holy Bible, *New International Version,*® *NIV.*® Copyright © 1973, 1978, 1984, 2011 by Biblica, Inc.™ Used by permission of Zondervan. All rights reserved worldwide. www.zondervan.com.

Library of Congress Cataloging-in-Publication Data

Elam, Jason.
  Inside threat : a Riley Covington thriller / Jason Elam and Steve Yohn.
     p. cm.
  ISBN 978-1-4143-3173-7 (pbk.)
  1. Terrorism—Prevention—Fiction. 2. Football players—Fiction. I. Yohn, Steve. II. Title.
  PS3605.L26I57 2011
  813'.6—dc22   2011016087

Printed in the United States of America

17 16 15 14 13 12 11
 7   6   5   4   3   2   1

DEDICATION

LORD, WE THANK YOU first and foremost. You more than anyone know the miracle of this process. We ask that You continue to use this series to surprise people with Your truth.

To Tami and Nancy and all of the kids: Your love and support mean everything. This book wouldn't have happened without you.

To Matt Yates: You have moved from agent to friend to brother. We so appreciate all that you and the rest of the Yates & Yates team have done.

To Karen Watson: We could say the same about you, obviously, replacing *agent* with *publisher*, *brother* with *sister*, and *Y&Y* with *Tyndale House*, and probably getting more team-specific by including names like the editorially amazing Jeremy Taylor, the artistically spectacular Dean Renninger, and the assistantly irreplaceable Stephanie Broene, but other than that . . .

ACKNOWLEDGMENTS

And finally, to all of you who have been reading through this series. Thanks for your unfailing support and encouragement. Picturing your smiles and laughter is what keeps the fingers moving over that laptop keyboard on those cold, lonely, basement mornings.

SATURDAY, SEPTEMBER 10, 11:35 A.M. EDT

WASHINGTON, DC

The September sun soaked into Scott Ross's face so deeply that he could almost feel his skin browning. *Yeah, baby, brush a little butter on me, and you'll cook up a nice golden, flaky crust.* The leaves around him hadn't started to drop yet, and the breeze that rustled them smelled fresh and clean—not always a given in the nation's capital.

The moment of peace contrasted sharply with the insanity taking place around him. For Scott, as director of the counterterrorism division's Special Operations Group Bravo, life was always a little crazy. But whenever a credible tip came in on an impending attack, it was Katy bar the door.

Scott and his team had gotten the call less than twenty minutes after Malik Abdul-Tawwab walked into the Washington, DC, Metropolitan Police Fourth District station.

Less than half an hour after that, Scott was in an interrogation room getting the scoop.

Malik Abdul-Tawwab was a young, second-generation American Muslim who had been frustrated with his life. With no work and no prospect of that situation meaningfully changing, he had become bitter toward the land of his birth. It wasn't long before he found himself drawn to a radical group that had formed within his mosque. The talk of jihad, threats of revenge, and promises of a better life for all Muslims struck a chord with him. Gradually what he once had considered *his* homeland transformed into *their* homeland.

Then, three weeks ago, this ten-person cell received a call informing them that it was time to put their talk into action. That night, the imam asked for a volunteer who was willing to become *shahid*, a martyr for the sake of Allah. All ten members of the group raised their hands, including Abdul-Tawwab. All were ready to kill; all were ready to die. However, only one was needed, and the one chosen was a seventeen-year-old named Taqi Abdur-Razzaq.

Although disappointed for himself, Abdul-Tawwab was happy for his friend and proud to be part of an operation that would strike terror into the corrupt hearts of the American public.

At least, he had been proud. Then the other attacks had started happening.

The first took place eight days ago. An American-born Muslim walked into the Alamo in San Antonio, Texas, and opened fire with an assault weapon, killing eight and wounding twelve before an off-duty police officer managed to put him down with a .45 cal to the chest.

Four days after that, a young Islamic man on a helicopter tour over Gettysburg, Pennsylvania, pulled the pins on a couple of M67 grenades. According to witnesses on the ground, it looked like the pilot had yanked the chopper to the left just before the explosions. As a result, the wreckage crashed into a field rather than the intended crowd that had gathered to watch a Civil War reenactment. Even so, four were killed, and seventeen were wounded by the flying debris, including a five-year-old who was blinded by a severe head wound and a three-year-old who would never walk again.

That's when the reality of what Abdur-Razzaq was about to do set in. And the following day Malik Abdul-Tawwab walked into the police station. That was three days ago.

"Foxtrot One, this is Foxtrot Three. You still awake?" Gilly Posada asked through Scott's earpiece.

"Yeah, Foxtrot Three. Ready and raring to go."

"You sure? 'Cause I've got you in my scope, and you look like you're in happy, happy dreamland." Posada was one of two snipers Scott had positioned in the vicinity of this bench.

"I told you I'm awake. Now point that thing somewhere else before you put someone's eye out."

Gilly Posada was one of seven "Foxtrots" Scott had scattered near the reflecting pool that stretched between the Washington Monument and the Lincoln Memorial. The *Foxtrot* moniker itself was Scott's idea and had much less to do with the NATO phonetic alphabet than it did his favorite album by the band Genesis, whose 1981 *Abacab* Tour T-shirt he was currently sporting under a heavy, green army trench coat.

Alongside Posada was his spotter, Ted Hummel. Matt Logan was manning a second sniper rifle, with Carlos Guitiérrez spotting for him. And Kim Li and Steve Kasay were on a bench across the pool from Scott, battling away on a plastic chess set.

According to Abdul-Tawwab's story, he had seen a map of the planned attack that showed Abdur-Razzaq coming along the reflecting pool toward the steps of the Lincoln Memorial. Once there, he would seek out a tour group, then detonate an explosive vest. That was plan A.

Abdul-Tawwab also claimed that they were having trouble,

putting the vest together, since none of them had done it before and they were mostly working off Internet sites. So if the vest turned out to be a no-go, plan B was to open up with an automatic weapon and take down as many people as possible—not quite as effective as the vest, but effective enough.

Back at SOG Bravo headquarters, Scott's team of analysts had been monitoring cameras at the four key entry points of the reflecting pool plaza. Each possible suspect was quickly scanned through facial recognition software. So far, though, no hits.

Patience was not a virtue that came naturally to Scott, and his antsiness was starting to burn off the groove he was getting from the sun. *Come on, hajji wannabe, show yourself. I want to get home in time to put James to bed.*

It was nearly two years since Scott had sustained multiple fractures of his leg during an operation to stop an electromagnetic pulse bomb. While in the hospital, the infatuation he had for his lead analyst, Tara Walsh, soon turned into mutual admiration and, finally, love. These two examples of opposites attracting were married eight months later.

Soon after, Tara discovered she was pregnant—a fact that inspired Scott to insist for the next six weeks that everyone at the office call him Captain Testosterone, much to Tara's chagrin. Then, six months ago today, little James Gerald Ross was born— James for Scott's former boss, killed in the line of duty, and Gerald for the late father of Scott's best friend, Riley Covington.

Seriously, if this waste of oxygen makes me miss my boy's—

"Foxtrot One, this is Base. I think we've got him," came the voice of analyst Evie Cline.

Scott fought hard not to react. "How sure are you?"

"I'd say 85 percent. This facial recognition software is crap."

"I need better than that. Where is he?"

"We just got the hit, and he's already about to pass you. Sorry, Foxy, but as I said, this facial recognition software is slower than—"

"Don't need a metaphor, just a description," Scott said, as, with a groan, he slowly spun his feet to the ground. As he did, a young African American man in a black jacket and a black cap turned quickly toward him. Scott stared at the ground and scratched his marriage-expanded belly.

"He's an African American male, black jacket, tan pants, black baseball cap."

Swell, he thought as he peripherally watched the suspect slide past. The young man was still watching him, so Scott loudly hawked up a large wad of phlegm and watched it slowly drop to the ground.

"Ewww," Evie said, along with at least three of the Foxtrots.

Scott got up and stretched, then casually started following Abdur-Razzaq. The easiest thing would have been to let Posada or Logan send a 7.62 full metal jacket into this fellow's cranium. However, he needed better than 85 percent to give that order.

Besides, I want to talk with this idiot.

"Foxtrot Six and Seven," Scott said softly to Li and Kasay, "start arguing over the chess game. I want him looking somewhere other than back at me."

Suddenly, a string of profanities echoed across the reflecting pool. Li was standing over Kasay and pointing at the board.

When the would-be terrorist's head was turned toward the ruckus, Scott quickened his pace, making up quite a bit of ground.

Now, Kasay flipped the board off the bench and stood up chest-to-chest with Li.

"Careful, boys, we don't want DC's finest stumbling in on us." Scott had purposely chosen not to inform the MPDC of the details of this operation as a protection against heroes and leaks—both of which could get a lot of people killed.

As they neared the end of the pool, the number of tourists began to grow. Scott quickened his pace. Abdur-Razzaq had just moved into a crowd at the base of the steps leading up to the memorial, when he turned around. His eyes locked onto Scott's, and Scott knew he was burned.

"Put your hands up," Scott commanded, quickly drawing his harnessed Bushmaster assault rifle from under his jacket. "Put up your hands! Now!"

But rather than surrendering, Abdur-Razzaq clenched his arm around the neck of one of the now-screaming onlookers and placed a pistol to her temple. "Drop your weapon, or I swear I'll blow her head off," Abdur-Razzaq yelled.

Part of Scott was relieved that this homegrown terrorist cell's apparent incompetence in all things explosive had kept him from being diced into small morsels. The other part was ready to kill this weasel.

"You drop your weapon," Scott yelled back for lack of a more creative option.

"You drop yours!"

"You drop yours!"

The voices of Li and Kasay joined in as they finally pushed their way through the fleeing mass of bodies. "Drop your weapon now!"

Instead, Abdur-Razzaq pushed the barrel of his pistol harder against his hostage's head. "I'm going to put a bullet in her, man! I swear I will! On three she's going to die! One! Two!"

"Whoa, whoa, whoa," Scott called out, moving his weapon out perpendicular to himself. This situation was way out of hand. "No one needs to die today."

Slowly, he lifted his rifle's harness over his head and laid the weapon on the ground. "See, weapon's down."

"Now those two," Abdur-Razzaq said, motioning toward Li and Kasay.

"Wrong-o, wingnut," Li answered. "How about I give you until three before I put 115 grains of lead into that empty brain cavity of yours?"

Still looking at Scott, Abdur-Razzaq answered, "Tell him to drop it! I'm not messing with you!" Sweat was pouring off the young man's face, and Scott could see scared determination in his eyes.

"Agent Li, hostile attitudes like yours don't fully meet with our government's new kinder, gentler policy toward whacked-out terrorist nut jobs. Put your weapons down," Scott said, his voice growing firmer with the last sentence. "Now!"

Li and Kasay obeyed.

Turning back toward Abdur-Razzaq, Scott said, "So, the weapons are down. What now?"

"Now? Now I die a *shahid*, and I take you American pigs with me," he said, still clutching the woman tightly but pointing the gun at Scott.

"Wait, wait, wait," Scott said, lifting his hands up. "What do you mean 'you American pigs'? Dude, you're as American as baseball, hot dogs, apple pie, and government-owned motors! Don't be giving me 'you Americans.'"

"Shut your mouth! You don't know what you're talking about! I don't belong to this nation of infidels! I belong to the nation of Allah's warriors!"

"And I belong to the nation of tall, goateed fat guys," Scott said, trying to buy time, praying for Abdur-Razzaq to make a mistake and give him an opening. "Allah's warriors? Give me a break! I've seen your file, man. Your real name's Byron, for the love of—"

Scott felt the bullet strike his chest even before he realized Abdur-Razzaq had fired. As he fell backward, two sounds echoed in his ears—the report of Abdur-Razzaq's gun, and the *thwip-pop* of the head shot coming from one or both of his team's snipers.

Scott landed with a splash in eighteen inches of water. As he lay there groaning, two thoughts played in his mind—*Thank God for the inventor of Kevlar* and *I'm going to be hurting for a good, long time.*

CHAPTER TWO

"*FM, no static at all . . .*" Donald Fagen sang through the earbuds. Walter Becker picked up the guitar riff, which ultimately led into Riley Covington's favorite part of the song—Pete Christlieb's smooth sax solo. It transported him to a warm Southern California night, the lights of the city stretched out below him, the sweet, rich smell of jasmine thick in the air. *Yeah, that's—*

The sound of air brakes popped Riley back into reality.

"Cleveland," he grumbled to himself as the team bus came to a stop in front of the Hyatt Regency, "the 'Well, she's got a nice personality' of American cities."

"What are you mumbling about over there, Pach?" tight end Don Bernier asked from across the aisle. *Pach* was Riley's nickname from his time playing with the Air

Force Academy Falcons and came from a comparison to the fast, hard-hitting Apache attack helicopter.

"I was just saying how thrilled I am to be back on the beautiful shores of Lake Erie."

"Come on, buddy, it's no different than any other city. It's got a hotel and a stadium. Beyond that, who cares?"

"True enough," Riley said, as he dropped his iPod into a small duffel and stood up to go. *Another city, another game— maybe we win, maybe we lose—another flight back to a city that's home but not really home, all to start another week of practice to prepare for another game. It's all feeling so . . . what's the word? Not monotonous . . . Meaningless. That's it; my life is starting to feel meaningless.*

Getting back into football had been a difficult decision for Riley. Two years ago, when New York City was rendered uninhabitable by an EMP attack, Riley had abandoned the rest of the football season in order to aid the refugees who were waiting their turn to be transported to safety. It had taken nearly two months to evacuate the last of those who wanted to leave the city. But finally it was time for the replanting of the Big Apple to begin.

Riley, his bodyguard and constant companion Skeeter Dawkins, and his friend and former teammate Keith Simmons were each faced with a decision—should I stay or should I go? There was plenty of work that could be done helping out the thousands of workers that now were descending on the city. But their hearts had really been drawn to the victims of the attack. Becoming part of the rebuilding support staff didn't have that same sort of emotional pull.

After a few evenings of debate, the friends decided to part ways—Riley and Skeeter to Riley's home in Kenai, Alaska, and Keith back home to Denver. As the months went on, their paths continued to diverge even further. While Riley and Skeeter took the time to collect moose and bears and very large salmon,

Keith took his time to collect kids—NYC refugees, to be precise. By the time he was done, nine of the ten bedrooms in his house had little munchkins sleeping in them; he was sleeping in the tenth.

More than eight thousand children had been left parentless as a result of that terrible day. There were some whose parents had been killed, but there were also some whose parents just hadn't been able to locate them. Sometimes it was because the kids were too young to be able to communicate who they were; others were just too traumatized. For a time, the reuniting of a parent with his or her child was almost a nightly story on the evening news—two came from Keith Simmons's own house. But soon, the reunions trickled to weekly, then monthly, and now they had almost stopped.

Riley filed into the hotel lobby, where a team staffer handed him an envelope with his key in it. Seeing he was only on the fourth floor, he opted for the stairs instead of waiting for an elevator.

His feet echoed up the thinly carpeted stairwell as, for what seemed to be the thousandth time, he seriously questioned his decision to return to football.

Admittedly, a large part came from simple boredom. You can only shoot so many elk, and you can only dig so many clams.

The need to be challenged, to constantly be pushing himself beyond what he should be able to do, was a big part of what made Riley who he was. It was this drive that had helped him to excel in everything he had attempted—Air Force Special Ops, football, paramilitary, even bringing comfort to the hurting. "If you're going to commit to something, give it all you've got," his late father had told him many times.

I've got no challenge anymore, he had thought. *Nothing to strive for. But if I come back to football after two years off, that would be a huge thing! And on top of that, if I made all-star? I mean, who does that?*

Reaching his floor, Riley entered the hallway.

Having made the decision to reenter football, the first challenge he had faced was the Washington Warriors owner, Rick Bellefeuille. Rumor was that the two weeks Bellefeuille had spent trapped in a New York football stadium had mellowed the man. However, if that was true, it certainly wasn't evident in the conversation Riley had with him.

A very long two hours passed while Riley struggled to keep his pride and anger in check. Finally Bellefeuille had agreed to allow him back on the team on the condition that Riley cut his salary by a third and double his required public relations appearances. So Riley had swallowed his pride and signed— and spent every day thereafter wondering what he had been thinking.

The key card slid in and out, the light turned from red to green, and Riley opened the door to his room. It looked like every other hotel room he'd been in. He dropped his duffel onto the bed—a valet would be up later with his overnight bag—grabbed a bottle of water from the mini-fridge, and fell into a chair by the window. Pulling back a corner of the curtain, he saw that the only thing outside was Cleveland, so he kept the drapes closed.

Turning the TV on to FoxNews, he saw a big ALERT banner. A senator was holding a press conference at the Lincoln Memorial. He mentally tuned it out.

Soon after the incident earlier today, a shaken Tara Ross had called Riley to say that Scott had been shot but was okay. A couple of hours later, Scott himself had called to give him a rundown of the op as only Scott could. When the laughter had finally died down and they said their good-byes, Riley was left with a feeling of relief that Scott was all right but also with a twinge of jealousy.

Hadn't Riley always been the one who had it all together? Wasn't he the one with the sense of purpose to his life? Now, here was Scott Ross saving the world one terrorist at a time; here was Keith Simmons saving the world one kid at a time; and here was Riley Covington saving the game one tackle at a time.

Give it this season, just to show you can *come back,* he thought. *After that, you . . . Wait, isn't that Senator Andrews?*

Riley quickly turned the volume up. He still didn't pay much attention to the words. Based on the story Scott had told him, the senator was probably less than a hundred yards from an active crime scene. Andrews had chosen the timing for his presser just right, so that the lights from the memorial were starting to glow in the growing dusk, while the white lights from cameras revealed him in all his congressional glory.

Media hog, Riley thought.

But the senator wasn't the reason Riley was watching so intently. It was on the fifth question, when the camera widened to catch a view of Carl Cameron taking his turn from the front row, that he saw her. Off to the senator's right, staring intently into the crowd, stood Khadi Faroughi. Then just that quickly, the shot tightened again, and Khadi disappeared.

Riley grabbed for the remote to rewind the picture, then realized he wasn't at home and there was no DVR. He put the control back on the table and continued to watch. But soon the senator finished his moment of exploitative grandeur, and the shot cut back to the Fox studios, where a panel was waiting to analyze the man's words.

Riley turned off the TV, then stretched out on the bed and stared at the darkening ceiling. Khadi looked as beautiful as ever, with her dark hair, olive skin, and sharp Persian features. And beyond just her physical appearance, there was a self-assuredness—a sense of strength and control—that only heightened her beauty and appeal.

As he lay there, his mind played through scenes of his and Khadi's time together. There were good memories—hours spent talking through life, laughter over shared cups of coffee, accidental touches, intimate words. There were also not-so-good memories—angry prayers to God for allowing him to fall in love with a woman he couldn't have, holding her bleeding body after she had been shot, saying good-bye.

According to Scott, Khadi said she had made the decision to leave SOG Bravo because she was tired of being a target for bad guys' guns. But when he pressed her, she admitted that there were just too many memories of Riley there for her to stick around. She needed a clean break. She had heard of an opportunity in a firm that provided security to senators and congressmen, and she had decided to take it.

Riley had received an e-mail from her soon after she left telling him of her decision—really flowering up why this was such a great career move for her—and wishing him the best. He hadn't responded. He hadn't known how.

That had been eighteen months ago. Every now and then Riley found a way to get some information about her from Scott, but when he heard she had started seeing a guy from the FBI, he stopped asking.

"Not that I know of," had been Scott's response when asked if Khadi's new man was a Muslim. *And that's what burns me most of all. The one thing that kept us apart—her Islam and my Christianity—doesn't even matter to her anymore.*

Riley lay there a long time brooding in the slowly deepening darkness until someone pounded on his door and announced, "Team meeting in ten" before continuing down the hall.

"Another night, another meeting," Riley said to no one as he grabbed his notebook and headed out of his room.

"And I'm calling for a top-down investigation into these events. Everyone needs to be examined. Why should Homeland Security Secretary Stanley Porter feel safe in his position when the American people don't feel safe in their own homes?"

Khadi Faroughi did her best not to roll her eyes. *Mr. Opportunity* was the nickname given to Senator Clayson Andrews by all but his most senior staff members, because he never missed a chance to get his face on camera. Now he was calling out Stanley Porter, her old boss at the counterterrorism division—a man who had probably over the years had a hand in saving more lives than the number of votes this blowhard had received in his last election.

"Does this mean you're calling for Secretary Porter's resignation?" asked an MSNBC reporter who was known for being especially dim.

"Certainly not . . . yet," Andrews answered, letting his trademark smile creep onto his face—the smile that had helped him win three terms in the Senate and bed somewhere around half the female lobbyists in town. "Seriously, I'm not calling for anyone's head. All I'm doing is calling for an investigation. These attacks have to stop. And if this current crew at Homeland Security can't do it, then we need to get some people in there who can. The lives of the American people are too valuable to worry about tramping on anyone's feelings or whether or not somebody loses their job.

"Next, let's go to . . ."

Tyson Bryson, Andrews's chief of staff and a man whose parents had apparently hated him since birth, leaned forward and whispered something into the senator's ear. Khadi immediately went on alert.

"Actually, ladies and gentlemen, it looks like my time is up. Thank you for your time, and may God bless America."

As the senator backed away from the podium, Khadi stepped to his right side, while J.D. Little, the second member of the senator's two-person security detail, flanked his left. They didn't expect any trouble, but on a night like tonight, you never knew.

Khadi had argued vehemently against holding the press conference right next to where the thwarted attack had taken place. Not only was there the usual danger of the random wacko, but there was also the very real possibility of a secondary strike—a second gunman or an explosive device set to detonate on the first responders and the crowds that had gathered to watch. But the lure of the photo op was too great for Mr. Opportunity. So he went, putting himself, his staff, and his security detail at risk. All so he could get those pearly whites on the network news.

"Guess you were wrong, Faroughi," Andrews said as they walked toward the waiting limo.

"We're not to the car yet, sir," Khadi replied, using the word *sir* to replace the one she really had in mind.

"You worry too much," he said with a wink.

"And you worry too little. Besides, worrying is my job."

"I've told you before, Khadi, if you want a job with a little less worry and a lot more fun, all you've got to do is—"

"Please duck your head, sir," Little said to the senator as he opened the door for him.

"What? Oh, yes. Thanks, Little," Andrews said as he climbed into the vehicle.

Thank you, Khadi mouthed to Little.

Little shook his head and rolled his eyes in response.

It had taken the senator exactly six hours from the time Khadi first began her position in his security detail to make a pass at her.

She had been sent to his house by Congressional Protection, Inc., a small, very specialized, and very solid security firm. She arrived at 5:00 p.m. for an overnight shift. All was quiet until 11:00 p.m. She was standing in front of a bank of television monitors when she heard someone enter the security office. She watched the senator's approaching reflection in the glass of the screens. He was wearing magenta silk pajamas and he carried a drink. The smell of the alcohol arrived well before he did.

"Care for a little drinky-winky, my lovely Persian queen?" With one hand he held the glass in front of her, while his free hand slowly slid down her side from rib to thigh.

Never taking her eyes off the monitors, Khadi said, "I'll give you three seconds to take your hand off me before I shoot you in the kneecap. Then I'll go upstairs and tell your wife why you're down here bleeding."

"Oh, my . . . I guess I should have expected the infamous Khadijah Faroughi to be a fighter," an undeterred Andrews said with a laugh and a squeeze to Khadi's backside.

Before the senator had time to react, Khadi whipped her pistol out and pressed it to his forehead. His glass dropped to the ground and the front of his silk pajamas darkened.

Through gritted teeth, Khadi said, "Senator, I will watch over you and protect you. You can call me at all hours of the day or night, and I will come running. I will fight for you and I will die for you, because that is my job. But one thing I will not do is allow you to disrespect me. Do we have an understanding?"

The senator didn't respond. He just stared with terrified eyes.

Realizing that holding a gun to a US senator's head probably wasn't a great career advancement move, she lowered her weapon and turned toward the monitors.

When she heard the door to the office latch closed, she dropped into a chair, put her head in her hands, and cried. *What have you done?* she thought. *You left the one job you've ever had that you absolutely loved. You were born for SOG! Why would you do such a stupid thing?*

But she knew why she had done it. There was never a real question. The fact was that Riley Covington's ghost was all over that office. Everywhere she looked, she saw him—laughing with Scott, looking over Evie Cline's shoulder, sharing a Gatorade with herself out in the courtyard.

She couldn't do it. She had to move beyond Riley, and the only way to do that was to get away from the Special Operations Group.

Now here she was, crying in an office, the stench of urine and bourbon in the air, having been groped by a senator, and quite possibly facing charges for assault with a deadly weapon.

But surprisingly, the next morning the senator came down like nothing had ever happened. The incident was never mentioned then or since. He still made verbal passes at her almost daily, but he never again touched her.

After that initial horror, Khadi's life had developed a routine. She found new friendships. She was even spending some time with a real up-and-comer in the FBI. Sweet guy, hardworking, great looking, treated her like a princess; he was everything a girl would want, but . . . *but he's not Riley Covington*. There was still just something missing.

As she slid into the limo and sat across from Andrews, who was clearly only half listening to Bryson's ramblings, she wondered what Riley was doing. She knew he was in Cleveland. *But it's not like I'm following his every move. Everyone knows the Warriors are playing an away game against the Bulldogs this weekend.*

Poor guy's got to be worried sick about Scott. Even with all the junk Scott put him through, Riley was always such a good friend to him. But that's just the kind of guy Riley is.

"So, Khadi, about this other job," the senator said with a wink.

Khadi shook her head, stared out the window, and dreamed of what her life could have been.

SATURDAY, SEPTEMBER 10, 4:35 P.M. EDT
DEARBORN, MICHIGAN

The building shook with the sound. Even above the din of the machinery—and the voices struggling to be heard over that machinery—it was clear what was happening outside. Another Michigan thunderstorm.

Majid Alavi shook his head angrily. He knew what this meant. After nine hours of making sure the Visteon's transmission control modules would actually shift Ford vehicles when Ford vehicles need to be shifted, he would get to go home to his third-floor apartment to clean up the puddle that would inevitably have formed somewhere in his bedroom or hallway.

"Never on the tile," he grumbled, "always on carpet." His temporary home was permanently musty and, depending on the level of humidity outside, carried a varying level of odor reminiscent of teenage locker room.

As he was about to curse under his breath,

a thought hit him. *But wait, tonight is different. What do I care what happens to that dump? Let the roof cave in and the apartment flood. It's not my problem anymore.*

Another blast caused Alavi to look up toward the factory's high windows. He noticed several others doing the same thing, slipping their earphones back to see if they could catch the next strike. His eye caught that of his cousin, Kaliq, who smiled and used his hands to imitate a missile striking the ground and the subsequent explosion.

Alavi grinned and nodded, then turned back to his work. Kaliq would be one of the few that he would actually miss. His cousin understood the stakes. He hadn't caved in to the lure of American decadence.

Although born twenty-two years ago in Mishawaka, Indiana, Alavi considered himself no more an American than Osama bin Laden. He was a Muslim first and foremost, and the followers of Allah were not limited by man-made borders. Allah was his president and almighty king, and the domain of his king was worldwide.

Ninety minutes later, Alavi was dodging puddles left behind by the afternoon squall. The parking lot hadn't been repaved in what seemed like decades, part of a Chapter 11 cost-cutting decision. The result was an enormous stretch of asphalt that contained more lakes than Minnesota and Manitoba combined. As Alavi and the other employees made their way to their cars, he imagined the view from high above must resemble that of a mass of small frogs hopping their way through bumper-to-bumper traffic.

The lingering humidity from the warm storm caused his shirt to cling to his torso. He knew his physique was surprisingly muscular for his seemingly wiry frame. From the time he was a teenager, Alavi had considered his body a tool for Allah. He constantly exercised and was very careful about what he ate. He took care of himself the same way he was so meticulous about cleaning his guns, and for the same reasons. You never knew when Allah would call you up for service, so you had to be ready.

"Majid, wait up!"

Alavi turned to see Kaliq splashing toward him. When he reached his cousin, Kaliq put an arm around his shoulder.

As they walked, Kaliq said, "So, you're really going through with it."

The sentence came off more as a question than a statement, and Alavi at first wasn't sure how to answer him.

"Allah has called us to serve him in the name of jihad. Do you doubt that what we're doing is right?" Alavi asked defensively.

"Of course not, cousin," Kaliq answered quickly, steering them both around an old white and rusty Taurus in order to avoid a particularly expansive lake. "You know better than that. You saw how desperately I begged the imam to let me participate."

"You're right. I'm sorry. I would have loved to have you alongside me. But you know as well as I that the correct decision was made. You have a family at home to take care of."

"Bah," Kaliq said with a dismissive wave of his free hand.

As they walked, they took less and less notice of the puddles. Once shoes and pant legs reached a certain level of soaked, it just didn't matter anymore.

Alavi knew that it was hard for Kaliq to see him go. Kaliq's family had pushed him into a marriage when he was just eighteen to a girl that he didn't love and hardly even knew. In the four years since then, she had only managed to give him two daughters, no sons, and a lot of headaches.

As the cousins had spent their teen years with just two houses separating them, they had always talked about fighting together. They had dreamed up plots to strike devastating blows upon the Great Satan. Often their ideas would become bigger and bigger and the results more and more ridiculous until they would both end up losing themselves in laughter the rest of the night.

Through it all, there was one thing they knew. They were going to fight for Allah, and they were going to do it together.

But now that the time had actually come, one cousin was going while the other was staying behind.

"There are other ways to carry out jihad than becoming *shahid*, dear cousin," Alavi said.

"True. But none so glorious." The disappointment in Kaliq's voice put Alavi at a loss for words. They continued walking in silence.

The cousins came to a stop next to Kaliq's Jeep Cherokee.

Alavi was surprised to see tears in his cousin's eyes as Kaliq said to him, "Go with God, my brother. Take courage from the righteousness of your actions. And may *al-Malaikah* guard your every move."

"And may the angels watch over you, too," Alavi said, pulling Kaliq into an embrace.

After a moment, Alavi let go and walked away without saying another word. As much as he loved Kaliq, his cousin was now of the past. And as he was trained to remember, the past is past. All family, all relationships, everything was now in Allah's hands. From here on, nothing mattered except the future, the mission, the calling.

Alavi threaded through two more rows of cars before he came to his little black Focus. Suddenly, a thought struck him, and he began to laugh as he looked around the parking lot. *How is it that we can despise this capitalistic system so much, yet when it comes to cars, we all still buy American?* Shaking his head, he got into his tiny Ford.

With one last look to confirm that he had, in fact, put his bag on the backseat this morning—trainings past echoed in his brain: *Stupid, little mistakes are the ones that get you killed before you accomplish your mission*—he started the car, backed out, and headed south.

CHAPTER FIVE

SUNDAY, SEPTEMBER 11, 12:40 P.M. EDT

CLEVELAND, OHIO

"Okay, Riley, now tell me how you're feeling right now—I mean, *really* feeling."

"Angry."

"Good, good. Now, try putting that into a sentence. Like, 'I'm really feeling angry right now because . . .' You know, then you can fill in the blank with whatever. Just remember to make it real, make it raw! Go!"

Riley stared at the producer—*Narbinger? Narvinger? Novinger—that's it, Mike Novinger—*trying to keep control. *Come on, watch what you say! Don't forget you've got a mic on! Think about it before you open your mouth! WWJD, buddy!*

Typically, with a little bit of mental reasoning and a few deep breaths, Riley was able to maintain a solid handle on his words and actions. Unfortunately, this time his inner monologue didn't quite have the desired effect on his outer response.

Slowly standing from his bench in the Cleveland Bulldogs' visitors' locker room, he leaned into Novinger's personal space. He could feel his face reddening, and he fought to control the volume of his words. "You want to know what I'm feeling? Really? Then how's this? I'm really feeling angry right now because I've had a camera in my face since 7:30 this morning!"

"But that's just part of—" the producer sputtered.

"*And* . . . I'm really, *really* feeling angry right now because some obnoxious little Chris Berman wannabe keeps asking me every five minutes what I'm feeling and why it is that I'm feeling the way I'm feeling! *Comprende?* That clear enough for you?"

"Sure, Riley," Novinger stammered. "You know, I don't mean to be such a pain. I'm just trying to do my job the best I know how."

Riley sighed deeply and looked toward the ground. It was true that, ultimately, this guy wasn't to blame. Instead, his anger should be directed toward the owner, Rick Bellefeuille. He was the one who contacted HBO and offered up the ultimate subject for their new PFL series, *Sunday Warriors*.

He could imagine Bellefeuille's pitch: *"Who better to follow around the entire day of the game with three cameras, multiple mics, and a producer/sports psychologist who could really get into the mind of the player than the ultimate Sunday Warrior—Captain America himself, Riley Covington?"*

Great plan, Bellefeuille, and if you get your team a little more publicity and yourself some extra spending cash in the bargain, well then that's just bully for everyone around. Everyone except for the zoo animal you're putting on exhibit!

Lifting his head so that his mouth was right next to Novinger's ear, Riley put his hand around the back of the man's head and said, "Listen, I know you're only doing your job. It's just that I don't like your job. And I don't like that I've been forced to be part of your job. So I'll tell you what: I'm going to go hit the head. While I'm gone, I'll see if I can get myself back into the 'It's okay, Riley, you're only going to be exploited for one day' frame of mind. Deal?"

"Sure, Riley. It's a deal."

Riley could feel his hand dampening with the man's perspiration. He started to let go, but then clamped his hand tighter. "One more thing. I'd consider it a great favor if you muted my mic for the next five minutes. Some things are just personal, and if anything like that made it into your little show, well, let's just say you've read my bio—you don't want to have Captain America out gunning for you, do you?"

"Of course not. I mean, of course so," Novinger grunted as Riley gave his neck a final squeeze. "I mean, no problem; we'll mute the mic."

Riley released the man, then walked past two of the cameramen. As he did, he heard Novinger whisper, "Did you get all that?"

He turned his head in time to see one of the boom mic operators holding a thumb up. "Frickin' awesome," the operator whispered back.

Shaking his head, Riley continued onto the sticky tiles of the bathroom and shower area. Immediately, the stench hit him—a miasma of odors emanating from years of opponents' nervous stomachs combining with this week's new offerings.

Swallowing back a gag, Riley found an empty stall and closed the door behind him. Thankfully, he didn't really have to go—the thought of any part of his anatomy actually coming into contact with that chipped, semi-whitish fixture caused another wave of revulsion. He was just looking for a place to get away for a few moments, and this was the one place he hoped he could get at least a semblance of privacy.

Well done, he chided himself. *You lost your cool and gave them exactly what they wanted.* He punched the metal divider with his taped and gloved hand, rattling the whole rickety stall system and causing groans of protest from a few of the players who were leaning against it trying to regain their composure.

"Sorry, guys," Riley called out. Then the picture flashed in his mind of all these huge, tough guys sprawled on this disgusting floor leaning against these just-as-disgusting dividers, and he began to laugh. It started small but quickly grew. Soon he had tears pouring out his eyes, and he was having a hard time standing up.

Meanwhile, the door slammed on the stall next to him, and someone noisily barked out the contents of his stomach. This sent Riley over the edge, and he dropped onto the seat of the toilet.

"It ain't funny, Pach," a voice grumbled from next door.

"Sure it is, Panda," Riley answered merrily, recognizing the voice. "Every week, you sound like you're giving birth to a baby through your esophagus."

"Bite me," Panda answered, starting to laugh himself. "By the way, this week it's a boy."

Five minutes later, Riley emerged from the bathroom. He and Panda had gone back and forth about the newly arrived baby, covering topics from his name to his skin tone to his future college education.

The protests from the other stalls finally shut them up, and they quietly stepped from their stalls. It was a respect thing. Each player got ready for a game in his own way. The one element that was typically honored by all was quietness. The two apologized to their teammates, then snickered on their way out.

Riley arrived back at his locker and the waiting crew. But not before deciding that he was taking himself way too seriously. His pride was getting in the way again—an affliction that he constantly found himself battling. It wasn't easy keeping a small head when there seemed to be a television, newspaper, or magazine story every other day that talked about how he was America's hero and the greatest thing since frozen waffles.

The worst thing he could do would be to start believing his own press. Chasing down glory eventually turned into a losing proposition—it always did. Ultimately, why should he care what people thought of him? Whose affirmation was he trying to gain, after all?

He remembered the apostle Paul writing, "For to me, to live is Christ and to die is gain." So his life wasn't really about himself anyway. *Just be yourself and try to show Jesus in how you're living. Beyond that, who really gives a flying flip?*

As he sat down at his locker prepared to apologize to Novinger, he could see that the producer had tears in his down-turned eyes and was desperately trying to suppress a grin. Riley looked around and saw that the rest of the crew were in various failing stages of laughter suppression.

"So I'm assuming you didn't mute the mic," Riley said to Novinger, causing a brief snigger from two of the cameramen.

The producer tried a couple of times to answer, but each time ended up looking at the bench again—his shoulders silently bouncing up and down.

Riley could see that they were beginning to attract attention, which could mean trouble. He was about to tell Novinger that he and his crew better cool it, when he saw defensive coordinator Mick Fields come stomping through the locker room.

Too late.

"What's the matter with you people? Are you a bunch of amateurs? Aren't you supposed to be from HBO, the big leagues? In case you haven't noticed, I've got a team here trying to get ready for a PFL game—that's the Professional Football League, the big show—and you're all here tittering like a bunch of schoolgirls reading a *Tiger Beat* magazine! Well, I'm not having it! Get out of my locker room—all of you!"

Novinger began to pull out a piece of paper from his back pocket. "But we've got permission from Mr. Bellefeuille to—"

"Save it! I don't care if you've got a signed affidavit from the

Almighty executed by seven flaming archangels; I won't have you disturbing my locker room. Now get out! You can catch up with Mr. Superstar on the field!"

As the crew gathered up their equipment and headed toward the doors, the crimson-faced coach swung around to Riley. "And you—don't think I won't throw you out with them!"

"Sorry," Riley said sheepishly. "My bad. Seriously, Coach Fields, it won't happen again."

Fields glared at him for a time. Seeing the sorry look on Riley's face mollified him somewhat. Grunting, he turned to go.

"Oh, Coach, one more thing," Riley called after a few steps. Fields stopped and slowly turned, fire in his eyes. "If you happen to see a little kid named Ralph back in the bathrooms, would you mind sending him my way?"

Originating from just beyond the doors of the locker room, the sound of the HBO crew completely losing it echoed through the tunnels of the stadium.

CHAPTER SIX

SUNDAY, SEPTEMBER 11, 2:35 P.M. EDT
CLEVELAND, OHIO

The eyes—watch the eyes! Riley backpedaled, staring hard at the Bulldog tight end. He felt his cleats tightly gripping the turf. A salty bead of sweat slipped into the corner of his mouth.

He's gonna break! Keep with him! There!

The tight end's eyes glanced right. It was just a flicker, barely noticeable, but that was all Riley needed. *Sorry, son, this is the big time!*

But as soon as Riley committed to the right, the tight end bolted left. Riley tried to cut back, but it was too late. He had already lost two steps and the advantage.

All he could do now was chase as the tight end pulled in the pass and tacked on another fifteen after-catch yards. Sammy Newman, the Warriors' free safety, was the one who finally managed to trip the Bulldog up, sending him sprawling. As the tight end flew toward the ground, Riley launched himself into the man to finish off the play.

Unfortunately, the collision happened a fraction of a second too late for the referee. Riley groaned as he watched the yellow flag drop to the grass inches from his face.

The tight end—*Lendell . . . no Temple, second-year guy out of Penn State*—rolled out from under Riley, then turned and offered him a hand up. Riley grabbed it, feeling a bit like an old man being offered help up a flight of stairs.

"Nice juke," Riley said after he was on his feet.

Lendell just grinned at him, then jogged back to his huddle.

As the ref announced to the world Riley's late hit, a hand tapped his back. Turning, he saw second-string linebacker Noah Keaton standing next to him.

"Coach sent me in, Pach," Keaton said.

Riley looked toward the sideline and saw Mick Fields waiting for him. Ten yards to Fields's right, he saw head coach Scott Medley glaring at him. He was about to ask which coach, when Medley lifted a clipboard to his face and turned away. Fields, on the other hand, had not taken his eyes off of him.

This should be fun, Riley thought as he jogged toward the sideline.

Fields didn't wait for Riley to reach him. Running onto the field, he launched in. "Really, Covington? Is that really all you've got? Because that second-year boy just schooled you! Seriously, what were you thinking? Crap play like that just ain't going to fly—especially not from you! Because I know your salary, son! I know how much Bellefeuille is dishing out for you each year!"

I'm not in the mood for this. I'm truly not in the mood.

Riley didn't bother to look at Fields. Instead, he just kept walking, forcing the coach to follow next to him. As Fields screamed, Riley led him on a maze through the players standing along the sideline, circling around the benches, and edging between the phone bank and the Gatorade table. All the while, though, Fields never left him and he never shut up.

I'll grant him one thing—he is persistent. He's like a little yappy terrier that you just can't shake off.

"In fact, I can tell you your salary per game—per play, even! The way I figure it, Mr. Bellefeuille and the fans of the much-storied Washington Warriors just dished over right around $10,000 for you to miss that coverage. Or we could say it was approximately $350 for every yard you just gave Cleveland!"

He's good with the numbers, too! Very impressive, Riley thought as he gave an embarrassed nod to one of the Bulldog cheerleaders who had been intently watching the whole incident. He did an about-face and headed back toward the team. *I've got to find a way to lose him before I end up saying something I'm going to regret.*

"Don't think you're getting rid of me, Covington! You're going to hear what I have to say!"

Finally, Riley saw his salvation. Moving toward the field, he made a quick right in front of a Fox Sports tech holding a parabolic audio dish. Fields, who was cut off, stumbled into the man, and then in turn was rammed by the HBO Steadicam operator who had been marching behind the two-man parade.

Seizing the opportunity, Riley ducked into the mass of players. Behind him, the crowd roared their approval for something that was happening on the field. *Good to know I'm not the only one stinking rocks today!*

Sliding his helmet off, he fought the urge to throw it at . . . what? A bench? Coach Fields? Bellefeuille's private box?

I got it! How about those obnoxious Dog Pound fans with their Bulldog masks and their creative speculations into my lineage? Riley made the mistake of looking in the direction he was thinking. This sent the Dog Pound into a barking and howling frenzy.

Ultimately, none of the options seemed practical or productive, so he settled for sitting down by himself and sulking. To say that Riley was having a bad game today would be like saying the Titanic was suffering from minor structural damage. His game was going down fast and it was going down hard—a fact that was as obvious to him as it was to the coaches. This was the first time that he could remember ever being pulled from a defensive series.

The crowd behind him roared again as the stadium announcer proclaimed another Bulldog first down.

A hand landed hard on Riley's shoulder. He looked down at it. Dirt formed a black crescent on the tips of the fingers, and three of the green-stained joints were oozing blood at varied rates. Following the arm up, he saw Don Bernier scowling at him.

Suddenly, the scowl transformed into a grin. "Well, Mr. Covington, I would venture to say that it truly sucks to be you!"

Riley chuckled in spite of himself. "Yeah, how many people hate me right now? I think I've got fantasy team owners all over the nation cursing my name."

"Not if they drafted Lendell," Bernier responded, just before dancing back to avoid a rapidly swinging forearm.

"Dude, I don't know what's wrong with me today," Riley said when Bernier came around to the front of the bench. A groan sounded from the crowd—*Finally, a good sign!*

"It's easy," Bernier said as he grabbed a water bottle from a passing trainer. He squeezed the contents all over his face, only aiming into his mouth for the last four seconds. After shaking the water off, he continued, "You're thinking too much. You're overanalyzing. You're forgetting the fundamentals. You're letting your outside life affect your inside game. You're putting matter over mind. You're letting your form determine your function. You're not dancing with the one who brung you. You're putting on the Eminence Front. You're black and white, but you're not red all over. You're—"

"All right, all right, you've made your point—I think," Riley interrupted, laughing again. "Now, please, can't you just go away and let me self-loathe in peace?"

Bernier leaned in close to Riley. "And most of all, mi amigo, you're forgetting that when it's all said and done, this is just a stupid—"

Riley cleared his throat hard, cutting off Bernier's final word and causing the HBO audio guy to curse and snatch the earphones off his head.

Don't forget . . . Riley mouthed, then pointed to where the mic was tucked in his pads. *"Don't say anything near me you don't want Bellefeuille and millions of others to hear,"* Riley had warned his teammates in a meeting last night.

You could say a lot of things about football, your team, even the coaches. But you never let them hear you say it's just a game. Because then they start questioning your heart.

After a moment, recognition showed in Bernier's eyes. Standing up, he stuck his finger in Riley's face and, starting out slowly but building up steam, shouted, "What I meant to say is this is just a stupid way for you to be playing the game. Yeah, that's it. You get with the program, mister! Because, by gum, if my beautiful children, Ryan, Emma, and Leah, and my enchanting wife, Heather, could hear me now, I'd tell them that I love them and that I have too much pride in my profession to be playing as poorly as you are today!"

By now, Bernier was starting to draw a crowd. "And besides that, you slacker, you good-for-nothing ne'er-do-well, our beloved Mr. Bellefeuille deserves better! He is without doubt the greatest owner the PFL has ever seen. Not only is he wise and gifted and a paragon of virtue, but he is also kind and, I'm not afraid to say it, remarkably handsome! So you give him your all! He deserves it! You hear me? You give him your all!" Bernier's voice cracked in the final words of his speech. Then, giving Riley a quick wink, he turned and stomped away.

Most of the players who had gathered followed Bernier, laughing and slapping his back. When the crowd finally thinned, there stood Coach Fields. Not surprisingly, he didn't look pleased.

"Phone," was all he said; then he walked away.

That's just great, Riley thought. With Coach Medley and all the defensive staff currently on the sidelines, there was only one person left for him to talk to by phone.

Riley crossed behind the benches. That route took him a little closer to the stands than he wanted to get, and he had to endure the Bulldog fans' analysis of his play. Finally, he reached the phone bank, and there, lying on a table, was a single handset off its cradle. Before reaching for it, he quickly downed a cup of Gatorade from the next table over and threw the cup to the ground. He could feel Rick Bellefeuille's eyes on him from above.

Heaving a deep sigh, he picked up the receiver.

"Covington here."

There was silence on the other end.

Another groan came from the crowd, and Riley saw the field goal squad head out onto the field. He waited.

"Hello, this is Covington."

Still he waited.

Looking up, he tried to spot Bellefeuille's box. After a few seconds, he saw him. He was presently occupied yelling at the Warriors' director of player personnel. Riley turned back to the field in time to see the Bulldogs' kick go through the uprights. The stadium erupted in cheers and music.

I'll give him a couple more—

"You're doing this on purpose, aren't you, Covington?"

Riley spun around to see Bellefeuille with the phone in his hand, staring down at him from three stories up.

"Excuse me?"

"You're doing this on purpose! You're pissed because I forced you to have that HBO crew tailing you all day! So you're tanking it!"

Riley felt his temper rising. You could question a things about him, but don't you dare go attacking his inte, or his work ethic. "Listen, Mr. Bellefeuille, if you think—"

"No, you listen, Covington! I let you back on my team because you asked me nicely! Because you came with your little sob story about how you needed to try to make your comeback to prove to yourself and to the world that you could still do it!"

"That's not exactly how—" Riley tried to counter.

But Bellefeuille was in talking mode—not listening. "And what did I do? I said yes! Sure, Riley, we'll give you another chance! You've been there for us; we want to be there for you!"

Riley shook his head. Bellefeuille was twisting the whole situation around. "That's not at all what—"

"And all I ask in return for your chance at recapturing your stardom, not to mention millions of dollars of my money, is that you play hard on the field and you do some interviews! Is that asking too much? Is it?"

Feeling that maybe Bellefeuille was actually wanting an answer, Riley ventured, "Well . . . no, sir, but—"

"But instead what I get is a frickin' prima donna—"

"Listen, I'm no prima donna!"

But Bellefeuille hadn't paused long enough to hear Riley's protest. "—who's gonna play hard when he wants and tank it when he wants! Well, listen to me, Covington, this is no game—"

"Well, technically—"

Bellefeuille's voice somehow increased an octave and multiple decibels. "You want to be a smart guy? You want to be funny? This is not a game; this is business! This is all about dollars and cents! And when something no longer is bringing me dollars, it stops making sense!"

On and on Bellefeuille went, while Riley looked up at him. *This is ridiculous*, Riley thought as he moved the phone away from his ear and let it cradle horizontally in his hand. He was pleased to see Bellefeuille's rage hit an all new level.

Then Riley's eye caught something on a table next to him. *No, man, you can't do that! That would just be so wrong! So wonderfully, wonderfully wrong!*

He quickly glanced at the HBO cameras around him, which had been joined by a Fox Sports handheld. *Come on, remember—what would Jesus do?*

Actually, in this situation, that's fairly debatable. The question I should be asking instead is what would Scott Ross do? And as far as the answer to that question goes, there is no debate.

While Bellefeuille's voice echoed through the handset, Riley stretched out the phone cord and walked to the table.

SUNDAY, SEPTEMBER 11, 2:50 P.M. EDT
WASHINGTON, DC

Scott ran the DVR back again, then paused it.
He had already watched the segment twice,
and now he was waiting for Tara to get back
from getting little James up from his nap.
With the flat screen ready, he quickly looked
around for something he could use to clean
up the mess from the Yoo-hoo spit take that
had just redecorated the coffee table.

*It's on our coasters. It's on the candles. It's on
Tara's* Food & Wine *magazine. Crud, it's even
on our wedding album!*

He spotted a decorative blanket that Tara
used to accent a corner of the couch he was
on. But when he reached for it, the pain from
his chest bruise caused him to pull up short.

"You were not just going to use my chenille blanket to mop up your mess, were you?"

Scott looked over and saw Tara standing there, looking as beautiful as ever and as
frustrated as usual. Baby James was squirming
in her arms, wanting to get to Daddy.

"Don't worry, I called up the Captain, and he said it was okay."

Tara just stared at him.

"Get it? The Captain? Captain and chenille? Sounds just like Captain and Tennille? Work with me, babe."

Scott could see just the faintest movement at the corners of Tara's mouth, which was all the encouragement he needed to plow forward. He stood up and moved toward her.

"Come on, 'Love Will Keep Us Together'? 'Do That to Me One More Time,' which, for the sake of the little dude-a-mus here, we will assume is referring to the desire for another shiatsu foot massage."

Tara's resolve broke and she started laughing now. Sliding up against her, Scott wrapped her and the baby in his arms and began slowly swaying with them.

"And of course, the greatest of all, folks," he continued in a bad Casey Kasem impersonation, "the one that zoomed to the top of the charts, the animal love ballad to top all other animal love ballads, 'Muskrat Love.'"

As the threesome danced around the room, Scott sang, with Tara soon joining in:

And they whirled and they twirled and they tangoed
Singin' and jingin' the jango

"I have no idea what that means," Scott whispered to James.

Floatin' like the heavens above
It looks like muskrat lo-o-o-o-ove.

Scott tried to end the dance with a dip, but his chest caught him up again. Unfortunately, Tara was already on her way back, and all three of them ended up in a laughing heap on the hardwood floor.

"I told you, baby," Scott said to Tara, "once you give in to the dark side, there's nothing but good times ahead."

He still couldn't believe that she was his, or that he was hers, or that they were each other's, or whatever the politically correct phrase was. It was nothing short of a miracle that they were together.

In a conversation on their honeymoon, Tara had admitted to him that she'd spent much of the last few years in a love-hate relationship with Scott. She respected his intelligence, courage, loyalty, and surprisingly to her, his leadership skills. Also, his willingness to sacrifice himself for his country and his friends was well beyond most people she had ever met.

But on the flip side, she had said that his lack of professional discipline, his disregard for authority, his passion for sarcasm, and most of all, his insistence on wearing T-shirts celebrating the tours of bands who had probably been broken up or dead for decades had all combined to make sure that no love connection would ever be made between them.

Then came the daily visits to the hospital. It was during those long visits, she had told Scott, that she really had a chance to see the character beneath the frungy exterior. It was then, also, that she had given up her mission to change him and had decided to start trying to love him as he was.

Now, two years and one baby later, Tara took time to remind him daily of how lucky she was to have a man like him. And to Scott, who had never really known what family love was and who deep down had the self-image of a hairless terrier, those words were like gold.

"How'd you like that dancing, Jimmy-Jer?" Scott said, lying on his back and tossing James above him. Each throw caused him to wince in pain, but his boy's laughter made it worthwhile. "Yeah, I know you! You got the moves! You like to rock it! You like to get down! Admit it, you dig it when this white boy plays his funky music!"

Scott brought his knees up and laid James against them. He quickly glanced at Tara, who was watching him with love in her eyes.

"You ready to work it, son?" He started dancing the boy's chubby legs while he laid down a beat. James was giggling uncontrollably, causing spit to fly everywhere. "Uh . . . oh yeah . . . uh, uh, uh, break it down."

"Pardon me, MC Scott," Tara broke in, laying a hand on Scott's shoulder.

"Just a sec. Drum solo." Scott took James's arms. "Doog-a-doog-a-doog-a-doog-a-doog-a-doog-a-crash-crash." Then raising James's arms up, he said, "Thank you, folks! I'll be playing here all week!"

Tara shook her head, laughing. "You realize that our boy doesn't stand a chance of being normal?"

Scott just grinned.

"I hate to break up the concert, but what's up with the mess? Is there a reason Yoo-hoo is all over the floor and apparently the coffee table, too?"

Scott put James's hands up to his chubby little cheeks. "Oh, my! That's right! I've got to something to show you and mommy! Come on!"

"Scott . . . the mess?"

"Sorry, you're right. James, wanna play Indy 500?"

Sitting James on the floor, Scott said, "Here we go! Vroom, vroom! Rev that engine! Yellow, yellow, yellow, green!" With the sound of peeling out, Scott began scooting James all around the floor. "Watch out for the parked car—you don't want to be like Mario Andretti," he said, curving around a large decorative vase, which held three brown-painted bamboo stalks that Scott had never quite figured out the purpose for.

"Scott Ross, you are not using my son as a human mop!"

"Of course not, baby! He's just driving the track. It's pure coincidence that his super-absorbent patooski is soaking up the spill. *Errrrk!*" Scott made a quick turn of James, just missing a table leg.

When the floor was dry, Scott took James to the couch and sat down with him on his chest. Tara was just finishing cleaning the liquid off the coffee table. After dumping the paper towels, she sat next to him.

"Uh, I think your son needs a change. He seems to be a little moist underneath," Scott said trying to hand James over.

Tara responded with a slap to his arm. Then she picked up the remote while Scott grumbled to James about his derelict mother.

She pressed play, and the frozen Fox PFL logo spun on the screen, then shot off the top right. Full screen were the two announcers for the Washington Warriors–Cleveland Bulldogs game, Clay Sturgis and Tim Anderson.

"*Well, just when you think you've seen everything the PFL has to offer,*" Sturgis started out.

"*No doubt,*" Anderson tagged in. "*While you were away, folks, the action here didn't stop—at least not on the sidelines.*"

The picture of the announcers switched to a bouncy close-up shot from across the stadium of Rick Bellefeuille. He appeared very upset as he spoke into a telephone handset.

"*Obviously, with his team down by twenty-eight points early in the fourth quarter, Rick Bellefeuille is not a happy man,*" Sturgis said. "*And right now he's letting somebody know it. And who, Tim, is the lucky recipient of his wrath?*"

"*Why, it appears to be America's hero, Riley Covington,*" Anderson answered.

The television screen switched to a split screen. Bellefeuille was relegated to the left half, while a tight shot of Riley on the sideline filled the right.

"*There's no doubt that Superman has been fed a kryptonite sandwich by the Bulldogs today. And it appears that Bellefeuille is letting him know what he thinks about it.*"

"Poor Riley," Tara said.

"Just watch."

"Now, there's nothing new about a player getting chewed out by an owner," Sturgis said.

"Although Bellefeuille is one of the few who actually does it during the game," Anderson added.

"True. What is unusual, however, is Covington's response."

As Sturgis said this, Scott and Tara watched Riley let the phone fall away from his ear and lie horizontally in his hand.

"He did not," Tara said with her mouth hanging open.

"Shhh, it gets better!"

". . . seen a player do this with an owner," Anderson continued. *"And judging by Bellefeuille's reaction, he's not seen it either."*

On the screen, Bellefeuille was in meltdown mode. He was wildly swinging his free arm, causing all of his staff to move to a safe distance. His wife could be seen in the corner of the box with her mouth hanging open, covering the ears of their tween-age daughter.

"It's probably good we don't have audio with this shot," Sturgis said.

"You got that right. But we haven't seen the best of it yet. Watch what Riley does next."

As Scott, Tara, and an estimated 205 million other people watched (whether now, during later sports reports, or after the video went viral online), Riley walked to the Gatorade table, lifted the white plastic lid off the big orange bucket, and dropped the handset in.

"Aughhhh," screamed Tara. "He didn't! He didn't just do that!"

Scott tried for some smart comeback, but he was laughing too hard to get any words out.

"Put it back," Tara cried. "Play it again!"

Scott quickly rewound the DVR. This time they watched it muted.

"Look at his face," Tara said through teary eyes, ever the analyst. "He's trying to decide what to do. Then watch . . . right there! That's when he got the idea. Now he's mulling. . . . He's thinking about the outcomes—you can see it in the way his eyes are darting up to Bellefeuille, then over to the bucket. And there! That's when he decides to do it. And we both know that once Riley decides to do something, he doesn't stop until it's done. Splash!"

"You know, we got to get you back in the office more, woman," Scott said, impressed.

"No one better," she said with a grin.

After rewinding the DVR one more time, he turned to James, who was busy peeling the cracked and faded sun off the Utopia 1977 Ra tour T-shirt his dad was wearing. "Look at the TV, little dude-a-mus," Scott said. "It's Uncle Riley."

"He's not interested, my dear."

"He needs to be. Come on, watch this, buddy."

Scott tried to direct James toward the screen by shaking a grenade-shaped rattle in front of it—a baby gift from the guys on the ops team.

Finally satisfied that James was facing in the right direction, he slowed the recording to half speed and began his own description of the action.

And when the handset began its descent into the tub, Scott became very serious and whispered into his child's ear, "That, dear boy, is your Uncle Riley. Do you know what he's doing? He's sticking it to the man. Learn well, my son. Learn well."

"Kid doesn't stand a chance," Tara said with a sigh, then fell back into the couch.

CHAPTER EIGHT

SUNDAY, SEPTEMBER 11, 3:15 P.M. EDT
WASHINGTON, DC

Majid Alavi's hand struck hard against the man's face, the pop caused by his cupped palm echoing through the warehouse. The man spun a quarter-turn but didn't go to the ground. Two more pops sounded, then a voice said, "Again."

Stubble scratched across Alavi's palm as another connection was made. The man dropped to his knees. Alavi slid his hand back and forth on his jeans trying to erase the tactile sensation of the hit.

"Again."

This time the man was left sprawled out on the dusty concrete. Alavi looked around and saw that one of the others was also laid out, while a third was raising himself up from a squatted position—defiance was on his face.

"Very good," said Saifullah. He stood on a small platform set against one wall of the overheated warehouse. He looked every bit the Islamic cleric with his robe, his *taqiyah*, and his salt-and-pepper beard tight on his face.

But there was something unusual about him—something hard to nail down that separated him from most of the imams you might find in American mosques. Most believed it had to do with his eyes. Some said they were empty, soulless. Others that they were filled with rage and vengeance for centuries of oppression. Still others said they could see the fires of hell burning in them. One thing they all agreed on was that life was better when Saifullah was looking at someone else rather than at you.

The cleric continued, "You all know the words of the Koran where Allah states, 'Let there arise from among you a small group of people, inviting to all that is good. They enjoin the good, forbid the evil, and it is they who attain success!'

"You are that people! You have been called out, and you have answered the call! May the strength of our benevolent God be upon you!"

Murmurs of approval spread through the twenty-four men, each handpicked for the mission. Majid Alavi made sure his face showed the gravity of the blessing Saifullah was pronouncing over them. But inside, he was smiling. In fact, he was more than smiling; he was exulting! After all this time, after all the preparation, finally he was to fulfill the destiny prepared for him long ago, before time began.

"As our passage says, to attain success we must forbid the evil! These men did not do that! Thus, they had to be reminded of the need for purity in all our thoughts and all our actions!"

Deep down, Alavi had to admit that he didn't feel that the infractions of these three men merited the punishment they received. After all, two of them were now bloodied simply for having been found with fast-food wrappers in their cars. "A lack of physical discipline," Saifullah had pronounced.

The third, the one who stared defiantly, had been an hour

late for his rendezvous. When asked what had happened, he refused to give a reason. Even now, ten hours later, no one knew what had delayed his arrival. *That one probably does deserve the discipline; these others, not so much.*

When Saifullah had pronounced the punishments, all three men submitted willingly. And Alavi, second in command to Saifullah and one of three members trained outside of the US, took his place as an enforcer.

"What say you now?" Saifullah asked the three men.

The first two dropped to their knees and placed their foreheads on the ground. "We throw ourselves upon the mercy of Allah," they said in unison, as they had been taught.

However, the third man—Quraishi, Alavi thought his name was—dropped only to one knee and mouthed the formulaic words. *I wish he had been mine. There would not be that much defiance left in him still. He is a man who bears watching.*

Saifullah accepted the men's apologies with a nod, and then continued while Alavi and the others joined the rest of the group cross-legged on the floor. "We must keep a sharp edge to this team. We must shed the last vestiges of this decadent culture from our souls. We must separate ourselves out, so that we can do what our weak sisters cannot.

"There is no denying that many of our fellow Muslims have softened. They feel guilt at our successes, shame at what Allah has accomplished through the glorious actions of the *shahid* who have gone before us. They forget that if anyone is ashamed of Allah in this life, Allah will be ashamed of them in the next!"

Again, a murmur of approval swept through Saifullah's audience. Alavi nodded. Sweat trickled in beads down his neck, and he could feel the moisture spreading on his back, giving him a little relief from the wet heat of the musty building.

"We are doing the work of Allah, and we must remember that he will accept nothing from us except our best! We live to serve! We live to die!"

With that, Saifullah turned and left the stage. Around him, the men stood to go. However, Alavi remained seated processing the cleric's words. There was something about them that seemed different—a little off. Maybe it was just that the way Saifullah spoke was so different from what he had heard among the mullahs during his six-month training in Somalia.

His message has been Americanized, Alavi thought. *That's what it is! Phrases like "sharp edge" and "team" and "nothing but our best"—you don't hear those in the Middle East. The brilliance of Saifullah is that he is coming at us as both a coach and a spiritual leader. He knows who we are. He knows what will motivate a squadron of warriors who happened to have had the misfortune of growing up in America.*

Alavi looked around at the men of his team. They had arrived last night and early this morning, coming from places as diverse as Dearborn and Dallas, San Diego and Seattle, Memphis and Miami. All ready to fight. All ready to die.

No two stories were exactly the same as to how these men had metamorphosed from American boys to jihadists. Yet each probably had similar elements: some level of poverty, experiences of discrimination, a lack of hope for bettering their circumstances, and a radical mentor to piece everything together.

The beginning of Alavi's turn toward radicalism occurred quite unexpectedly. He was a fairly happy eleven-year-old, living in a moderate Muslim family in Mishawaka, Indiana. He played third base on his little league team and was two-year school spelling bee champion for his grade.

Then, on this very day all those years ago, the planes crashed into the twin towers of the World Trade Center, and Alavi's life changed. He was on the school bus when the first plane hit. After arriving at school, his class followed the events throughout the morning, everyone stunned, including Alavi.

Then came lunch break. Alavi was throwing the baseball with his best friend, just as he did every day at lunch. They were trying to distract themselves the best they could from the events on the East Coast. Suddenly, he was surrounded by six other boys.

"Hey, raghead, you must be cheering the guys on those planes," one boy said, giving the young Alavi a push.

"We don't even know who flew those planes," Alavi shot back. "It could have been anyone!"

"Yeah right. Everyone knows it was some camel jockey, just like you," another said, also giving a push. "Look around you. Everyone else is all crying and stuff, and you're here playing ball like nothing happened."

"No, like he knew it was going to happen," a third said from behind, giving young Majid's head a hard push forward.

"Knock it off," Alavi's buddy said, trying to elbow his way into the circle. But he was yanked backward by a couple of onlookers and shoved to the rear of the growing crowd.

"So, come on, raghead," the first boy taunted. "How'd it feel to see your cousins crashing those planes? Huh? How does it feel to know your family killed all those people?"

Alavi knew he was in trouble but couldn't find a way out. Panic welled up inside him as words continued to be said and he continued to be pushed. Then came the first punch. After that, it was a free-for-all. By the time a recess aide got there, Alavi was on the ground, a bloody mess.

But I didn't cry! No matter what they threw at me, I didn't cry, he remembered with pride, even this many years later.

The boys were suspended for three days, but Alavi never went back to that school. Not that he didn't want to. But the principal of the school was concerned for his safety, so she recommended he study at home.

Then, a week after the attack, Alavi's dad was unexpectedly laid off from his job as manager of a clothing retailer. The higher-ups had cited a history of poor store performance, but Mr. Alavi knew that sales had actually been up that year. The rumor around corporate was that there had been customer complaints about having a man with an Arabic name running the store, and some had vowed not to return.

After scrambling for employment for a month—there weren't a lot of "Muslim Wanted: Apply Within" signs around the Mishawaka area at that time—Mr. Alavi found a job through his sister at a factory in Michigan. So the whole Alavi family—Dad, Mom, Majid, and his little brother, Hatim—packed up and moved to Dearborn.

The positive side of the move was that Dearborn was thick with people just like themselves—Arab background, moderate Muslim. The negative side was that a junior assembler in a factory didn't make near the same kind of money as a manager of a clothing store. Typically, the Alavi family spent the final few days of each month eating rice and curds until the paycheck came and they could start the cycle again.

America! The great melting pot where everyone is welcome—as long as you have white skin and are a Christian, Alavi thought, letting his tongue dance in the gap where one of his upper left bicuspids had been until that morning on the playground.

America! Where they stick their noses into everyone else's business, then cry when that nose gets hit! America! The great imperialist that commands smaller nations by feeding them foreign aid, then forcing them to do their bidding like a pimp running a crack whore! America! Who, like an old plantation owner, is too fat and lazy to do any work on their own, so instead they exploit the slave nations of the world to do their work for them! They import everything, and the only thing they export is the moral filth of their culture!

Alavi stood and moved across the warehouse to where his cot was, one of eight in the small area belonging to the squadron he would command. He sat down and began dismantling his Glock 21 .45 for a cleaning, carefully laying out each piece on an olive green blanket. *Well, we are the wake-up call! We are retribution! We are the Vandals to this modern-day empire! And before they know what hits them, Rome is going to get sacked!*

SUNDAY, SEPTEMBER 11, 3:30 P.M. EDT
CLEVELAND, OHIO

The gold coin twinkled as it spun between Riley's thumb and index finger. Although it was still the fourth quarter of the game, he was showered and dressed and sitting in front of his locker. Word of what was now being referred to as the Gatorade Incident had spread quickly. Within three minutes, Coach Medley had come to the bench where he was sitting and told him in no uncertain terms that he was no longer welcome on the sidelines. Riley was all too happy to oblige.

He flicked the coin again with his right index finger and watched it spin. The walk back to the tunnel had been interesting. It was the first time all day that he had been cheered. Even the Dog Pound was giving it up for him. All the random comments had eventually coalesced into a resounding chant of "Phone Boy, Phone Boy, Phone Boy" that had spread throughout the stadium. He had smiled and waved to the crowd before going under the seats, knowing that on a day like today, he could use all the friends he could get.

Riley flicked the coin again. This time it went bouncing across the carpet. He jumped up after it, stopping its roll with a stomp of his foot. After picking it up, he sat down at his locker and examined it. The reverse side had the Statue of Liberty on it and made it clear that the coin's value was one dollar. On the obverse side was a picture of a president. *Zachary Taylor,* he read, *12th President, 1849–50. I know there's a story to that short tenure, but for the life of me, I can't remember what it is.*

Placing the coin back between his thumb and index finger, he spun it again. The only positive thing to come out of the situation so far was that he was no longer wired for sound. Mike Novinger from HBO had removed his mic so that he could shower. When he came back out, he fully expected to have the mic replaced. But Novinger didn't approach him. Even the cameras kept a respectful distance. The only explanation he could think of was that Bellefeuille had demanded they back off.

As he sat there, Riley entertained himself with thinking of all the things he wished he had said—all the comebacks he could have nailed Bellefeuille with, all the zingers that would have rocked the man back on his heels. *Why am I always so good thirty minutes after the fact? I desperately need to take a course at the Scott Ross School of Witty Repartee.*

Suddenly, the activity around him began to increase. The rising scramble of the Warriors locker-room minions told him that the game was just about at an end. He craned his neck so that he could check out the big screen that was hanging on the wall above and to the left of him. Sure enough, there was 1:03 left and the Bulldogs were going to kneel it out.

Riley pocketed the coin and prepared to meet the press onslaught. *Lord, help me to not do anything even more stupid than what I've already done today.*

The doors burst open, and his teammates began filing in.

Riley kept his head down, not wanting to put anyone in an awkward position. In the PFL, the doghouse is a lonely place to be. Most players try to shy away from demonstrating any support, in case it could be perceived as choosing sides against the ownership.

Add to that the lousy performance not just from Riley but from the whole team, and he didn't expect a whole lot of post-game banter.

As the foul-smelling men moved past him, a dirty cleat kicked up against his Merrell; then a small paper cup dropped to the ground. Looking up, Riley saw it was Don Bernier, who just kept walking without acknowledging him. He fished the cup from the floor, wondering what his friend was up to. It didn't take long to figure out. On the inside of the green Gatorade cup, Bernier had used a grease pencil to draw an angry face with a phone to his ear and smoke curling up the sides.

Riley laughed to himself as he balled up the cup, destroying the evidence. Then, after thinking a moment, he unwrinkled the waxy paper, folded it into thirds, and slid it into his pocket. *You never know when you might need to remember that you're not alone.*

Minutes later, the press was let in. Almost everyone bee-lined to Riley.

"What made you do it?"

"What was Bellefeuille saying to you?"

"Have you apologized?"

"Are you going to be suspended?"

Hmmm, suspended? Hadn't thought of that.

Putting up his hands to silence the questions, Riley began a response that he had been mentally rehearsing. "Listen, what I did out there was—"

"I'm sorry, folks, but Riley won't be taking questions right now," said Jonny Wiens, the Warriors' head of public relations, pushing his way through the mass of reporters.

"Come on," *Pro Football Weekly*'s Gus Verdant protested, "you can't cut him off. He was just answering."

With a professionalism that only experience can bring, Wiens brushed off the protests. "Again, I'm sorry. Riley will be available sometime this week for comment. For now, he's needed elsewhere. All right?"

Groans and curses answered Wiens as he took Riley by the arm and pulled him away. Riley followed easily. He didn't really care where he was being led. He was just happy it was away from the press.

The two men walked past the lockers, Wiens keeping his hand on Riley's arm. *Ahhh, heading out to freedom,* Riley thought as they moved toward the exit.

But just before they reached the rear doors, Wiens stopped. He pulled Riley around so that his back was to a wall that appeared to have been hastily covered with a Washington Warriors banner.

"Listen, Riley," Wiens began in a low voice, poking his finger in Riley's chest, "I just wanted to get you away from them so we could talk."

"I know Bellefeuille's probably through the roof with this thing, but he—"

Wiens threw his hands up in the air and shook his head violently. "That's where you're wrong. Sure, Mr. Bellefeuille's seriously ticked at you, but he's loving the whole situation."

"Loving it?" Riley said, confused. "I'm not sure I'm following—"

"Oh, come on, Riley," Wiens said very loudly, again throwing up his hands. He stepped away for a few moments like he was trying to regain his composure. When he came back, his finger was in Riley's face.

"Think about it," Wiens said quietly. His face was turning a dark red, and beads of sweat were rolling down his face. "This is a boon for Bellefeuille. His face will be everywhere. People from all over the world will be hitting the Warriors website. He couldn't have asked for a better PR gimmick."

Nothing was making any sense. The incongruity between Wiens's words and his actions was getting to be too much. Riley grabbed Wiens's finger. "First of all, get your finger out of my face! Second, what's with the . . . wait a second. The banner, the lighting . . ."

Riley let go of Wiens's finger and stepped back.

"No, keep it going. That was great," Wiens said, cowering a bit, like he was afraid Riley was going to hit him.

"This is a setup—a photo op!" Riley looked around the locker room and saw that they had drawn the attention of everyone in the room. Every eye, every camera in the room was pointed in their direction.

"You weasel," he said, turning back to Wiens. "Is this all part of Bellefeuille's big plan to exploit the situation?"

"What do you think, Riley?" Wiens was back in his face again, appearing to be madder than ever. "You play along, and Mr. Bellefeuille will pretty much let the whole thing blow over. No suspension, just a minor fine. We figure a press conference on Tuesday when you can publicly apologize. Then Mr. Bellefeuille will forgive you—after all, who wouldn't snap after all the death-defying things you've done over the past few years? Finally, you shake hands and the show's over."

Riley was stunned. While Wiens panted "angrily" in his face, he just stared back, amazed at the man's brazenness. *What am I, a circus animal? Next thing you know, Bellefeuille's going to have me jump through a flaming hoop—he'll probably sell the show live on pay-per-view! Seriously, is this really what I want my life to be?*

"Come on, Riley. Come at me one more time, while we still have their interest. Then we'll call it a day. I promise."

The whirr of cameras was the only thing that broke the unnatural silence of the locker room. Riley placed his hand on Wiens's chest and slowly pushed him back a step.

"That's it," Wiens said. "Just finish the show."

Riley's fists balled together at his side. Through clenched teeth, he said, "Mr. Bellefeuille wants a show, huh? Okay, I'll give him a show."

Both of Riley's fists moved up in front of Wiens's face, causing the man to involuntarily suck in his breath. Then, one finger at a time, Riley let his right hand open. "Nothing there," he said.

Riley slowly opened his left hand. "Nothing there."

Riley's face broke into a wide smile. "Abracadabra." He reached behind Wiens's left ear and pulled out a gold Zachary Taylor coin, then held it up for all to see. "Ta-da!"

There was a moment of silence, while everyone tried to process what they had just witnessed. Then everyone, players and press alike, burst into laughing applause.

Riley was still staring at Wiens, who was turning a much darker red than his manufactured emotions had produced. "Please tell Mr. Bellefeuille that I hope he enjoyed the performance."

Without acknowledging the cheers, Riley moved toward the exit. Then, stopping suddenly, he turned back toward Wiens and flicked the coin. Instinctively, Wiens caught it.

"Sorry, that was almost my bad. Your ear, your coin." And with a wink, Riley went out the doors.

CHAPTER TEN

SUNDAY, SEPTEMBER 11, 8:30 P.M. EDT

LEESBURG, VIRGINIA

This is so much more house than I need, Riley thought as he watched the garage door make its slow ascent. *It's just stupid! Stupid! What was I thinking?*

The three-story colonial was located next to a small lake in Leesburg, Virginia. It was a beautiful brick home with a decked-out interior and a decent-size yard, sitting on the end of a cul-de-sac. He had thought of buying something cheaper—maybe even a townhome. After all, he was still paying on his place in Kenai, Alaska, and his house in Parker, Colorado.

At least the Parker home was being used. Six months ago a family connected with Keith Simmons's refugee work moved in. Riley had decided to let them live there rent-free, so they could better carry on their ministry. *Seven New York City orphans—what must they be doing to my carpet? Oh well; everything is replaceable.*

Riley eased his black Durango into the garage, parking it next to Skeeter's Chrysler 300. The realities of his past had nixed the townhome idea. You just never knew when someone was going to get it into their head to put an end to Captain America once and for all. If that situation were to arise, it was better to have a little room between yourself and your neighbors.

So he had settled on this beauty. The neighbors were nice, and after the initial freak-out of having Riley Covington on the street, they treated him fairly normally. The HOA stocked the lake, so he could fish off his little dock. And best of all, the Warriors' headquarters was just a quick fifteen-minute drive up the Harry Byrd Highway.

But despite all those positives, he still felt guilty every time he pulled up. *This thing was about three hundred grand more than you should have paid for a house. And what are you doing with five bedrooms? Maybe you should get Skeeter to run a bed-and-breakfast out of it, so the extra square footage doesn't go to waste.*

Riley swung open the Durango's door with a *thwunk*, adding another crease to the multitude that already existed in the Sheetrock wall. *That's what this place is missing! Maybe they could have dumped one of the bedrooms and put in an extra couple hundred square feet of garage space!*

The Virginia evening felt hot and muggy after the truck's air conditioning. He pulled his bag out of the backseat and walked into the mudroom.

"Lucy, I'm home," he called out as he slipped his shoes off.

The response he got from Skeeter was just as he expected—silence. To say that Skeeter Dawkins was a man of few words was like saying that outer space was a place of little gravity.

Riley walked through the kitchen, tossing his keys on the counter, and spotted Skeeter in his usual chair, the ever-present book in his hands.

"Watcha reading now?" Riley asked, plopping himself down on the couch opposite his friend.

Skeeter held up the book.

"*Agricola and Germania* by Tacitus," Riley read. "I don't even know what that means."

"Agricola was his father-in-law."

"What? Whose father-in-law?"

Skeeter pointed to Tacitus's name on the cover. Then he turned his attention back to the book.

"And Germania is obviously Germany. So this Agricola was a Roman guy who was involved in conquering Germany," Riley deduced.

Without looking up from his book, Skeeter pointed toward Riley and then tapped his own temple a few times.

"You know, I've been thinking about getting a dog. Figured at least it might give me a little more conversation."

"Mmmm," Skeeter replied.

Laughing, Riley got up and stretched. "You see any of the game?"

"Been reading."

Skeeter didn't usually watch Riley's games. He was much more of a basketball fan. Tonight, Riley was glad of that fact.

"Getting something to drink," Riley said, moving toward the kitchen. "You want anything?"

"I'm good."

You know, a dog might not be a bad thing. Got enough hunt clubs around here. I could train him to . . .

Riley stopped as he opened a cabinet to get a glass. All his dishes and glasses were gone. In their place stood rows and rows of green paper Gatorade cups. He spun to look at Skeeter and caught his eyes quickly dropping back to the book. Nothing, though, could disguise what the laughter was doing to his six-foot-seven frame.

Riley looked in the next cabinet and found the same thing. Opening three more doors gave him the same result.

"Skeeter, all of our cabinets seem to be filled with Gatorade cups," Riley said, trying to stay serious.

"Mmmm?" Skeeter replied, a lot higher than usual.

"Do you possibly know how this might have happened?"

Putting down his book, Skeeter said, "Don't know." Then, spreading his fingers, he waved his hands in an outward arc. "Must have been . . . magic."

Seeing Skeeter do that was as funny as the prank itself. When Riley could speak again, he said, "Very nice, Skeet, very nice."

Leaving the cups alone, Riley pulled a can of Diet Coke out of the fridge and headed for the den. As he was closing the door, he saw that Skeeter was still slumped down in his chair laughing—book dumped on the floor.

Riley snatched a handheld from his desk, stretched out on a couch, and dialed Scott Ross's number. As it rang, he took a deep swig from his can, then set it on the floor.

"Is this the Great Covitini?"

"Really, Scott?" Riley chided, as he pulled a throw pillow from behind his back and tossed it on the floor. "You've had how many hours to think this through, and that's the best you could come up with?"

"Yeah, that was pretty lame. How about, 'The Mysterious Covington, where the phone is quicker than the eye'?"

"Probably ought to stick with Covitini."

"My thoughts exactly. Now, let's hear it—leave nothing out. What in the name of Ann-Margrock were you thinking?"

Riley took another pull of his Diet Coke. "Dude, I have no idea. At the time, dropping the phone into the bucket seemed like the most logical thing to do."

"Forget that! That I understand perfectly. In fact, I'm going to burn that little scene off of my DVR so I can show it to James on a regular basis as he gets older."

"Always happy to be a role model."

"What I can't figure out is the whole locker room thing.

One minute you're getting a new orifice bored out by Dr. Suit, and the next you're pulling a coin out of his ear! Classic! I mean, that was bizarre behavior even by my standards!"

It was good to talk to Scott. *Even when you think you've quite probably screwed up your whole world, Scott'll find a way to grab the situation and put a big red clown nose on it.*

"That was the thing. Wiens—that's Dr. Suit, head of PR—he wasn't chewing me out. He was definitely trying to make it seem that way with his arms all monkey-flailing around. But his words were like, 'Mr. Bellefeuille wants to make this work out. Just go along with the program. Yada yada yada.'"

"No way! Tara, you were right, baby! Suit-dude wasn't laying into Riley." The sound was muffled, like he was holding his hand over the phone. "Okay, that's fine. Whatever. What? No, I'm not going to ask him right now. . . . Listen, we'll talk about it later. . . . I said, we'll talk about it later."

While he waited, Riley turned on the TV. ESPN was showing him pulling the coin out of Wiens's ear. On CNN, he watched himself drop the phone in the Gatorade bucket. He flipped it to CNN Headline News and saw himself pulling the coin out of Wiens's ear, but from another angle. On FoxNews, Sean Hannity had convened a Great American Panel to discuss the incident. MSNBC was showing a slow-motion shot with his hand highlighted as he slipped the coin out of his pocket.

Too bad Olbermann's gone. This would have been another great right-wing conspiracy for him.

Scott came back on the line. "Hey, sorry about that. Me and the missus had a little discussing to do." Riley could hear the tension in his voice.

"So, what aren't you going to ask me about right now?" Riley shut off the TV.

"Never mind. Finish your story."

"Not much else to say. He told me to give the media a show, so I gave them a show."

"You're beautiful, man," Scott said, laughing. *That's the great thing about Scott. His emotions are like the weather in Colorado. You don't like what you've got? Give it a few minutes.* "You keep pulling stunts like that, you're going to make yourself famous someday. What's the scoop now?"

"Who knows? On the flight home, they were talking to me some more about a Tuesday press conference for a public apology."

"You gonna do it?"

"I haven't gotten that far. They're also considering releasing a statement saying they want me to be evaluated for post-traumatic stress disorder," Riley admitted, a little embarrassed to be saying the words.

"You? PTSD? Dude, you're the most balanced person I know—well, next to Skeeter."

Relief spread in Riley. He didn't realize how nervous that possibility was making him until he actually verbalized it. "So, I'm not nuts?"

"First of all, PTSD is not technically nuts," Scott said, taking on a mock-academic tone. "Second, it's not like you decked the dude or started shooting the place up or something. All you did was dump a phone into a Gatorade bucket, then pull a coin out of a guy's ear during an argument on national television—which as I'm hearing these words spoken out loud does in fact sound approximately two large steps beyond the far side of Whac-A-Mole."

Riley sat up and started spinning the TV remote on a nearby coffee table. "Thanks, buddy. You're always the encourager."

Scott laughed. "Yeah, it's a gift. Listen, Pach, you're at a place in your life where whatever you do next is really your call. You want to stay in football? You play Bellefeuille's game. You want to get out? You get out. It's not like you need the paycheck. You could buy me ten times over."

"Not with the way your eBay bids are going up."

"Sweet. Gotta check that out. What I'm saying is, if you're done with the game, then be done with the game. The return for you torturing yourself is diminishing rapidly."

Riley didn't answer right off. Just like that, Scott had gotten to the source of his frustration with his life. *But what should I do? If I stay, I could—*

"And don't try to figure it out right now," Scott said, interrupting Riley's thoughts. "You yourself told me never to make major decisions when you're tired or in a weird place. You're two for two."

Riley chuckled. He took a long drink from the Diet Coke, stifled a belch, and said, "You're right. Enough about me tonight. Now, what does Tara want you to ask me?"

"Good turnaround, my friend. Nicely played."

Silence filled the connection. Riley began tossing a baseball-size rubber ball against the brick fireplace in front of the couch.

After three catches, he said, "Oh, Scotty?"

"Okay, man, so everything was going great today. We're playing with James, watching the game, laughing together. Then suddenly she drops this bomb. She's like, 'Scott, you know you could have died out there yesterday.' I say, 'Yeah, but I didn't.' And she's all, 'Scott, you know you're a dad now. James needs his father. What if you had been killed?' And I say—and here's where, admittedly, I may have gone a bit the wrong direction—so I say, 'Look at me, baby! Guys like me are a dime a dozen at any bar in DC.'"

"Couldn't you have just pulled a coin out of her ear?"

"Would've been a better play because, let me tell you, it was not pretty. She's all . . . Actually, I'm just going to stop there. You made me promise once that I'd never talk bad about my wife in front of anybody. So I'm just going to shut up."

"Crap," Riley said, as the ball bounced off of his hand and onto the Diet Coke can, spilling its remaining contents out on the carpet.

"What? Dude, that's what you told me."

Riley was on his feet looking for something to clean up the spill. "No. You did the right thing. I just . . . never mind. What's the question?" Not seeing anything to soak up the pop, he pulled off his shirt and began mopping up.

"Should I step out of ops? Tara wants me to ride a desk."

The door to the den opened, and Skeeter looked in, obviously alerted by the sudden commotion. Riley was kneeling on the ground, naked from the waist up, phone cranked on his shoulder, holding his shirt to the carpet.

Skeeter shook his head and said, "You need a hobby, man." Then he closed the door again.

Riley sighed, then laid another part of his shirt on the spill. "Listen, I can understand what she's saying. Yesterday probably scared her spitless. You ever consider any other options?"

"Like . . . ?"

"I don't know. Private security. Something like what Khadi does. Or even starting your own firm. I've told you before I'd back any business venture you wanted to step into." Lifting his shirt, he felt around the floor. *Feels all right. Let's hear it again for dark brown carpet.* He tossed the wet shirt toward the door to deal with later.

"I know. I appreciate it. But can you picture me yessirring and nosirring some rich, old-money dude or his spoiled, entitled, punk son? I'd probably end up shooting the kid myself—and the dad."

"Yeah, or dropping them in a bucket of Gatorade."

"There you go."

"Well, just be thinking of options. A wise man recently told me never to make important decisions while you're tired or in a weird place."

"Sounds like a smart guy."

"Occasionally," Riley said as he lay down on the couch, his bare back squeaking against the leather. "Now go find your beautiful wife. Apologize to her. Admit you're a pig and that you'll at least think about her question. Then make up however you young married kids make up these days."

"Usually it's a few hands of gin rummy; then we hold hands watching the sun set."

"Sounds nice."

"Or we just have sex."

"TMI!"

"Later, buddy."

Riley hung up the phone feeling a lot better than when he had picked it up. *It's good to have options. A little prayer, a little time, things just might work out after all.*

ELEVEN

Khadi tried to laugh along, doing her best to keep her emotions in check. But she had a feeling that her fuse didn't have much further to burn. She was sitting at a crowded table in an upscale coffee bar in downtown DC. Tightly packed around her was her usual Monday morning group.

To her left in the circle was Jonathan Kattan, then Josiah, Korinne, Kierra, Jordan, Jackson, Jed, and finally Audrey, who was on Khadi's right. All were involved in security or law enforcement, and all were single.

Six months ago, everyone except Audrey had been part of an obnoxious How-to-Be-olitically-Correct-When-You're-Taking-Down-Perps kind of seminar. At one point, they had been separated by gender and alphabetized by name. Then the boy Js had been put together with the girl Ks to role-play some extreme, totally illogical scenario that the seminar leader—who obviously had no law enforcement background—had come up with.

No one took the assignment seriously, and they ended up laughing their way through it, much to the chagrin and anger of the facilitator. When the goofing didn't end after the exercise, they were eventually, very politely, asked to leave.

They all hit a coffee place afterward and had been getting together every week since then. Audrey had joined the gang soon after at an invite from her roommate, Korinne.

"The Gatorade thing—that I can understand! I mean, I can't tell you how many times I've wanted to do that to my boss," Jordan said. "And with all the stories you hear about Bellefeuille? You gotta respect Covington for that."

"Sure," Kierra agreed. "But the coin? What was that?"

"That was sheer craziness," Josiah said. Then, mimicking Riley's trick, he said, "Nothing up my sleeves. Presto!" And he pulled a packet of Sweet'N Low from behind Korinne's ear.

They all burst into applause. Even Khadi clapped, although her insides were twisting in knots. She felt like she should be defending Riley, and she probably would have if Jonathan hadn't been sitting next to her.

The two of them had been dating for a few months now—nothing serious . . . yet. He had asked her in the past about her history with Riley, but she had always tried to brush the questions off or change the subject. For some reason, she felt that her relationship with Riley was just too personal or private or, maybe, painful to talk about with anyone else. That time of her life was like a treasure to box up for herself and bury deep down in her heart. Although it was seeming more and more lately that she hadn't buried it deep enough.

"I was listening to the Sports Junkies on the Fan this morning. They said that there was a rumor going around the Warriors' facility that Covington might be going for a psych evaluation," Jackson said.

Jonathan leaned back in his chair and put his arm around Khadi. "Come on, he may be a lot of things—arrogant, a little too perfect—but he's not crazy."

"He's not arrogant," Khadi blurted out.

"What?" Jonathan asked.

"You said he's arrogant. He's not arrogant in any way, shape, or form. Your saying that shows that you know absolutely nothing about him," Khadi said, a little more defensively than she had intended.

A joking *ooooooh* went around the table.

"Listen, Khadi, I know he's your friend," Jonathan said, trying to get himself out of a bad situation. "There's no doubt he's got to be a good guy if you were that close to him. I was just saying—"

Khadi leaned forward, away from Jonathan's arm. "I know what you were 'just saying.' I know what all of you were 'just saying.' And what I'm 'just saying' is that you don't know him, so you really have no right saying any of it!"

"Khadi, sweetie, we're sorry if we said something wrong." Always the peacemaker, Kierra took Khadi's hand in both of hers. "We were just joking around. We didn't mean anything by it. Promise."

Khadi sat quietly for a moment. She knew she wasn't angry with them. She was angry with herself for caring. She was angry that she felt the need to defend Riley. She was angry at the tears that were in her eyes.

Sliding her chair back, she said, "Look, I'm sorry, guys. Jonathan, I shouldn't have snapped at you—I shouldn't have snapped at any of you. It's just . . . I don't know. I think I better go. I need to drive all the way out to Mr. Opportunity's house."

"Please stay, Khadi. Let the old fart wait," Korinne said.

"No, I better go." Khadi stood up.

Jonathan rose too. "Let me walk you out."

"No, please . . . please, Jonathan," she said, putting her hand on his chest. Then she turned and left.

Remarkably, when she had parked this morning, she had found one of the very rare Washington, DC, meters that was within a few blocks of where a person actually wanted to be, so the walk to her BMW was short.

After sitting for a couple of minutes with her blinker on, someone finally waved her out into the lane. With DC traffic, she was looking at a minimum of forty-five minutes to get out of the city proper and to Senator Andrews's house. She turned on the radio, which just sounded like a bunch of noise. She turned it off again.

Tears were still in her eyes, and she desperately wanted to cry, but she wouldn't let herself. *You promised yourself you wouldn't. You've cried enough tears over him. It's done! It's over!*

She took a few deep breaths, then occupied her time by trying to change lanes—always an exercise in patience. *Why couldn't I have kept my mouth shut? They weren't trying to be mean. It just . . . kind of came out that way.*

Poor Riley, though. I can't imagine what he's going through today. He was always so great when other people were having a bad day. How many times did he cheer me up? I hope Scott or Skeeter can give him a boost—although Scott will probably end up saying exactly the wrong thing, and I'm sure Skeeter won't say anything at all.

Khadi laughed to herself as a wave of nostalgia hit her. There had been a lot of great times amid the bullets and bombs. They really had been like a family.

I wonder . . . She looked at her phone. *After all the times he was there for me, it would be nice to . . . No, that would just muddle it all up again. There's a reason things are like they are. To step back would just lead to more confusion and more pain.*

But as she drove, she found that she kept glancing down at the phone. Finally relenting, she picked it up and tapped number five—Riley's designated speed dial, right in the middle—bringing up a picture of him and a little green Call button. She knew it was silly to still have him there, especially because it had been almost two years since she had spoken with him. But there was a comfort in knowing he was still just a phone call away if she needed him.

Like he needs you now, she thought as she looked at his face, his eyes, his smile, his hair that always looked like it could have used just a touch more intentionality. *Just press the button. He'd love to hear from you—you know he would! Just press it!*

But instead of calling, she set the phone on her leg. *You can't go back! It's too hard! You just can't go back!*

Resolved, she turned her attention back to the road. But a sound caught her attention. It was like a tinny voice saying something indiscernible. She checked the radio, but it was off. Still the voice went on, almost sounding like it was saying her name.

It was driving her crazy trying to figure out where the sound was coming from. Then her stomach clenched. Looking down at the phone on her leg, she saw a timer counting: 00:00:45, 00:00:46, 00:00:47.

I must have hit Call when I put the phone down, she thought, panicking. *What do I do? Should I hang up? Should I answer? I'm such . . . an . . . idiot!*

She picked up the phone and put it to her ear.

"Hello? Hello? Khadi, is that you?" Just hearing Riley's voice sent her heart racing and her stomach flipping.

"Hi, Riley," she managed to get out.

"Oh, man, Khadi! It's so good to hear your voice! How're you doing?"

Riley seemed genuinely happy to hear from her, which answered one of Khadi's concerns.

"I'm good, I'm good. Work's good. Family's good. Everything's good."

"Good," Riley said. "I mean, that's really great to hear. Scott tells me that you've been working for Senator Andrews. I've even seen you on television a few times."

"Yeah, he's always ready for a photo op. We call him Mr. Opportunity," Khadi said, wondering why it was seeming so hard to have a normal, nonstilted conversation with this man she had spent so many hours with.

"Mr. Opportunity. That's funny. Sure seems to fit him."

"It does."

An awkward silence ensued.

Riley finally broke it. "I've got to tell you, I'm surprised by your phone call this morning. Thrilled, but surprised."

"Oh, well, I was watching the news yesterday. . . ."

Riley groaned.

"Exactly, so I thought you might need a little boosting up."

Riley laughed. "Yeah . . . well, thanks. I do. I'm not sure what happened yesterday. It wasn't one of my bright, shining moments."

"I disagree completely. I thought it was very . . . I don't know . . . very you," Khadi replied, trying her best at encouragement.

"Actually, it was probably more Scott."

"Or maybe even Gooey," Khadi said, referring to a particularly bizarre member of the CTD analyst team.

They laughed together, then fell into another awkward silence.

"So, how's your mom?" Khadi asked.

"Great, she's great. Got the goat farm back up and running. Said Dad would have wanted it that way. I didn't have the heart to tell her how much he hated those goats deep down. She asks about you all the time."

"Oh? Well, send her my love next time you talk to her."

"Will do. She'll be thrilled."

Another silence.

"Well, I better run. I'm just pulling up at the senator's house," Khadi lied.

"Mr. Opportunity!"

"Yeah, Mr. Opportunity. Well, it was really great catching up with you, Riley."

"You too. You made my day—seriously. I've really . . . I don't know. I've missed you, Khadi."

Khadi stayed silent for a moment, trying to keep herself under control. *And I've missed you too, Riley. So, so much.*

"You take care, Riley. And keep away from those Gatorade buckets," she said with a weak attempt at humor.

"You got it, Khadi. Take care."

Khadi pulled the phone away from her ear and watched through tear-blurred eyes as the timer flashed 00:02:59, 00:02:59, 00:02:59, and then Riley's face disappeared from her phone.

MONDAY, SEPTEMBER 12, 7:35 A.M. EDT
LEESBURG, VIRGINIA

Riley stared at the phone, wondering what
had just happened. *After two years? Just out
of the blue?* He dropped back into his chair
and tossed the phone onto the kitchen nook
table. *I can't believe she . . . I mean, just out of
nowhere . . .*

Skeeter, who had stepped into the great
room when the call first came, sat at the table.
Taking a large bite of his Cholula-smothered
Denver omelet, he asked with his mouth full,
"You okay?"

Riley nodded absently, then seemed
to connect with Skeeter's question. "Yeah,
I think so. That was so weird. She sounded
so . . . I don't know . . . distant, different."

"Time'll do that."

"I guess so," Riley responded, lifting a
piece of omelet but never quite getting it to
his mouth. He dropped his fork and pushed
his plate back. "She just sounded so sad. It's

almost like this was a cry for help. You know, I wonder if I should call her back to see if everything's okay."

"Wouldn't," Skeeter said, tackling another chunk from his plate.

"Why? What if she needs me? Maybe she just couldn't bring herself to say anything? We had these awkward pauses, almost like she was trying to get the courage to ask me something." Riley stared at the phone that seemed to be crying out, *Pick me up! Pick me up!*

Skeeter put down his fork and wiped his mouth with a napkin. "Used to have a dog, Comanche. Okay dog as dogs go. But hooked on the white bread—couldn't get enough. I give Comanche a little white bread, he'd do anything for me. He'd walk with me from home to hell and back, as long as I kept feeding him the white bread."

Although there were usually points to Skeeter's stories, they weren't always easily accessible. This one seemed to bring a new depth to the word *obscure*.

"So, you're saying . . ."

Skeeter picked up his fork and used it to point at the phone. "White bread."

Riley watched his friend shovel another bite into his mouth. *Am I that easy? Is that what he's saying? Give me a phone call, and I'm panting like Pavlov's dogs?*

"You love that dog, Skeet?"

Pushing his empty plate away, Skeeter downed the last of his coffee and shrugged. "Don't know. Probably."

At least that's something. At least there's some possibility that she—

"Didn't respect him, though. He was way too easy."

That was like a blow to Riley's gut. Love and respect always went hand in hand for him. No respect, no love.

"Got film today." Riley slid the plate with its half-eaten omelet across the table to Skeeter, who accepted it with a nod.

As he brushed his teeth, he wrestled with whether Skeeter's story really applied to Khadi and him. For it to be true, Khadi would have to be using him—for companionship, for affirmation, for something. She may have loved him, but it wasn't a real love. It was a "what-can-you-give-me" kind of love, not the other way around.

But that just didn't sound like her. Nothing about her ever said *user* to him. No doubt about it, there was real love there— once.

He stepped into his bedroom and went to his sock drawer. Running his hand underneath the balled-up pairs, he found the strip of leather he was looking for. He pulled it out and held it in front of him. Hanging at the end of the leather thong was a ring that Khadi had given to him the last time he had seen her. It had belonged to her grandfather and had the words *truth*, *integrity*, and *honor* inscribed on it in Farsi.

As he watched the gold slowly twist, he thought, *I understand what Skeet's saying. I don't want to just grab any little bite and explode it into some big thing. But there's no doubt that what we had was—is?—real.*

Truth, integrity, honor—I've forgotten a bit about those words lately.

He was replacing the ring among his socks when he stopped and pulled it out again. Taking the thong in both hands, he slid it over his head and tucked the ring under his shirt. *This may be as close as I get to her today, but at least it's closer than I was yesterday.*

MONDAY, SEPTEMBER 12, 8:20 A.M. EDT
ASHBURN, VIRGINIA

There were the expected things—a Gatorade bucket in his locker, a Monopoly Get Out of Jail Free card, a pile of dollar coins, a musical greeting card that played "They're Coming to Take Me Away, Ha-Haaa!"

But two items did stand out from the crowd. One was an underwater phone—a device that Riley could not think of a single practical application for. The second was a guillotine that was supposed to allow you to cut off your hand, then magically have it reappear attached to your wrist. The trick looked pretty cool. However, as hard as he tried to find volunteers, he couldn't find anyone willing to give it a shot.

Despite the joking around Riley's locker, the mood in the locker room was fairly subdued. Everyone knew what was in store for them, and when the time came, Riley filed down the hall with the rest of the team to the main amphitheater to watch film. If you had a good game, film time was wonderful. There was praise from the coaches. There were high fives from your teammates. It was a fun event and a great ego boost.

However, if your game was bad, three hours in the film room could seem like the worst eight hours of your life. Every mistake was played and replayed. You were expected to give answers to unanswerable questions, like "Why'd you let that happen?" and "What were you thinking?" It was frustrating and humiliating.

Because of the horrendous game the team had played, the film time went much as expected. The only positive for Riley was that the whole team had stunk, so he wasn't consistently singled out. However, he did get his share of onscreen lowlights.

Sitting in the cool air of the amphitheater, he often found himself wondering what had happened. His mistakes were rookie mistakes—missed coverages, bad reads, weak tackles. At one point, he watched as an easy interception bounced right off his numbers, eliciting a groan from the entire room.

As much as he told himself he didn't really care about football, he was still embarrassed. *I can't believe that however many millions of people watched me suck this badly! I've got friends and family who saw this. And I can't imagine what the blogs are saying. I guess my only hope is that my on-field suckiness will be overshadowed by my off-field stupidity.*

Mercifully, the film got to the fourth quarter, and he tuned out the analysis. He closed his eyes, put his head back, and slowly twisted back and forth on his swivel chair.

But then, after the final play, he felt an elbow to his arm. He looked up to see the screen filled with him dumping the phone into the Gatorade bucket.

A few players hooted, then quickly fell silent as Coach Medley glared at them. Next came the coin incident with Jonny

Wiens. One player called out "Presto" when Riley pulled the coin out, causing snickers throughout the theater.

The film ended, and the lights came up to full.

Coach Medley stood in front of the team, arms folded, looking straight at Riley. Finally, he said, "Gentlemen, I think Riley has something to say to Mr. Bellefeuille, Mr. Wiens, and the rest of his team."

What? What is this? Come on, Coach, this isn't how to play this! Don't be forcing my hand this way!

All eyes were on Riley, and he was steaming inside.

He eased himself up. With a penitent look on his face, he slowly pivoted so that he had a chance to look at everyone on the team. "Mr. Bellefeuille, Jonny, my fellow Warriors. It was a strange day all around yesterday. Things were done, and stuff was said. And I guess . . . I guess I probably need to clear the air. When I was with Jonny, the word I said was *abracadabra*, not *presto*, as is currently being reported in the press. I just wanted you all to know that."

The theater erupted in laughter. Riley gave small, contrite waves and nods as he settled into his seat. Looking around at the team, he spotted Coach Medley glaring at him. With a smirk, Riley locked eyes with him until eventually Medley turned away.

All around him, players were calling out to him and giving him thumbs up. Apparently, the fear of retribution had flown out the window. Riley took it all in with smiles and waves. But inside he was thinking, *Well, that's strike three, son. It's going to be interesting to see if you've just struck out.*

MONDAY, SEPTEMBER 12, 6:50 A.M. CDT

OKLAHOMA CITY, OKLAHOMA

Allen Barr turned his dusty, dimpled grey Ford Taurus left off of NW 39th Street into the Dunkin' Donuts parking lot. He circled around to the back of the store because at this time of day the front parking was always taken. He was ten minutes early for his meeting, but past experience told him that it could take that long to find an open table.

After finding a spot, he turned the key and pulled it out. The car answered by rumbling for a few seconds. Then it knocked a little before finally settling into a long series of clicks.

That can't be good, Allen thought. *Then again, what can you do? Unless the car fairies come down in the middle of the night to fix it, it's just going to have to keep complaining every time I shut it down.*

Since his divorce three years ago, money was extremely tight. Alimony and child support took a significant portion of his paycheck each month. But he didn't begrudge it. He was still madly in love with his wife, and he knew that he was the reason they weren't together.

And his kids—they were the light of his life. Two girls and a boy, all under ten. He was striving to rebuild a relationship with them, and so far it seemed to be working.

No, Allen didn't care how much of his check they took or how hard he would have to work. The entire blame for his current life's situation fell on his own shoulders. He had made his bed . . .

Two men in flannel jackets and gimme caps walked out the front doors of the donut shop, the second one holding the door for Allen, who nodded his thanks and stepped in.

There are few things like the smell of a donut shop, he thought as he deeply inhaled the thick, doughy sweetness. Quickly scanning the restaurant, he saw two tables open with only one customer in front of him. *This just might work out!*

When it was his turn, he ordered an iced chocolate bismark, a strawberry cheese Danish, and two coffees. After paying, he said, "Thanks, Lenny," not expecting any response. In return, he received just what he hadn't expected. In fact, it was the same response he received every day from the store manager.

Lenny is not a man who is happy in his work, Allen mused. *Lord, bring some happiness into his life. Bring somebody or something. Lenny needs a little boost of love.*

A two-seater was open, and Allen took the seat facing the door. He set the Danish and a coffee on the table in front of the other chair. Marty would complain that he paid again, but Allen felt it was only right. After all, Allen was the reason they were here. He was the one with the problem. He was the one who had blown his life. He was the one who had destroyed his family. Having Marty there to hold him accountable during the rebuilding process was certainly worth a Danish and a cup of coffee a day.

About five tables away was a four-top. A member of

Oklahoma City's finest was seated in each chair. Allen watched until one of them caught his eye. Almost imperceptibly, Allen nodded and gave a thumbs-up. The officer nodded in response and turned back to the conversation.

The first time he had seen Officer Donny Marden in the donut shop, he had almost turned and walked back out. But then he thought, *That's what the old Allen would do. Man up!* So he had instead walked straight up to the man and introduced himself. Marden vaguely remembered him and seemed a little suspicious of the interruption. But after Allen described his journey and the changes he had made, the policeman had actually stood up, shaken his hand, and wished him luck.

That was huge for Allen, because Officer Marden had technically been the one who had pulled the pin on the grenade that blew up his life—although Allen knew that when it came down to it, it was all his own fault. It was Officer Marden who had pulled him over that night on I-44. It was he who had given Allen the field sobriety test. It was Officer Marden who had put the cuffs on him. But it was Allen himself who had fifteen minutes earlier gotten in the car knowing full well that he already had two DUIs behind him.

That arrest had cost him his license and ninety days in jail. It was also the final shove that sent his job and his marriage plunging into the abyss. In the weeks that followed his arrest, he spun so far down into depression that alcoholic homelessness or suicide seemed his only options. Not that there was much difference—one just being a slower way to reach the same end.

One day, as he sat in that county cell wallowing in self-pity over what he had made of his life, he heard a voice from the other side of the bars.

"Allen? Allen Barr?"

Without answering, he looked to his left and saw a man with a gentle face and biceps the size of his own thighs.

"Hey, Allen, I'm Larry Soady—one of the chaplains here.

Sorry it took me a few days to get over to you. How're you holding up?"

Allen looked around his small cell, then back at the chaplain. "Now that's a stupid question."

Chaplain Soady smiled. "Yeah, I guess life looks a little brighter from this side of the bars. Anyway, I just came by to see if there was anything I could do for you?"

"Get me my family back. Get me my job back. Get me out of this place."

The smile stayed on Soady's face. "Well, my friend, I can't help you with those things, but maybe I know someone who can."

Allen's anger flared. "Yeah, I know. I've heard it all before. 'Jesus loves me, this I know'; 'There's no sin too great'; 'Shall we gather at the river?' Yada, yada, yada. Just stow it! You can keep your Jesus and all your happy little promises that go along with him. My philosophy is God helps those who help themselves."

Soady tapped his wedding ring on the bars and said, "Maybe it's time to start thinking about a new philosophy. Listen, anytime you want to talk, shoot me a kite and I'll be here."

Over the next two weeks, Chaplain Soady came by every couple days—always with a smile on his face, always unfazed by Allen's attitude. Finally, either by sheer determination or maybe pure stubbornness, he wore down Allen's defenses.

"Okay, Larry, talk to me. Tell me what I need to hear," he said skeptically one day when they were sitting at a table in the common area. The television was so loud that all the other prisoners were talking even louder just to be heard. Allen leaned in so he could hear.

"I don't know who you're thinking Jesus is," Larry began. "I don't know if you think He's just waiting for you to screw up again so that He can come down on you. I don't know if you think you're beyond His reach because of how you've messed up your life. But John 1:17 says, 'For the law was given through Moses; grace and truth came through Jesus Christ.' Jesus isn't about the rules. You get right with Him, and the rules take care of themselves. He's about grace. Do you know what grace means?"

"I know it's 'amazing,'" Allen said with an uncomfortable chuckle.

"It is that. Grace just means getting what you don't deserve. Like winning the lottery without ever having bought a ticket. Through Jesus, everyone has won a ticket-free lottery. But not for money—for something better, something bigger. Money's going to get spent or stolen or absorbed into the bottomless pit of the IRS. But the prize we've won never fades or is lost. And it's one of the few things the government can't put its hands on—eternal life."

"You know, Larry, that's great for when I die. Great to know that I don't just fade into oblivion. But look where I'm at! I've got nothing! I need a here-and-now Jesus, not just a Jesus who's waiting at the finish line."

Larry's trademark smile crept back onto his face. "That's just the thing, buddy! He's full of grace *and* truth. It's the truth that keeps us going here. He has all the right answers. A life following Him is a life following the path that your Creator created you for. So no matter how bad your life gets, no matter what problems come your way, you can still have peace, joy, contentment. How? Because you're following the Truth. So you know you're not alone. You know you're doing the right thing."

Twenty minutes later, in the noise of that common area, Allen was praying for the first time in his life. It was a prayer asking for forgiveness from God. It was a prayer that confessed his belief that Jesus Christ had died and rose again for him. It was a prayer committing himself to trying with everything he had to live the way the Lord wanted him to.

Allen took a sip of his coffee and looked around the donut shop. *I wish I could say things have been rosy since then. But at least I'm making progress. And I know God loves me, and that gives me a peace like nothing I've ever felt before.*

The front door pinged, and Allen looked over, expecting to see Marty. It was just two stoner teens looking like they wanted to feed a craving. Checking his watch, he saw that it was five after. *Strange, Marty's never late.*

Upon Allen's release, Chaplain Soady had connected him with a church that had an Alcoholics Anonymous–like program. The twelve steps were pretty much the same, but they put the name Jesus down as their Higher Power. Marty, sober for eighteen years, had become Allen's sponsor. Now, even when the temptation to drink again was at its worst, through prayer and picturing Marty sitting across from him in this donut shop, he was able to fight through it.

The door pinged again and Allen looked up, again expecting to see Marty. Instead, it was a young man with olive skin and jet-black hair. He was carrying something, and when Allen looked to see what it was, his whole world suddenly shifted into slow motion.

The man shouted something unintelligible as he turned his back to Allen. The automatic weapon in his hands began firing at the table with the police. Officer Marden's throat burst open, and more rounds shook the three other officers to the ground.

For an instant, Allen wondered if this was just someone who had it in for the police. But he had seen the news reports of the other attacks, and when the gunman continued firing at the other tables, he knew this wasn't revenge—it was jihad.

I can't let this happen! Three steps and I'm on him! Lord, give me strength!

As he launched up and took the first step, the faces of his beautiful daughters and precious little son flashed in his mind. *Lord, protect them. Keep them. They're yours.*

In his second step, he saw his wife. *Forgive me, sweetheart. I pray you find the Jesus I have, then pass Him on to the kids.*

As he took his third step and reached his arms out to grab the gunman, something slammed into his back. He pitched forward and fell onto the shooter's legs. Two more shots sounded from behind him as Allen hit the ground, and the young gunman collapsed on top of him.

The pain in his chest was unbearable, and he was feeling incredibly cold. The other body was pulled off him, and someone was talking to him. Although he knew that man was speaking English, none of the words were making sense to him.

And they seem to be getting smaller . . . shrinking, drifting, fading . . . fading. Pain's fading. Oh, Jesus . . . fading. I'm fading. . . . I'm fading. . . .

FIFTEEN

MONDAY, SEPTEMBER 12, 1:00 P.M. EDT

WASHINGTON, DC

"Widen it out a bit," Evie Cline commanded a grumpy Gooey.

Gooey always loved an audience, particularly when he was about to do something really cool. But he didn't appreciate—or desire, or need—any help from the peanut gallery.

A brilliant analyst with satellite and surveillance, he was the oddest of the odd ducks that worked in the RoU (Room of Understanding—a name Evie had determined was less confrontational than War Room) of the counterterrorism division's Special Operations Group Bravo. Crowded around his desk chair were the other analysts of SOG Bravo: Evie Cline, Joey Williamson, and Virgil Hernandez.

"A little bit more," Evie continued, reaching her hand for his mouse. "Come on, just a little bit—"

"Would you shut up?" Gooey said, blocking her with his shoulder. "It's not like this is my first rodeo."

"*Bzzzz,*" Hernandez called out, giving Gooey two slugs in the arm. "Pay up!"

Recently, the team had put out a tired cliché jar, labeled with the phrase "Oh No You Di'int," right next to their curse jar, which bore the label "You Kiss Your Mama with That Mouth?" The sanction for minor infractions like "keeping it real" and "staying on the cutting edge" was one dollar. However, if you stooped to uttering especially heinous phrases such as "noodling it out," "don't go there," and "What up?" (particularly if combined with the word *dog*), the price started at two dollars and went up from there. So far the highest fine was four dollars paid by Scott Ross when he gratuitously added a delayed "Not!" to the end of a sentence.

"Dude, I'm busy," Gooey said. He nodded toward a corner of his desk where sat a Velcro flip wallet that was possibly once yellow but was now some other sort of noncolor. "Just take it out."

"I'm not touching that," Hernandez countered as he poked at it with a pencil. "I don't want my fingers smelling like gravy or pork rinds or some other rancid food item for the rest of the day."

"Then shut up and let me work."

Evie, Hernandez, and Williamson all shared a look.

"*Tsk, tsk, tsk.* Sounds like somebody got up on the wrong side of the sty today," Evie said disapprovingly.

Gooey spun around. "Listen, guys, I'm trying to get something done, something you three apparently aren't capable of since you're spending all this time over here! So if you're going to hang out over my shoulder, breathing down my neck, I'd appreciate it if you'd maybe shut up so that I can get some work done! What do you think? Would that be okay with you?"

The three analysts stared at him—shock and anger on their faces. Gooey could certainly be temperamental at times. But very rarely did he stoop to this kind of disrespectful outburst.

Then Gooey's face broke into a wide grin. "Aughhhh, I got you! What a bunch of suckers, making it that easy! Go on, pay up!"

Voicing their respect, the trio walked over to the last of the three jars—the gullible jar. On its label stood Bugs Bunny holding a carrot like a cigar. A voice bubble above his head read, "What a maroon!" They each dropped in a five-dollar bill. These infractions cost the most; being gullible was thought by the analysts to be the worst of all crimes.

Swiveling back around, Gooey seized the mouse and continued his work. The gang crowded around him.

"Okay, there he is," Gooey said, zeroing the screen in. "He looks like he's alone."

"All the better to minimize the collateral damage. Don't want more people mad at you than is necessary," Williamson pointed out.

"Wor—exactly," Gooey agreed, catching himself before he was out another two bucks.

"What are you using to take him out?" Evie asked. She was leaning in so she could better see their target.

"Come on, you know me. I'm going to drop the hammer on him."

"The big hammer?"

"Is there another?" Gooey took a big breath, laced his fingers, popped his knuckles, and exhaled. "Okay, guys, here goes!"

From the right of the screen, an avatar that looked somewhat like Gooey—except he was thin, sported a neon green mohawk and warpaint, and was dressed only in a loincloth—dropped to the forest ground. In his right hand he held a war hammer that was twice his own size. Before the other avatar on the screen had a chance to react, the hammer came down with a deep *thump*, flattening it. A message came up: *kissmedownunder has been destroyed by epluribusgoonum.*

Cheers went up all around Gooey, as he muttered, "Take that, you Australian wallaby lover. I hope a dingo eats your baby."

A chant of "USA, USA, USA" echoed through the small room.

Scott, hearing the celebration, came walking out of his office. "Who was it this time?"

"Kissmedownunder," Gooey answered proudly.

Scott stopped. A look of appreciation spread across his face. "You've been after him for weeks. Congratulations, Gooster. Now, how about you all join me around the table. Break time's over."

Sounding an obligatory "Awwww," they all quickly obeyed. Even though they looked and acted like a bunch of National Mall buskers, they were still some of the best counterterrorism analysts in the country. They loved to mess around, but they took their jobs seriously. The knowledge that their successes and failures meant the saving or losing of people's lives constantly weighed on them. Thus the hard work and long hours to get the job done and the regular bouts of obnoxious stupidity to keep themselves sane.

Scott looked around the table at his team and wondered where to begin. This was his first time back into the office since the shooting on Saturday. His desk was piled with paperwork that needed to be filled out and reports that needed to be filed regarding the incident. However, even with all the mucketymucks wanting fast answers, he still had managed to buy himself a day at home with a quick call to Secretary Porter.

But now he was back. It was game time again.

"Anything I need to know before we begin?" Scott asked, as he titled a yellow legal pad sheet *Staff Meeting: September 12—SR, EC, JW, VH, G.*

"Just that we're glad you're okay," Evie said, getting up and opening her arms to give Scott a hug.

Okay, this is a little weird, Scott, who had never been much of a hugger, thought, *but how do you say, "No, please don't hug me"?* He put his pen down, stood up, and put his arms out for Evie. But just before they connected, she leaned back and punched him hard on his chest, right on top of the bruise.

"Evie! Holy mother of St. Lucius!" he cried out, doubling over, then falling back into his chair. Times were tight for the Ross family now that James had been born and Tara wasn't working. Every dollar of fine he paid was a dollar of food snatched from his baby's mouth, a fact Scott tried to keep in mind even as he rode the tide of pain that flowed through his body. "Ohhhh, tie me kangaroo down, sport! Crap biscuit, crap biscuit, crap biscuit!"

Evie showed no pity while she watched Scott try to ease back to normalcy. Meanwhile, the other three guys were in a debate as to whether *crap biscuit,* though not an actual swear word, was still worth fifty cents in the jar per usage.

"What was that for?" Scott finally croaked out.

"For getting yourself shot, Señor Stupido," Evie said, the rest of the gang drawn back in now. "What's the matter with you? You've got Tara to think of now. And even more than that, you've got James. I'm not going to let my godson go through life without his dad!"

"You're not his godmother," Scott pointed out.

"Yeah, whatever—maybe not in your eyes."

"Whose else's eyes count?"

"'Whose else's'?" Hernandez asked, looking at Williamson, who just shrugged in return.

"Listen," Evie said, refusing to let go of her point. "All we're saying is that it's not just all about you anymore. You've got to start thinking about your family."

Scott tested his chest with a light touch, then quickly pulled his hand away. "I appreciate what you all are saying. I got the same speech from Tara last night. Trust me, I don't have a death wish. It's just that sometimes out on the field, things happen."

Evie started to say something, but Scott cut her off. "However, that being said, I do promise to try my best to avoid all rapidly flying lead if I can help it. Deal?"

They all nodded their heads skeptically.

"Good. Now, barring any other unnecessary acts of violence, update me on Oklahoma City."

Hernandez answered. "Looks like sixteen casualties with nine dead, including four cops and the shooter."

"And a Good Sam," Evie added. "Guy was lunging for the bad guy when he got in the way of a round from a plainclothes officer behind him. Let's see how the media blows that out of proportion."

"So that's four attacks in less than two weeks. What are we missing?"

Williamson jumped in to answer. "Part of our problem is that they're not using traditional lines of communication. Since all of our perps are American, none of the noise is coming from outside the country. Everything is in-house, so to speak."

"Plus, they've created their own language, almost," Hernandez added. "There's a terrorist-speak that is very Americanized. They understand it, but to us, it just blends in with everything else."

"You're saying there's nothing that our COMINT resources are programmed to intercept," Scott asked.

"Bingo. Now the one thing that we have going for us is Malik Abdul-Tawwab. Out of his interrogations, we've been getting some trigger words. Unfortunately, they're fairly common phrases."

"Phrases that tie in perfectly with their new preferred methods of communications—texting and social networking sites," Evie said, completing Hernandez's thought. She slid a paper she had been writing on to Scott. "These guys are smart and they're savvy. Take a look at that message."

Scott read it over: *rofl! ur such a sweet<3! ilu bff!* He slid the paper back. "Text speak! Can't stand the stuff. What does it say?"

Without looking at the message, Evie translated, "'Rolling on floor laughing! You are such a sweetheart! I love you, best friends forever!' This was the last message Abdur-Razzaq received on his cell phone prior to his attempt on the National Mall. Abdul-Tawwab has already confirmed that the 'ilu bff' was the final go-ahead for the mission. He thinks the middle part may have something to do with the problem with the vest, but he wasn't in the communications side that deeply."

"All that to say, you can see our problem," Williamson said. "This text could be sent from one twelve-year-old girl to another twelve-year-old girl a thousand times a day across the country. There's no way for us to filter them out. And as far as social networking sites, they're potentially on Facebook, Twitter, LinkedIn, Classmates, even MySpace—although they may be the last people in America actually using that particular forum."

"Okay, you've given me the problems," Scott said, scribbling some more notes on his legal pad. "How about some solutions before we have another punk bin Laden wannabe blow up the St. Louis Arch?"

"Abdul-live and Abdur-dead are the keys," Gooey said. He scratched something off his front tooth, looked at it, then sucked it off his finger before continuing. "They're linked. I've got the hard drive from the stoolie's computer here in-house. I was able to hack and upload sniper-bait's hard drive before those donks in the FBI snagged it out of his apartment."

"Sniper-bait?" Evie asked. Williamson pretended to take two shots at Hernandez, who in turn lifted his hand off the back of his head.

"Ahhh," Evie said with a nod.

Gooey plowed on. "What we're doing is tracking down every connection they've got on their networking sites, then, in turn, following those relationships out. Any 'friend' or 'buddy' or 'classmate' where the networking profiles don't match the rest of the computer's activity will be flagged for us to check out."

"Do you realize how deep that could get?" Scott asked, tossing his pen down. "Think how many computers are out there with teenage girls spending their afternoons on them messaging their friends, while the girls' dads spend their nights surfing for pictures of naked cat jugglers. It's just not practical."

A big grin spread across Gooey's fleshy face. "Have faith, my friend. As my confirmation teacher used to say, 'With Goo, all things are practical.'"

"Confirmation? You?" Hernandez said, giving voice to the surprise that was on everyone's faces.

"You betcha! Signed, sealed, and just waiting to be delivered! Can I get a witness?"

"Why do I have a feeling St. Peter isn't going to be signing for that delivery at the pearly gates?" Williamson said.

"Okay, guys, reel it back in," Scott said, knowing he had about ninety more seconds of their attention span before all was lost. "If this is what we've got, then this is what we've got."

"Profound," Evie said. The others nodded appreciatively.

Scott stood. "What I mean is, keep running this lead. Right now, it's the best we have. But don't get locked in. This is a whole new paradigm we're operating in. The rules are different, and the only thing we know is that we don't know what we don't know."

Two Evie Cline punches on the arm later, Scott pulled out his wallet, dropped two dollars into the "Oh No, You Di'int" jar, and grumbled his way back to his office.

CHAPTER SIXTEEN

MONDAY, SEPTEMBER 12, 2:15 P.M. EDT

LEESBURG, VIRGINIA

Riley dialed his phone, then slipped a hands-free device onto his ear. He always felt like a dork when he wore it, so he only put it on when he was driving. *I never could understand the people who walk around all day with their little cyborg-looking command modules hanging off their ears, flashing a little blue electronic heartbeat every few seconds. They say cell phones will give you brain cancer; how about having some foreign, wireless object sticking in your head eight hours a day?*

"Hyello," a voice answered on the other end.

"Hey, Grandpa."

"Riley! How's it going, son? Been watching the news; sounds like you had a full weekend."

Riley gunned around some slow traffic, then eased back into the right lane. "Yeah, it's been a bit unusual."

"I've got to say, you have us all wondering

just what it is you're going to do next." Riley could hear the laughter in Grandpa's voice.

Riley and his grandfather had always had a close relationship, made more so by his decision to join with Grandpa's Air Force, rather than his dad's Navy. Then, after Dad had been murdered two years ago by a terrorist group, Riley realized that his grandfather was the last man he had in his family. As a result, he had come to rely heavily on him for guidance and direction.

Mom was wonderful—full of love and encouragement. She was the one who sent the care packages. She was the one who was always checking up on his friends. She was a nurturer through and through.

But Riley didn't feel comfortable burdening her with his problems. She had experienced more than her share of pain in her life. And now she had enough problems of her own living as a widow.

Grandpa, on the other hand, was the source of wisdom. He was the straight shooter. He had shoulders a mile wide that were ready for whatever Riley needed to dump on them. And he knew how to get through to his grandson like no one else.

When Riley was little, they had a yellow Lab named Princess. Once, Princess got tangled in a wire fence. Her leg got cut up pretty badly. The vet stitched her up, then gave Riley's dad antibiotic pills to give to the dog to avoid infection. That night, try as they might, they couldn't get Princess to keep the pill down. Finally, Dad had torn a piece of bread, wrapped it around the pill, and gave it to the dumb dog, who swallowed it right up.

Thinking of that story always brought Grandpa to mind. It might be that you didn't want to hear about something—you refused to accept the truth. But Grandpa had a way of wrapping it all up in a tasty morsel, and before you knew it, you had swallowed it whole.

"If you really want to know what's next, how does this

sound to you? The Warriors suspended me today," Riley said with a little more anger in his voice than he was expecting.

"Suspended? Well, yeah, I guess I shouldn't be surprised after yesterday."

Taking a deep breath, Riley said, "Well, it actually wasn't over what happened yesterday. They were ready to let that go. All I needed to do was formally apologize."

Riley told Grandpa of the incident in the film room earlier in the day. He could have sworn he heard the old man stifle a laugh at the end of his recitation, but it was hard to tell long-distance.

"So, you refused to apologize, even though you knew you were in the wrong?"

"I guess you could put it that way," Riley said, easing onto an off-ramp and up to the light.

"Interesting," Grandpa replied, still with a lilt to his voice.

"Anyway, Coach Medley dismissed everyone from the room except me. I waited there in silence for about ten minutes until Mr. Bellefeuille came in. The two of them conferred quietly for about three minutes, then Medley asked me, 'Do you want counseling to get to the root of your psychiatric issues?'"

"And your response?"

"Something along the lines of 'Your mama.'"

"Classy."

The light changed and Riley turned left, passing under the highway. "Yeah, maybe not the best choice of words. Well, Medley and Bellefeuille talked a little more, and then Bellefeuille handed Coach a piece of paper and walked out of the room—never once did he look at me.

"Medley called me down and handed me the paper that Bellefeuille had given to him. 'This is going to be released to the press this afternoon,' he says. 'Read it so that you're not surprised.'"

One more left turn and Riley was in his neighborhood. "I can't tell you exactly what it said, but it was something like

'Riley Covington has been an American hero both on and off the field, blah blah blah. However, the Warriors organization has seen some changes recently in his behavior. We're concerned it could have something to do with the physical, mental, and emotional trauma he experienced, more blah blah blah. After consulting specialists in post-traumatic stress disorder, for his own sake and that of the rest of the team, we are placing Riley Covington on paid compassionate leave until he is professionally evaluated and pursues any recommended courses of treatment. Thus far he has rejected the options we have offered him, and we can only encourage him to reconsider. Our thoughts and prayers are with him, etc. The end.'"

"Hmmm, so you're not suspended? You're just on leave?"

Riley gave an obligatory wave to his neighbor two doors down, then pulled into his own driveway and put the car in park. After switching the air-conditioning to low, he put his head back and closed his eyes. "It's semantics, Grandpa. Either way, I'm on the shelf."

"But not if you were to do the evaluation, right?"

"I'm not suffering from PTSD! I'm just fed up with all the crap that comes with playing in the PFL. Football used to be fun. It used to be a game. Now it's just a business, and I'm only a product. I don't know. I think I'm just done with it."

"Perfect! Then you've got your wish. Sounds like Bellefeuille gave you exactly what you wanted."

"Grandpa, that's not . . ." Riley stopped and thought a moment. *You know, he's actually right. If it weren't for most of America thinking I've gone gonzo, the situation couldn't be more perfect.*

"And I know what's going through your mind, Riles. But who cares what other people think of you? You got to make sure you're right with God and with the people who love you. Let Him take care of the rest. You start worrying about everyone else, you'll end up driving yourself crazy."

Riley smiled to himself. He pulled out his pocketknife and began scraping off some dried smoothie drips from his center console.

"You're right; you're right," he said as he wiped the pale orange flakes from the blade onto his shorts and continued scraping. "I guess I just don't like people thinking I'm nuts."

"Probably save you from having people cut in front of you in line at the grocery store."

"And no one will dare complain if I have more than ten items in the express lane," Riley said, wiping off his knife one more time, then folding it and slipping it back into his pocket. He licked his thumb and rubbed off the final smoothie remnants. "Yeah, I can see really making this work for me."

"Riley, just trust God to lead you in the situation. And remember that no matter how bizarre your behavior gets—"

"Hey, that was your fault, mister," Riley interrupted. "You're the one who taught me that coin-from-behind-the-ear trick twenty years ago."

"And your mom was sure to call me last night and remind me of that fact. *Mea culpa*, my boy. Anyway, just remember that no matter what, you are loved by your grandpa, your mom, and most of all, your God."

"Thanks, Gramps. I love you too."

Yeah, that's what grandpas are for, Riley thought, as he parked the truck in the garage. *Putting everything back into perspective.* After slamming another dent into the drywall, he lifted his fishing pole and tackle box off a narrow workbench and headed down to the dock.

SEVENTEEN

Majid Alavi glanced impatiently at his watch—2:37 a.m. He turned to his partner, Ubaida Saliba, who circled his hand, indicating he also was anxious to get things moving.

"Let's go," Alavi quietly demanded of the man who was busy working the lock on the window.

"Shut up and let me work. You hired me to do a job; now let me do it," he hissed back. "And back up. Give a man some room."

This third man—this specialist—went by the street name Touch and was supposed to be the best at what he did. And what he did was get people safely and quietly into places where they weren't invited.

I don't care about his reputation or his skills, Alavi thought. *He's still the weakest link in this mission.*

The three men, dressed all in black, were huddled outside a rear window of an average-size, two-story, brown brick home in

Bethesda, Maryland. Inside the home slept the chaplain of the United States Senate, Daniel Musman, and his wife of fifty-three years, Elsa.

A barely perceptible click sounded from the window, and Touch gently slid it to the left.

"You're sure about the alarm," Alavi asked.

Touch looked offended by the question. "Do I tell you how to do your job? The alarm's taken care of. You think I'd be opening the window if it weren't?"

"Okay, we shouldn't be more than ten minutes," Alavi said, ignoring the man's attitude. *There'll be plenty of time to deal with that later.* "Stay low and don't get seen."

"Pffssh, please." Touch cradled his hands, and Alavi put his right foot in. He hoisted himself onto the window ledge and into the house. Saliba followed seconds later.

Alavi took just a moment to catch his bearings. The air inside was warm and had an ethnic odor of cabbage and some sort of meat. A quick sweep with a red-light flashlight showed him that the way was clear to the stairs. He nodded to Saliba, and the two men crossed the room—Alavi taking the lead, Saliba behind carrying a silenced Glock 21.

Just prior to mounting the staircase, Alavi had a moment of hesitation. He took a quick look back at the window. *I just don't know how much I can trust Touch. The last thing we need is for this petty thief to slip in and steal some bauble or trinket without me knowing. That could bring the whole plan crashing down.* He considered keeping Saliba downstairs just in case Touch tried anything, but he couldn't afford to be without him if things took a wrong turn upstairs.

It's in your hands, O Allah. I will trust you to keep the animal on his leash.

Softly he ascended the steps, caressing them with his feet like he was shown during his training in Somalia. As he walked, his mind flashed to when he was a kid watching reruns of the television show *Kung Fu*. Countless afternoons, he and his friends would pretend to do the rice paper walk, gently gliding their way through the room of candles. *"When you can walk the rice paper without tearing it, Grasshopper, then your steps will not be heard."*

After reaching the top, he allowed himself one more sweep of the red light to ensure there was a clear path to the bedroom three doors down. Quietly, the two men moved past the second door where the wife was sleeping, a long-ago banished victim of her husband's snoring and apnea. When they reached the third door, Alavi turned around.

Looking Saliba in the eyes, he gave a slight nod. His partner nodded his readiness back.

Alavi turned the handle and eased the door open. The bed was large, with its four posts sticking straight up in the middle of the room. To the left of the bed was a door that led to a master bathroom; to the right was a sitting area with a floral chair and ottoman. A suit was laid across the ottoman with a shirt and tie on top; shoes with socks stuffed in them sat on the floor.

A low hum sounded through the room, and it was toward that hum that Alavi moved. When he reached its source, he looked back at Saliba to confirm he was in position. As was the plan, Saliba was standing at the foot of the bed with the gun pointed toward Musman's head.

Alavi breathed in deeply and let the air slowly exhale from his mouth. The whole plan was riding on these next couple minutes. If he blew this, not only would he dishonor himself and his family, he would disappoint Saifullah and Allah himself. *Give your servant strength. Give your servant stealth. Give your servant success.*

Turning his attention back to the small, humming machine, Alavi gave it a quick examination. It was the exact model of CPAP that he had practiced on. Air was sucked in through a filter on the back of the device and then pumped out a tube that connected with a mask on the chaplain's face. The pressure of the air was such that it kept the old man's upper airway open and unobstructed, alleviating the apnea and the snoring that typically accompanied it.

Alavi slipped a small, thin screwdriver out of his pocket. Reaching around the back of the machine, he pried off the air intake cover. He pinched out a charcoal filter and set both items on the end table. After putting the screwdriver back into his pocket, he removed another item—a small silver atomizer.

As he held the cigar tube–shaped device with one gloved hand, he used the other to pull a thick cloth filter over his nose and mouth. Immediately, he felt his air severely restricted. But the temporary discomfort was more than worth the risk of the alternative.

He removed the cap, positioned the atomizer at the air intake, then closed his eyes and turned his head. *One, two, three sprays. It's done.*

Quickly, he capped the tube and slid it into his pocket. The saxitoxin, also known as shellfish toxin, would take effect any second, and Alavi didn't want to be around when it did. Virtually untraceable, the poison paralyzed the nervous system, causing nearly immediate death. With the already-failing health of the aging chaplain, the hope was that there would be only a cursory postmortem investigation and that his peaceful passing in the night would be viewed by friends and family as God's blessing for his many years of faithful service.

Reaching behind the CPAP, Alavi replaced the filter and snapped on the cover. He nodded to Saliba, who began moving toward the door. Alavi started to follow him when he was stopped short by a hand around his wrist.

He turned toward Musman and saw him staring back wide-eyed. The old chaplain was trying to say something, but his lips formed only empty words. Saliva began running out the corners of the clear plastic mask, and his breathing consisted of short gasps of air. Alavi tried to pull his arm free, but the dying man's grip was like iron.

The seconds seemed like hours. Alavi wanted to escape the accusation and fear that were in Musman's eyes, but he couldn't bring himself to turn away. Finally, the lips stopped moving, the grip relaxed, and Alavi was able to break free. But as he fled toward the door, he knew he would forever have the picture of that man's dying eyes embedded in his brain.

Back at the window, Alavi was relieved to see Touch waiting outside the house. First Saliba dropped out; then he followed. Touch slid the window closed and expertly snapped the screen back in place.

Ten minutes later, the three men were turning from Old Georgetown Road onto Wisconsin Avenue. Touch, who was sitting in the front passenger seat next to Alavi, hadn't shut up since they had pulled away from the chaplain's house.

Laughing, he said, "You sure you won't tell me what you guys picked up? It's driving me crazy!"

"You were hired for a job. You did the job. You were paid well for the job. That's all you need to know," Alavi answered angrily. In the rearview mirror he connected with Saliba. *Now*, he said with his eyes.

"Don't go getting like that with me, man," Touch replied defensively. "You told me you were going in to lift something. But when I see you guys going in with nothing, then coming back out with nothing, it makes me wonder what—"

A bullet from Saliba's silenced pistol stopped Touch short. His head flew forward, then snapped back as the seat belt restricted his movement.

"That was none too soon," Alavi said as he wiped some red mist from his cheek.

"If he never shut up in the car, there's no way he could have kept quiet on the street," Saliba agreed.

Three blocks down, they turned into an alley and parked.

Saliba got out of the car and opened the passenger door. He was about to pull the body out when Alavi stopped him. After a quick search, Alavi found Touch's wallet in his left front pocket.

"Give the cops a little more of a challenge identifying him," he said.

While Saliba pulled the dead man out and dropped him to the wet asphalt, Alavi looked in his wallet. He pulled out Touch's driver's license—Wesley Kelley, it read.

Wesley, huh? No wonder you went by Touch.

He heard the door close and saw that Saliba was back in the car wiping his hands on his pants. After slipping the wallet into his pocket, he put the car in gear. *Twenty minutes to our parked car, and another thirty to the warehouse. All in all, it couldn't have gone much better. Thank you, Allah, for success. What you have begun, let these hands finish in your name.*

TUESDAY, SEPTEMBER 13, 2:05 P.M. EDT

WASHINGTON, DC

"We all grieve the passing of Chaplain Daniel Musman, and we pray for his dear wife, Elsa, his children, Brian and Stephanie, and his numerous grandchildren. Chaplain Dan, as I used to call him, was a good man—a man who made an impact on this world, a man who made an impact on me. I remember when I came to Washington nearly sixteen years ago, Chap walked up that first day to this green, wet-behind-the-ears senator who, champing at the bit to begin his fight for truth and justice . . ."

Leave it to Clayson Andrews to turn a tribute to a dead Senate chaplain into an homage to himself, Khadi Faroughi thought, standing six feet to the left of the senator. They were on the steps of the National Cathedral, its neogothic facade rising more than three hundred feet behind them. Andrews, as usual, was behind a bank of microphones. A little more than twenty reporters were listening to him and taking notes. Beyond them, a crowd of fifty-plus onlookers had gathered.

"'Senator Andrews, my friend,' he said—even that first day he called me 'my friend,' something this young, wide-eyed idealist needed to hear . . .'" The senator's voice cracked, causing Khadi to roll her eyes behind her dark sunglasses.

Listening to his pathetic emotional prattle was almost more than she could bear, especially after what had happened just a couple of hours ago. She was still shaken and was having a hard time grasping the reality of the situation.

She and J.D. Little had been going through the usual pre–photo op preparations when Tyson Bryson had called her into his office. As the senator's right hand man, Bryson technically was her supervisor, so she obeyed.

Bryson's office was decorated in what might be called modern brownnose. There were Clayson Andrews campaign posters and memorabilia covering every wall and every shelf. The photos on his desk and bookshelf were mostly of Senator Andrews meeting some head of state with Bryson somewhere in the background, often only able to be spotted by a child skilled in the art of *Where's Waldo?*

Bryson sat on the corner of his desk, and he motioned for Khadi to sit in a red plush chair in front of him. Although she didn't like being this close to him, she obliged.

"How are you, Khadi? You look well," he said with a smile on his face that made her skin crawl.

"I don't mean to be rude, Tyson, but J.D. and I are trying to get things ready for the National Cathedral presser."

"Always business, aren't you? Well, okay then, let's get down to business." Reaching behind, he lifted a 10x13 clasp envelope from his desk. "You know, Khadi, a big part of my job is to make sure that the senator is protected from those around him."

"Funny, I thought that was my job," Khadi said sarcastically.

"So it is. But who is there to protect him from his protectors?"

Khadi stared blankly at Bryson. *Where is he going with this?*

"I've spent some time researching your background, Khadi."

Khadi leaped out of her chair. "You what? What gives you the right to go digging into my life?"

"Shh, shh, shh," Bryson said condescendingly. "Please sit back down. I think you're going to want to hear what I have to say."

What does he have? It couldn't be anything! I've passed so many clearances—I'm clean as a whistle. Curiosity, however, got the best of her, and she sat.

"There's a good girl," he said, almost causing her to leap up again. "Now, your background is spotless, Khadi. I must commend you for that. Always doing the right thing. Always faithful to the cause. Unfortunately, the same can't be said for everyone in your family."

Khadi's spine stiffened. *What does he have? Did one of my brothers do something stupid?* "I'm listening," she said quietly.

"I'm glad, because what I have to say to you is very, very important. In this envelope, I have your parents' application for political asylum dated back thirty-some-odd years ago. Unfortunately, as I examined it I found—how should I put it?—some discrepancies."

"Discrepancies?" Khadi asked, her blood growing cold. "What kind of discrepancies?"

"Oh, a little stretch here, a little fudge there. Each one maybe not enough to raise a red flag. But put together? They scream for action to be taken."

"Action? What do you mean by *action*?"

"Oh, nothing much. Just prosecution. Quite possibly deportation."

Khadi was again on her feet. Grabbing Bryson by his lapels, she said, "I swear, if you do anything to harm my parents, I will make your life a painful hell—then I'll kill you."

But the normally easily cowed Bryson wasn't visibly fazed

by Khadi's outburst—apart from a little moisture appearing on his upper lip.

"I suggest you sit down, Khadi," he said calmly. "Right now, I'm the only person standing between your parents and a return trip to the Islamic Republic of Iran."

Khadi's head was spinning. *Could he really have evidence that my parents lied on their application?* Releasing Bryson's suit jacket, she eased herself back down.

"Let me see the envelope," she demanded, holding out her hand.

Dropping it back on his desk, Bryson said, "No, I don't think so."

"Then how do I—"

"You know it's true, Khadi. Deep in your heart, you know I wouldn't make this kind of accusation if I couldn't back it up."

Which is true, Khadi thought. *Although Bryson is a man of many disgusting qualities, stupidity is not one of them.* "Why are you telling me this? What do you want?"

"Ah, now we come to the crux of the matter, don't we? How much is this information worth? What are you willing to give in order to keep your family safe and sound in their happy little life here in the Land of Opportunity? I already know you don't have much money to give—I've seen all your bank records."

Again, Khadi stiffened. She felt violated by his deep searching into her life. Her stomach felt queasy, and the air in the room was beginning to taste stale.

"So I thought to myself, 'Self, if not money, then what does the lovely Khadi Faroughi have to offer me?' It was then I realized that I had just answered my own question. A lovely young lady like you, a reasonably attractive young man like myself . . ."

The bile in Khadi's stomach rose into her mouth, and she swallowed it back down. *He's not really suggesting what I think he's suggesting, is he?* But the lecherous smile on Bryson's face answered her question for her.

"Not in a million years," she said slowly, emphasizing each word.

"My, my, won't your parents be disappointed. But that's okay; maybe it won't be so bad. I hear the welcome-home committee for returning political refugees is very warm and hospitable," he said with an evil smirk.

"You're a disgusting pig," she spat out.

"Maybe so, but I'm the disgusting pig who's holding all the cards. I'll give you a week to think about it. You can go now."

Gratefully, she hurried out of Bryson's office, went right into the bathroom, and threw up.

She still felt the same queasiness now as she listened to the senator.

"'Senator Andrews, my friend, you make sure you do what it is that the good Lord called you here to do. But remember, Washington is a tough town. So while you're here doing what you were called to do, make sure you don't let this city change who you are.'"

Looking up toward heaven, a single tear rolling down his cheek, Andrews choked out, "I didn't let it change me, Chaplain Dan. Now, you can see clearly from your side of eternity that I'm still that same wide-eyed idealist. Thank you, Chap! Thank you!"

Andrews held a thumbs-up toward the sky long enough for the photographers to snap the shot before he turned back to the crowd. After dabbing his eyes with a handkerchief and taking a deep breath, he continued. "The reason I called this press conference in this particular location is that I have been given the somber honor by Elsa Musman and family to announce a memorial service for Chaplain Daniel Musman on Thursday, September 15, at 10 a.m. This service will be held in a venue befitting such a great man—" Andrews swept his arm back— "the majestic National Cathedral."

As Khadi's eyes panned the crowd, her mind began racing.

Thursday? Why Thursday? Isn't that a little fast? Surely they can't expect to get everything together in just two days?

Khadi's real concern, however, had nothing to do with the practicality of the preparations in so short a window of time. What she saw was the door slamming closed on her long weekend off.

Tomorrow evening, Ramadan would begin. This holiest of months on the Muslim calendar was a time for followers around the world to fast and pray and dig deeper into their faith. It was a time of commitment and sacrifice. It was also a time for families and celebration.

Late tomorrow night after her shift ended, she was planning to drive to her parents' spacious home in Arlington, Virginia. Her brothers and their families would already be there, most likely bedded down for the night. The next morning before dawn, they would get up, have a light breakfast, and go outside to watch the sun rise, bringing with it the beginning of Ramadan.

The day would be spent fasting from food and drink. It was natural for everyone to get a little bit crabby while the body adjusted to the deprivation, and that's why it was so helpful to have family around. The men would spend the time talking, praying, and going to the mosque. The women would fill their day with taking care of the kids and preparing for the evening's feast.

Finally, the family would all gather outside to watch the sun drop down below the horizon. When the last of the rays disappeared, they would let out a cheer, because now it was time for the *iftar* to begin.

Iftar was the celebration of breaking the day's fast. Typically throughout the month, it was done with just a normal meal. However, this first day was special. From everyone together eating their ceremonial first fig to when they all leaned back in their chairs full to bursting with their mother's amazing cooking, it was a night of joy and laughter and love.

It had been years since Khadi had been able to join her family for this tradition. She was so excited to see her parents. And the incredible women her brothers married were more like true sisters to her than in-laws.

Family, Khadi thought as she watched a man reach into his camera bag. *That's what I need right now.* When she saw that what he pulled out of his camera bag was in fact a camera, she let her gaze move on. *I need to be around people who love me with no questions asked, with no expectations. I need to be touched, hugged. I need to hear someone tell me how special I am. And now more than ever, I need to see my parents. I need to ask them about their application for asylum. I need to hear from their lips what the truth is. I absolutely have to see them!*

But she knew that the possibility of this actually happening had just decreased dramatically. Anytime the senator went to a public event, it was all hands on deck. It didn't matter if you were scheduled for a kidney transplant; you'd just have to say, "Sorry, Doc" and wait until the next organ came up for grabs.

Andrews was wrapping up, so Khadi casually moved closer to him. J.D. Little did the same to flank his other side. Glancing over their exit route, Khadi saw Tyson Bryson watching her with a smug smirk on his face. *He knows exactly what this is going to cost me, and he's getting a kick out of it.*

The senator gave a final thanks to the assembled masses, then pointed one last time to the skies while a beatific smile spread across his upturned face. After the clacking of the camera shutters died down, he turned and moved toward the street where his car awaited him.

Bryson met them halfway down. "That was beautiful, Clayson. Heartfelt. I could really sense your love for that wonderful man."

Andrews snorted. "The old windbag gave the longest prayers of anyone I've ever heard. I swear, if I stepped out of the chamber at his 'Dear Lord,' I could be back up from the commissary carrying a toasted bagel with cream cheese and a coffee long before he hit 'amen.' Maybe now they can get someone in there who knows the meaning of the words *brief introductory prayer*."

"You're right, you're right," Bryson agreed as he slid into the back of the limo behind Clayson. "What a gasbag!"

Khadi stepped in next, followed by Little.

The car pulled out, and she turned her attention toward the side windows. Bryson began going over the senator's schedule with him, but Andrews wasn't looking at his chief of staff. His eyes were locked on her.

Khadi tried to ignore his gaze, but she kept finding herself looking at him out of the corner of her eyes, trusting her dark sunglasses to hide the fact that he was getting under her skin.

When she could take it no longer, she slowly turned her head and said, "May I help you, Senator?"

"I was just wondering what you thought about the memorial being scheduled on Thursday?" he said with a Cheshire smile.

"What I think is that you and your cronies are rushing the celebration of a good man who gave more than twenty years of service to this country so that you all can still get an early Friday start to your weekend getaways."

"Oooooh, such ugly cynicism from such a beautiful face," Andrews said, his smile widening even more. "Is that really what's got you troubled, Khadi?"

Don't spar with him, her common sense screamed out to her. *This has nowhere to go but downhill!* But still she found herself saying, "Isn't that enough? 'Let's get him in the ground as soon as possible, so that I don't miss my Friday a.m. tee time'?"

"Ouch!" Andrews said, clutching his heart. Next to him, Bryson giggled. "No, Khadi, I have a feeling that the lack of a fitting tribute for our dear departed Christian chaplain is not what's really bothering you. I think that just maybe you are being disingenuous with me. Are you, Khadi? Are you being disingenuous?"

"I'm not having this conversation with you here," Khadi said angrily. "And especially not with him here." She indicated Bryson with her head, then turned back to the window.

But Andrews wasn't through with her. "This doesn't have anything to do with your little vacation, does it? *Tsk, tsk, tsk.* Alas, things happen. When you think about it, it was kind of insensitive for the old blowhard to die when he did." Bryson cackled with laughter.

Khadi just kept looking out the window. She was angry with herself for the tears that were filling her eyes and thankful once again for the glasses that hid them.

"I know you're disappointed. But don't worry; there will be other times. Your little Muslim holiday comes around once a year, doesn't it?"

But that's not the point, Khadi thought, her face tightening. Her hatred for this man grew with every word he said. *This is family tradition! Besides, I need this! I need it now—this year! I have to see my family!*

"Besides, it's not all bad." Andrews leaned forward and whispered conspiratorially, "If you happened to sneak something off the after-service buffet, I promise not to say anything."

It wasn't his words that set her off; it was the accompanying wink. Before she knew it, she was lunging across the limo for the senator. In the span of a second, her hands reached out for his designer suit, a satisfying look of terror appeared on Andrews's face, and nearby Bryson lifted his embossed leather portfolio to protect his face.

But then it all went wrong. Her forehead hit something hard, and her momentum was stopped flat. She pulled back and saw that the hard thing she hit was Little's mouth, which was just starting to bleed from the upper lip.

"Stand down," Little commanded her. "Stand down!"

Khadi quickly faded into the corner of her seat.

Now that Little was between them, Andrews regained his courage. "Who do you think you are coming at me, little girl? You're nothing but—"

Little spun around at him. "And you need to let it go!"

"Let it go?" Andrews repeated incredulously. "She just tried to assault me!"

"Let it go!"

"Forget that! I want you to arrest her!"

"Let . . . it . . . go!"

"And who do you think *you* are? Apparently, you've forgotten that I'm a United States senator, and you . . . you're just a glorified rent-a-cop!"

Khadi could see the back of Little's neck redden. "I may be a rent-a-cop, but I'm also the guy who knows all the juicy little secrets that the press and your wife would love to hear."

"That's blackmail," cried Bryson.

In one sweeping motion, Little snatched Bryson's prized leather portfolio with one hand while the other pulled a combat knife from under his pant leg. The blade sliced, and the folder was halved down the spine. Little sheathed his knife, neatly stacked the two pieces of the ruined portfolio, and handed them back to Bryson.

"Blackmail's an ugly word, sir," Little said to Bryson, who rapidly nodded his agreement.

Turning to Andrews, he said, "Now, please, Senator. I'm asking you to let this go. The situation got out of hand. You pushed too far. Khadi reacted. Let it go."

Khadi could see the rage in Andrews's face. But then it softened. Always the politician, Andrews had the ability to turn emotions on and off like a light switch.

"Of course. You're right, Little. Things just got out of hand. I'm sure Khadi will accept my apology, as will you. In fact—" he gave Khadi his syrupy, Vote for Andrews smile—"just to make it up to you, why don't you take tomorrow off. Relax. Get a manicure. See a matinee. Just make sure you're here early for the memorial service on Thursday morning."

Khadi didn't respond—didn't even look at him. In fact, she barely even heard him. Instead, her mind was filled with thoughts of CTD and just what it would take to convince Scott to let her back in.

The club arced down and connected with the ball. *Keep your head down. Follow through.* No matter how much Riley had played the game, no matter how low he could bring his handicap, the swinging of a golf club never came naturally to him. Thus, at every shot, whether using wood, iron, or putter, he found himself always repeating the same mantra. *Keep your head down. Follow through.*

As his club came to a rest above his left shoulder, he looked up and watched his ball fly straight down the fairway. After a few seconds it dropped, bounced, and rolled to a stop on the edge of the low rough, about seven feet behind Skeeter's ball.

Picking up his tee, he noticed that Skeeter was already walking back to the cart.

"What? No 'Good shot'?"

Skeeter grunted. "Little short."

Riley laughed. The two friends had remarkably similar games. Typically they matched each other shot for shot—the winner often decided by one lucky chip or one chunked putt.

As reward for his victory in the last round they had played at the TPC at Avenel, Skeeter got in behind the wheel of the cart. Riley slid his driver back into his bag, slipped a Colorado Mustangs club cover over it, and dropped in next to him. Skeeter popped the brake, and the cart accelerated. Riley lifted his hat off and enjoyed the feel of the air rushing across his sweating face. Even though the temperature was only 84 degrees in Leesburg, Virginia, the humidity level matched the number.

He took a long pull from his Diet Coke, then leaned back and enjoyed the view. The course they were on today, Raspberry Falls Golf & Hunt Club, was set amid lush green rolling hills. A gentle breeze rustled the countless trees, and the singing of birds carried across the swaths of open spaces that had been carved out of the forest. And if that wasn't enough beauty, when you got to some of the higher tee boxes, the views of the many ridges of Catoctin Mountain were just this side of spectacular.

The course itself was also amazing. Gary Player had designed it in a Scottish links motif—uneven fairways that took a little getting used to and deep pot bunkers that must be avoided at any cost. The little twists and tricks of the course ensured frustration for the first-timer. And it usually took until round three or four before a player could really start getting a feel for its personality.

Unfortunately, most nonmembers never made it to rounds three or four. For ordinary, off-the-street schmoes, being able to schedule a round—especially with a two-person party like Riley and Skeeter's—was extremely difficult and ridiculously expensive. Riley, however, was no ordinary nonmember, no off-the-street schmoe. His reputation as Captain America, Savior of the Nation, Hero to All Who Love Freedom and Justice, smoothed over the first hurdle of booking a tee time, and the ridiculous amount of money paid to him to run after men who were carrying a leather prolate spheroid took care of the second.

Heroship does have its privileges, he thought as they pulled up near their balls. Both rested on the left edge of the fairway, fear of the long bunker off the right side having caused Riley and Skeeter to overcompensate their shots.

Before they jumped out, Riley pulled the scorecard. "Okay, looks like the green is surrounded by these nasty pot bunkers. But the bunker to look out for is just to the right of the green. It's so big they gave it a name."

"Which is . . . ?"

"Myrtle Beach."

"Because . . . ?"

"It's as big as Myrtle Beach."

"Makes sense."

Riley figured he had about 140 yards to the green, so he pulled out his seven iron, lined up his shot, and swung. *Keep your head down. Follow through.*

When he finally looked up, he saw his ball veering slightly to the right. It landed with a puff of sand.

"Life's a beach," Skeeter said as he walked toward his ball.

"Then you die," Riley finished for him.

As he watched his faithful companion line up his shot, he knew it was time for them to have the talk. They were on hole sixteen, and Riley had been trying to find a way to broach the conversation since the first tee.

How do you tell a guy it's time for him to move on? For the past few years, Skeeter had provided Riley an invaluable service. He had been the eyes in the back of Riley's head, the extra gun when things got messy. He was Riley's protector, his guardian, his confidant, his friend.

Now, however, it seemed like the need for a full-time bodyguard had passed. The threats against Riley had diminished to the point that he was only bothered by a couple cranks a month—and even those could usually be dealt with by just ignoring them.

When it came down to it, he felt that by letting Skeeter stay with him, he was holding him back. The big man had way too much to offer, way too many skills that could be put into use saving the country or even saving someone else, somebody more important, who was in real danger.

But Skeeter had made a pledge to him. He had sworn that he would watch over Riley—that he would give his life for him if necessary.

He'll never back off from his commitment. That's simply not who he is. The only way it might possibly work is if I release him from it.

As Riley watched Skeeter send his ball into the same bunker, a picture flashed in his mind. He remembered a scene that had been repeated in several movies from when he was young. A boy had a dog that he had found. That dog became his constant companion. He protected him and loved him. But then came the tragic day when, for some reason, the boy would have to send the dog away. He would tell the dog to go; then he'd try to chase him away. Finally, with tears streaming down his face, he'd throw rocks at the dog until the animal finally slunk away with a look of heartbroken bewilderment on its canine face.

Back in the cart, he looked at the massive man who sat next to him. *Throwing rocks at this guy would be a good way to get my butt kicked from here to next week.*

They pulled up near the green and got out their sand wedges and putters. They walked over to Myrtle Beach and grinned at each other.

"Pretty nasty," Riley said.

"Mmmm-boy," Skeet answered with a nod.

Riley stood in the sand and tried to clear his mind of everything but the shot. He took a couple of practice swings over his ball, then lofted it high. Sand sprayed in an arc up the side of the bunker. The ball bounced on the green, rolled toward the cup, and stopped four feet shy.

"Not bad, beach boy," Skeeter said as he moved toward his ball.

Riley didn't reply, his beautiful shot going right by him. Instead, he was too busy role-playing the conversation in his head. He quickly replayed all the answers he had come up with to Skeeter's inevitable objections. He ran through how he would defuse his friend's rising anger.

Remember, he's going to be hurt. Don't take to heart the things he's going to say. He'll be speaking from emotion—from his heart and not his head. Don't let yourself get caught up defending yourself. And don't back down from your decision.

Skeeter took a swing, sending his ball arcing onto the green. Its path left him about ten inches short of Riley's ball.

Riley picked up the rake and started smoothing the sand. *Now! Do it now! Do it because the heartbreak has to come sooner or later, and you can't keep putting it off! Do it because this is sounding more and more like a breakup with a girlfriend, and it's starting to get a little creepy!*

"Hey, Skeet," Riley called out, saying a little prayer in the back of his mind. "Got something I want to talk to you about."

"Shoot," Skeeter replied, laying his wedge on the edge of the green and carrying a putter to his ball.

Riley dropped the rake and walked up to the green. Standing back out of club reach, he said, "I'm not sure how to tell you this, and I hope you don't take anything that I'm about to say wrong. You have been the best friend-slash-bodyguard I could have ever hoped for. You have saved my life on multiple occasions. You have always been there for me. You are truly one of the most amazing guys I know. But . . ."

He paused as he tried to figure out just the right words to say. Part of the awkwardness of the moment came from the fact that he was talking to Skeeter's back. The rest of the man was standing over his ball lining up his putt.

"But . . . I'm sorry, man, but I just think it's time you moved on to something better for your life."

"I agree," Skeeter said. His putter smoothly rocked forward, tapping the ball with just enough force for it to roll five feet and drop into the cup. "Par for me."

Riley stood, leaning forward on his putter, his mouth hanging open.

Skeeter smiled. "Come on, it wasn't that good of a putt."

"You agree? Just like that?"

"You'd rather I didn't agree?"

Riley was fully flustered. He'd been prepared for rage, for hurt, for argument. The one thing he had never planned on was agreement.

"No, it's just that . . . I mean, I figured you'd . . . You agree?"

"Pach, I swore to you that I'd watch out for you as long as you needed me. Best I can see, you don't need me so much anymore. Honestly, I'm getting a little restless living this cushy life. It ain't me. I just didn't want to go until you were ready for me to go."

Shaking his head, Riley moved toward his ball. He started lining up his putt, then turned back toward Skeeter.

"Just like that? I mean, I've got a whole speech planned for you—all the reasons why you've got to get out there and live your life."

Riley watched Skeeter's slightly smirking face a moment longer, then faced his putt. But before he swung, he spun around again.

"You know what you're going to do instead?"

"Scott's given me a standing invitation. Figured I might jump in with him."

"So, you've got this all planned out?"

"For the most part."

After another moment, Riley turned back to his ball.

His mind was reeling. He was surprised to discover that he was a little bit hurt that Skeeter was so ready to leave him, and not just ready, but had been planning it for what appeared to be no small amount of time. But then he caught himself when he realized just how twisted that line of thinking was.

Face it; it really couldn't have gone much better. Skeet's going to move on with his life, and you're left to pursue whatever it is that God's going to lead you to next. You're in a good place now. Life may have been tough lately, but there's no denying it's on the upswing.

Expelling his breath, Riley eased the club forward and gave his ball a solid tap. *Keep your head down. Follow through.* The ball trekked its way across the short stretch of grass to the cup, where it skirted around the inside of the lip and back out, rolling to the left, at which point it caught a downward slope that carried it another eight feet before it came to an abrupt stop against the edge of the fringe.

CHAPTER TWENTY

TUESDAY, SEPTEMBER 13, 8:10 P.M. PDT
SANTA ROSA, CALIFORNIA

The smoke was so thick in the car that it was becominging too much even for Donnell Marcum, a man who had smoked two packs a day for the last twenty years. But he didn't dare put down the window. No one could know he was in the parking lot.

Another straggler rolled in, and Donnell eased his body sideways onto the seat until the lights passed. The meeting had begun ten minutes ago, and he figured people would still be coming for another ten—*after all, these people are living on California time.* Then with a smile, he added, *Or you could say they're living on borrowed time.*

It was three years back and forty miles south that Donnell had first been exposed to the radical teachings he would eventually embrace. He was in San Quentin serving a stretch for armed robbery—not his first time enjoying the hospitality of the California Department of Corrections and Rehabilitation.

The Muslims had always been around, and he had respected them—you had to respect them . . . or face the consequences. But he had never felt a draw to be part of them. Too many rules. Too much "we." He was a loner—always had been, always would be. Connections held you back. Relationships brought responsibility.

Sure, while in prison he had joined the Black Guerrilla Family. He even had a guy tattoo a black dragon with the numbers 2-7-6 over it to show his loyalty. But that was prison life. In prison, you do what you have to do—and one thing you never do is go it alone.

Outside's different. Outside you could make it on your own. Outside you made up your own rules.

So he'd lived out his sentence as part of the family, until one day another BGFer shorted him on a cap of green. This dude was a BGF lifer and way up the ladder. But that didn't matter. You try ripping off Donnell Marcum, you're going to answer to Donnell Marcum.

Donnell had confronted the guy in the yard. Soon fists were flying, and Donnell was pounced on by four other BGFers. By the time the guards came, he was a bloody mess.

After his time in the hospital and in solitary, he truly was on his own. The BGF didn't want anything to do with him, and he obviously wasn't going to the Aryans or the Mexican gangs. It was then the Muslim brotherhood reached out to him. They were the ones who took him in, gave him a home, and covered his back.

As he spent time with them, he learned that while there were rules, they were rules with a purpose. Not only did they exist to please Allah, but they also were there to please the guards and the prison officials. And pleasing others meant one word—freedom!

If you please Allah, you are free from the cares of this world and the next. You serve him well in this life, he will reward you in the next.

If you play the game and please the prison toads, you get freedom of another kind. You leave their little hellhole, you leave their watchful eyes, and you receive freedom to do what Allah calls you to do.

So, he threw himself in completely with *Jam'iyyat Ul-Islam Is-Saheeh*. The Assembly of Authentic Islam gave him purpose he had never felt before, and finally he found himself really wanting to belong—to be part of something bigger.

And as he listened to the leaders, his hatred for America and Israel grew. But his patience and self-control grew in the same measure. Two and a half years later, he was paroled. And this time when he walked out those gates, there was a JIS car waiting for him.

For the past six months, he had been living in Oakland rent-free in a small apartment that sat adjacent to a JIS mosque. His days were spent in study or listening to the imam. His nights were spent fervently praying for the opportunity to be used by Allah.

His time finally came three days ago, when the imam called him into his office following the *Dhuhr* prayer. Ammar Kazerooni offered Donnell some lunch, but he declined. Even though he had thirty-five years under his belt—and countless parole hearings—this was probably the most nervous he had ever been in a meeting. It was the first time the imam had ever called him into his office. The news had to be important.

"Are you ready to fight for Allah?" Kazerooni had asked.

"I'm ready to die for Allah!"

"Are you? Are you sure?"

"I will do anything for my God," Donnell insisted.

"Anything?"

"Anything!"

Kazerooni stared at Donnell awhile, as if trying to decide if he could trust him with an important piece of information.

"I promise you, Mullah, whatever you say, I will do. Let me prove it to you."

After a few more moments, Kazerooni said, "I believe you, Donnell. I believe you will do whatever Allah calls you to do."

Just hearing those words sent Donnell's heart soaring. In that moment, he knew that even if he was called to assassinate the president himself, he would find a way to do it.

"What I'm about to tell you is very secret. No one must know. Am I understood?"

"Yes, sir."

Kazerooni lowered his voice to just above a whisper. "Something big is about to happen. I can't tell you what. I can't tell you where. I can't even tell you when. But just know it will be big. And we have been asked to help."

"Anything, Mullah. I'll do anything."

"I know you will. We have been asked to create a diversion of sorts. You know of the attacks that have been taking place around the country?"

Donnell nodded. Of course he knew. He had heard them from the imam's own mouth during services and had laughed and rejoiced with each blow struck against the enemy.

"The purpose of these attacks is to draw attention away from the big event. Sometimes if there are enough flies swarming your face, you don't see the bull behind them. We have been asked to be one of these flies. Do you understand, Donnell?"

Donnell felt he knew where this was leading, and he could hardly contain his excitement. "Yes! Yes, I do. By making smaller attacks, we will draw manpower and other resources away from the agencies who are tasked to monitor anti-American activities. That way they will be looking the other way when the big punch comes."

Kazerooni smiled. "Exactly! And I have chosen to give you

the privilege of carrying out this attack. By agreeing, you will not only gain honor and praise in this life but a martyr's welcome in heaven."

"Just tell me! Whatever it is, I'll do!"

That conversation had led to Donnell's being here, outside this building, watching the last of the procrastinators enter through the glass double doors. The clock on the dash said 8:25. He took one last deep drag on his cigarette, then stubbed it out in the overflowing ashtray.

He stepped out of the car and moved to the trunk, popping it open with his key fob. He slid two .45s into the rear of his waistband and filled the pockets of his windbreaker with six more clips. He would have felt better with an automatic weapon, but getting one into this meeting undetected would potentially have been difficult. *Instead, I'm going to have to kill them the old-fashioned way—one at a time.*

He hoisted a gym bag onto his shoulder and walked toward the building. Just outside the front door stood a white board:

North Bay Patriots
Tonight, 8–9:30 p.m.
All are Welcome!!

You may want to rethink that last line, Donnell thought as he pulled open the door. Across the entryway through another set of closed doors, he could hear someone speaking. He was saying something about taking back America and the evils of Washington. *"Evils of Washington," huh? Maybe we have something in common after all,* he thought with a smile.

Stepping to the right side of the outer doors, he set down the gym bag. From inside, he removed a hammer and one small nail. With one practiced swing, he embedded the nail about a third of the way into the wall six inches up from the floor.

He replaced the hammer and moved the bag back to the

other side of the doors. Once the bag was down again, he fished out from its corner a small tab with a round hole punched in it. Attached to it was a thin wire that fed out as he walked back toward the nail. He slipped the tab over the nail and returned to the bag. Reaching in, he flipped a toggle, then zipped the bag back up.

A little surprise for anyone trying to run away. Or for any first responders who might think about coming to help.

He faced the inner doors. Taking a deep breath, he prayed, "O Allah, you gave me back my life when I had thrown it away. And now, in reverent gratitude, I give it back to you. You are great, O my God!"

He pulled both doors open and stepped in. The room was filled with over a hundred people. All were facing a man behind a podium with an American eagle emblem on it. *Perfect!*

Reaching with both hands behind his back, he grasped the two .45s and pulled them out. But before they had cleared his back, a woman in a seat next to him cried out, "Gun!"

Surprised, Donnell hesitated a moment, and that moment was all it took for him to lose his advantage. Instantly, ten, fifteen, twenty—more than he could count—people stood up, guns drawn, facing him.

Shouts of "Put the gun down!" and "Drop it!" mixed with the screams of those nearest him. There was chaos all around him. Instinctively, his hands went up over his head, and he saw some of the men begin to approach him.

But then he remembered why he was here. *There is no honor in being arrested! There is no honor in saving your life! I'm here to become* shaheed! *I never planned on getting out of here alive to begin with! To your glory, Allah!*

With a cry, he brought his guns back down. But before he could get a shot off, the air filled with the sound of gunfire. All over his body he felt impacts, and he flew back through the doors.

Panic filled him. This wasn't the way things were supposed to happen. He didn't know how many times he had been shot, but he knew he was in major trouble. He couldn't move his left side, and the room was spinning around him. In that moment, the most basic of instincts kicked in—survival. *I've got to get out of here!*

He could hear shouting and commotion just behind the doors. Half running, half stumbling, he made for the exit.

Gotta get through! Gotta get home!

He punched the crash bar on the front doors just as the first of his pursuers slammed through the doors behind him. None of them lived to know what hit them.

CHAPTER TWENTY-ONE

Majid Alavi murmured a greeting to the man guarding the warehouse door, then slipped out into the warm night. He was leaving a very unpleasant meeting. They had just heard of the botched attack in California, and Saifullah was fuming.

"That's what we get for trusting the JIS! Prison rats! Gutter trash!"

"But we still accomplished our purpose," Alavi had protested. "Many more people focused on that incident."

"Bah! Quit defending them! They gave all of Islam a black eye with their incompetence! Our goal with this whole operation is to wreak as much devastation and carnage as we possibly can. This fool squandered his opportunity."

Outside, Alavi breathed deeply, letting the fresh air fill his lungs. Although it was a fairly large warehouse, it wasn't big enough to mask the smell of twenty-four hot, tense, sweaty men, and the old odors of gas and grease that had absorbed into the cement floor over the years just thickened the atmosphere that much more.

As number two, he was one of the few allowed outside. For all others, stepping a foot through the door meant severe punishment. Saifullah had made it clear how dangerous it would be to have fifteen or twenty men standing outside an abandoned warehouse smoking and shooting the breeze.

"That's how people get seen. That's how plans fall apart. All we need is one drive-by police cruiser, one helicopter flyover, one drunk bum looking for a reward, and our mission is done," the old man had chided them.

Alavi tucked himself into the blackness next to an empty Dumpster and sat on the ground. The metal was warm against his back, and an ancient sour smell lightly tainted the air. Even so, it was still better than being inside.

The night sky was clear and dark—no moon, and only the brightest of stars breaking through the ambient light of the city. He pulled an apple out of one pocket, pulled a knife out of the other, and sliced off a piece, which he ate off the side of the blade.

The darkness just before Ramadan, he mused. *The blackest night of the year.*

Alavi's father used to tell him how this particular night symbolized the darkness of the world prior to the first revelation to the prophet Muhammad. No one knew the truth. Sinfulness and idolatry filled the earth. It was a night to remember what we once were—and who we might still be without Allah's message to his creation.

But then, when the sun set the next evening, everything would change. The moon would begin to make its appearance again. Light would be restored to the darkness, because this was the day that the great angel Jibril gave the first words of the Koran to Muhammad.

"That is why Ramadan is the holiest of all the months, Majid," his father had said on one of the dark Mishawaka nights of

Alavi's childhood. *"That is why we dedicate ourselves to prayer and fasting for that period. You see, tomorrow night the first crescent of the moon will show, reminding us that the true light of Allah's revelation has entered the world. That is why we hold the symbol of the crescent so dear. It is our reminder of Allah's wonderful gift to us."*

Alavi carved another piece of the apple and snapped a bite from it. His dad had seemed so strong back then—invincible. And he seemed to know everything. So many nights they would sit on the back porch with all the lights off. He would lean against his father's chest and listen to story after story. But then . . .

No, that's for another time. Now is the time to remember the good—to hold tight to the love and laughter of my family.

As Alavi turned the apple in his hand, he felt a soft spot just beneath the skin. With a quick pull of the blade, he removed it and flicked it to the pavement.

"Why is the Koran so special?" he remembered asking. Then, trying to mask the hurt and shame in his voice, he added, *"My friend Mike from school says that his dad said that the Bible is God's only word, and that the Koran is just a bunch of nonsense."*

His dad's chest had tensed briefly, then eased back to its usual solid softness.

"Mike's dad is simply ignorant. Do you remember what I told you was the difference between ignorance and stupidity?"

"Ignorance means you don't know. Stupidity means you don't know and you don't care that you don't know."

"Exactly. Mike's dad is probably not meaning to be cruel. He is just deceived—ignorant. The Bible is truly a good book full of God's revelation. It has the messages to Adam, the Suhuf Ibrahim, the Tawrat of Moses, the Zabur of David, and the Injil of Jesus. All full of wisdom. All useful tools in submission. But the revelation to Muhammad—oh, what a glorious gift it is! It is the culmination of all other revelations! It is Allah's perfect message!"

"And since it was first given in Ramadan, we give that month over to fasting and to prayer to better understand what Allah has

told us," the young Majid had said, repeating what he'd learned at the mosque.

"You're a smart boy," his dad had responded, giving him a squeeze. *"So we can't get angry at Mike or his father. Instead, we should feel pity for them, since they don't know the wonderful gift Allah has given to the world."*

What warmth, what security Alavi had felt when that arm wrapped around him and held him tight. But those days were gone now. In the time leading up to the move to Dearborn, his dad had changed. He had become defeated. The man who had once stood proud and had walked with purpose now had shoulders that slumped as he shuffled around the house.

Why? Alavi threw the apple across the wide parking lot. It skittered over the asphalt until, with a metallic shudder, it came to an abrupt stop against a chain-link fence. He wiped his knife on the leg of his pants, folded it up, and returned it to his pocket. *Why did you let them beat you, Dad? Why did you just take it? Why didn't you fight back?*

Tears formed in his eyes, and his throat constricted. But just as quickly, he forced the emotions back down.

I understand. You couldn't. It just wasn't you. But don't worry; the next generation of Alavis has reached its time. I will avenge you and restore honor to our name. I will fight the war you couldn't fight. I will cause pride to well up in your heart, Dad, the way you once caused it to well up in mine.

He took one last look at the night sky, then stood, stretched, and began a slow walk to the door.

Tomorrow night the crescent will appear, and Ramadan will begin. Then, the next morning, after the Suhoor *meal, the fasting will commence. Only this fast will be different from any other. This fast will not be spent in quiet study. No, this year I will fast with action. It will be a fast of service. It will be a fast of violence and vengeance. It will be a fast leading to death—most likely my own, but most definitely that of many others. It will be a fast of jihad.*

WEDNESDAY, SEPTEMBER 14, 2:45 P.M. EDT

WASHINGTON, DC

Khadi Faroughi took a deep breath. She had no idea what to expect when the door opened. Had it been long enough that the welcome she received would be forced, with wide smiles, stiff hugs, and overblown greetings—*"Wow, Khadi, it's sooooo great to see you! You're looking sooooo good!"*—that would quickly fade into an awkward silence?

Who said, "You can never go home again"? she asked herself. *Wasn't it Thomas Wolfe? I'll ask Scott, the human encyclopedia. Without a doubt, he'll know. Speaking of . . .*

She looked at the familiar glossy black door again, one she was in the peculiar role of having to knock on, something she'd never done in the past. How many times had she barged through that door on some sort of mission—analysts or ops team in tow?

This is my element, my habitat. Now I'm standing on the outside looking in like an old man who desperately wants to walk through the house he grew up in but is too timid to leave the car. She was tempted by a momentary impulse to punch her old code into the touch pad, just to see if it would work.

So much was riding on this moment—her future, her happiness, her life's purpose. *I honestly can't imagine spending the rest of my life protecting Mr. Opportunity and other amoral, self-important political hacks like him. That decision is already made. I'm out of there! But is this really the best alternative? Am I just running back to what's familiar?*

Remember how much this job takes out of you. Remember the hours. This place takes over your whole life. That's one of the reasons I left to begin with. What will happen with Jonathan? I might as well say good-bye to any future with him if I return here.

But do I really care?

She stared at the door for a time, trying to keep back the name that was forcing itself into her thoughts. Finally, she gave in. *And what about Riley? What would he think? Would he see this as some feeble attempt to try to get closer to him?*

Ultimately, though, does it really matter? After the way I treated him on Monday's call, the whole Riley issue is probably moot anyway.

She set her heavy shoulder bag on the floor and looked at it with a twinge of embarrassment. It was full of presents for the analysts who were waiting beyond the door in the Room of Understanding—little things from special moments or inside jokes. Suddenly, the goofs that seemed so fun at the store now seemed foolish, like she was trying too hard. Tears welled in her eyes as she pictured the fake smiles the trinkets would bring, the rolled eyes that would be exchanged as soon as she turned away.

What have I given up? What was I thinking? These people were my family! You can't just walk away from family! But that's exactly what I did. And now I want to come back like some prodigal who realized that life isn't all that good away from home.

What makes me think Scott will even take me? Sure, he's made lighthearted offers in the past, but was he just being nice, encourag-

ing me? Like when you invite someone to come to a concert with you when you know full well they'll be out of town. The last thing you expect is for them to actually take you up on your offer.

She looked up at the door, then at the bag. *This is stupid! You can't go home again!*

Picking up the bag, she turned to go. But the electronic sound of a bolt being drawn stopped her. The door flew open, and there stood Scott and the rest of the gang.

"What are you doing?" Scott cried out. "We've been standing here in an odorous cloud of Gooey's foot sweat watching you on the video monitor for five minutes."

"Hey, my feet sweat," Gooey protested. "I can't help it. It's what they do."

"It's hard to get over it when the smell is still clinging to my clothes when I get home at night," Virgil Hernandez said.

Khadi watched this exchange with an ever-increasing sense of relief. This was her family—her bizarre, irreverent, oftentimes dysfunctional family. And she loved them.

Suddenly, arms were all around her, hugging her, pulling her in, slipping down into her bag after she let the word *presents* slip out of her mouth.

"Back off, everyone. Give the girl some room," Scott commanded. When no one listened, he added, "So she can pass out her gifts."

Everyone obediently took two steps back.

Khadi started to say something, but emotion stole the words away.

"You okay?" Scott asked, pulling a handkerchief out of his pocket. But after examining it, he thought better of the gesture and tucked it away.

"Yeah," Khadi answered, drawing in a deep breath, then slowly letting it out. "I was just wondering who the fool was that said you can never go home again."

"I think that was Thomas Wolfe," Evie Cline offered.

"That's what I—" Khadi said, before Scott interrupted, his head shaking.

"Actually, it was the Moody Blues. Side two, cut three of their *Every Good Boy Deserves Favour* album."

"You're both wrong," said Gooey. "It was from a *Ren & Stimpy* Christmas episode. Can't remember the name of it, though."

Hernandez and Williamson quickly took sides, and a debate began to heat up. Khadi watched with wondered amusement until Scott noticed her smile.

"Hang on, gang! Am I to assume that was a rhetorical question, Miss Faroughi?"

"Nothing's rhetorical with this group," she answered. Her eyes began to well up again. "It's just so good to see you all again."

A second round of hugs ensued, and then Khadi passed out her presents. Evie received a long, slender box that held a single white rose to go in the bud vase of her VW Beetle. Hernandez and Williamson were given a new set of Stiga table tennis paddles to use when the long days ran into each other and they'd drop a net onto the conference table to hold Ping-Pong tournaments.

As she reached in for Gooey's present, she suddenly realized what had been bothering her. Everything had felt like coming home, but still there was something different about the place—something just off enough to be slightly unsettling. And now it hit her. It was the smell. Gone was the heavy, buttery air that usually filled the room—the pungent aroma that permeated the walls and ceiling, causing mooches from the other offices to come knocking on the door most afternoons looking for handouts. She turned to where Gooey's full-size carnival popcorn cart had stood for the last year and a half and saw that it was no longer there.

"It's gone. I'm sorry, Gooey, I didn't know," she said as

she handed him a popcorn-seasoning sampler that contained flavors like malt ball, gummi bear, and sardine-dill.

Ignoring her apology, Gooey's eyes lit up. "Sweet! These are awesome!"

"Don't worry; the cart's not gone, just temporarily incapacitated," Scott said. "Gooey blew a heating element, so he traded the tech geeks in advanced weaponry a month's worth of free popcorn to repair it."

With everyone focused on their gifts, Khadi gave a little nod toward Scott's office. Scott nodded back.

"Hey, gang! Enough goofing. We've got a world to save. Time to get back to work."

There was a little bit of grumbling, but not a lot. Within seconds, the analysts were back at their stations, totally focused on the tasks at hand.

Something must be going on around here, Khadi thought. *They didn't put up much of a fight.*

"Come on back," Scott said with a smile, leading the way to his office.

"What's keeping the kids so occupied . . . if I may ask?"

"You may. There's tons of chatter going on," he answered over his shoulder. "Mostly about more of these smaller-scale attacks. We've got warnings all the way from Des Moines to Dubuque."

"Wow, Des Moines to Dubuque? What is that, 150 miles? You guys must really be stretched."

Scott stopped and turned. "Okay, Bangor to Bakersfield. That better?"

"Much. Speaking of attacks—how are you doing?"

Lowering his voice, he admitted, "Still a little sore. Gotta tell you, it freaked me out a little more than I'm letting on."

"As it should. You going to be okay?"

"Yeah, just have to process a little more. Having a little squirt at home changes things."

"Again, as it should. So, do you see any connections within all this intel—any threads tying the attacks together?"

"Some. All the players are homegrown. All individuals or small-cell. I'm just looking for a bigger picture to all this other than them wanting to be a giant pain in the collective American keister."

Khadi thought for a moment. "Could they be white noise? You know, trying to distract you from a bigger play?"

Scott nodded thoughtfully. "Yeah, could be. That would certainly give a purpose. Give me a second." He moved off toward Evie. "Go ahead and make yourself comfortable," he called back to her.

That was easier said than done. The room he called his office was really little more than a closet. There was just enough room for his desk, an executive chair, and a rolling secretary's chair that was missing a caster. It was on this second chair that Khadi now precariously balanced herself.

"So, no present for me?" Scott asked a couple minutes later as he breezed into the room and began organizing into a pile some papers that were spread across his desk.

Here goes, she thought. "Don't you think it would be bad form for one to butter somebody up with a gift just before asking said person for one's old job back?"

Scott stopped short, his eyes lifting to meet Khadi's. She could tell that he was trying to read whether or not she was serious.

Leaving the papers where they lay, he sat down and said, "Well, truthfully, I've never really seen anything wrong with buttering someone up, especially if I'm the butteree."

She bent down to her bag. When she came up, she was holding an infant onesie. It was black and on the front were written the words:

Mommy's All Right!
Daddy's All Right!

She could see Scott's face light up.

"Wait for it," she said. With as much flair as she could muster, she flipped the outfit around. On the back was written in a half-circle arc:

They Just Seem A Little Weird!

"No way! Tara is going to kill you," Scott shouted as he snatched it out of her hands. "It's awesome!"

It was so good to hear Scott laugh—to see the sheer delight he took in the moment. When he laughed, everything seemed right in the world. Somehow, some way, all things would work out, and good would always find a way to triumph over evil.

Please, God, let this work out. Let him say yes.

"Yes," Scott said, the smile still big across his face.

"Yes what?" Khadi asked, taken off guard.

"You buttered me up for a reason. I'm telling you it worked. When can you start?" he asked, folding the onesie and setting it on his desk.

"Don't you want to hear why? I've got a whole sob-story speech prepared for you."

Scott leaned back in his chair and folded his hands behind his head. "You know, as appealing as that sounds, I think I'd rather just say yes."

For what seemed like the hundredth time today, Khadi's eyes filled up with tears. She was coming home. Back to the people she loved. Back to where she was making a difference, protecting people who truly deserved protecting.

"Now, of course, we're going to have to start you at the bottom. Wouldn't be fair to everyone else if we just put you back in your office. I figure maybe we'll start out with you assisting Evie and let you work your way up."

"Of course," Khadi said, her heart falling as she tried to keep a smile on her face. "That would only be fair."

Wow, that was unexpected. But then again, why should it be? Why should you expect to be able to simply waltz back in and . . . Her thoughts were brought up short by a mischievous grin that was beginning to spread across Scott's face.

"Jerk," she said with a laugh, relief flooding her body. "But seriously, I'd be willing to step into whatever job you want me in. I don't care where or what it is. I just want to be in a place where I can most help out the team. I know I have no right to expect—"

Scott held up his hand to interrupt her. He was still laughing. "Please, Khadi, stop! You're slipping into your prepared speech, and the absolute pitifulness of it is going to either have me crying or busting a gut laughing."

"So I'm back in?"

"You're back in."

"At my old job?"

"At your old job."

"At my current salary?"

"This is the government."

"It was worth a shot," Khadi said, amazed at how quickly their old bantering habits fell back into place. "When can I start?"

"You tell me," Scott said, picking up the onesie and admiring it one more time.

"Let me give my two weeks to the senator today. How about September 28?"

"Perfect. I'll have Gooey move his boxes out of your office, and we'll give it a coat of fresh paint."

"Ummm, I almost hate to ask, but . . ."

Scott leaned back in his chair so that its back was against one wall and his feet were propped against the wall opposite. "Not much to it. It's just the typical guy finds apartment, guy moves into apartment, guy's seven-foot boa constrictor busts out of its cage and escapes into the walls of the apartment building only to be rediscovered when it falls through a bathroom vent fan onto the lap of another tenant who just happens to be availing herself of the facilities at that precise time, guy gets evicted story."

"Happens all the time."

"No doubt. So Gooey's been in a motel for the last couple of months, and he needed a place to store some of his stuff. Just a heads-up, though. When you start, you may want to bring a supply of scented candles."

"Already on my list."

"It's good to have you back on the team, Agent Faroughi," Scott said.

"It's good to be back, sir," Khadi said with a wink.

WEDNESDAY, SEPTEMBER 14, 6:20 P.M. EDT
WASHINGTON, DC

Majid Alavi eased the white utility van through the open warehouse doors, then watched in the rearview mirror as they closed behind him. Suddenly, there was a thump on the side of the van. He spun around. Then another, and another. Soon it sounded like a storm of hard, meaty hailstones was raining blow after blow on the side panels.

Then a chant began outside. Alavi chuckled as he made out the syllables—*Mc-Don-Alds, Mc-Don-Alds, Mc-Don-Alds*. He glanced to where Ubaida Saliba was crouched with a hand on the door handle. Alavi nodded, and Saliba slid back the door.

A cheer rose from the dancing, chanting warriors.

"Form up," Saliba called out. Immediately, the men formed a line, albeit with plenty of good-natured jostling and gibing.

Alavi unbuckled his seat belt and joined Saliba. As the men stepped forward one by one, Alavi handed each a bag containing a quarter-pounder and a large fries, while Saliba pulled a large Coke from one of the six full cardboard drink carriers he had been frenetically trying to keep from tipping over.

For most of the return ride from the last McDonalds—they had gone to four, so as not to raise suspicion by ordering twenty-four identical value meals from one location—their conversation had been reduced to "Slow down!" "I am going slow!" "Go slower!" "Any slower and I'll be going backwards!" "Just slow down!"

"Allah bless you," Saliba said to each man as they took their meals. Alavi remained silent, watching the gleeful expressions on the faces of these chosen few who had existed the last few days primarily on cheeses and vegetables.

Ramadan would officially begin at sunset. At that point, Saifullah wanted all the men to be fed and ready to focus on God and on the task at hand. But in the few hours of daylight that remained, he had decided to boost the men's morale by sending Alavi and Saliba on an old-fashioned fast-food run.

Alavi had briefly considered pointing out the inconsistency of Saifullah's now providing the very food for which three days earlier he had caused two of the men to be beaten. Prudence won the day, and he had decided against it. He knew there was always a deeper reason for whatever the old man did.

The answer came later in the day. "If you teach your men to respect you, they will go to their deaths for you," the wise imam had eventually told Alavi, while handing him the keys to the van. "But if you teach your men to love you also, they will still go to their deaths for you . . . but with smiles on their faces."

The last man in line received his meal. *Mission accomplished,* Alavi thought. Smelling the fries had created in him a ravenous hunger.

He reached to grab the final two bags for himself and Saliba, but found a third still remaining. Looking out of the van, he searched for anyone not eating. It didn't take long for his gaze to fall on Quraishi—the defiant one from the first day's beating—still sitting on his bunk sharpening his knife. The man's eyes were on Alavi as he slowly stroked his blade across the stone.

Alavi held up the white paper bag. With a defiantly bored shrug, Quraishi slowly and deliberately sheathed his knife and slipped the stone into a small pouch, which he set squarely in the middle of his pillow. Then, easing himself up, he stretched and began a casual stroll toward the van.

Who does this idiot think he is? Alavi wondered as he felt the heat beginning to rise in his face. Many of the men were watching Quraishi, more and more heads turning with each relaxed step he took. Some of the men were grinning and elbowing each other. *His fans,* Alavi thought. *Something's got to be done about this guy. This whole week, it seems he's made a point of trying to challenge me and to weaken the authority structure Saifullah has worked so hard to establish.*

Slowly, with a bored look on his face, Quraishi continued his approach. When he was about ten feet away, an indignant Saliba yelled out, "Who the—?"

But Alavi silenced him with a raised hand. A self-satisfied smile appeared on Quraishi's mouth. *He thinks he has me cowed. Seems it's time for an example to be made.*

Alavi sized the man up. Quraishi had about three inches and forty pounds on him. *Proceed carefully but conclusively with this one.*

The big man finally arrived in front of the van's side door and stood staring at Alavi. Every eye in the warehouse, including, he was sure, those of Saifullah, was on the threesome.

"Hungry?" Alavi asked.

"I could eat," Quraishi said smugly, holding out his hand for the bag.

Taking hold of the bag from underneath, Alavi lifted it towards Quraishi. But before the other man could take hold of it, Alavi turned it over. Fries needled to the ground, and the cardboard box holding the burger bounced once, ejecting its contents, which landed in an elongated three-layer stair step on the dusty ground.

Never once taking his eyes from his adversary's, Alavi reached toward Saliba, who deposited a Coke in his outstretched hand. He tipped it and squeezed until the lid shot off, spewing its sticky liquid onto Quraishi's boots and pant legs. As the events took place, Alavi could see the other man's expression turn from anger to rage to dark hatred.

Reaching for the final two bags, Alavi said in a low, firm voice, "Get a mop and clean this mess up. Or else someone's liable to slip and hurt themselves."

He had just shouldered past Quraishi, when he heard, "Give me your bag."

"Sorry, no time for you to eat," he answered without stopping or turning around. "You've got work to do, mop-boy."

"I said, give me your bag." These words were followed by a snatch at the bags Alavi was carrying. With surprising speed, Alavi brought his right elbow arcing backward, catching Quraishi on the temple. The man grunted, stumbled, but didn't go down. Using his momentum, Alavi completed his body twist and drove the steel toe of his left boot into Quraishi's jaw with a sickening crunch.

The force of the blow spun Quraishi around, landing him on his back. Letting his momentum carry him through a complete circle, Alavi slid the knife out of his thigh sheath, dropped to one knee, and plunged the blade deep into the rebel's neck.

"*Astaghfirullah,*" Alavi whispered with his eyes closed, seeking forgiveness from Allah. With two hands, he pulled the blade out, then wiped it on the dead man's shirt. Standing up, he turned to the two men who were nearest to him. They were staring at him with eyes as big as their hamburger buns.

"Finish your meals; then clean this up, please." They quickly nodded their assent.

To the rest of the assembled men, he said, "A cancer needs to be removed as soon as possible, or eventually it will spread to the whole body. This man has reaped what he sowed. His fate now rests in Allah's merciful hands. He missed his opportunity for martyrdom and now must wait to see what his life has earned him. *Inshallah*, he may be in paradise, or he may not. It is only for Allah to decide. I apologize for having put a damper on your celebration."

Still holding the two bags, he walked toward the office. Through the glass in the door, he saw Saifullah and Adnan Bazzi, the third of the three team leaders, watching his approach. As he neared, Saifullah took a seat at a conference table inside the office, while Bazzi opened the door.

As soon as he entered, Alavi deposited the bags on the table and knelt before Saifullah. "Please forgive me."

Saifullah's hand rested on his disciple's head. "You did what needed to be done. That one has been trouble from the start. It is as Allah wills. Now please, rise and eat."

Alavi took a seat across from Saifullah, while Saliba sat to the leader's left. Bazzi already had his meal spread out at Saifullah's right.

"Are you sure you won't have my meal?" Alavi offered the imam.

Saifullah shook his head slowly. "No. I'm afraid I have my meal right here," he said, indicating a plastic Pepcid bottle that was sitting on the table.

Alavi opened his bag and inhaled deeply the warm, heavy scent of the fries. But instead of the anticipation he usually felt at that aroma, this time it turned his stomach. And by the third packet of ketchup that he squeezed into the open lid of his cardboard burger container, he could take it no more. He pushed the meal aside—disappointed and slightly nauseated.

He saw that Saliba had done the same thing. However, Bazzi, who had the benefit of distance, continued to scarf down his meal.

"I'm sorry this unfortunate incident has stolen your appetite, my friends. You'll need your strength tomorrow."

"We'll eat before the sun comes up in the morning, Teacher," Alavi said. "That should give us what we need for the day."

"Very well. Now, let us begin."

For the next hour, the four men talked through the following day's attack, step by step, move by move. Whereas on Monday, when they first rehearsed the events, the process was choppy, awkward, with each man trying to figure out how his part fit in, now it was like a flowing narrative—a four-man recitation of a memorized presentation.

When they reached the end, Saifullah said, "*La hawla wa la quwwata illa billah*. There is no power or strength except with Allah. He will determine the ultimate success of our mission. We must simply follow the plan he has given to us.

"Tomorrow, when the gunfire starts, you must observe your men closely. Most will follow the plan perfectly. However, because this is the country of their birth, there are certain things you must watch for.

"There are some who may feel the fires of revenge against past wrongs burning out of control. As a result, they may resort to unnecessary violence and cruelty. There are places for these things, but they must be controlled. Sloppiness due to unbridled aggression puts us all in danger.

"Others you must watch for signs of doubt. Many have mentally accepted the fact that these men and women are their enemies. However, when the bloodshed starts, they may begin seeing old friends or loved ones in the faces of the infidels. These are ones who can be compromised by compassion as time goes on. They are the potential chinks in our armor. We must be diligent in watching them.

"Yes, Saifullah," the three team leaders said in unison, while Alavi stole a glance at his discarded quarter-pounder. Time was creating a separation from his previous actions, and the hunger in his stomach was beginning to make the cold burger look more appealing. He forced himself to turn away.

"Now go and get your teams together. Rehearse the plan with them again. Watch their eyes to see which of them you may need to spend more time with. Then pray with them. At 8:30, I'll lead in prayers and give an address for the advent of Ramadan. Everyone must be in bed for lights-out at 9:30. Now go, and may God go with you."

Alavi left the office and approached his already-assembled team. He glanced toward where the attack had taken place and was gratified to see no sign of any violence. After sitting down with his men, he looked each one in the eye. He opened his mouth to begin his speech to them but found that he had lost his train of thought. Instead, his mind was filled with the aroma, the texture, the taste of a stale quarter-pounder and cold, soggy fries.

This could turn out to be a long, hungry night.

WEDNESDAY, SEPTEMBER 14, 7:45 P.M. EDT
WASHINGTON, DC

"I'll let them know. . . . Love you too."

Tara ended the call and set the handset on the kitchen counter. Riley could see just a hint of aggravation on her face, but she quickly hid it behind a smile.

"Scott says to apologize and that he'll be home in about ten minutes."

"No problem. This way we get you all to ourselves. Right, Skeet?"

Riley turned to get an affirmation, but Skeeter never heard him. He was too engrossed in the book he was reading. The best Riley could figure out, it was about this caterpillar that just kept eating everything in sight until he made himself sick. It was Skeet's fourth time through, and he seemed to still be as fascinated with the story as baby James, who was nestled snugly in the crook of his massive dark arm.

"A salami? A lollipop? A cherry pie? That's

nothing for a silly caterpillar to be eating," Skeeter's deep voice softly rumbled across the room like the tremble of a thunderstorm heard from miles away.

"Can't get enough of seeing that," Tara said, moving up to where Riley was seated on a stool.

"Too cool," Riley agreed. "Reminds me of when we were in New York after the attack. We actually started something called Uncle Skeeter's Story Time, and kids from all over the refugee camp would come running each afternoon at 3:00. There would always be a big clamor over who got to sit on his lap while he read. Finally, Skeet would lift two kids out—never the same ones twice—and drop them on his legs. He'd put his arms around them, and they'd hold the book while he read—turning it to show the pictures when Skeet'd tell them to.

"It was an amazing thing to watch these kids whose lives had totally fallen apart laugh and cheer and dance around, even if just for fifteen or twenty minutes. It truly was remarkable. . . ."

Riley's voice trailed off as his mind drifted back to those terrible days. So much death, so much sorrow, so much hopelessness, so many tears. The faces of the victims—men, women, children, old, young, dead, alive, somewhere in between, dirty, bloodied, crushed—still visited him in his dreams.

The sound of a refrigerator closing snapped Riley back to the here and now. He saw that Tara had moved away from him and was laying out ingredients on the counter—onion, green pepper, olives, pepperoni, pineapple, cheese.

"Sorry, I kind of lost myself there for a minute," Riley said, embarrassed.

Tara smiled. "Occupational hazard. Scott does the same thing."

Riley took a knife and a green pepper and began cutting. "What about you? You spent enough years in CTD."

"True, but I was never ops. I read about the things you guys did, but I never actually saw them."

"You ever regret that?"

"Are you kidding? I like being able to close my eyes at night without seeing whatever it is you guys see."

Riley smiled at Tara, but he knew his smile was hollow. He turned his head back to the cutting board. "You know, right off the top of my head I can think of about twenty-nine other topics of conversation that would be both cheerier and more interesting."

"Hear, hear," Tara said, dumping a can of olives into a bowl, then popping one into her mouth. "Let's talk about football."

Riley looked up to confront Tara's laughing face. "You know, that wasn't even nice."

"Here, help me out," she said, tossing him a jar of pizza sauce.

Riley quickly dropped the knife and caught the jar. He was thrilled when he had seen that they were going to make home-made pizzas tonight. Not because it was necessarily his favorite meal, but because it was fun, simple, and best of all, cheap.

In the past, whenever Riley and Skeeter had come over for dinner, Tara had always felt like she had to make a big production of it. The recipes would be intricate; the ingredients would be expensive; the china would be gleaming. Tara would spend most of the night scrambling to make everything perfect, and Scott would become more and more subdued.

"I wonder what was up with Scott tonight," Riley had said to Skeeter a few weeks ago on their way home from a dinner that probably could have earned Tara Michelin stars.

"It's the money," Skeet said.

"What money?"

"Think about how much jing they laid out making that dinner."

A wave of shame and anger came over Riley. *How could I*

have missed it? I'm such an idiot! Living in my world of way too much, I keep forgetting the struggles of those just getting by. Since Tara stopped working, they're down to one salary in the household— and a government one at that.

"Dude, you're awesome. I'm calling Scott and demanding he let us pay for the dinner tonight."

He pulled his phone from his pocket, but before he could dial Skeeter snatched the phone from his hand.

"No, you're not."

"I'm not?"

"You're not. Come on, Pach, you're not really this clueless, are you?"

"No," Riley responded defensively. *What the heck is Skeet getting at? Why can't I just pay for the stupid meal—I'll even throw in a little extra to help out.* "But let's just say—for argument's sake only—I was. What would you tell this hypothetically clueless, pretend Riley was the reason for not paying for dinner?"

"Because you'd embarrass them—"

"You mean, hypothetically clueless, pretend Riley would embarrass them," Riley corrected.

"And you're not going to tell them to stop making expensive dinners because of their financial situation either."

"I'm not? I mean, he's not? Then what, pray tell, is he going to do?"

Refusing to play along, Skeeter said, "You're going to tell them that you don't like the fact that Tara is always running around and missing the company. You spend your life eating fancy meals, and you'd just like some good, old-fashioned, everyday, real-people food."

"Ahhh, that would probably seem like a really good plan to hypothetically clueless, pretend Riley."

So here they were tonight, eating homemade pizzas with packaged meats, jarred sauce, and premade, store-bought dough. And Riley couldn't be happier.

Riley loosened the lid from the jar and slid it back across the counter to Tara.

"Thank you, kind sir."

"It's good to have Captain America around the house."

"Tru dat," Scott said as he walked from the mudroom into the kitchen. "What up, Cap?"

Riley leaped up, and they did the manly one hand shaking, one hand double-clapping the back thing. Scott next went to Tara, gave her a kiss, and whispered something to her that made her smile and give him one more kiss.

Then he moved toward Skeet and James. Holding out his arms, he said, "How's daddy's big man?"

Skeeter looked up from the book and said, "You best be talking to me, because you ain't getting the boy."

James, who got a big smile when he saw his dad coming over, turned and laid his head on Skeet's chest when he heard the man's voice. Scott pulled up short.

"Don't worry, buddy," Riley said. "It's like guys and the rumble of a Harley. You can't explain why, but you could waste a whole day just sitting there listening to it."

Somewhat mollified by Riley's explanation, Scott leaned over and kissed James on the top of the head. To Skeeter he said, "You can have him now, but he's not going home with you."

"We'll see," Skeeter replied, turning his attention back to a new book, this one about a bear who was determined to stay awake until Christmas morning.

"You want to go get changed, honey?" Tara asked.

"Into what?"

"He's got a point," Riley said, knowing that for Scott getting changed from a day at the office meant changing from a black Ozzy T-shirt to a black Dio T-shirt.

"Well, then take the cheese and make yourself useful," Tara said, tossing Scott a bag.

"So, did you have fun storming the castle?" Riley asked, grabbing a handful of veggies to spread around the first pizza.

"Well, I didn't get shot today, so that's a plus."

Tara punched him in the arm. "That's not funny."

"You guys got anything going on?"

"Mostly we're just trying to figure out these attacks. They're so random. We've got the ones that have already happened, and intel is going through the roof saying there's more to come."

"You know who it is?"

"On the surface, it's just a bunch of homegrown *hajjis*. Guys pissed off—"

Tara elbowed him and nodded toward James.

Lowering his voice, Scott said, "Guys angry at America because they're not able to make something of their lives, so they use their religion as an excuse to blow stuff up."

"But it's weird that it's all happening at once, don't you think?" Tara said. "For a while, nothing. Now, all of a sudden it's all over the place."

"That's what's been bugging me," Scott said, sprinkling a final, thin layer of cheese over the first pizza. "There's got to be some unifying factor."

"Could they be distractions designed to draw your attention away from some major thing?" Riley asked.

"Funny, that's what Khadi said."

Riley stopped short, a pepperoni hovering over the second pizza. "Khadi? When did you talk to Khadi?"

As Scott and Tara exchanged glances, Riley heard Skeeter stop midsentence. A moment later, he softly started up again: "He stands with a stretch and a great big sigh. 'I hope I can make it. I do want to try. . . .'"

"Scott?"

Scott laughed. "Dude, I've got the biggest mouth ever. I mean, ever! Remember that time when we were going to surprise Posada for his birthday? Remember that? I went off and—"

"Scott, when did you talk to Khadi?"

As quickly as the laughter started, it stopped. With venom in his voice, he said, "What, is there a crime in that? Are you going to start telling me who I can and can't talk to?"

"Didn't buy the laughing bit. I'm not buying the angry one either. Why can't you just tell me when you talked to her?"

Scott sighed, beaten. "Because one question will lead to another, and I don't know how much I can or should say."

Scott was always so free with his information, so when he clammed up, Riley knew something big was going on.

"I'm not looking for you to betray any confidences. Just tell me this: is she doing okay?"

Again the glance to Tara. "She's all right. Going through a bit of a tough spell."

"Is there . . . I mean, you'd let me know if there was something I could do to help, right?"

"Of course."

Stillness hung over the kitchen betrayed only by the steady movement of hands over pizzas and the low verbal rumble from Skeeter's corner.

Without looking up from his work, Riley said, "Did she . . . ask . . . You know, next time you talk with her, tell her I said hey. Tell her I'd like to . . . Tell her I said hey."

The rest of the night went great. The pizzas were great, the conversation was great, the obnoxious banter was great, the games of hearts after James went down were great. Scott was elated that Skeeter had decided to rejoin CTD, and for a while the two of them talked through logistics. Riley was thrilled that everything was working out so well for all of them. It was great . . . just great . . . absolutely, positively, flippin' great.

And at 2:47 a.m., when he looked at the clock on his nightstand, he was still thinking about just how great everyone's life was. *Everyone's except mine . . . and apparently Khadi's. But I can't* help her. And she can't help me. Because we've got this thing, this massive whatever-it-is between us that keeps us apart.

So I'll just stay miserable, and she'll just stay miserable, and together we'll separately live out our miserable lives. And it'll be great. It'll be just great.

CHAPTER TWENTY-FIVE

THURSDAY, SEPTEMBER 15, 6:15 A.M. EDT
WASHINGTON, DC

Khadi had been thinking about her parents all morning.

What do I do about this Bryson thing? I can't let him proceed with any actions. He's got enough connections in government to push a prosecution through, or at least an investigation. Who knows? He might even get Andrews in on it—a little revenge for his own failed attempts at me.

I'm sure I could end the whole thing with one word to Scott. He and a few of the ops guys would be glad to give Bryson a late-night visit that would ensure the matter was never mentioned again. But can I really put him and the rest of the guys at risk like that?

Untouched, the corn flakes in the bowl in front of her slowly softened in the milk. A spoon, which would eventually be returned clean to the drawer, lay next to the bowl. Khadi knew she should eat, knew that today was going to be a tough one and that she'd need all the energy she could get, but still the milk warmed as the flakes wilted.

Got to get it out of your mind! You've got too much on your plate for today. Focus on happier things—happier times.

Right now, my family is having a big suhoor *meal, gathering their strength in order to endure the struggles of the first day of the fast. Even though it's a solemn occasion, I can still picture my mom's smile and my dad's loving winks. They'll eat together; they'll pray together; then my dad and brothers will go off to the mosque. That's when the real fun at home will begin.* At the Faroughi household, most of the rest of the day would be spent laughing and playing as the family prepared the iftar feast for tonight.

While she slowly dipped a teabag in and out of a mug, reminiscences of the past danced in her mind's eye—the mayhem of flour fights that would break out among the ladies of the extended family, the laughter and the blushing of the younger girls because her mom's sharp wit had struck again, the hugs, the accidental brushes, the impromptu neck massages, the kisses, the touches . . . *You know, that's what I think I'm missing most—the touches.*

She let the teabag sink to the bottom of the mug and dangled the string over the lip. The world of a single, career-driven woman was typically not one of a lot of physical contact—at least not the kind that was welcome. Of course, there *were* plenty of ways to feel touch, and plenty of men out there ready to give it. *Maybe that's what this whole relationship with Jonathan is about—I just need to be touched by someone. And he does seem to really care for me.*

But that's not what I really need. I need to feel arms of love around me. Touch that's backed by more than just emotion or passion. I want to feel the touch that comes from history, experience, blood, soul—from people who know me through and through and still love me—my folks, my family, old friends . . . Riley.

She laughed softly to herself. *There you go again—pining*

like a schoolgirl. What's done is done, and you did it. Think of how many other women across the country are sitting right now at their tables thinking of the wondrous Riley Covington, wishing they could meet him, imagining what life would be like to be Mrs. Covington, totally unaware that in real life . . . well, in real life he's even better than they're probably imagining. How many of them would give everything to have had the chance with him that you had, and that you blew?

Taking the string from her cup, she began to wind it tightly around her left index finger, turning the tip of her finger a dark red. When it was fully wound, she used a spoon to press the excess water out of the tea bag. Satisfied that she had excised every last drop from the pouch, she held it over a paper towel she had folded into quarters and let it drop. It quickly unraveled as it fell until it hit the end of the string with a bounce and a spin. After letting it rotate for a few moments, she rested it on the paper square.

She didn't know when in her childhood she had started this little ritual. She just knew that tea didn't taste like tea if she didn't get a chance to drop that little pouch. Her mom used to gently tease her as together they'd watch the bag spin. The only difference between the ritual now and then is that this teabag was destined for the trash. Growing up, it would have gone into one of three bowls marked *first*, *second*, and *third*. Her mom insisted on not throwing away a teabag until it had its full four uses wrung out of it—a practical holdover from the spare years following their flight from Iran in the late 1970s.

Khadi smiled sadly as she thought of the watery tea that her family would probably be drinking today. *Oh, I miss them,* she thought as she took a sip from her mug, then carried it to the sink, where she poured it out.

At least I know they're thinking of me. As she collected her uneaten cereal and dumped that down the sink too, she wondered, *What do they think of me? They say they're proud of me. But*

I still know that Dad wanted me to be a doctor. And Mom's always worried that I'm going to get myself killed.

After running the garbage disposal and placing the bowl and mug on the top rack of the dishwasher, she walked to her bedroom and pulled a rug from her closet. *But I really do think they're proud. "And that one is our Khadija, the one who's always out saving the world,"* she'd overheard her dad saying to some people at a fund-raiser she had attended with her family. *Funny how that's stuck with me these last couple of years.*

After rolling out the rug on the living room floor, she went into the bathroom. Without plugging the drain, she started the water in the tub. First one foot, then the other went under the water for a thorough scrubbing. Next, her arms and hands took the plunge.

Following a quick dry with a towel, she padded back into the living room, turned off all the lights, and knelt on her prayer rug. The sun was just coming up, and the new light of dawn began to drive the shadows from the room.

Banishing all other thoughts from her mind, she began to recite a prayer that she had prayed on this special morning ever since she was old enough to speak—a *du'a* of commitment for the first day of Ramadan:

> *"Allah, on this day make my fast the fast of those who fast sincerely and my standing up in prayer of those who stand up in prayer obediently. Awaken me in it. . . ."*

THURSDAY, SEPTEMBER 15, 6:53 A.M. EDT
WASHINGTON, DC

". . . from the sleep of the heedless, and forgive me my sins, O God of the worlds, and forgive me, O one who forgives the sinners."

Majid Alavi kept his forehead on the ground a moment longer before rocking back into kneeling position. To either side of him were Ubaida Saliba and Adnan Bazzi, facing him was Saifullah, and behind him knelt the twenty remaining *shahids*.

"Today is Allah's day," Saifullah called out. "Today is our day! My faithful students, my courageous warriors, my dear children, this day let there be no fear of death, for death ushers the martyr into the presence of our God. Let there be no fear of pain, for pain only purifies us and keeps our wits sharp. Let there be no fear of guilt, for what we carry out today is a righteous sacrifice to a worthy God.

"Know this day that Allah is proud of what you do, your family is proud of what you do, all Islam is proud of what you do . . . and I am so very proud of what each of you is about to do. While I may be called the Sword of Allah, today it is you who will take his blade in your hands and fight.

"Now take some time to prepare yourselves before Allah. Your team leaders will call you together at the proper time."

As people began moving around him, Alavi closed his eyes and continued kneeling on his rug. A thought had been bothering him ever since the imam had begun speaking—*I wonder how Saifullah's words would have been different if this team had been raised in the Middle East instead of here in America.*

His mind drifted back to his time in Somalia. During his half year there, he had witnessed only one suicide team being sent out. It was the first time he had ever experienced anything like that, and the vision of these men ready to sacrifice themselves for the sake of Allah had seared itself into his memory.

He remembered his own rush of adrenaline as he watched the men stand before the cameras and tape their farewells. Then they went before the imam, who had spoken words to them that had been much more centered on the wickedness of the enemy and the future support of the martyrs' families.

Here in America it was all about the martyr himself. Was he doing the right thing? Would people remember him with pride? *Here, we have been saturated in a me-centered culture. Saifullah does not fight that; he uses it in his discourse. They . . . we can't stand the thought of our family and friends being disappointed in us.*

That thought opened up a sore spot for Alavi that he quickly tried to cover over with prayer. But soon enough, his mind drifted back to his family.

There's no way Dad's going to understand this—not now, not this side of Paradise. But one day he will. One day he will see the justification of my actions. In fact, he'll even celebrate it.

Oh, Allah, I know that what I'm doing is right. Please let my father see that truth. Please protect him from unnecessary shame. Forgive him if he doesn't understand your call to me. He's a broken man; he doesn't think clearly anymore. He's lost sight of all that you are. You are a God of mercy; extend mercy to him, I pray. Then I can go to my death truly at peace.

With a deep inhale, he pushed himself to his feet. Silence filled the large warehouse as each man spent time with his thoughts or his prayers or his doubts. Quietly, Alavi moved back to his cot. As team leader, he didn't have the same luxury of time. There was too much to be done. Everything had to be gone over one last time. Everyone had to be fully prepared.

For this to come off right, it would take discipline, determination, courage, and ruthlessness, and even then they'd need a large amount of divine assistance. If this were to fall apart, it could give all of Islam a black eye. However, if they pulled it off, it would shake the foundations of America, knocking it off balance for years to come.

CHAPTER TWENTY-SEVEN

THURSDAY, SEPTEMBER 15, 9:50 A.M. EDT

WASHINGTON, DC

"Tell me about it," Scott yelled as he charged out of his office. The Room of Understanding was a flurry of activity as everyone was busy pounding keyboards and clicking mice.

"Looks like two gunmen at a Krispy Kreme in Little Rock," Virgil Hernandez reported from his workstation. "Opened fire as soon as they walked in."

"Another donut shop? Are you sure they're *hajji?*"

"Don't know of any Arkansas white trash militia that shouts *'Allahu akbar'* before they start firing."

Scott slid in behind Hernandez and watched a CNN news report over his shoulder.

"Did they get them?"

"Come on, Scott," Hernandez answered, aggravation evident in his voice. "It's a donut shop. Four cops dusted them before they even knew what was coming."

"Yeah, didn't happen that way last time,"

Scott grumped. On the screen a banner read *Five dead in Krispy Kreme shooting*. "Looks like the cops didn't get them soon enough, either."

"Got another one," Evie Cline called out.

Scott ran to her. "Report!"

"It's not even on the news feeds yet, but seems some whack-a-doo just opened fire in Caesars in Vegas."

"That couldn't have lasted long," Scott said, wondering to himself what connections there may have been between the two attacks. "Even this early in the morning, they've got security there that makes the Secret Service look like the neighborhood watch."

Evie read down the flash for a moment, "One perp . . . two dead . . . looks like they took him down by hand. . . . Definitely Islamic extremist."

Scott stood up and looked around. "What's going on?" he barked. "Why didn't we know about this? Virgil? Joey? Gooey?" Seeing the analyst's station empty, he asked, "Where's Gooey?"

Without looking up from his screen, Joey Williamson answered, "He's been in and out all morning. Bad pizza, he said."

"Got another one," Hernandez said. "A bus in Sacramento. Five dead, seven wounded, perp in custody."

"Come on, talk to me! What's going on?" Scott was in the middle of the room. He was hanging on to a chair at the conference table, struggling to resist the urge to chuck it across the room. He closed his eyes and tried to concentrate.

"Physics class at Ball State," Evie called out. "Don't know the numbers. Perp's dead."

Come on, think! Think! What is this? It's obviously coordinated, but to what end? In the distance, Scott heard something about Tampa and a diner, but he was too focused to process the details. Sweat began beading on his head; his grip on the chair grew tighter. *What are they trying to prove? This isn't a show of strength. Too much little stuff. Maybe they can show numbers with what they're doing, but not strength.*

A Fort Wayne grocery store and an auto auction in Pittsburgh. . . .

It's just too much! It doesn't make sense! If they really wanted to terrorize, they'd do one a day for a week or a month—really get people looking over their shoulders. But a flurry all at once?

Another grocery store, this one in Boise—

"Stop!" Scott yelled. "Everybody just shut up!"

A hush quickly fell over the room. "Conference table—now!"

"But there's still—" Hernandez started to say until a glare from Scott shut him down.

The team quickly took their seats around the long table, including Gooey, who must have returned while Scott had his eyes closed.

"What's going on?" Scott demanded.

"Hard to tell when we're over here and our computers are over there," Gooey complained.

"That's not what I mean. What's really going on here? I'm looking for a motive for all this—something bigger than 'Let's make the bad Americans scared.'"

"You mean, like what Khadi said," Evie agreed. "Is this all part of something bigger? Are they trying to distract us from something else?"

"Bingo," Scott said, and for once no one clamored for him to drop a buck in the "Oh No You Di'int" jar.

"But what could be bigger?" asked Williamson. "It's not like these amateurs could get their hands on a nuke."

"Word," Gooey agreed, deciding to exploit the moratorium on the cliché jar for all it was worth. "They'd be all over a nuke like white on rice, like cats on mice, like dots on dice, but for now that's just not how they roll."

Smiling despite himself, Scott said, "Thanks for clarifying that, Goo. I agree that we're not necessarily looking for bigger in scope, just bigger in impact. Precision, pinpoint—like a well-directed blow to the solar plexus rather than a club over the head. Think of the chatter you've processed over the last week. Any of the locations of these attacks a surprise to you? Evie?"

"None, except Sacramento—"

"Saw that one," Hernandez said with a quick raise of his hand.

"Okay, and Ball State."

"Muncie, Indiana."

"Duh, Muncie," Evie said, smacking herself lightly on the forehead. "Thanks, Virge. And judging by what else I've seen, I'd be very worried if I were in Houston, Cincinnati, Tucson, or Clovis, California."

What's going on here? There's got to be a thread—got to be a purpose. Scott sat silently with his eyes squeezed shut, the thumb and index finger of his right hand massaging the bridge of his nose. Everyone knew to be quiet when they saw him like this—nobody wanted to be the one who threw the wrench in his high-torque mental machinery.

"Okay," he finally said. "Let's pull it back one more level. We've been following this line of chatter because *a*, it was related to the earlier attacks of the last few weeks, and *b*, it thus had the highest level of urgency. But what other threads have we set aside in pursuit of this? In other words, pretend none of this exists. What would you be focusing on instead?"

"Big stuff happening in Londonistan, rumors of a nasty shipment coming across the border from Mexico, and a moderate elevation of the usual rumblings here in our lovely adopted hometown," Gooey said.

More to himself than anyone at the table, Scott said, "The Brits can take care of London. The nasty stuff on the border . . . How nasty is nasty, Gooman?"

"Sounds like some heavy weapons, but no reason to hatch this elaborate a plot."

"Honestly, Scootie," Evie chimed in, "I'm most concerned about the hometown chatter."

"First of all—Scootie?" Scott said. "Second of all, how concerned are you?"

Gooey jumped in. "I'd have been spending all my time on it if these other threads weren't having us running around like a bunch of one-armed paperhangers."

Scott asked, "So what are the specifics?"

"No specifics," Williamson said. "We just know they're talking. It's serious enough that Secret Service has been notified, as has security at the Capitol."

"No specifics in the chatter leaves us with the news. What's happening around the city today? What could they be trying to draw our attention from?" Even as he was saying the words, a tense fluttering was beginning in his stomach. Something was happening today. He remembered hearing about it—even talking about it—but he just couldn't put his finger on it.

"The only thing out of the ordinary I know of is the funeral at the National Cathedral," Evie said.

The funeral—that's it! Khadi and I talked about it. But a funeral doesn't really fit the profile of a well-designed, planned-in-advance conspiracy, does it? "A funeral's kinda hard to plan for. Remind me how Chaplain Whozit died again."

"It's Chaplain Daniel Musman," Evie answered. "Died Monday in his sleep. I'm pretty sure it was a heart attack."

The details were beginning to fall into place for Scott. "He was pretty old, wasn't he? Was there an autopsy?"

"I'm not sure. I can check," Evie said sliding her chair back.

"No, don't bother. I'd bet woodchucks to wombats there wasn't." Tension filled Scott's body, and his leg started bouncing like a piston on hyperdrive. "I was talking with Khadi about this yesterday. She's going to be there with her senator, along with a bunch of other congressional folk. Guys, I'm getting a bad feeling about this."

"Ditto," Gooey said.

Jumping up from his chair, Scott began pacing. "Okay, here's how we're going to play this. Evie, you call FBI. Fill them in and get them on board."

"Scott—" Evie said.

"Goo, you start acquiring feeds on every camera surrounding the cathedral."

"Scott—" Evie tried again.

"Joey, you—"

"Scott!"

"What?" Scott yelled back at her.

"You realize that they scheduled the funeral for 10:00 this morning?"

"Thank you, Evie! I know that already! Your point?"

In reply, Evie just nodded to the digital clock that hung over the door to the Room of Understanding. In big red letters it read 10:09 a.m.

Scott's response would have cost him eleven dollars in the "You Kiss Your Mama with That Mouth?" jar—if they had been keeping count.

THURSDAY, SEPTEMBER 15, 10:10 A.M. EDT
LEESBURG, VIRGINIA

Riley rounded the corner and continued down the sidewalk. His legs were starting to ache, but he wasn't sweating quite as much as usual. It was the time of year when the mornings were just starting to cool down, providing some welcome relief from the still-hot afternoons.

He admired the oaks lining the street and tried to picture what they would look like in another month or so when the colors were blazing. *I can't wait for fall,* he thought. *The sights, the smells—the only thing better than watching the leaves fall is the smell of the freshly raked piles in the crisp October air.*

Besides, remember where you could be instead. I'm thinking Bernier and the rest of the boys over in Ashburn aren't enjoying their morning workout quite as much as I am.

Riley's world had changed quite a bit since his "woe is me" whine-fest last night. His sleep had been restless, and he had woken up tired. The last thing he wanted to do on a morning like this was to spend time in his daily devotional. He was still pretty ticked at God, not at all happy with His plan. But then something Riley's dad used to say squeezed its way through his unrighteous indignation: *"It's usually in those times when you don't want to hear from God that He's really got something important to say."*

Funny how even now after he's been gone two years, Dad's still giving me advice, Riley mused as he opened his Bible that morning. For the last couple of weeks, he'd been reading Isaiah—an interesting book, but sometimes a little hard to fully understand. Today, however, that wasn't the case. He was in the forty-sixth chapter, and he read these words:

> I am God, and there is no other;
>> I am God, and there is none like me.
> I make known the end from the beginning,
>> from ancient times, what is still to come.
> I say, 'My purpose will stand,
>> and I will do all that I please.'
> From the east I summon a bird of prey;
>> from a far-off land, a man to fulfill my purpose.
> What I have said, that will I bring about;
>> what I have planned, that I will do.

Suddenly, all his bellyaching about his life seemed like just that—bellyaching. God had His big plan for the world, and He had His little plans for His people. Riley had two options: whine and complain and be useless, or get on board. His prayer this morning had been for God to renew his joy, to change his attitude, and to help him remember that his life was about others and not about himself. And in that moment, he felt a freedom that he hadn't felt in months, like a burden had been lifted from his shoulders.

It's amazing what a little perspective can do, he thought as he jogged past the colonial houses with their manicured lawns and their towering trees. Looking ahead he saw a pretty, petite brunette walking a very large, very black, very well-controlled Newfie. *That thing's got to hate the summers.* He laughed.

He smiled and said hi to the young lady as he came alongside her. She initially gave him the "I'm-used-to-being-hit-on-by-every-doofus-who-jogs-past-me" nod, until she seemed to recognize who he was. But by the time she got her "Oh, hi" out, he was already past. *Too bad. She was a cutie. But it's probably for the best. She had that "love me, love my dog" air about her, and that's just a little too much dog to love.*

Speaking of dogs, with Skeeter moving out soon, maybe it's time to revisit getting a slobbering beast of my own. That's a pretty big house for just one sentient being to exist in. He rounded another corner and started up his cul-de-sac. He was at the end of his five-mile circuit but had no idea how long he'd been gone. Dumping his workout watch was one of his sacrifices to this newfound freedom.

What breed should I look at? Don't want one of those yappy puntable pets. But I also don't want one of those Wookie-size furballs that'll have me using a roller on my clothes every time I leave the house. How about a bulldog? If I could train it to not chew everything in—

Riley's train of thought was broken by a silver Mercedes coupe pulling down a driveway right smack in front of him. He tried to stop in time, but his momentum was too much. He thumped against the front fender and his knee caught the edge of the wheel well.

The door flew open. "Riley, I'm so sorry," said his neighbor—*Roy? Rich? Rob?*—as he jumped out. "Are you hurt? Do you need me to call 911?"

Riley, who had bounced off the car but kept his feet and was now limping around trying to walk off the pain, said through gritted teeth, "No, I'm good. Give me just a second."

"Seriously, Riley, I can't believe I did that! Are you sure you don't want me to call anyone?"

"No thanks. No worse than running headlong into an offensive lineman," he said, trying to keep the tight smile on his face. *Walk it out. Come on, walk it out.*

"Can I at least get you a cloth for your knee?" Roy/Rich/Rob asked.

Riley looked down and saw for the first time that he was bleeding. Not stitches bad, but bad enough to start a trail down his leg.

"No, seriously, I'm good."

"I still can't believe it. I am so sorry. I'm just a little freaked out by all the stuff that's going on. I was turning the car radio to the news station and just plain didn't see you. Totally my fault. Again, I'm so unbelievably sorry."

"Forgiven," Riley said, the pain beginning to subside. *Come on, here's your chance to use your newly rediscovered joy.* "I just hope I didn't hurt your car."

A light seemed to go off in Roy/Rich/Rob's head, and he quickly turned to his coupe. After examining it, he breathed a visible sigh of relief. "No, she's good."

She? That's a man who loves his car. Bet he's even got a name for her. "So, what's going on that's got you all freaked?"

The neighbor looked at Riley with big eyes. "You mean you don't know? I thought you of all people . . . There're terror attacks all over the place. I'm talking like everywhere."

On hearing this, Riley started to back away toward his house. "Everywhere like everywhere? Or everywhere like here in the States?"

"Here in the States. Las Vegas; Fort Wayne, Indiana; Houston, Texas—all across the country. These Islamic terrorists are going into places and shooting them up."

By now Riley had turned toward his house and was awkwardly limp-sprinting across the two lawns that would lead him to his garage.

"Sorry again, Riley," the neighbor called.

Riley gave a wave in return. He quickly punched in the code that raised the door, then ran through the garage into the house. Stopping in the kitchen, he dumped a couple handfuls of ice into a dishtowel and carried it into the family room. Skeeter was already there with the television on. He was sitting on the edge of the couch with his elbows on his knees.

"It's bad," Skeeter said as soon as Riley sat down. "So far, ten incidents in ten different cities. At least thirty dead—perps all dead or in custody."

Riley placed the towel on his knee and winced. "All *hajji*?"

"American *hajji*."

"Really? All of them?"

"Best they can tell so far." Skeeter seemed to notice Riley's knee for the first time. "What happened to you?"

"Hit by a car. No major."

Seemingly satisfied by the answer, Skeeter turned back to the TV. The picture was divided into quarters, with aftermath scenes from Las Vegas, Houston, Pittsburgh, and Muncie, Indiana, filling the screen.

"Should you get down to CTD?" Riley asked.

"Tried calling Scott, but he was too busy to talk. Did talk to Gilly, and he told me to hold off. It's still in the analysts' hands. He'll let me know if it looks like ops is going to come into play."

The two of them watched the reports for a while, then Skeeter stepped away. When he returned, he was carrying a large gauze bandage and some Neosporin.

Riley took them. "Thanks." He lifted the bloody towel from his knee and looked at the damage. There was a ragged gash, but it didn't look too deep. He squeezed some ointment onto it, rubbed it around a bit, then covered it with the bandage.

"So, are you thinking what I'm thinking?" he asked Skeeter. "What's next?"

"Exactly. I'm sure that's the question that's got Scott and the gang going crazy."

Riley leaned back on the couch and mentally tuned out the commentary on the television, instead focusing on the pictures. *Lord, You showed me this morning that You are the One who's in control and that You've got a plan. But I gotta admit, it's a little hard to see it right now.*

Let these people feel Your arms of love. It's won't be easy for them—trust me, I know. Just let them see You.

After a few more minutes, Riley got up and headed to the shower. As he leaned his hands against the tile wall and let the hot water rain down his neck and back, he prayed, *And, Lord, use me to help. If You've got a place for me in the midst of all this, just show me. I'll go where You want me to go, and I'll do what You want me to do. I'm a tool in Your hands—use me.*

Khadi held the hymnbook and sang:

> "A mighty Fortress is our God
> A bulwark never failing."

As a member of a minority religion in a Christian culture, she was used to these types of situations. Growing up, the families of some of her Muslim friends would get upset at their children being exposed to Christmas in school or hearing stories of the Easter bunny from friends. She, however, never really minded. Easter meant candy, and Christmas meant days off from class. On top of that, her parents often felt bad that all her Christian friends were getting presents, so she'd end up scoring a few guilt gifts.

Now everything was changing. These days, you couldn't even say, "Merry Christmas" in a store—in a "Christian" nation. She remembered her dad telling her when she was eight, "Nobody has a right not to be offended. Just remember who you are, and let others have their fun."

And I replied, "And if I make their fun my fun, then we all have more fun together!" Dad laughed his deep laugh and gave me a hug. How I love that man!

"Lord Sabaoth His name
    From age to age the same . . ."

What is a Sabaoth*? Sounds like Sabbath—the Jewish day off. Got to be tied to that somehow.* Khadi looked around at the people in her row and across the aisle. *I'm guessing none of them have a clue what it means either, but still they keep on singing. And why not? It is a pretty song.*

Senator Andrews caught her looking around and glared at her. In response, he received one of the first genuine smiles she had ever bestowed upon him. *In your face,* she tried to say with her grin.

This morning before the funeral, she had told him of her decision to leave his employ and return to CTD. He had pitched an absolute fit, accusing her of everything from disloyalty and cowardice to being a closeted lesbian.

Then the threats had begun—"You'll never work in this town again!" and "I could put you in jail for how you've threatened me!" A reminder that she already had another job and that there were very good reasons for her threats, ones that his wife would probably be interested to hear, quickly shut down that line of attack.

Finally came the promises—promises of more money, more flexibility in her schedule, and more time off. He swore that he would never make another pass at her and would cut out completely the crude comments.

It was about that time that the creepiness of having a sex-addicted senator begging her to stay with him started jittering her insides. She left the room and didn't see him again until they were preparing to leave. Thankfully, Charlotte Andrews, the senator's wife, was with him, buffering his usual piggish behavior.

"My husband tells me that you are leaving us," Charlotte had said formally after giving Khadi's black dress a condescending once-over. Even though she tried to fight it, Khadi immediately became self-conscious of how she looked in what was the nicest outfit from her closet. "I wish you luck on your next adventure. We will miss you."

Khadi knew that neither of those last two statements were true. She had always felt that Charlotte saw her as some sort of rival for her husband's affections. As a result, her demeanor toward Khadi had always been one of intentionally cold indifference.

She's another person I won't miss. But the one I definitely will miss is J.D.

J.D. Little was disappointed to hear her news but not surprised. Gracious as always, he had wished her luck and promised to do everything he could to deflect the wrath that was certain to come from the senator.

Khadi looked down the row to her partner. *I wonder if there might be a place for J.D. at CTD. He deserves better than a life protecting Mr. Opportunity and others like him. I'll ask Scott.*

The hymn finished, and everyone sat down. Khadi was surprised to see how many people had shown up. There had to be nearly four hundred people in the vast sanctuary. She couldn't tell for sure without turning around again, because Senator Andrews had jockeyed for a place in the second row just behind the family.

Seated to her left was Kirstin Evert, wife of the Senate minority leader, Bill Evert, who was sitting on the other side of his bride. And next to him was the controversial Speaker of the House, Cristy Johnston, along with her husband, Lance.

On Khadi's right sat Tyson Bryson, causing her to cheat

herself as far to the left side of her chair as propriety would allow. He had asked her again this morning whether she had thought about his proposal. Her response would have made her mother blush.

Charlotte Andrews sat on the other side of Bryson. Next to her was the senator, and finally, J.D., who was on the inside aisle. *Funny how it is so much more important to Andrews to show that he needs personal bodyguards that he gave up the visibility of the aisle seat. Who could ever hope to understand these guys?*

Up front on the beautiful wooden platform, standing behind an even more beautifully carved wooden pulpit, Brian Musman, son of the deceased chaplain, began reading the obituary and memorial. Although looking and sounding like he might lose it at any moment, he was doing a good job. Khadi found herself rooting for him to make it through.

The clutch purse on her lap began vibrating. There were only two things in that purse: a cell phone and a Smith & Wesson Model 66 .357 Magnum Snub. She opened it and reached for the phone.

Scott's number was on the caller ID. *Probably forgot where I was,* she thought as she hit End and slid the phone back into her purse. Thirty seconds later, she felt another single vibration. *Good, he left me a message.*

Bryson turned to her, pointed to the purse, and whispered, "This is a funeral!"

"Ah, well that explains why I haven't seen any clowns yet," she whispered back, causing him to redden and turn back to the front.

Her purse vibrated again, making enough noise for Mrs. Evert to turn to her.

"I'm sorry," Khadi said reaching for the phone. "It's official business."

Evert nodded like a woman to whom the words *official business* had been used over her lifetime to justify any and every questionable activity under the sun, save those that actually might be considered by the everyday voting taxpayer as *official business*. Khadi fought the urge to say, "No, really," and instead just looked at her phone.

This time it was a text from Scott: *Call me NOW!!*

At funeral. Call in hour, she typed back. Embarrassed, she slipped the phone into her purse.

Brian Musman had finished his memorial in one piece. Now a little girl, presumably one of the granddaughters, was walking up, carrying a piece of paper. She couldn't have been more than seven. She was wearing a pretty little black dress that flared out with ruffles at the bottom. Khadi felt her throat begin to constrict and her eyes begin to moisten.

Now it's your turn to keep it together, she chastised herself.

Turns out that the paper she was carrying was a letter to her grandpa.

"Dear Poppy," she read.

Khadi's purse vibrated again. This time she got glares from up and down her row and from a lady in front of her who might have been one of the chaplain's sisters.

She opened the text message from Scott and read, *NO!! DANGER!! CALL ME NOW!!!* Immediately, Khadi's heart began racing. She looked to her right and saw that J.D. was watching her. She pointed to her phone and cut her hand quickly across the air indicating that it was something serious. J.D. pointed for her to go.

"Are the angels beautiful, Poppy?" Khadi heard as she began excusing herself across the laps of the most powerful people in the Senate and the House of Representatives. She heard gasps and whispers from behind her, but she kept pushing on. Once she made it to the outside aisle, she headed toward the back of the sanctuary. Every click of her heels seemed to echo through the high vaults of the Gothic cathedral. After passing several rows, she reached down, slipped off her shoes, and jogged the rest of the way barefoot.

When she finally made it to the rear, she dialed Scott.

"Just listen," he said, answering on the first ring. "We've got reason to think that there may be a terrorist attack aimed at the cathedral. Look around and tell me what you see."

Instantly, all her anger at Scott vanished and she was in protect mode. She scanned her surroundings, taking special note of the people in the congregation. "I don't see anything out of the ordinary. What am I looking for?"

"Don't know. There have been ten terrorist attacks across the country in the last thirty minutes."

Khadi felt the air leave her lungs, and her knees felt weak.

Scott continued. "They were all homegrown perps. We're thinking you may have been right about your distraction theory. DC was the focus of one of the outside threads. And you are right in the middle of the only event of significance taking place in this city today."

Khadi realized Scott was only playing a hunch. But the hunches that came out of the RoU more often than not turned into reality. She looked to the ceiling—nothing. She looked for explosives up the enormous pillars—nothing. She looked for nervous shifting or excessive sweating among the attendees—nothing.

"I've got nothing, Scott," she finally said, hoping beyond hope that this would be one hunch that didn't pay off. She shivered, not knowing if it was nerves or the cold seeping from the tiles into her bare feet.

"Good!" Scott said, a little relief coming into his voice. "I need you to keep your eyes open, though. And didn't you say there was a reception afterward? That's probably an even more dangerous setting than you have now."

"Got it. Does this mean I'm officially on payroll?" she asked feebly, trying to lighten the tension.

"Just keep your eyes open," Scott said, uncharacteristically letting her joke fall to the ground.

Khadi ended the call, and it wasn't until a full thirty seconds had passed from the time she had rung off that she heard the bootsteps—and then the screams began.

THURSDAY, SEPTEMBER 15, 10:25 A.M. EDT
WASHINGTON, DC

If you have enough men and you move quick-
ly enough, you can do just about anything you
want, Majid Alavi thought as he ran through
the south entrance of the National Cathedral.
Adrenaline-fueled sweat dripped down his
face, and he could feel his heart racing.
Behind him were twenty-two other jihadi
warriors divided into three teams. Saifullah
also ran as a *de facto* member of his team, and
Alavi hoped the old man could keep up.

Two vans full of armed men dressed all
in black had obviously attracted attention
when they pulled up to the curb on South
Road. But they moved so fast, there was no
time for anyone to react until they were well
past. By now, he was sure, scores of 911 calls
were being made. *But they'll be too late. This*
place is ours.

A couple of rent-a-cops had stood on
either side of the vaulted entrance. A silenced
shot from his weapon had taken out the

right-side security guard, and one from the second on his team, Hassan Fadil, had dropped the guard on the left. From there it was a quick sprint up the remainder of the Pilgrim Steps and through the doors to the south seating area.

Alavi burst into the sanctuary and was immediately taken with the massive size of the building. *Focus,* he commanded himself. Gasps sounded all around him as he ran to the stage—his hard boots joining forty-four others in creating an unholy clatter on the tile floor.

Spotting his target, he leaped onto the platform, took the pastor or priest or whatever he was by the head, and pressed his assault weapon to the man's temple.

"Nobody move!" he yelled, leaning into the lapel mic that the man was wearing. Black spread through the sanctuary like ink from a leaky pen as his men rushed down the aisles.

This is the critical time, he thought. *If we can just get into position, we've got them. But if some hero fires on us, it's going to be a bloodbath.*

"I swear, if I see one gun drawn, this one's getting a bullet in his head and the rest of these men are going to start firing!" His eyes scanned the audience down the long nave. Screaming had started, and people were beginning to panic. *Come on, just a few more seconds.*

"Why are you doing this?" asked the pastor, whose breath reeked of coffee poorly disguised by mint.

Alavi answered by pushing the barrel of his rifle harder against the man's head, eliciting a strange half grunt, half squeak.

Three men from his team had run to the north seating and taken up position there. Two more stood just below him with their weapons trained on Senator Bill Evert and Speaker of the House Cristy Johnston. Next to him on his right was Fadil—his rifle searching the congregation. And two steps behind him, he hoped, was Saifullah, but he didn't want to turn around to check.

Ubaida Saliba's team was now in position. The nave was

divided into four seating sections—two in the front and two in the rear. Each quarter had two warriors facing it, one on the inside aisle, one on the outside. All had their weapons tucked tight and ready to fire.

This place is huge, Alavi thought, the first moments of doubt beginning to creep in. The schematics and pictures had shown the place to be big, but he was learning just how impossible it was to truly experience the vastness of the space without stepping into it. *There's no way we can control every eventuality within this scenario.*

A movement by a man in the second row caught his attention. His right hand had shifted toward the inside of his jacket.

"Second row aisle!" he yelled to Fadil, but his team lieutenant was already on his way, apparently having seen the movement himself.

"You don't have to do this," the pastor said.

"Shut up," Alavi hissed, moving his hand from the man's forehead to the top of his head. He grabbed a handful of hair and yanked back. The pastor's body stiffened.

"Give me your gun!" Fadil screamed, his rifle pointing at the man's face.

"What gun?" the man protested, raising his hands.

"Give me your gun, now!"

"What gun? I don't—"

The man's words were cut short by a round from Fadil's weapon. Blood and gore burst from the back of his head. A lady in the row behind also dropped from the bullet that had passed through and hit her in the chest. The bloodied gentleman sitting next to the dead man, whom Alavi recognized as Senator Clayson Andrews, jumped sideways onto his wife, who began screaming uncontrollably. More screams erupted all around, and Alavi could feel a shift in the tension. *Got to get control of this, or it's going to snap!*

A quick look to his left showed him that most of Adnan

Bazzi's team was in place. Each one of them had been carrying two large duffels that were now piled stage left. Four men were working with the bags, and two were controlling the south seating area. He had to trust that the other two were clearing out stray people from the choir area behind him.

"Got it!" Fadil called out, lifting the large-caliber pistol he had pulled from the dead man.

"Check his waist and ankles, too," Alavi ordered, knowing that professional security, which that man clearly appeared to be, rarely carried only one weapon.

Dropping his own weapon to his side, he pulled out a combat knife. Panic sprang to the pastor's eyes, as Alavi spun him so that he could face him. He brought the knife down, slicing open the man's long, ornate robe. Sheathing his knife, he quickly saw what he wanted. He unclipped the lapel mic from the robe and pulled the transmitter box from the belt that was holding up the pastor's khaki shorts, then pushed the pastor off the stage.

The man stumbled down the three steps and fell headlong across the tiles. Regaining his feet, he hurried to the widow of the chaplain, who seemed to be having some sort of breathing fit and had slipped down onto the kneeling bench.

A scream louder than the others cut through the din. Looking up from the mic he was clipping onto himself, Alavi saw that another muffled shot had been fired halfway back on the right.

"Silence!" Alavi commanded. When the quiet was slow in coming, he fired three shots from his unsilenced pistol into the air. "Silence!" An uneasy hush quickly fell on the congregation.

He had a clear view of them now. Men and women, young and old. All dressed in their finest—some to show respect, others just so they could be seen looking good.

There were a handful of children scattered around, and they were Alavi's only regret. *But Allah has placed them here for a reason. They too must be considered means to accomplish our end.*

In many faces, he could see people who were rightfully terrified, some even fainting. But in some eyes, he could see anger and even purpose. These were the ones that had to be neutralized immediately.

"I want all guns out now!" Alavi demanded. "You have seen that we are not afraid to use our weapons! All guns now!"

Nobody moved. An unspoken battle of wills had taken hold. Alavi knew that the last thing these well-trained security professionals and government law enforcement agents wanted to do was to give up their weapons.

He eyed a man in the front row. *Don't recognize him as a senator or congressman—probably just family. He'll do.* He pointed his pistol at him and fired. The man crumpled and fell to the ground.

A scream came from the man's wife, so Alavi shot her, too.

"When I give an order, if it is not obeyed immediately, one person dies. If I find a gun on anyone—and you all will be searched—you will watch ten people die, then you too will die. If anyone hurts one of my men, you will watch twenty people die, then you too will die. I trust I have made myself clear.

"I want all guns out now! And trust me, if you try anything heroic, many, many people will die!"

Each of the four members of Bazzi's team who had been unloading the duffels now lifted a bag to his shoulder and began circulating through the sanctuary. Alavi watched as gun after gun was handed butt-first to his men, who deposited them into the duffels.

A hand fell softly on Alavi's shoulder, causing him to start.

"No more killing for now," a calm voice said quietly in his ear.

"Yes, Saifullah."

"If you can help it."

"Yes, Saifullah.

"Hurry, please," Alavi called out to Bazzi's men. The only

sounds now in the vast sanctuary were the sounds of boots on tile, the metallic *chink* of guns dropping on each other, the occasional whispered curse by those handing over their weapons, and the low, audible bed of muffled sobs.

But as he watched and listened, a new sound crept into the eerily silent cathedral—sirens. He knew that it wouldn't be long now until law enforcement tapped into the cameras mounted throughout the enormous sanctuary. When that happened, he wanted to already have everyone sorted into smaller, more containable groups. Right now, his men were simply too spread out for safety.

Despite all the adrenaline pumping through his system, Alavi felt his stomach growl. *The first day of Ramadan is always the hardest,* he thought. *Almighty Allah, accept my hunger as a sacrifice to you. Use me and my brothers this day to accomplish your will. Bring your truth and your law to this wicked land. Give us victory in your name.*

THURSDAY, SEPTEMBER 15, 10:25 A.M. EDT
WASHINGTON, DC

When the footsteps first began echoing off the arched ceiling, Khadi ducked behind one of the many pillars that ran the length of the nave. She reached into her purse, removed its contents, then scanned the back of the church and spotted what she was looking for.

Trying to keep the pillar between herself and the front of the church, she raced to the back wall. As she ran, she speed-dialed Scott.

"Nobody move!" she heard a voice say over the cathedral's sound system.

Scott answered on the first ring.

"What's—?"

"It's starting. Multiple gunmen. Mute your phone; I'm going to try to keep the line open."

Pulling some brochures forward, she slid the gun and then the phone into an information rack. She prayed that Gooey would be able to enhance the audio enough to make it useful.

The voice on the microphone said something else, but the screams had already started and it was impossible to make out his words. Taking a deep breath, she stepped back into the open. Immediately, one of the men in black spotted her. His assault weapon pointed straight at her. Khadi recognized it as an AK-103—*Probably got it from the Venezuelans; they're manufacturing those things down there now, and they'd be pleased as punch to help deal us a blow.*

"Get over here and sit down!"

Khadi let out a scream, and pointed to herself.

"Yes you! Get over here now!"

Prissily, she scampered—still barefoot—to where the man indicated. *Look helpless! Gotta buy time!*

"Please don't shoot me! Please don't shoot me! I'll do whatever you say! Just please don't hurt me!"

Just then, a particularly desperate scream sounded from the front of the sanctuary. Khadi looked in time to see J.D. Little drop to the ground, the back of his head gone.

She swallowed back the raging *NO!!* that formed in her mouth and tried to transfer the emotion to a look of fear and desperation. Dropping into the chair the gunman indicated, she put her head in her hands and began to sob.

A tender arm went around Khadi's shoulders, and the tense air was discordantly filled with the smell of lilac.

"There, there, dear. We'll get through this," a woman's voice said through vocal chords that sounded like they'd been scuffed by many years of usage. "I can't say I've been through worse, but the Good Lord's always found a way to help me survive, no matter the situation."

Khadi could feel the woman start when she whispered to her in a tone thickened by frustration and rage, "Is he gone?"

"What was that?"

"Is . . . he . . . gone?"

"He's moved forward, if that's what you're asking. But he's still nearby."

Khadi looked up and saw that the gunman was no longer looking in her direction. She had just begun counting the enemy force, when that same terrorist got into an argument with a man about seven rows up from her. Without warning, the gunman raised his silenced rifle and shot the man. Complete chaos ensued as the man's wife draped herself across her fallen husband, even as others instinctively pulled themselves away from the gore.

Three shots rang out from the front of the church, startling everybody to attention. In a moment of bizarre dissonance, Khadi realized that even with everything that had taken place over the last five minutes, those were the first unmuffled gunshots she had heard.

"Silence!" came the command from the man on the platform.

The screaming ceased, but the crying continued. It was a sound that wouldn't leave the sanctuary for hours to come, Khadi knew. Eventually it would become no more than white noise, the basal hum from which all other sounds grew.

"Give me a pen," Khadi whispered to the older woman next to her as she began counting again.

"Who *are* you?" The woman was now looking at Khadi with nearly as much fear as she seemed to have for the terrorists.

"I'm sorry to be curt. My name is Khadi Faroughi. I work with the counterterrorism division of Homeland Security."

The man up front was saying something about collecting guns.

The woman's face lit up. "Khadi Faroughi? I thought I recognized you. I've seen you in *Time* magazine. You're friends with that football player, Riley Cunningham, aren't you? My name is Gladys Cook, and I'm—"

Another shot rang out, followed closely by one more.

"Oh my, that's terrible—just terrible," Gladys said.

"Again, I'm sorry to be so short, but I need a pen." Twenty-four was the number she counted, although she couldn't be sure whether there was anyone outside of her view.

Gladys began rummaging through her purse. "Don't you worry about me, honey. You just do your job. And I'll just sit here and pray—that'll be *my* job."

The man up front was threatening to kill a lot more people if his orders were not obeyed. Khadi began scanning the pillars until she found what she was looking for, no more than twenty feet from where she sat.

"I've got ballpoint or permanent," Gladys whispered, holding a pen in each hand down below the sight lines of the gunmen.

"Thanks," Khadi said, taking the ballpoint. "I'll take some hand sanitizer, too, if you have it."

In numbers large and thick enough to fill her entire palm, Khadi wrote *2* on her right hand and *4* on her left.

"Gladys, stop looking in your purse for a moment," she said, taking her neighbor by her cold, bony hand. "I want you to tell me when they're not looking. Can you do that?"

"Listen, honey, you're talking to a member of the World War II WAC. Whatever you tell me to do, you can consider it done."

"You're wonderful," Khadi said, giving the woman's hand a quick squeeze, then releasing it.

As soon as she let go, Khadi began loudly sobbing again. She dropped her head and covered her ears with her hands. Gladys's arm went around her shoulders once more.

Seconds later, Khadi heard the voice of the man who had ordered her to her place.

"Shut up! Tell her to shut up," he said.

"Oh, go away," Gladys said defiantly.

Did she seriously just tell the rifle-wielding terrorist to go away? Khadi marveled.

Again, Gladys spoke, "And you can point that thing some-where else. Are you going to shoot a defenseless, ninety-year-old woman? What do you think your Allah-god would say about that? Now scoot and let the poor dear get it out of her system!"

A few moments passed, then Gladys whispered, "Okay, you're clear. I think you have about two minutes before the men collecting the guns get here."

Still sobbing, Khadi opened her hands away from her ears and toward the surveillance camera she had spotted up on the pillar. She knew that the first thing Scott would do when he tapped into the feed would be to look for her. She wanted to reward that loyalty with some information. Hopefully, the sob-bing fit would attract his attention, so he could see her message.

"He's turning," Gladys said.

Khadi clamped her hands back on her ears.

"Clear," Gladys said again.

Khadi again opened her hands. She counted to fifteen, then lifted her head.

"I don't have any hand sanitizer, but if you're looking to clean the ink off your hands, I do have a bottle of water."

"Perfect," Khadi said, letting Gladys pour a little onto her palms. She began rubbing them together. "Did you really tell that guy to scoot?"

Gladys winked at her. "Don't get on the wrong side of a tough old lady who's got nothing to lose."

Khadi checked her palms to confirm that the numbers were gone, then said, "You just be careful. I want to see both of us get out of here in one piece."

"You just worry about saving yourself and all these other people. Let me worry about me."

The men with the duffel bags were getting closer. After the threats the man up front had made, she prayed they wouldn't find the gun she had hidden. *Deep breaths—analyze the situation.*

The men passed by, not giving her a second glance. When they reached the rear of the sanctuary, they jogged back up to the front and placed the bags on the stage behind the man with the microphone. As they did that, for the first time Khadi really took notice of an older man standing behind and off to the right of the main guy.

He's got to be the one in charge. The one with the mic is the general, but that old man is the commander in chief.

"Now, I want all cell phone batteries," said the general. "As the bags come by, I want cell phone in one hand and battery in the other. Again, same rules apply. If I find a cell phone battery not turned in, people will die."

The men began moving down the rows again. One by one, the thin plastic batteries dropped into the bags.

"How do you get the battery off of this thing?" Gladys asked, picking at her phone with a rose-pink fingernail.

"Let me help," Khadi said, taking the phone and snapping the battery off the back.

"Why do they just want the batteries?"

Handing the phone back, Khadi answered, "Without a battery, the phone is useless. However, with the battery all sorts of things can be done. It can be turned on remotely, it can be used to pinpoint location, it can be tapped into and used as a listening device."

"Oh my, no wonder I don't like them. That's simply Orwellian."

"You don't know the half of it."

An argument broke out ten rows up.

"I don't have a phone," a man protested, desperation in his voice. Khadi recognized him as a congressman, Dennis Robbins, from one of the Midwest states.

"Everyone has a phone," the terrorist with the bag countered.

"What I mean is that I do have a phone, just not with me. I forgot it at home this morning."

"Liar! Where is your phone?"

"I swear, I don't have it!"

The man with the bag nodded to his partner standing next to him. The gunman reached across three people, grabbed Robbins, and lifted him out.

The man with the bag pressed the muzzle of a pistol to Robbins forehead. "What's your name?"

"Robbins. Dennis Robbins. Congressman," he sputtered.

Khadi saw the two terrorists exchange a glance.

"What's your cell number? And if you give me a wrong number, I'm pulling the trigger!"

Robbins rapidly rattled off a number. Then sucked in a breath when the gunman lowered the pistol and pulled a phone from his own pocket.

The terrorist dialed the number Robbins had given, then held the phone to his side. A mechanical hum sounded in the sudden quietness. The woman who was sitting next to Robbins's empty seat gasped.

"She didn't know it was in there! I swear! I put it in when—"

Robbins's protests were silenced by the stock of an AK-103 coming down across his head. He dropped to the ground. The men began kicking him with their boots, continuing until there was no more movement. The man with the bag knelt down and felt for a pulse on Robbins's neck. Satisfied with what he felt, he nodded to the other man.

Standing back up, he said to the quaking woman, "Give me his phone."

With trembling hands she pulled it out of her purse and passed it to him.

"Do you swear before God that you had no knowledge of what this man did?"

"I-I s-s-swear," she said, barely keeping control.

"Very well." The terrorist popped the battery off the back of the phone. The battery went into his bag, but the phone he dropped onto the tile floor. Lifting his leg, he drove his heel onto the phone, crushing it.

"A warning: do not mistake my mercy for weakness," he said. Then he moved on.

Why did it matter that he was a congressman? Khadi asked herself. *Other peopple have been killed without a second thought. But the congressman was just beaten.*

Then another thought hit her.

"Oh no," she said out loud.

"What is it?" asked Gladys.

The man with the bag was now only four rows away.

"I dialed CTD, then stashed my phone in the back of the church. They'll want to know where it is."

The man stepped forward a row.

"Then take mine," Gladys said.

"No way. They'll want to know where your phone is."

"Take it . . . and trust me," Gladys ordered, putting her phone and battery into Khadi's hands, then wrapping her small fingers around Khadi's, sealing the deal.

The man with the bag moved forward another row and glared at Khadi and Gladys. Khadi slowly raised her hands with the battery in one and the phone in the other.

After collecting all the batteries from the row in front, he stepped next to Khadi. She handed him the battery from her hand, followed by one after another as all the batteries were passed down the row.

"Where is your phone?" he asked Gladys.

"I don't carry one of those gadgets. They're annoying and rude," she answered matter-of-factly.

"Everyone has a phone," the man countered angrily. "Give me yours!"

"Listen, young man, I didn't have a phone in my house until after I was married, and somehow I found a way to get along just fine. So, I'll be danged if, just because it's the twenty-first century, I'm going to be tied to one of those devices twenty-four hours a day!"

"I don't believe you! Everyone has a phone!"

"I don't care what you believe! And you watch your tone with me, young man! I didn't make it to ninety years old just to have nasty young punks like you give me sass. Besides, you should be ashamed of yourself! I can hear in your voice that you're American born and bred. If I were your mother—"

The gunman had heard enough. He leaned in and pulled his hand back. Khadi lunged forward and grabbed his arm before he could strike. Her grip was strong, and he looked at her, surprised.

"I'm so sorry," she said, quickly softening her grip. "My grandmother doesn't always know what she's saying. Please, forgive me. I'll control her."

Leaning back out of the row, the man said, "You'd better."

"Control me? You're going to control me? Listen, little girl, I remember putting you over my knee and spanking your bare behind when you were just a tyke, and I'm not afraid to do it again today."

"Just shut her up," the bagman said before moving on.

"I will. Thank you," Khadi said. "Grandma, hush now."

The men with the bags finished their circulation and returned to the front. A group of them conferenced with the general, then moved to the side wings of the sanctuary. Soon all the people from that seating area began moving into the nave.

Once everyone was in the main sanctuary, the terrorists began a long process of sorting people into groups. Khadi could count three. One seemed to be collecting all the celebrity politicians. Another contained primarily women and the few children that were in the building. The third seemed to be a hodgepodge of those who didn't really fit into either category.

Helpless and frustrated, all Khadi could do was watch.

Please, Scott, come up with something fast. I don't know what they have in mind, but I do know that this isn't going to end well.

But what about you? You need to do something. You can't just wait for Scott while this whole thing goes down! Do something!

Try as she might, Khadi was at a loss. Deflated, defeated, she sagged into her seat. Soon a cold, bony hand opened Khadi's fist and slipped into her grasp. She turned to Gladys and saw her smiling.

"Just give it time, dear. God always finds a way."

Khadi did her best to smile back. She covered Gladys's hand with her own. *Okay, God, Gladys says you're going to find a way. If you're going to do it, you better do it quickly, or else you're going to end up arriving a little too late, and this party will be over—for all of us.*

**THURSDAY, SEPTEMBER 15, 10:40 A.M. EDT
WASHINGTON, DC**

"I don't care about the difficulties, just get me a feed and find her," Scott commanded Gooey, who was frantically typing on his keyboard.

His words elicited no response from the analyst, nor did he expect one. He was just blowing off steam, and Gooey was the closest one to him. The Danish he'd had for breakfast felt like it was burning a hole in his throat, so he popped a couple of Tums from a roll he kept in his pocket.

He leaned over the media tech's shoulder and eavesdropped on his conversation while watching the dual computer monitors. Gooey was on the phone with Todd Shupe, head of security at the National Cathedral.

Seeing right away the hopelessness of the situation, Shupe had dismissed his entire security staff so they could try to make it off the grounds without getting killed. He, however, had remained behind in the main security office set in the northeast corner of the building.

Shupe had been speaking with the Metropolitan Police when Gooey had cut in. From listening to Gooey's side of the conversation, the MPDC had not been happy about his arrival and demanded he get off the line. But the analyst had quickly decided that it was a better option for the police to go, and had bid them *sayonara* from the call. Now he was walking Shupe through how to give him total access to the cameras and their stored memory.

"Now just type in the password *Shamu the mysterious whale*. . . . No, it's from that U2 song, you know, 'It's all right, it's all right, it's aaaall right.' . . . Yeah, I know. I've since been informed."

A small screen popped into a corner of the right monitor. It showed the inside of the National Cathedral. Scott leaned in. He could clearly see movement—people being organized into groups.

"Beautiful, buddy," Gooey said to Shupe. "Now just hang on while I see if I can . . ." Another small screen popped up. On it was a vertical list identifying *Camera 1*, *Camera 2*, all the way down to *Camera 12*. Gooey double-clicked *Camera 1*, and the same shot came up that was on the other screen, only this one was time-coded three hours earlier.

"Got it! You're the—" Gooey stopped short. "Todd, what's going on? Todd?"

Scott looked at Gooey and saw panic on his usually slack face.

"What?" Scott mouthed.

Gooey slammed a button on his phone, triggering the speaker.

"*Who are you talking to?*" a voice yelled on the phone.

"*I told you, I was talking to my wife!*" another voice protested.

"*Liar! I'll give you one last chance to tell me the truth!*"

There was a pause, then the sound of a scuffle. Then the second voice said, *"I hope you all burn—"*

His words were halted by a *whump! whump!* There was some rustling around, and then the first voice, much clearer now, said, "Who is this? Tell me who this is!"

All the analysts had stopped what they were doing and were staring at Scott. Rage filled Scott's heart. *All the good ones—all the good men and women die first!* Every fiber of his being cried out for him to somehow climb through the phone and beat this man to a bloody pulp before finishing him off with a bullet to the brain. *You gotta let it go. Keep it under control. Breathe.*

He lifted Gooey's earpiece from the analyst's oily head and held the microphone to his mouth.

"Who are you?" he said through clenched teeth.

"I don't answer questions; I ask them. Now tell me who you are!"

Interesting accent—he's got a little bit of the South in him.

"Okay, you want to know who I am? I'm Scott Ross, director of the counterterrorism division's Special Operations Group Bravo. You'll recognize me as the tall, goateed guy behind the rifle that puts the bullet between your eyes."

The line clicked dead.

Taking a deep breath, he gently placed the earpiece on the desk. Looking around the room, he saw everyone still watching him. "What? You got nothing to do? Get back to work! Evie, check and see if the ops team is ready to go, then keep working to enhance the audio from Khadi's phone. Joey and Virgil, I still want to know who these people are." Turning back to the monitors, he said, "Gooey, make these screens larger."

Gooey didn't move. Scott turned and saw tears in the analyst's puffy eyes.

"Listen, man, I know," Scott said softly. "I know what you're feeling. It sucks, but it's reality. Shupe's a hero, and we'll make sure everyone knows it. Now it's time for you to be a hero again and help save the rest of those hostages. Got it?"

Gooey grabbed a small ceramic Yoda figurine from off of his desk and hurled it across the room, where it shattered against the wall. He crossed his arms, and the tears began to trickle down his cheeks.

I don't have time for this! Come on, think of something! An idea popped into his head.

Scott leaned down and whispered into his ear, "You realize you've just defeated a formidable Jedi Master with one swing of your arm. Now, let's find a way to harness that amazing power and use it for good and not evil."

Gooey turned, and through the tears Scott could see a twinkle back in the man's eyes. The analyst snatched two brown Taco Bell napkins off a stack he kept on a corner of his desk and wiped his eyes. Then he honked his nose with such volume that Scott was sure it threw off the migratory patterns of countless flocks of Canada geese.

Reaching for the mouse, Gooey brought both video feeds up to full screen.

"You're the man, Goo," Scott said, putting a hand on his moist shoulder. "Let me keep watching live. You cycle through the cameras and give me any that show the sanctuary interior. Then start running through stored video and find me Khadi."

"Will do," Gooey answered.

"Ops ready in five," Evie called out.

"Got it," Scott acknowledged.

The shot he was looking at showed the front quarter to third of the seating and the chancel area. At the front of the platform stood one man. He seemed to be directing things. There was a flurry of activity all around him—men with guns (he couldn't see how many) and hostages aplenty (again, number unknown).

Then something caught his eye. Amid all the activity, there

was one stationary element—an older man, standing back and to the right of the main guy. *Now we see the brains and the heart behind the attack,* Scott thought. *They've got their own junior bin Laden calling the shots.*

His screen suddenly divided in half, then into thirds, then fourths, then fifths, then sixths. Each window showed a different angle of the sanctuary.

"These are the best cameras," Gooey said, reaching into a drawer and pulling out a mouse. He snapped a Bluetooth receiver off the mouse's bottom, and slid it into a USB port on the back of Scott's monitor. "You can resize any window by pulling a corner. Double-clicking will make it full screen."

"Perfect," Scott said, taking the mouse. What he saw in the windows didn't give him much comfort. There were a minimum of three hundred hostages, and he counted at least sixteen terrorists.

He glanced at Gooey's monitor and saw the same six windows, but Gooey had his moving at least five times normal speed. Scott marveled at the analyst's ability to cycle through so much video moving so quickly, while still absorbing all the content.

"Remember, we talked to Khadi during the service, so she's probably somewhere toward the back," he said to Gooey, who again didn't feel a need to acknowledge Scott's words.

"Got her," Gooey said a moment later. A cursor sped across Scott's monitor and double-clicked the feed from Camera 4.

Khadi was sitting on the aisle looking even more beautiful than usual in her fancy black getup. Senator Andrews was nowhere around her. *Of course, Andrews would be up front where he could be seen. Khadi must have found a seat when the action started.*

Scott could see she was scanning the cathedral, analyzing everything that was going on. *Good girl. Take it all in.*

The picture split in half again, and a time code appeared on the top of both windows.

"Ops in three," Evie called.

"This is from when the action started," Gooey said, "Camera 1 and Camera 4."

Scott watched as the scenario unfolded in triple time. He saw the gunmen running in, Khadi being hurried to a seat, the shooting of J.D. Little—a man he had only met once but had heard good things about from Khadi. There was another shooting of a man near Khadi.

Then Khadi began fidgeting around. She was whispering with the old woman next to her. There was some activity that was blocked from the camera by the man sitting in front of her, and Khadi began a crying fit.

What are you doing? Scott wondered. Seeing the action at this high speed took away too much of the reality of the situation, and he was having difficulty processing.

"Slow it down to real time," Scott said. Gooey complied.

One of the gunmen came back, but the old lady seemed to talk him away. Then Khadi, head in hands, turned her palms directly to the camera.

"Full screen!" Scott yelled, even as Gooey was double-clicking it.

"Ops in one," Evie said.

"Tell them to hold! I'll be there soon as I can!"

"Done," Evie acknowledged.

With Camera 4 full screen, Gooey backed it up a few seconds, then zoomed in on Khadi. The picture took a moment to depixelate. As he ran it forward, they watched Khadi turn her hands toward the camera. On her right hand was written the number 2, and on her left the number 4.

"What a stud-chick," Scott said under his breath. Khadi closed her hands to her head for a few moments, then opened them back up.

"Gooey, I want these feeds all sent to my handheld."

"Got it."

"Evie, get out word to all agencies that there are twenty-four perps and that we have a person on the inside. Then call Tara and ask her to come in—she can bring James if she can't get a sitter. We need her oversight. Then find everything you can on the layout of the cathedral—from the outside grounds to the inside guts of the building—and send it to me. Guys, any luck on ID?"

"Not yet," Hernandez answered.

"Come on, I need that information, like, yesterday!" Backing away from Gooey's workstation, he said, "I'm out with the ops. Update me immediately with anything and everything. Got it?"

"Yes, sir," the analysts called out, all the fun and games out the window.

Scott turned and ran through the door toward the back parking lot where the ops team was impatiently waiting for him.

THURSDAY, SEPTEMBER 15, 10:50 A.M. EDT

LEESBURG, VIRGINIA

After Riley finished dressing, he walked downstairs to an empty house. Stuck to the blender that Skeeter knew would be his next stop was a note. *Nothing like being a creature of habit,* he thought.

He pulled it off and read in Skeeter's surprisingly flowing script, *Gilly called. Catch you up when I can.* A twinge of jealousy panged his heart when he read the words.

What's that about? You're the one who doesn't want to be in ops full-time. Remember the whole "It's not my calling" speech you gave to Scott a couple months back? He pulled a bag of mixed berries out of the freezer, then snatched up the remote control and turned on the kitchen TV.

Over a flowing animated background floated eight boxes, each showing the aftermath of one of the many attacks of the day. One of them expanded to full screen, and he watched for a minute while a Fox Pittsburgh reporter gave the latest on the attack at the auto auction. Fourteen dead and twenty-six wounded; perp among the dead.

The picture minimized, and one of the others zoomed up full screen, showing a diner in Tampa, Florida. More blood, more mayhem. Riley turned back to his blender. After dumping some berries in, he slid a can of protein powder over. As he scooped, he thought, *But even though I don't feel ops is my calling, somehow I always end up back in it. I'm like the reluctant warrior. You know, that'd be a good name for my biography*—Riley Covington: Reluctant Warrior.

He dipped a plastic measuring spoon into a bag of whey and emptied it into the blender. *Hey, nice one, buddy! It only took you five minutes to take this whole tragedy and make it about yourself.*

He walked to the refrigerator and retrieved a carton of soy milk. *Lord, forgive my self-focus. There are so many people hurting. Please help them.*

His prayer was halted by a news alert graphic flying across the television screen followed by video of the National Cathedral. Something triggered in his mind. *What's going on at the cathedral?* A sinking feeling filled his chest as he watched the story. He set the soy milk next to the blender. His hands were shaking.

"Gunmen have taken over the National Cathedral. In a coordinated attack, multiple armed men dressed in black military clothing stormed the National Cathedral during the memorial ceremony for longtime Senate chaplain Daniel Musman. Early reports are that more than three hundred were in attendance, among them Speaker of the House Cristy Johnston, Senate Majority Leader Dennis Nettesheim, Senate Minority Leader Bill Evert, and numerous other senators and congressmen."

Suddenly, all Riley's fear and anxiety coalesced into one word—*Khadi*.

He ran from the kitchen, searching for his cell phone. He

tore through the mudroom, then upstairs to his bedroom. Finally, he spotted it in the living room, where he had been watching the news reports with Skeeter.

Snatching it up, he speed dialed Scott. *Come on, answer the phone! Answer it!*

Scott's voice came on, not so politely inviting whoever was calling to leave a message and in no way promising a call back.

"Scott, what's happening with Khadi? Call me right away!"

He hung up, then dialed right back in the hopes that if Scott was only screening his first call, he might pick up the second time. It went to voice mail.

I gotta get to the RoU! I need information! He now began a frantic search for his keys, wasting precious minutes before finding them right where he always kept them—on the kitchen counter, hidden behind the carton of soy milk.

The home phone rang.

"Scott!" he said as soon as he pressed talk.

"Oh, I'm sorry, honey," his mom said. "Are you expecting a call? Should I hang up?"

Deflated, he said, "I am, but . . . no, don't hang up. Is everything okay?" He really needed to get going, but ever since a terrorist had taken his dad's life two years ago, he lived in fear that the same could yet happen to his mom. And with everything going on . . .

"I'm fine. I just wanted to find out how you were feeling with all these horrible things going on."

Riley breathed a sigh of relief. "It's all a bit unbelievable."

"It certainly is. You have to wonder at the mind-set of these people. And to think, so many of them are our own neighbors! What's this world coming to?"

"I know, Mom. It's crazy. How are you doing with it? I know these things always bring up memories of . . ." his voice trailed off.

"Of Dad? That's kind of why I was calling, sweetheart. It's

just . . . it's hard watching this stuff all by myself without him around. Jerry—Dad was always the one who could put these things into perspective. Then they took him, and . . ."

"I know, Mom," Riley said, his throat lumping up. "Dad had a way of looking at the big picture and making everything seem like it was going to be all right."

Silence hung over the line. Part of Riley wanted to get off the line and get moving. But the better part of him kept him glued to this spot with the phone in his hand. He began scratching at the grout between the tiles with his fingernail.

Riley's mom broke the silence. "So you answered 'Scott.' Is he supposed to be calling you with some information on what's happening?"

"No, I had left him a message when I realized that—" Riley stopped himself. His mother loved Khadi dearly. Did he really want to burden her with this? Would that be fair to her? Besides, he realized, she'd probably also figure out that he was leaving to do something about it, and she'd try to stop him, and it would turn into a big thing—a big thing that he had neither the time nor the emotional energy to deal with right now.

"You just realized what?"

"I just . . . I just realized that Scott is involved in this National Cathedral thing," Riley said, immediately feeling guilty for lying.

"I figured he would be. How can I be praying for him?"

Maybe God's using my lie for good. Nothing wrong with getting people praying. "Just safety. Pray for safety and wisdom so that he can save those people."

"I will." Now his mom's tone changed, "You know, Riley, you never were a very good liar, especially to your mother. So tell me what you were originally going to say."

Busted. "Mom . . ." he began, trying to come up with the right words to say. "Mom, it's Khadi."

"What about Khadi?" she asked quickly.

When Riley didn't answer right away, she added, "Come on, Riley. That precious girl is like a daughter to me. You tell me what's going on with her."

"Okay, okay. You know the thing at the National Cathedral? Well, it started out as a memorial service for the Senate chaplain. So quite a few senators and congressmen were there, including—"

"Including Senator Andrews. Which means that Khadi is inside there. Oh no."

Riley dropped onto one of the stools that lined his kitchen island. His forehead fell into his hand.

"I know, Mom. That's why I didn't want to say anything. The good news is that they don't seem to be reporting it like all the others—you know, go in and shoot up the place. It sounds more like a hostage situation. So there's a much better chance that she's still safe."

"Oh, dear Lord. Why Khadi? Father, she needs you more than ever right now. Touch her heart. Protect her body."

Riley tried to keep his emotions in check, something that is very difficult with one's mother on the other end of the line.

"So I suppose you're contacting Scott so that you can help try to rescue her?" Sorrow and resignation filled her voice.

Riley said nothing.

A minute passed before his mother spoke again, this time with steel in her voice. "Riley, I want you to listen to me closely. Your dad and I had only been married six months when he shipped off for Vietnam. I prayed and worried every single day he was gone. They were the most difficult days of my life until . . . well, until you went to Afghanistan. Then I prayed and worried every day that you were gone.

"But even though they were hard days and I did worry, I still had a peace that God would take care of you. Prayer will do that for you. Do you have your Bible near?"

Riley looked over to the kitchen table, where he had been

having his quiet time with the Lord over breakfast. There it sat—that worn black book with the packing tape holding the cover together. Written in its margins were the notes from a decade of sermons, Bible studies, and personal study times. It was like an old friend—a faithful companion that had carried him through good times and bad.

"Yeah, Mom, it's right here," he said, getting up.

"Turn to Philippians 4:6-7."

Riley stopped and sat down. This was one passage he knew.

"Do you have it?"

"I've got it," Riley said, closing his eyes and picturing the familiar words on the page.

"It says, 'Do not be anxious about anything, but in everything, by prayer and petition, with thanksgiving, present your requests to God. And the peace of God, which transcends all understanding, will guard your hearts and minds in Christ Jesus.'

"Riley, that's why I never tried to stop you or your dad. And I never made you feel guilty for going. Because you were in God's hands. And also because I could never make you feel guilty for being who you are.

"I've always thought of you and your dad like the knights of old—you know, wild yet chivalrous. Every time you enter a room, all the good people naturally feel safer and all the bad people begin to get nervous. It's who you are. It's what God created you to be.

"So with that being said, I want you to know that you have my full blessing to go out there and save that girl. I wouldn't have it any other way. And if something happens to you . . . well, just . . . just know that God always takes care of His children.

"I love you, Riley, and I'm so proud of you. Now, please, do your mother a most blessed favor and tell her you love her . . . then hang up the phone."

It took half a minute before Riley could get the words out. "I love you, Mom."

He held the phone to his ear a few moments longer before he pressed End. The phone dropped to the counter, followed by his fist. His fist rose and dropped three more times before he launched up from the stool.

He ran to his bedroom closet, where he kept a small gun vault. Most of his weapons were back in Colorado, but he still kept a fairly impressive miniarsenal here in Leesburg.

After punching six numbers into a keypad, he laid his thumb on a biometric pad. The lock clicked, and he opened the door. He pulled out a Kel-Tec P-32 in an ankle holster and strapped it on his right leg. Next he removed his Smith & Wesson M&P Compact .40 and clipped its holster onto his pants in the small of his back.

Looking up, he yanked on a shoulder holster, bringing it down with its hanger still attached. He cinched it on his torso, then dropped into it a Smith & Wesson Model 29 6½-inch .44 magnum. Images of Dirty Harry always popped into his mind when he carried it, making him feel a bit self-conscious. However, the thing could stop an elephant, and given the situation, the more power the better.

Slamming the vault door closed, he pulled on a black hoodie with *Thousand Foot Krutch* stenciled on it and zipped it halfway up. He quickly checked the mirror. The sweat jacket didn't do much to conceal the bulge under his arm, but it would have to do.

Ninety seconds later he was in his Durango, tearing around the corner of his cul-de-sac, not caring at all about the enormous chunk of drywall his truck door had just taken out of the side of his garage.

C H A P T E R

THIRTY-FOUR

THURSDAY, SEPTEMBER 15, 11:00 A.M. EDT
WASHINGTON, DC

So far it couldn't have gone much better, Majid
Alavi thought as he scanned the cathedral.
All the sentries were at their posts, and all
the stairways had been wired with explosives. A look into the Wilson Bay, down the
south side of the nave, confirmed that the
tech crew was busy wiring up the camera
and the Internet connection. Each of the
rooms adjoining the main sanctuary had
been searched and their occupants captured
or dispatched. All this without losing one
single man to injury or death.

*Allah, you are with us today. Thank you for
honoring our Ramadan sacrifice.*

Saifullah walked up next to him. "Do we
have a final count?"

Alavi nodded as he looked out at the
three groups that were now being individu-
ally searched for any weapons or communication devices. He pointed to the largest group
and said, "That is the release group. It has

249—women, children, elderly, and the excess men we don't have need for. I've also included some of the security people because, as we said, it's better to have them outside than in here conspiring."

Saifullah grunted. "I'm still not fully comfortable with that decision, Majid. Won't they take out valuable information?"

"They will," Alavi agreed. "However, probably not much more than what the Feds are already getting right now through their surveillance devices." He tilted his head toward the ceiling and the mounted cameras. "And as we have discussed, the benefits of keeping the surveillance devices active outweigh disabling them."

Saifullah nodded. "Once we demand the constant Internet feed on Saturday, people all over the world will be able to watch what is happening here twenty-four hours a day."

"And they will, too. The world is full of voyeurs. They'll keep us open on their computers continuously, just waiting for something to happen. And as they watch, fear will embed deeper and deeper into their psyches."

"And followers of the faith will draw more and more strength from us."

"Exactly," Alavi said. "So, yes, law enforcement will draw information from the released hostages and from the cameras, but we don't really expect this is going to go the full thirty days anyway. Of course, if you want to retain the hostages, we will do as you say, but my recommendation is to stay to plan."

"No, send them," Saifullah said, waving his hand. "You are right. How many are in the second group?"

Alavi pointed to another cluster of bodies, mostly men in suits. "That is our fodder group—the expendable ones. There are twenty-five. We're holding on to them primarily to keep the number of hostages up. And they will be the ones we will use if we have to make a point."

Saifullah turned toward the final group, located nearest to

the front. "And in that group are our illustrious senators and congressmen."

"Yes, sir. Twenty-nine senators and thirty-seven congressmen—sixty-six total, fifty-nine men and seven women."

"Very good," Saifullah said softly.

Both men studied this assembly of diverse characters. While all these legislators had power, it was easy to tell which ones had achieved it based on character and which ones had bought, schmoozed, or cheated their ways to the top. The ones with character were cooperative in action but bore an underlying defiance in their attitudes. The burning behind their eyes bespoke a warning to Alavi and his men. These were the ones who would have to go first.

But a larger majority of the congressional members were carrying on just as he had expected—crying, begging for their lives, making unfulfillable promises—*Much like they do on the campaign trail*, Alavi thought with a smile. *They are spineless, sniveling vermin. Vermin that will soon experience the extermination that all pests deserve.*

"How long do you think we have until the Americans try a rescue?" Saifullah asked.

Alavi thought for a moment. "Judging by the growing assemblage outside, I'd say not long. Fifteen minutes—twenty, tops."

Again, Saifullah grunted. "Then we'd best get our first message out and slow them down. Has the tech team prepared for the video recording?"

Alavi removed a small walkie-talkie from his belt. "Tech, this is Lead."

A moment later, a voice responded, "Go ahead, Lead."

"What's ETA for going hot?"

"Two minutes for video. Ten for uplink."

"Roger. Lead, out."

He turned to Saifullah. "Let's go do it. We aren't uplinking this first message anyway."

Saifullah nodded, and the two men began walking toward the Wilson Bay and the video camera. "Two, this is Lead," Alavi said into the walkie-talkie as they rounded the chairs on the south side of the nave. He could feel the eyes of many of the hostages on them as they walked.

"Go ahead, Lead," Ubaida Saliba responded.

"The imam is ready for his first vid. What's the ETA on the first vest?"

"Thirty seconds. We're ready for you."

"Excellent. Send him over immediately. I'm with the imam, so you take the conn," Alavi said, directing Saliba to take their place on the stage at the front of the sanctuary.

"Ten-four. Out."

The surreal nature of his situation momentarily disoriented Alavi as Saliba signed off. In his mind, he was transported to the backyard of his parents' house. It was as if the war games of his childhood were suddenly being played out in real life. As he thought of it, he realized that much of the déjà vu he was feeling originated in the terminology they were using.

When Alavi had returned from his training in Somalia, he was determined to do everything exactly as he had been trained. But as soon as he began drilling the young men in the warehouse this week, he realized that very few of them understood a single word of the technical military jargon he was using. And why should they? True military training was an experience that they never had a chance to share.

What they did share, however, was a childhood watching *Power Rangers*, *X-Men*, and *Transformers*. Later, most of them had graduated to *CSI* and *NYPD Blue*. Recognizing that, Alavi took a bold step. He dumbed down their communication from complex military parlance to a commonly understood blend of superhero- and cop-speak. Suddenly everyone knew exactly what everyone else was saying and what was expected of them.

Now here he was, leading a band of real militants, shooting real bullets, fighting in the name of Allah, and using the language he grew up hearing come out of the mouths of Red Ranger and Optimus Prime. *Better quit thinking about it, or you're going to freak yourself out,* Alavi thought, shaking his head.

They walked through a small arch and into the Wilson Bay—a cutaway of sorts along the southern wall of the nave. In it was the final resting place of President Woodrow Wilson— *The only president buried in Washington, DC, if I remember my history correctly. Those windows are beautiful,* Alavi thought as he looked around.

Three large stained glass windows filled the area with a rainbow of light. One figure caught his eye. At the bottom of the left mosaic, a brown-skinned, red-hooded, young-looking figure stood staring at him with large, clear eyes. His arms were outstretched and his hands were turned such that it looked like he was about to pull himself out from the window and into the room. The overall visual was accomplished so effectively that it was a bit disconcerting, and he turned away.

The camera was set below the windows facing Wilson's stone casket. Through them Alavi could see the north side of the nave. Unfortunately, the square footage of the area was a little less than they had anticipated and would be cramped for some of what they had planned. But they could probably make do.

"Where are you taking me? Please don't hurt me! I've got a family!"

Ah, our friend is arriving, Alavi thought, turning toward the eastern arch. A man in a black suit and a teal-and-gray tie stumbled through the entrance, followed by one of Saliba's team.

"What is your name?" Saifullah asked him.

"Please don't hurt me! I've got a—"

Saliba's man drove the butt of his rifle into the man's hip, dropping him to the ground. "Answer the man's question," he demanded.

"Dermott Lawrence," the man croaked out, trying to ride through the pain.

"Ahhh, Congressman Lawrence," Saifullah said. "If I am not mistaken, you are from New Hampshire, are you not?"

Lawrence nodded emphatically.

"That's fine, Mr. Lawrence. Now, I am about to record a video. Your job is to be my model—seen but not heard. Just another pretty face for the camera. Do you understand?"

Again Lawrence nodded.

"Very good," Saifullah said. Turning away from the camera, he looked across the nave. The seats were filled with people of the first group—the release group. Seemingly satisfied, he turned back to the camera. "Lift him up, and let us begin."

Alavi grabbed the congressman by the jacket collar and lifted him to his feet. The cameraman pressed a button, counted down with his fingers—*three, two, one*—and then pointed at Saifullah.

"This is for the person or persons leading the rescue attempt only. If I find that this video has been released to the public, I will kill five hostages. I trust you will take me at my word. Otherwise I will have to prove my sincerity.

"We have 340 hostages. Of those 340, sixty-six are members of your legislative branch of government. If you attempt a rescue, please know that we will open fire on the hostages, not on our attackers. Our goal will be to achieve the maximum amount of damage. The dead will easily reach triple digits. And if you think that maybe you can beat us to the trigger, then hopefully this will still your hand. . . ."

He nodded off-camera, and Lawrence stepped into the picture. "Unbutton your jacket please, Congressman," Saifullah said.

Lawrence did so, revealing a vest loaded with explosives.

"We have fitted most of your senators and congressmen with these."

Alavi knew that was a lie. Logistically, they could only get ten vests assembled and into the cathedral. But that was still enough to cause all the damage they needed.

"All I need do is press a button, and they will all vaporize along with everyone within twenty yards of each of them. So please don't make me do it—it's a nasty way for anyone to die."

Saifullah placed a hand on Lawrence's shoulder and encouraged him back off the screen.

"At 1300 hours eastern time, a live feed will be going up through the Internet. Attached to this disc, you have found written the link to this feed. I want all the network and cable news channels to have access to this link so that the people of America may watch our message live. If anything is done to interrupt that link, there will be consequences. I trust I make myself clear on that point.

"Also on that piece of paper is a number for a cell phone. I will expect a call from you five minutes after the live feed has concluded, but not before. Again, I trust I make myself clear."

As Alavi watched, the old imam's eyes hardened.

"Please understand that we are all prepared to die, and we fully expect to meet Allah before this is all over. It is up to you to decide how many will come with us. I pray for the sake of the hostages that you make the right choices."

"How close are we?" demanded Secretary of Homeland Security Stanley Porter. He was standing at a Formica table bolted to the floor of an FBI command center truck parked on an asphalt loop just seventy yards from the front entrance to the National Cathedral. Crowded around the table two and three deep were the head of the Secret Service, Craig LeBlanc; FBI Director Edward Castillo; MPDC Chief Jim Sprecker; and several seconds, vices, and unders. But even with all these high-powered individuals present, all rarely seen at an active crime scene, the man to whom he was directing the question was Scott Ross.

"We're green in ten," Scott answered.

"Can you ensure the safety of the hostages?" Castillo asked.

"Of course he can't, you idiot," answered the always-abrasive LeBlanc. "You got twenty-four psychos with automatic weapons and a few hundred hostages. Use your brain!"

"Listen, if you're going to get personal with this—" Castillo charged back.

"Gentlemen," Porter interrupted, "if you two are going to bicker through this meeting, I'm going to throw both of you out. This is my show; you're here at my discretion. Got it?"

Without waiting for an answer, he turned back to Scott. "Can you estimate casualties?"

"I really can't, sir. Our only daylight option is to go in hard and fast. But they'll see us coming. It could very well be a bloodbath."

"Can we chopper down and go through the stained glass windows?" Porter said, using his fingers on a cathedral schematic to demonstrate his proposal.

"That's part of the plan. However, our problem is that you've got a huge mass of people down here," Scott said slapping his long palm down on the middle of the sanctuary. "You'll be showering everyone with large shards of glass. And with all the firing going on, ops'll have an extremely difficult time sorting out the *hajjis* from the hostages."

"I'd prefer we used the term *perpetrators*," Castillo interjected.

"Oh, grow up," LeBlanc countered.

"I need to say that I don't feel comfortable with this," Sprecker said. "They've got to have a purpose to this other than just killing everyone outright. Otherwise, they would have done it when they first went in."

"My thoughts exactly," Scott agreed. "The very fact that they are separating them into groups indicates a larger scenario."

"And one of those groups is full of senators and congressmen," said LeBlanc. "Now I'm willing to bet that they aren't separating them out so they can say, 'Sorry, didn't expect they'd be here,' and release them. Like I said before, I've got specific orders from the president himself to make sure no harm comes to any member of that congressional delegation."

"At least not to anyone of his party," said a voice from the third row of onlookers.

"Who said that?" Porter said, slamming his fist down on the table.

After a moment, a hand went up. It was an FBI assistant-vice-undersomething. "Sorry, sir, just some misplaced levity."

"You want to know what's misplaced? You," Porter hissed. "Get out of here before I bust you down to investigating dollar-store shoplifting. In fact, everyone get out, except for the techs, you, you, and you," he said, pointing to Castillo, Sprecker, and LeBlanc. Scott didn't move from the table either.

"Listen, you can't—" A look from Porter stopped Castillo's protest dead.

"That should take care of the levity," Porter said. "Right now everything's theoretical anyway until the president and his joint staff give us a thumbs-up."

"Just what are we authorized to do, if I may ask?" Sprecker said.

"Prepare and monitor. Right now the president is looking for information he can act on. I'm betting right now one or more of his joint chiefs are wanting us to fly over and bomb the crap out of Iran. The others probably have their own countries they want taken out. Fact is, the president can't authorize anything until he knows who these bozos are and what they want."

"If they take this place out," LeBlanc said angrily, "I say we level Mecca. Then we can take out Medina just for good measure."

"Brilliant," Porter said sarcastically. "Apparently you're not too keen on holding on to your job. Hopefully we can all pretend we didn't just hear—"

"Someone's coming out," called a voice from the front part of the truck. While they all hurried to gather around a small surveillance screen, Scott took the opportunity to bolt out of the truck and toward to the front line of police vehicles.

As he ran, he pressed a button on his earpiece. "ID?"

Evie answered, "It looks like it's the little girl who read the paper during the service—probably a granddaughter or great-granddaughter."

Just then, a girl of no more than eight wearing a little black dress that flared out with ruffles at the bottom appeared on the top step. She looked terrified and kept turning around to the front door. Hesitantly, she took one step down and then another.

"Skeet, go get her," Scott said into his earpiece. Skeeter was lying behind a low wall twenty yards from the entrance. Gilly Posada was lying next to him, and across the main path to the cathedral behind a matching low wall were Matt Logan and Carlos Guitiérrez. The rest of the CTD ops team—Kim Li, Steve Kasay, and Ted Hummel—were another ten yards back among the trees.

As soon as the words were said, Skeeter leaped up and ran across the open cement. The girl screamed when she spotted him and tried to turn back, but the big man swept her up in his arms and sprinted her to safety.

"Li, take Skeeter's place," Scott ordered as he ran to intercept Skeeter. He reached him just after he passed through the line of cars. Already, there was a crowd pushing in around Skeeter.

Scott shouldered his way through and heard Skeeter's deep bass saying, "Shhh, shhh, it's all right, sweetheart. Skeeter's got you now. Shhh."

The girl was no longer screaming. Instead she had her arms wrapped tightly around Skeeter's thick neck and was sobbing into his shoulder.

"She's got something taped to her back under her dress," Skeeter whispered to Scott. "It's hard and square."

"Everybody get back," Scott ordered. "She may be hot!"

The thought that this little girl might be carrying an explosive device sent most people running. Yet there were still quite a few who remained behind. One of them was a sweet-faced woman in an MCPD uniform.

"My name's Aynalem Kelemua," she said to Scott in a wonderfully sing-song African accent. "If you're going to be exploring this girl for explosives, you're probably going to want a woman nearby."

Scott smiled at her. "Beautiful. Thanks."

Looking at the rest of the people who had stayed close, he said, "I appreciate your heart, but you gotta move it back. Everybody back twenty yards, now!" Reluctantly, they obeyed.

"Her name's Grace," Skeeter said.

Scott nodded. "Hi, Grace. I'm Scott, you already know Skeeter, and this is Officer Kelemua," he said, reading her name off her tag. He knew she had told him her full name, but it had just gone in one ear and out the other.

"Do you know what they put on your back, Sweetie?"

Grace shook her head, still keeping her face buried in Skeeter's neck.

"Can you look at me, Grace?"

Again she shook her head. Scott looked to Skeeter.

"It's okay, honey. Scott's a really good friend of mine. He's really nice, and kind of funny looking, too."

This caused Grace to take a tentative sideways glance. Scott smiled and gave a little wave. Slowly, she turned and faced him.

"That's great, Grace. You are so brave. Now, I have something very important to ask you. Okay?"

Grace nodded.

"Did the bad guys say anything to you when they put this whatever-it-is on your back?"

Grace nodded again.

"Can you tell me what they said?"

"They said to give this to the person in charge. Are you the person in charge?"

"I am, sweetie. You did a very good job finding me."

She nodded again, then sniffed deeply. Scott used his end of his sleeve to wipe her eyes and her nose.

"They're really, really bad people, Mr. Scott. They hurt Uncle Denny and Aunt Lisa really bad." Then, dropping her voice to a whisper, she said, "I think maybe they're died."

"Oh, Grace, I'm so sorry," he said, as he gently placed his hand on her back. He sized up the attachment, then said to Kelemua, "I think we're good. By the feel of it, I'm betting it's a disc."

"Grace, sweetheart, is it okay if I get this little thingy off your back?" Kelemua asked.

The tears started fresh now. "Is it going to hurt?"

"I'll be very careful. I promise." Kelemua slowly reached under the girl's dress and ran her hand up her back. "How old are you, Grace?"

"Seven," Grace said through snuffs.

"I thought so. I have a nephew who's seven. His name's Jesse."

Scott watched the officer's hand working under the girl's dress. "It's definitely a plastic CD or DVD case," she said to Scott. Then turning back to Grace, she asked, "Do you like school?"

Grace nodded, then stiffened. It looked like Kelemua was picking at a corner of the tape.

"What's your teacher's name?"

"Mrs. Carr—OWWWW!" Kelemua had pulled hard at the tape. She pulled one more time and her hand came out from under the girl's dress. It was holding a DVD case with a disc inside. Covering the case were three long strips of silver duct tape.

"I'm so sorry, Grace," Officer Kelemua said. "It's all over now."

Scott took the disc and said, "We gotta go, Skeet. Grace, I am so proud of you. You were so brave."

But Grace wasn't listening. She was holding on tightly to Skeeter's neck.

"I have to go now, Gracie," Skeeter said softly. "Miss Aynalem will take care of you. She's a wonderful friend of mine too."

"I don't want you to go, Skeeter."

"I know, sweetie. But I have to. I've got to go get your mommy and daddy."

Grace leaned back and, through her tears, looked Skeeter straight in the eye. "Are you really going to get Mommy and Daddy?"

"I am."

"Do you promise?"

Skeeter kissed her forehead and said, "I promise."

Grace let go of Skeeter's neck and reached for Officer Kelemua. As soon as she did, Scott and Skeeter ran off toward the command truck.

When they arrived, the same gang of muckety-mucks was there waiting for them. Scott passed the disc to a tech, who slid it into a player.

They watched the message from Saifullah four times through. By the time the last cycle was complete, Scott knew three things. First, there was no way they were going through with the rescue attempt. Second, these guys were crazier and smarter than he had feared. And third, by the looks of what these psychos were laying out, he and the rest of the good guys were in for a long haul.

Riley threw open his truck door even before
he finished screeching to a stop. As he rounded the front of the vehicle, he noticed a sign
that said Loading Zone. *Good; maybe they'll
tow it while I'm getting Khadi. That way at least
I'll know it's safe.*

He took the steps up to the building three
at a time, brimming with confidence. And
why not? His plan was foolproof. He'd have
the front security call Scott. Even though his
friend might be reluctant to talk to him, he
couldn't very well turn away his best buddy
from the door. Once Scott agreed to let him
come back to the Bravo office, Riley would
simply refuse to leave. He would suit up with
the rest of the ops, and Scott would have to
either agree or have him arrested.

Sure, his friend would be pretty ticked at
him for a while, but oh well. It wasn't like
Scott hadn't forced Riley's hand a few times
in the past. Scottini, the Great Puppetmaster,

was the whole reason Riley was here in Washington in the first place, instead of back home playing for the Colorado Mustangs. This was only a small sampling of the payback his contriving little friend richly deserved.

Riley burst through the front doors and saw a long line at the metal detectors. It was worse than being at the airport. Each person was being thoroughly screened—IDs, belts, shoes, bags, everything.

I've got no time for this, he thought as he cut to the front of the line. Protests sounded from behind him.

"Sir, you're going to have to wait your turn," a very large, cammied Marine said, standing to meet Riley.

"I'm Riley Covington. I need—"

"I know who you are, sir. But Homeland Security has raised the threat level to high, so you're still going to have to wait your turn." The Marine took a step closer and lowered his voice. "And I'll tell you right now, if that cannon is still in your shoulder holster when you get back up here, you and I are going to have a real problem."

Normally, a man this size would have intimidated even the most confident of men, but Riley wasn't having any of it. Khadi's life was on the line. He had to get in to see Scott.

"We've already got a problem, Saur," Riley said, getting the man's name from his uniform. "And if you interrupt me again, you're just going to dig your hole deeper."

Apparently, this Marine wasn't used to receiving back talk, and a look of surprise showed in his eyes. But he quickly recovered. "Listen, if you want to make a scene, then make a scene. One football star getting carted off to prison isn't going to make much news on a day like this."

"I don't want to make a scene. All I want is for you to call Scott Ross and tell him I'm here."

Stepping back to try to defuse the situation, Saur said, "I'll be happy to call Mr. Ross for you . . . after you wait in the line."

Riley sighed. *Why does everything have to be so difficult? There is no way I can afford to wait the twenty minutes it will take to make it through that line. Time to change tactics.*

"Listen, Saur, I'm only asking because it's a matter of life and death. You see—"

"First of all, I never gave you permission to use my name. Second, if I polled everyone in this line, 75 percent of them would tell me they're here on a matter of life and death too. Now get . . . back . . . in line." With that final word, Saur turned to the people passing through the metal detectors.

Augh! What is with this guy? I'm so close! How do I break through?

Then a thought struck him. *Dare I resort to the nuclear option? Honestly, I don't see any other choice.* He pulled out his cell phone, scrolled down to *P* on his contacts, selected a number, and hit Send.

After a few rings, a voice answered. "Riley—while normally this would be a pleasant surprise, I'm sorry to say this isn't a good time right now, as you can probably imagine."

"I'm so sorry, Mr. President. I would never have called you if this were not a life-and-death emergency."

Two years ago, after all the events in New York, President Donald Lloyd had given Riley the number to his personal direct line. His reason for giving out such a valuable piece of information was that he was courting Riley for a job. Any calls he made using this top-secret number should have been related specifically to that job offer. But Lloyd had also said in passing, *". . . and if there's ever anything I can do for you, just let me know."* This was the rationale Riley now used for pulling out this ultimate ace in the hole.

"An emergency? Are you sure this can't wait, Riley? Like I said, this is not a good time."

"Again, I'm so sorry, sir. I have essential information regarding the National Cathedral attack that I have to get to Scott

Ross—" *only a little lie*—"but my way is being barred by a well-meaning but very stubborn Marine. It will only take thirty seconds of your time to clear my way."

"I'll do it in ten," the president said.

I can't believe he's actually going to do it! "Thank you, sir! I'll pass you over."

Riley tapped Saur on the shoulder. The Marine spun around.

"Call for you," Riley said. Saur glared at him, not taking the phone.

"Really, I think you're going to want to take this."

Finally, curiosity got the best of Saur. He snatched the phone from Riley's hand and said, "Who is this?"

He listened for a second, then very colorfully expressed his disbelief.

He listened a moment more, then suddenly straightened up. "Yes, sir. . . . I'm sorry, sir. . . . I will, sir. . . . Thank you, sir."

Saur hung up the phone, fixing Riley with an icy stare. "You can go through, but your gun stays here."

"Sorry, Marine. I think both my gun and I will both go through . . . or do I have to make another call? I think I have the secretary of defense on here somewhere," Riley said, beginning to scroll through his contacts.

"You sucked on Sunday," Saur said as he stepped aside to let Riley pass through.

Another round of boos and complaints sounded from the line, but Riley ignored them. Instead, he began sprinting down the long corridors. He ran until he came to the door he was looking for and slid to a stop.

He pounded on it. No answer. He pounded again. Still no answer. He pounded a third time. An electric lock disengaged, and the door opened. Evie stood in the gap.

"He's not here," she said matter-of-factly, then added, "The guard called and told us you were coming to see Scott."

"I need to talk to him," he said, hearing the desperation in his own voice.

His tone softened her a little. "I'm sorry, Riley, but he's not here, and he's not going to take your call."

"Please, Evie! How do you know he won't take my call? Did you ask him?"

Tears began forming in Evie's eyes. "Actually, I did—as soon as the guard called. He said to tell you to go home and that he'd call you first chance he could."

"No," Riley yelled, driving his fist into the door. Williamson, Hernandez, and Gooey all suddenly appeared behind Evie.

"Is there a problem?" Hernandez asked.

"No," Riley and Evie said simultaneously.

"No," Riley said again. Sorrow and embarrassment sucked the aggression from him, and he leaned against the doorjamb. "I'm sorry, Evie—guys. It's just I know Khadi's in the cathedral. I've got to find a way to get her out."

"I'm sorry too, Riley," Hernandez said, "but there's nothing we can do for you. Seriously. We love Khadi too, and you're just going to have to trust us to keep her safe."

Riley didn't say anything. His eyes dropped to the ground. He felt defeated.

"It's probably best you leave now," Hernandez continued, putting his hand on Evie's shoulder. "Riley, you know how we all feel about you. We're family. You have my word we'll let you know as soon as we hear anything about Khadi. Now, please let us get back to our work of saving her and all the others."

"You're right. You're right. I'm sorry."

Riley began to back away, and the door began to close.

Suddenly, it swung back open, and Evie wrapped him up in a huge hug. As she held him, she whispered, "Go there—to the cathedral. You can talk your way through the perimeter. Find Scott. He won't turn you away once you're there. I know he won't! But if he does, then call me and I'll call Kim. You know he could never say no to you. He'll get you in. Go there, Riley. Khadi needs you."

She gave him a firm kiss on the cheek and turned back to the door, where Hernandez stood holding it open. "I'm so sorry," she said one more time . . . and the door closed.

A minute later he was launching himself down the steps of the building. A member of DC parking enforcement was in the process of writing him a ticket, but he blew past her.

"Send it to me," he called over his shoulder, hopping into the Durango. Moments later he was in the flow of traffic, headed for the National Cathedral and the woman he needed to save.

THURSDAY, SEPTEMBER 15, 11:55 A.M. EDT

Even though they had been told to stare at the ground, Khadi still took every chance she could to steal glances at her captors. What surprised her was how young and nervous— even frightened—many of them were.

Sure, there were the tough ones—the General, Number Two (the guy who took the lead when the General left the room), the Attitude (the one that she and Gladys had had words with), Gropey (the scowling, dumb one who was a little too thorough with his frisking)—but they seemed to be in the minority. Most were in their early twenties and looked as if this was the first time they had held a weapon outside of some upstate Michigan jihadi militia day camp.

"Please don't do this! Please!" It was a woman's voice this time.

Khadi looked toward the Politicos, as she had styled the group of legislators. Speaker of the House Cristy Johnston was having a vest put on her. She was the sixth one. Khadi hurt for her. What terror she must be feeling.

How many more of those vests do they have? Just logistically, they couldn't have brought in one for each of the Politicos. That would have been too heavy. Besides, all their supplies—cameras, computers, food, explosive vests—had been brought in those sixteen duffel bags.

"Look down," the Attitude commanded as he walked by.

Khadi dropped her head.

"Careful," Gladys whispered.

Khadi knew she was about to be released—at least she was pretty sure. It was the only explanation for her group. *There are just too many of us. The food, the bathrooms—which, judging by the growing odor hovering above our group, is already becoming a problem—just the practical reality of having this many hostages is too much for this small a crew.*

Part of her felt guilty over her potential release. Shouldn't she be the She-Ra warrior giving it all to save the day? But deep down, she knew there was only so much one girl could do in the face of such heavy odds.

So instead, she settled her conscience with the unspoken promise to all who were sitting in the other two groups that she would gather all the information she could while here, and then once she was released, she would be back. She wasn't abandoning them; she was just going to get reinforcements.

Four more vests went on. Senator Andrews was not one of the ones who received one. *I wonder if that's good news or bad news for him,* she thought. She spotted him in the Politicos group. His face seemed puffy, and he looked like he had aged ten years.

Somewhere a few rows back, Charlotte Andrews sat on one of these comfortable padded seats. Earlier, as they were being sorted into the three groups, the senator's wife had somehow found a way to get next to her.

"Do something," she had demanded of Khadi.

"What exactly do you recommend?"

"I don't know! Something! You're the expert!"

Khadi knew this lady was scared, so she was trying to cut her some slack. But the arrogant blend of entitlement and condescension was really trying her patience.

"Okay, if I'm the expert, then this expert says that if I do anything, it will most likely get all of us killed."

Not used to hearing no from anyone but her husband, Charlotte had countered, "That's not good enough! I think you're just saying that because you're scared!"

"You bet I'm scared," Khadi agreed.

"You listen here! If either me or my husband gets killed here, I will promise you that you will never work in this town again!"

"First of all, I want you to think about the grammatical and logical inconsistencies in your statement. Second, the way this day has turned out, my future employment is way down my list of pressing concerns."

Khadi had turned her back to Charlotte, and when she turned around again, the senator's wife was gone. *Please, God, let me never have to see her face again!*

"May I have your attention?"

Khadi looked up and saw that the General had walked up and was addressing her group.

"I have good news for you. You will be released shortly. In the meantime, I must ask for your full cooperation. There are quite a few of you, and I want you all to leave here safely. So please, when the time comes, I will ask you to stand up row by row and walk out in single file. If you stand before your row is indicated, if you break line, or if you run in any way . . . well, let me just strongly encourage you not to do those things. Do we have an understanding?"

There were excited murmurs of affirmation from her group.

One woman asked, "What about our husbands? Will they be coming too?"

"Alas, they will not—at least not yet. There are still issues to be resolved with your government, and I'm afraid we must keep them a little longer. However, it is my fervent hope that an amicable solution can be reached, and you will be rejoined by your loved ones sooner rather than later. Now, are there any other questions?"

Hearing none, he said, "Very well. For now, please be patient and obey the rules. This will all be over for you soon." The General turned and walked away.

Is this guy a sociopath? What else could explain the disparity between the charming man who just addressed us and the one we saw earlier calmly shooting two people without a second thought? A chill ran up her spine.

Gladys gave Khadi's hand a squeeze. "It looks like this old broad may survive yet another adventure."

Khadi started to answer but stopped. Another voice had distracted her. It was a familiar one, and it came from the Grab-Bag group—the third group, so named because there didn't seem to be any connection between the members or any reason for them to be singled out.

"Sir? Oh, sir?"

She spotted him. *Tyson Bryson, chief aide to Mr. Opportunity, pig in every sense of the word. What's he doing? Best thing for you to do is keep your head down and try not to be seen, you idiot!*

One of the General's henchmen went toward Bryson. By the look on his face, his main goal seemed to be shutting him up as violently as possible. Bryson cowered under the man's upraised hand. He was doing his usual quick talking, but he was too far away for Khadi to hear what he was saying.

The man lowered his hand. He took a walkie-talkie off his belt and said something into it. After receiving a response, he took Bryson by the collar and lifted him from his chair. He half walked, half dragged the senatorial aide toward the General.

Oh, Tyson, you fool! What have you gotten yourself into? While the very thought of him disgusted her, she still felt just enough of a connection—maybe no more than a coworker bond—that she didn't want anything *really* bad to happen to him.

Bryson was thrown to the floor in front of the General. Words were exchanged. The General took a step back, seeming to consider something, then nodded his assent. Bryson spoke again, and a surprised look came across the General's face. Then it hardened.

"Where?" Khadi could hear all the way across the long nave.

Bryson lifted his hand, extended his finger, and pointed it right at Khadi.

Her heart sank. *Oh, Tyson, you didn't . . .*

It wasn't so much fear that she felt as the General and several of the gunmen made their way toward her. It was more of a resignation and a profound disappointment that someone, anyone, would actually stoop so low.

"Oh, my dearest Khadi," Gladys said, squeezing her hand so tightly that her joints hurt. "I'll pray for you, child. God will watch over you."

"Thank you, Gladys," she said, squeezing back.

"You! What is your name?" the General said when he was still ten paces away.

"What's yours?" Khadi responded.

The General nodded to another man, who stepped forward and slapped her hard across the face. She fell sideways onto Gladys and immediately tasted blood in her mouth.

"What is your name?" the General asked again.

"My name is Khadijah Faroughi. But you already know that."

"Where is your gun?"

"What gun?"

Again, a hand slammed down onto her face. Tears sprang

to her eyes, but only as a natural reaction to the pain. There was no sadness in Khadi's heart, only a raging fire of defiance.

"Where is your gun?"

"What, is there an echo in here? I said I don't have a gun!"

The hand came down again, but this time she was ready for it. She deflected it forward and countered with a straight-fingered stab into her assailant's ribs. He doubled over from the pain.

Her victory was short-lived as another gunman drove the butt of his rifle into her shoulder, spinning her to the ground. The pain was intense and her vision blurred for a moment. She felt two hands reaching to help her and saw Gladys's beautifully lined face leaning toward her.

The General stepped forward, grabbed Gladys by the hair, pulled her to her feet, and placed a gun to her forehead.

"Where . . . is . . . your . . . gun?"

Quickly, Khadi said, "In the back of the sanctuary—information rack full of brochures. There's a phone in there, too."

The General nodded to one of his men, who ran to the rear of the cathedral. As he waited, he never let go of Gladys's hair, and he never lowered the pistol. A minute and a half later, the runner returned. In one hand he had Khadi's phone and in the other her .357 snubbie.

The General released Gladys, who fell back to her seat. Taking the gun, he admired it. "Is this all? Just this one?" he asked Khadi.

"Just that one," she replied.

"I believe you," he said, smiling. He took a deep breath in, then exhaled. "Well, well, well, Khadi Faroughi, what an absolutely unexpected pleasure."

The last thing Khadi saw before she blacked out was the magnificent reflection of the stained glass windows on the meticulously polished nickel gun as it hurtled toward her head. *I always take good care of my weapons—always.*

THURSDAY, SEPTEMBER 15, 12:05 P.M. EDT

The traffic on Massachusetts Avenue came to an abrupt stop just north of Macomb Street. Riley's GPS was telling him that he still had a good half mile until he reached his destination. He had no problem determining in which direction lay the Cathedral Church of Saint Peter and Saint Paul—the official name of the National Cathedral, as his GPS system so helpfully informed him; he just had to follow the helicopters.

Riley looked ahead and saw absolutely no vehicular movement heading southeast. *Well, no guts, no glory!* Laying on his horn, he swung his Durango into the oncoming lane.

Not good! Not good! NOT GOOD! A car swerved left; he swerved right. He thought he may have heard the clash of metal on metal, but it was hard to tell over the crunch of his truck launching over the curb. He found himself speeding through a small, grassy park. *Watch for small people! Turn into the skid!*

He angled himself for Macomb Street,

dodged left, just missing a tree; found himself heading straight for a large, multipointed, metal fountain thingy; swerved right; mowed down a small sign of some sort, which made frightening sounds as it scraped across his undercarriage; bounced back over the curb; and slammed on his brakes, sliding the truck to a stop just inches from a small silver Acura.

This Acura, Riley quickly assessed, was the last car in a solid line of stationary vehicles that blocked the street for as far as his eye could see. *Last car until I arrived! Time to ditch the vehicle!*

To his left he saw a long building. The lettering to the side of the front doors read, *Washington Hebrew Congregation.* And right in front of the entrance lay a cement congregating area just the right size for a small group of Shabbat attendees or a large black Dodge Durango.

He quickly backed up, causing the car that had pulled up behind him to lay on his horn. He cut the wheel hard left, jumped the curb, and parked in front of the doors. On a whim, he left the key in the ignition, just in case they had to move it for services.

Even with all the activity around him, he covered the ground to the cathedral on foot in less than five minutes. As expected, it was a media circus. Every network was represented, and each of them had a truck. Satellite dishes extended from the roofs of the trailers into the sky, making the place seem like an urban space station.

After walking through the media maze, he came to the law enforcement layer. And it was impressive. There were police cars, Fed-mobiles, and SWAT trucks as far as he could see—probably enough to surround the whole of the cathedral grounds.

There was also the infamous yellow Police Line—Do Not Cross tape.

Riley ducked under.

"Hey," someone called out. "Hey, get back under that tape!"

Riley kept moving forward, hoping against hope that maybe the voice was addressing someone else.

A hand clapped on his shoulder. "Where do you think you're going?"

Riley turned to see a metro police officer. Two more were on their way to provide backup.

"Hey, aren't you Riley Covington?"

Riley tried to smile. "I am, officer. I need to get to Scott Ross, head of CTD's Operations Group Bravo."

"Is he expecting you?"

"Well . . . not exactly."

The two other officers arrived. "What's going on here?" asked the older of the two. "What are you doing beyond . . . ? Hey, aren't you Riley Covington?"

"That's who he is, Sarge. Says he's here to see some Steve Ross guy."

"Is he expecting you?" Sarge asked.

What? Do these guys work off a script? "As I was just telling . . ." Riley looked to the first officer.

"Marlin. Marlin Uhrich. That's Sergeant Ron Burchfield. And that's Eldon Auxier."

"Hey, guys," Riley said, nodding to each. "As I was just telling Officer Uhrich—"

"Marlin."

"Okay . . . Marlin. I just need to see Scott Ross. I've got very important information about what's going on in there."

"Can't you call him?"

"I can't get through. I need to get in to see him."

"That's the problem, Riley," Burchfield said. "We've got orders not to let anyone through this line who isn't carrying a badge. That includes you."

"Come on, guys. You've got to help me. I've got to get in there." *Why does everything have to be so unbelievably difficult?*

"Hey, Sarge," Auxier said, "how about if I go find this Ross character and see if he'll come escort him in?"

"Hmmm, yeah, good call. Any idea where Ross would be?"

"Just ask for the guy heading the whole show," Riley said. "If it's not him, he'll be standing next to him."

"On my way," Auxier said.

The sergeant seemed to be sizing Riley up. "Listen, I'd love to hang out here and get to know you—I'm sure you've got some pretty killer stories to tell. But I'm betting you're not in the mood to talk, and we've got a whole line here we've got to watch. Will you give me your word that you won't bolt from here?"

"I give you my word that I'll stand right here—unless Officer Auxier comes back here with bad news. Then, honestly, you're going to have to chase me down."

The sergeant thought for a moment, then a smile spread across his face. "An honest man. I like that. Well, let's just hope for both our sakes that Auxier comes back with good news."

"Thanks, Sergeant."

The two police officers walked off, leaving Riley to look around. He was surprised to see such a lack of activity around the cathedral building itself. Everyone seemed to be holding back. *There's got to be a reason for that. Usually, the more time you take, the more dangerous a situation becomes. You allow the enemy to set up, to entrench, to prepare countermeasures. Scott knows that—I taught him that lesson myself in Afghanistan.*

Time seemed to crawl while he waited. Several times he was tempted to run. Burchfield and Uhrich were busy and appeared to have forgotten about him. But his word kept him where he was—that and the fact that Sergeant Burchfield seemed like a pretty savvy cop. If he ran, he was almost sure that the Sarge would be right behind him.

Finally, he saw Officer Auxier break through the crowd. Following him was Gilly Posada. Auxier pointed Riley's way, and Posada clapped him on the back. Riley waved to Auxier, who nodded his head and went back to his place on the line.

"What are you doing here, Pach?" Posada asked as he walked up. He wasn't smiling.

"What? No hug? No 'How ya doing?'"

"Come on, man. Don't make this harder on me than it is."

"Make what harder?"

"Seriously, Pach. You know exactly. You gonna make me say it?"

"Scott sent you to deliver a message, so deliver it," Riley said. He knew he was being a jerk to a good friend. It wasn't Posada's fault he was in this position. But right now, this man was the only person standing between where Riley was and where he needed to be.

"Okay, you want to hear it? Here it is. Leave, Riley! Get out of here! You're not needed and you're not wanted! Anytime Khadi's involved, you're too emotional and too unpredictable! So I'm sorry, Riley, but you've got to go!"

"You done?" Riley asked.

Posada remained silent.

"Feel better?"

"No, I feel like crap."

"You gonna take me to Scott now?"

"You know, you suck, Pach! Seriously!"

Riley watched Posada with a sly smile. *This battle is so won!*

"Follow me," Posada said.

"Thanks, man," Riley said, putting his arm around his friend as he walked. Posada tried to shrug it off, but Riley kept it locked on.

He tried to pump Posada for information, but the ops man was having none of it. When they finally got near the command truck, Posada just pointed, then walked off.

Riley watched him go. *Never seen him that ticked before.* He shrugged. *He's a good enough friend. He'll get over it.*

Now, speaking of friends . . . He turned toward the truck. Two men in black suits were standing at the door. *I am* not *going through this a third time.*

He walked to the closest suit and said, "Send Scott Ross out here—now!"

"He's busy," the man said without emotion.

Riley pushed past him and began pounding on the door. "Ross! Get out here!"

The first suit grabbed Riley from behind, but Riley was able to spin him around so that he careened into the second suit. He pounded the door again. "Ross!"

Backups began sprinting in from all directions, and soon Riley was pinned to the side of the truck.

"Scott! Don't make me hurt these guys!"

The whole mass of people slowly tipped to the ground.

The truck door flew open and Scott came bounding out. "Get off him," he yelled. He began grabbing bodies and yanking them off. "Stand down, you idiots!"

Finally he got to Riley, who had the first suit in a headlock tight enough that the man was tapping the ground. "Tap all you want; this ain't the UFC," Riley said through gritted teeth.

Scott smacked Riley hard in the back of the head, and Riley let go. The suit sat up, sucked in a deep breath, then dropped again.

"I think I killed him," Riley said from his back.

"No, he's still breathing, you stooge," Scott replied, reaching a hand down to help Riley up.

Another suit, this one distinguished from all the others only by a little more gray around his temple, ran up to Scott and began cursing him eight ways to Sunday.

"Relax, Ringle," Scott said, putting his hand on the man's chest and backing him up a step.

"What do you mean, relax? I demand this man be put into custody! Did you see what he did to my guy?"

"Looks like a result of crappy training to me. He's lucky Riley held back."

Ringle knocked Scott's hand away. "Are you going to do something with this criminal, or do I need to go into the truck and talk with Director LeBlanc?"

"And tell him what? Your security man just tapped out due to rear naked choke hold? Trust me, LeBlanc would be on my side. Now run along, will you? I've got to talk to Mr. Covington."

"This isn't the end of it, Ross," Ringle said as he walked away. "Not by a long shot."

When Scott turned back, Riley was busy adjusting his various holsters—all of which had shifted around in the scuffle. All the laughs were gone now. It was one angry friend facing another angry friend.

"Why are you here, Riley?"

"Oh, shut up with the 'Why are you here?' Scott! You know exactly why I'm here."

"You shouldn't have come. You're just going to muddle up the works."

Riley laughed angrily. "Right. Admit it, Scott, you've been hoping the whole time I'd get here."

Now it was Scott's turn to laugh, but his sounded a little more uncomfortable. "Please! I've done everything I could to keep you away from here. How many times do you need to hear 'No'?"

"Let me get this straight. You're saying you tried to keep me away? Is that why you made Evie, the one with the heart of Charmin, tell me to stay away? And that's why you sent Gilly to the line to tell me to leave? You knew Evie'd tell me to come here, and you knew Gilly couldn't say no! So here I am, Scotty-boy," Riley said, tapping Scott on the cheek. "What now?"

Scott looked at the ground, saying nothing.

Riley put his hand on Scott's shoulder. "I'm here. Khadi's in there. Now you tell me how we're going to get her out."

"Okay, Pach. Come on in." Then under his breath, he said, "Ooooh, Porter's going to be so pissed."

"Tell him to meet me out here. I'll choke him out."

Scott laughed and opened the door of the truck. At the top of the steps, he turned and said, "But I didn't plan for you to come here. Get that out of your head."

"Yeah, whatever," Riley said. "Why do I feel like I've been masterfully played *again* by the Great Scottini?"

"Don't count on it. It'd take somebody really, really, really smart to be able to pull off that elaborate of a con on American hero Riley Covington," Scott said; then he winked and walked into the truck.

THURSDAY, SEPTEMBER 15, 12:45 P.M. EDT

Khadi awoke with a start. The tile beneath her cheek was still cool, so she figured she couldn't have been here long. The combination of waking up on the ground and the screaming pain in her head was very disorienting. Focusing on the red, green, and white diamond patterns on the floor for a minute helped her to feel a little more grounded. Finally, she tilted her head to the left so she could see up. A wave of nausea rolled up from her stomach, causing her to close her eyes and put her head back down.

A minute or so later, she tried again. This time, her stomach stayed put. Looking around, she could see that she was just inside an arched doorway—a camera stood under some stained glass windows. That was when the reality of her situation descended on her. She remembered where she was, and who all was beyond that arch. She felt like a condemned man waking up from a tropical dream only to see the bars and realize it's his execution day. His only chance at survival was a call from the governor. Khadi's only chance was for Scott to ride in with the cavalry.

A new pain suddenly made its presence known. Tugging gently at her arms, she realized that her wrists were zip-tied together behind her back. The sharpness of the pain told her that it was more than just tightness that was causing the pain; the plastic was cutting into her skin.

A hand grabbed hold of her hair and yanked her head up. The pain was so intense she cried out. Gropey's face appeared.

"Ah, so you're awake? Good. I have someone who wants to meet you." He let go of her hair, and since she had already been trying to pull away, her head slammed to the tile. Her vision grayed as she rode the pain wave.

Please, God, let me survive this. Give me the strength to help these people. When she could, she opened her eyes again. Across the room, through the tears, she was able to see an arched entryway that matched the one she was under. As she followed it up, she saw a statue of a man tucked in a tiny alcove just above the point of the arch. There was writing on his pedestal, but her vision was too blurred make out the words. She figured he was a saint or a disciple or something.

Although he was just a stone figure, there was something comforting about having him there looking down on her. He looked so peaceful, so . . . *compassionate* was the best word she could come up with. He made her feel like she wasn't alone, wasn't completely friendless—like someone was watching over her. *Don't you go anywhere,* she thought. *I may need you before this whole thing is over.*

There was movement in the arch below him, and in walked the old imam she had seen with the General.

"Sit her over there," he said, nodding to a stone bench built into the wall below the stained glass windows.

She was surprised by four hands lifting her up from behind

and carrying her by her armpits to the bench. Looking back to where she had been laying, she saw a small pool of blood and she prayed that someone would accidentally slip in it and crack his head open.

Following her gaze, the old imam said, "Clean that up."

Bummer, she thought turning her eyes back to the imam.

"So you're the guy who's going to burn in hell for all this," she said, more as a statement than a question.

"Khadi Faroughi," the old man said, ignoring the comment. "So, my dear sister in the faith, may I ask what you are sacrificing for Allah on this most holy first day of Ramadan?"

"Hopefully your life."

The imam laughed. "Well, that wouldn't be much of a sacrifice for you, would it?"

"I don't think your life would be much of a sacrifice for anyone," Khadi replied.

The old man's smile diminished for a fraction of a second, then spread again. "You know, you look much prettier in your pictures."

"My apologies. I was looking much fresher this morning before the General decided to pistol-whip me."

"The General? Who is . . . ? Oh, you mean Majid. Majid Alavi, my number one man. Believe it or not, he went easy on you. By the rules we had set down, we should have killed ten people and then you. He was actually quite merciful."

"I'm touched," Khadi said.

"You should be, Khadi. He has shown you mercy once, and he will not show it to you again. Nor will I."

For once, she didn't have a smart remark in return. Instead she was suddenly taken by the thought of how much she did not want to die. All the fearlessness Riley used to show about death, all the peace he had about what came after—right here, right now, she was realizing that she had none of it.

"You know, you are much more lovely when you are silent,"

the imam said. "Now you appear ready to listen. My name is Saifullah."

"The Sword of Allah," Khadi said softly.

"Yes, the Sword of Allah. Very good. And while Saifullah is simply a *nom de guerre*, it does describe perfectly who I am and why we are all here."

"Understood," Khadi said. *Be as agreeable as you can right now. The more time you buy, the better chance you have of surviving this, and hopefully bringing some people out with you.*

"I must tell you, dear sister, among the people I know, you are quite famous—or infamous. Yes, that would be a better term. So finding you here was quite a pleasant surprise."

"Why *are* you here?" Khadi asked. "What are you hoping to accomplish?"

"Big picture? Why, what every good Muslim wants—Sharia, of course."

Khadi shook her head. "And this is the means you are using? Killing people to force Islamic law?"

Saifullah spread his arm out over Woodrow Wilson's stone casket and toward the people in the nave. "These people? Why are you concerned over the lives of these people? Does not Surah Al-`Ankabut say, 'And who does more wrong than he who invents a lie against Allah or rejects the Truth when it reaches him? Is there not a home in Hell for those who reject Faith?' These people are full of lies about the true faith. Anything they experience is just retribution."

"But doesn't Surah Al-Baqarah say, 'Let there be no compulsion in religion: Truth stands out clearly from Error: whoever rejects evil and believes in Allah hath grasped the most trusty handhold, that never breaks'?"

Saifullah nodded in appreciation of Khadi's point. "That is true. Well said. But what you must understand is that nobody is forcing anyone to submit to the Truth. All are free to reject it—as long as they are willing to accept the consequences."

"But don't you see—?"

"Enough for now," Saifullah said, holding his hand out to still Khadi. "We are on a time schedule, and I have already spent too much time bantering with you. I want you to remain where you are. Pay close attention to what happens next, knowing that your fate will be similar."

Saifullah stood and exited the bay. Moments later, two of the men in black came in carrying a large, dark green plastic tarp. Knowing that tarps meant blood, Khadi watched in anticipatory horror as they unfolded it so that it covered the entire room, even tucking it under the tripod that held the camera.

As soon as they exited, Khadi heard a scuffle and some frightened, angry words; then a man in a black hood was pushed into the room, pleading and whimpering. He stumbled onto the tarp and fell, hitting his head on the corner of Wilson's tomb. Two men followed him in. Both had black knit masks on their faces; in the belt of one was a long-bladed knife.

Khadi was in full panic. *Oh, God, please stop this! Please don't let this happen—not here in America!* She had to do something. But with her arms bound, she was helpless. Then three more men walked in—Saifullah, Alavi, and a man who took up position behind the camera.

Saifullah stood in front of the lens, and Alavi came and sat next to Khadi. After pulling a pair of wire cutters from his pocket, he reached behind her and snipped off her zip ties. He slipped the cutters back into his pocket and removed her .357 from his belt. Placing it against her side, he whispered, "Keep your mouth shut and watch."

Tears streamed down Khadi's face. She couldn't believe what she was seeing. She was desperate to do something—anything—to stop this, not only because a person was about to be slaughtered but also because protecting this person was her job.

She had known who was under that hood from the moment she heard his voice. And her suspicion was confirmed when she saw the green, yellow, and black tie that Charlotte had given him for his last birthday.

But there was nothing to do but sob and watch. The cameraman pressed record, the hood came off, and Mr. Opportunity began his final photo op.

THURSDAY, SEPTEMBER 15, 1:00 P.M. EDT

Riley stood in a corner of the truck impatiently watching the players battle it out. Best he could tell, the head of the Secret Service didn't want to make a rescue attempt but did want to initiate a phone call. The FBI director wanted to make a rescue attempt and couldn't understand why Scott couldn't come up with a plan where no one would get hurt. The DC police chief wanted to hold off on everything until they received the first call. Scott and Stanley Porter understood that absolutely nothing was going to happen until they got a phone call from the White House, so they were ignoring all of them and seemed to be busy looking at a schematic of the crypt level of the cathedral.

Scott had made it clear to Riley that his role was to be neither seen nor heard, which was fine with him. He was content to absorb it all. The more he understood the situation, the better chance he had at success when it came time for him to make his move.

Unfortunately, what that move would

look like he still had no clue. Sneaking in to rescue Khadi was a pretty sure way to get himself, Khadi, or both of them killed. And even if he made it back out with her, the probable retaliation against the remaining hostages was a guilt that neither of them would be able to live with. Right now, it seemed as if his best option was to go in with the rescue assault if Scott would let him—as if Scott could stop him.

Whatever he was going to do, he needed to do it quickly. Right after he had entered the truck, Scott had received word from Evie that Khadi had been singled out and beaten, and now they couldn't find her on any of the cameras. The thought of her identity possibly having been discovered made Riley sick to his stomach. *They will have no mercy on her. In their minds, she is a traitor to her faith. Oh, Lord, please protect her.*

"Shhh, quiet," one of the techs said. He was sitting before a video monitor. "The stream is going to go live in five, four, three, two, one."

A picture appeared on the screen. On it stood the old man from the DVD. He was flanked by two terrorists dressed all in black with black knit masks covering their faces. Kneeling in front of the old man was a battered and bleeding Senator Clayson Andrews.

"RoU says it's being shot from Wilson Bay inside the cathedral," Scott confirmed. Riley looked at Scott, who mouthed, *Still no Khadi.* Riley nodded grimly and turned to the screen.

The old man began. "May the name of Allah the all-powerful, the merciful, the beneficent, be praised. And may the words of the Prophet spread throughout the world. To the people of America, I bring you greetings. I also bring you a warning—turn yourselves to the Truth while you still may.

"I am Saifullah—the Sword of Allah. It is not my real name, but my real name is not important. My army does not have a name. We are too diverse to be contained by any one name. But while we come from all parts of this country and all walks of life, there is one thing we share—a marvelous submission to Allah and a readiness to die in his name.

"Today is the first day of Ramadan, the most holy month of the year. Among some, it is traditional to give a present to a stranger on this day. They do this to demonstrate in a practical way the generosity and mercy of our God. Today, on this first day of the most holy month, I give to you a gift."

"The cathedral doors are opening," one of the surveillance analysts said excitedly.

"It's the hostages," Scott said, holding his hand to his earpiece. "It's the large group."

Riley pointed toward the door, but Scott held out his hand. *I'll let you know,* he mouthed. Riley again nodded, but his foot was tapping the floor. *Please, Lord, let her come out! Have Scott give me that nod! Bring her out, Father!*

On the smaller surveillance screen, Riley could see men, women, and children exiting the front doors of the cathedral. One by one they came out, tentatively at first. Then, as if energized by the sunlight, they ran—down the steps and into the arms of waiting members of law enforcement.

Outside the truck, what started as frantic shouts turned rapidly to cheers. People were clapping and whistling and hooting and hollering, all celebrating the safe release of so many innocent lives.

Riley glanced back at the larger screen. A look of smug satisfaction was on Saifullah's face.

Talk about manipulation. No doubt the imam can hear the cheers too. He's playing us like a fiddle. Riley looked down at Senator Andrews, kneeling on what appeared to be a tarp. *And he's not done playing, either.*

After almost five minutes, the last of the released hostages walked out of the church, and the doors closed. Scott shook his head again to Riley, who turned back to the screen.

The noise outside the truck was near deafening due to the

sheer number of released hostages and law enforcement that had flooded the area. The tech cranked up the volume, and everyone strained to hear.

"I trust you are happy with your gift," Saifullah said with a benevolent nod of his head. "I hope this will show you that we are not the animals your media will undoubtedly portray us to be. We are here for a purpose, and unnecessary bloodshed is not part of that purpose."

Saifullah's face hardened and his voice transitioned to a much darker tone. "That being said, there is blood that must needs be shed—necessary blood, guilty blood. The wars your government has waged in Iraq and Afghanistan have taken the lives of hundreds of thousands of innocents. Washington's unwavering support of the Zionist occupiers of Palestine has allowed a regime of hatred, violence, and death to masquerade as a legitimate government, while the true owners of the land wallow in hunger and squalor. And the treatment of political prisoners in Guantanamo Bay and other hidden sites around the world can be labeled as notoriously criminal at best."

Saifullah paused, letting the tension build. "We are prepared to forgive the ignorance of the American people. We will extend to you the benefit of the doubt that you neither knew nor understood the extent of your government's crimes. Turn to Allah for forgiveness and truth. Repent of your blindness. Accept the true peace that comes from leadership based on Koranic principles. If you do so, we will rejoice with you and welcome you into the brotherhood with singing and dancing.

"However, that mercy only extends to those whose sin is that of omission. There are still those who stand guilty of sins of commission, and those sins must be accounted for. Today, we have released the ignorant and retained the guilty."

A chill went up Riley's spine. He glanced around the room and saw everyone standing perfectly still—everyone except Craig LeBlanc, who was speaking softly into a cell phone.

Turning back to the screen, he prayed that he was not about to see what he and everyone else in that truck felt sure they were about to see.

"We are still holding ninety-one . . ." Saifullah's gaze momentarily went beyond the lens of the camera. "Ninety-two hostages," he corrected himself.

Riley's heart skipped a beat. He couldn't explain why, but in that moment he knew beyond a shadow of a doubt that Khadi was alive and in that room. *Protect her, Lord. Shield her from the enemy.*

"Today, and for the remaining twenty-nine days of Ramadan, one guilty member of your government will pay the price for his or her sins and for the sins of your government. It will be a just punishment, and I trust that this trial by fire will help release your nation's leadership from Satan's grasp.

"Hear me well: if any attempt is made to stop this just retribution, all will die—every last one. If, however, you allow Allah's sentence to be carried out, then at the end of the thirty days, all the remaining hostages will be released unharmed. I trust we have an understanding.

"Now let it begin."

Saifullah walked off camera.

The masked man to Senator Andrews's right grabbed him by the hair and pulled his head up. The second man held a piece of paper in front of his face.

"Please, I don't want to die," Andrews pleaded. "I have a family! Please!"

"Read it," the second man said, pointing to the piece of paper.

Through sobs, Andrews read, "I, United States Senator Clayson Andrews, am guilty of crimes against God and man. I have been a willing participant in the beating, rape, and murder of women and children throughout the Muslim world. I hereby repent of my sins and repudiate the heinous actions of the American government. What I receive now . . . Please . . . please don't . . ."

The second man hit Andrews in the back of the head and said, "Finish reading the paper!" Riley thought he heard a little Minnesota or at least Midwest in the man's voice.

Andrews could barely sputter the words out. "What I receive now is the just punishment for my sins. May Allah have mercy on my soul."

The second man pulled the paper away and stood straight up. "There is no God but Allah, and Muhammad is his prophet."

The first man joined him, chanting, *"Allahu Akbar, Allahu Akbar, Allahu Akbar!"*

The first man pulled the knife from his belt, pulled Andrews's head back to stretch his neck, and began sawing. At first there wasn't much blood as the dull knife began to break the skin, but then the blade cut across major veins and the arterial flow shot out across the room.

Riley tried to turn away, but he couldn't. It was so horrific, so beyond the pale.

A sigh puffed as the windpipe was opened—then the screen went black.

"What? What happened?" Porter called out.

"Someone shut down the signal," Scott said, hand to his ear. "It's out at the RoU, too."

Everyone who had the authority to shut down an Internet stream that quickly and that abruptly was standing in the truck, and they all looked accusingly at each other.

Finally, Craig LeBlanc said, "Listen, there's no way I'm going to let some crazy American raghead cut the head off of one of our senators live and in color for everyone on this god-forsaken planet to witness!"

"Do you realize what you just did?" Scott yelled back at him.

"Yeah, I saved a great American's dignity!"

"No, you killed people, you fool! You might as well have just pulled the trigger yourself because sure as I'm standing here, you just killed people!"

LeBlanc lunged for Scott. "Listen here, you hippie punk!" His sheer momentum threw Scott back into a bay of DVD recorders. He pulled back to hit Scott, but Porter grabbed his wrist. Twisting it around, he forced LeBlanc down to one knee.

"You were wrong to have done that, Craig," Porter said with one hand on Scott's chest and one holding LeBlanc's wrist. "Scott's right. There will be a penalty for what you did. Now walk out and cool off. We'll talk about this later."

Gradually, Porter let up on LeBlanc's wrist until the Secret Service head could stand. Then he let go, and LeBlanc walked out.

Turning to Scott, Porter said, "There are two ways to be right—the right way and the wrong way. Don't choose the wrong way again. Understand?"

"Yes, sir," Scott said.

Porter stepped away, and Riley stepped up.

"You okay, man?" he asked his friend, who turned around and began sliding DVD trays back closed again.

"You know she's sitting right there, don't you?" Scott said. His voice was pained, and he wouldn't look at Riley. "You saw his eyes—I know you did. Khadi was right there in that room."

Riley just nodded.

Scott was still breathing hard. "All I was thinking when that signal went down was that when this crazy fool hears what's happened, he's going to lash out at the first person he sees. Pray with everything you've got that either he or she is out of the room by then. Otherwise . . . otherwise, I don't know. Just pray, Riley. Please, man, just keep praying."

FORTY-ONE

Khadi had seen people die. She had even caused people to die. But nothing—absolutely nothing—could have prepared her for what she had just witnessed. In the minutes that followed, she forced herself to keep her eyes open because every time they closed, she saw the neck split halfway through, then finally separate. She heard the cries, the gurgles, the tears of flesh, the snap of cartilage. And that moment—that one moment—when Clayson Andrews's eyes froze in their terror and the light was extinguished.

No one deserves that. No matter who they are or what they've done, no one deserves to go through that agony. It's evil, pure and simple.

As Alavi supervised and Saifullah watched from the right archway, Senator Andrews's head was placed in a plastic garbage bag that was tightly cinched, then tied. The tripod and camera were lifted up next to her on the stone bench, and three men came in and began rolling the body up in the tarp. Khadi was surprised at their macabre efficiency.

"After you deposit the body downstairs," Alavi said to them, "be sure to really rinse down the tarp. Otherwise, it will foul very quickly. We only have two others, so we need to make them last."

"Yes, sir," the three said in ragged unison.

Once that task was done and the three had left with the body, two more came in with buckets and rags to scrub the walls and floor of any blood that had sprayed or had somehow spread past the borders of the tarp.

"So what did you think?" Saifullah asked Khadi, walking back into the room. Alavi stood and moved to the bay's entrance.

"I think you are all animals," she said, refusing to look up at him.

"Ha! And you in America are all soft. You send your military to commit atrocities around the world, but the moment it comes to your shores, you crumble, you break, you gasp in horror. 'I can't believe people would do such a thing,' you cry out. But your own military—your own young men and women—are committing the same acts on innocents in Iraq and Afghanistan."

"That's a bunch of lies, and you know it. Quit building straw men to justify your own sins."

"You talk of sins. You know nothing of sin! Until you see the mangled bodies, the orphaned children, the starving villages—all created by your government and your military—you have no right to talk to me about sins!"

"Is that why you're doing this? To force us to withdraw our troops?" she asked, finally looking up at him, mockery in her eyes. "If so, you're a bigger fool than I thought you to be."

Saifullah laughed and leaned close. "This isn't about a political agenda. I have no illusions of stopping any war. This is about revenge, pure and simple. Do you think anyone is going to get out of here alive? We'll slaughter these pigs one by one, while the sports dads and soccer moms look on in fascinated horror. Then, when Ramadan is over, we're going to blow this place up and everyone in it. It will be like when the mythical Samson collapsed the roof of the pagan temple on everyone below. It was a worthy sacrifice, an honorable death."

Although her heart ached at what she heard, Khadi wasn't surprised. "From the moment I saw you, I could tell you were an evil, two-faced madman."

Saifullah's hand slapped hard across Khadi's cheek. She dropped her face to avoid another blow.

"I had always heard you were feisty. We'll see how long that lasts."

"Long enough to put a bullet in your head," Khadi mumbled.

"What was that?"

Khadi looked up and stared him in the eyes. "I said, long enough to put a bullet in your sorry head."

Saifullah's smile faded and he held her stare. Finally he said, "Well, you had better do it soon, because your mouth has made you a liability. I have decided that tomorrow you will die."

Khadi tried not to let the fear show in her eyes, but she knew he had tagged her with a blow she couldn't hide. Dropping her head, she stared at the floor and tried to let his words fade from her consciousness—to pretend she wasn't really where she was and that she hadn't really just heard that today was her last full day on this planet.

Saifullah grunted with satisfaction.

Suddenly she heard urgent whispering. Keeping her head down, she glanced up and saw the cameraman in a quiet, intense conversation with Alavi.

"What is it?" Saifullah said.

"One moment, sir," Alavi said, holding up a single finger. He asked another question of the cameraman, impatiently listened to the answer, then drove his hand into the base of the man's neck, pinning him to the inside curve of the archway.

"And you are sure it was nothing you did?" he hissed, just

loud enough for her to hear. "You aren't trying to cover your own mistake?"

"No, sir! I swear! It was from the outside!"

"Very well," Alavi said, releasing the man. "Go."

The cameraman hurried away.

"The Internet connection went down," Alavi said, walking toward Saifullah.

"What? When?"

"During the execution. The ones who were monitoring the broadcast said that as soon as the first cut was made, the signal ended."

Saifullah stood and fumed. Then, turning to Khadi, he accused, "You see? This is why we will win! Unlike you, we are strong!"

"Unlike you, we are human," Khadi retorted.

Saifullah stepped toward her raising his hand. She lowered her head, preparing for the blow. It never came. Instead, she heard the two men in conversation.

"How much longer until the phone call?" Saifullah asked.

Alavi checked his watch. "Less than a minute."

"Give me the phone."

While Saifullah moved to the left archway with the phone, Alavi lifted himself onto Woodrow Wilson's stone casket and sat watching Khadi. She could feel his eyes on her but tried to block him out. She couldn't imagine what he was thinking about—what evil was mulling around in that mind of his. But she knew that if she spent too much time thinking about it, her thoughts would end up descending to the same dark places where his dwelled.

The phone chirped.

"To whom am I speaking?" Saifullah asked when he answered the call. "Scott Ross? I recognize your name. I think we may have a friend in common," he said, looking at Khadi. "Well, Mr. Ross, it seems you owe me an explanation."

At the sound of Scott's name, Khadi's heart soared. Suddenly, she felt hope again. Even though she had known that he and the rest of the team absolutely had to be out there, to know that Scott was leading the charge made it seem like maybe—just maybe—she would survive this after all.

After a long pause, Saifullah looked toward Alavi and shook his head. To Scott he said angrily, "I'm afraid your explanation is not acceptable. . . . Why, Mr. Ross? Because it's a complete fabrication, and I don't like being lied to. . . . You may apologize all you want, but there is still a penalty that must be paid. And I believe it must be one severe enough that you will think twice before going against my orders a second time." Saifullah turned toward Khadi as he said this.

The icy hand of fear gripped her heart, and all the hope she had been feeling just a moment ago was gone. *I'm going to die,* she thought. *Right here, right now. I'm going to die. Oh, dear God— Allah, Jehovah, whichever one you are; I don't know anymore—God, please let me live. Please, oh please, let me live.*

"Isn't it a little early in the game for you to be asking for mercy, Mr. Ross? . . . Yes, I understand this isn't a game. Please excuse my improper choice of words. . . . Because I am holding all the power. Why should I not be calm? . . . No, my mind is made up. A penalty must be paid and will be paid. Is this the number that I should use to contact you? . . . The discussion is over. I will be in touch. Good-bye, Mr. Ross."

Saifullah walked to Khadi and crouched down in front of her. "From what I remember reading, Scott Ross was the third partner in your sordid adventures with Riley Covington."

When Khadi didn't answer, he continued, "I wonder, could there possibly be a stronger message to him than to see your dead body roll out of the front doors?"

Khadi felt numb inside. She wanted to plead for her life—to promise him anything just to let her live. But something deep inside her—pride, hatred, loyalty, or simply training—caused her to swallow her pleas and remain silent.

"Look at me, Khadi."

Khadi kept her head down.

"I said look . . . at . . . me!"

Khadi raised her eyes to meet his.

He took hold of her chin. His hands were surprisingly soft and smelled like Jergens lotion. "Do you know the two things I hate most in this world? Disloyalty and cowardice. And while you have chosen incorrectly in your allegiances—a choice that will undoubtedly soon cost you your life—you are certainly neither disloyal nor a coward. However, the man who gave up your identity? He has both of those treacherous qualities. Do you know the man of whom I speak?"

Khadi nodded once.

"Did you know he made a deal with Mr. Alavi—your name for his freedom?" Saifullah shook his head. "*Tsk, tsk, tsk.* What kind of a man is that?"

Then, after a pause, he said, "I have decided that you will live to see tomorrow."

Saifullah released her, and she dropped her head into her hands and broke down. She hated herself for doing it—for showing that kind of weakness—but she couldn't help it. Her emotions had been such a roller coaster over these past hours; she had absolutely no control anymore.

Through her tears, she heard Saifullah grunt, then say to Alavi, "Bring me the one who betrayed her. He will be the one."

On hearing those words, her sobs increased even more. But this increase didn't originate in any sort of sorrow over Tyson Bryson being chosen or because she felt any compassion for him. Instead, it came from the fact that she knew deep down, in those dark recesses of the soul where few are brave enough to tread, she was glad that if someone had to die, he was the one.

You're safe now, Mom and Dad. Your secret, whatever it is, will die with him.

Crouching low, Riley, Scott, Skeeter, and Stanley Porter made their way along the police tape about a hundred feet back from the north side of the cathedral. Most of the noise and confusion nearby had died down. The released hostages had all been gathered in one area to await buses that would transport them to a facility where they could be debriefed. Now it was back to business as usual with police officers tucked behind their cruisers, guns pointed at the building where the bad guys were holed up with their hostages.

Stopping, Riley pointed to an entryway to the crypt level. "See? Over there. I'm just saying, those doors are going to be secured and possibly wired. But those windows—there're simply too many of them to wire up."

Porter nodded his agreement. Although he had initially made quite evident his lack of enthusiasm at Riley forcing himself onto the leadership team, he had apparently decided to live with it. Riley knew he had Scott to thank for that. *Will the wonders of the Great Scottini never cease?*

"Do we know where they lead to?" Porter asked.

Riley looked to Scott, who shrugged distractedly. "Downstairs?"

"Maybe you could get Evie to give us a slightly more precise answer," Riley said sarcastically.

"In a minute," Scott said.

Riley could see he was processing, so he decided to give him some space. Turning to Skeeter, he said, "I'm thinking that with some kind of diversion, we could have two teams of twelve—one east, one west—across the grass and through the windows in thirty seconds, forty tops."

"Mmmm," Skeeter agreed.

"But we've still got the vests," Porter said. "They're the wild-card that trumps all of our plans. All we'd need is one tripped alarm, one broken window, and the whole place could go up."

"That's what I'm wrestling with," Scott said. "I've got Gooey compiling the best enhanced shots he can of those devices. If we can figure out how they're put together, we can figure out a way to neutralize them."

Scott pulled a hand to his earpiece. "Evie says the front door's opening," he told the others, and they ran west toward the cathedral's entrance.

From their vantage point behind the lead cars, they watched as a single man poked his head out the door. A moment later he was pushed, and the door closed behind him.

His hair was disheveled, and his face looked like he had been struck a few times. He was jacketless but still wore an expensive-looking tie around the collar of his tailored white shirt. Over the shirt and tie, looking like the waistcoat of a mismatched three-piece suit, was a khaki green safari vest. The four front pockets of the vest bulged, and external wires connected all the pockets together. He carried an envelope in his hand.

"Get back! Get back!" Scott yelled to the cops who were running up to assist the hostage to his freedom. "Everybody back behind the line! I mean everyone!"

All the members of the advance team fell back. It was obvious the man had been crying. He tried walking forward but stumbled like it was closing time and he had just stepped out through the door of the corner bar. Grabbing hold of the railing, he found his legs and gradually began to make his way down, one shaky step at a time. The envelope crumpled around the handrail and crackled as it slid down.

When he ran out of handrail, he stopped.

After taking three deep breaths, he cleared his throat and said, "My name is Tyson Bryson. I have been asked to read a statement, after which I am to be released with the promise of no harm coming to those who assist me."

Yeah, right, Riley thought. *Ten to one they're just trying to draw us out so they can maximize the damage.*

"Everyone stay back," Scott ordered, and Riley was relieved to hear that his friend felt the same way.

With another deep breath, Bryson opened the envelope and extracted a single sheet of paper. He stared at it a moment, like he was trying to decipher a secret code. Suddenly its meaning dawned on him. "Oh, no," he said, and the paper and envelope fell from this hands.

"Down!" Scott yelled, but his command was cut short by a deafening sound.

Riley found himself thrown backward, then showered by glass from the windows of the police car he had half ducked behind. It was as if he had been hit in the chest by a home-run swing from an enormous foam bat, and he sucked in deeply, trying to replenish his air supply.

Slowly, he rolled to his side and pushed himself up to his knees. He knew that there was chaos all around him, but he had a hard time connecting with it. Everything was muffled, like when as a kid he walked around with the earflaps down on his dad's beaver fur hat.

As he surveyed the damage, he was relieved to see that it appeared to be mostly cosmetic. There were some cuts from flying glass on the faces around him, but for the most part everyone seemed to be in the same condition he was. *Thanks to Scott. If he hadn't kept everyone back, it would have been carnage.*

Speaking of Scott . . . Riley used the hood of the police cruiser to pull himself to his feet and began looking for his friend. He turned toward the cathedral and immediately wished he hadn't. There wasn't much left of Tyson Bryson, but what did remain was gruesome. Riley quickly looked away.

After passing four cars and stepping over twice that many groggy cops, Riley found Scott. He was talking into his cell phone—his earpiece was nowhere to be seen.

"Say that again; I'm having a hard time hearing you." Scott spoke at an unusually high volume. "Well, I'm sorry, but some psycho idiot just set off a body bomb about fifty feet from me. . . . Watch my words? You want me to watch my words after what you just did? Well how's this for watching my words—you can bite me, Mr. Saifullah! You and all your junior American *hajjis* who are bitter at the world just because some racist, banjo-playing inbreed pushed them down and called them a camel jockey when they were kids. You know what most people do when they get knocked down like that? They pick themselves back up and they make their lives better. That's what I did! That's what anyone with half a brain and an ounce of *huevos* does. What they don't do is feel so sorry for themselves that they take an assault rifle and shoot up a funeral! You understand? *Sie verstehen?*"

Through most of Scott's tirade, Riley was signaling for him to bring it down a notch. While he agreed with everything his friend was saying, Khadi was still in there—a fact that, judging by Scott's reaction, Saifullah had now just reminded him of.

"No, don't. . . . Please. . . . Listen, I'm sorry. I just had a bomb blow up in my face. Just . . . No, let's just . . ." Scott's face was scrunched up tight and his whole body was moving in tense, contorted motions. His fist slammed down onto the roof of a nearby cruiser, leaving a wide dent in the sheet metal. He locked eyes with Riley, and his face said it all—*Khadi!*

"Please stop! I'm sorry. . . . I swear, if you hit her again, I'll be the one pulling the trigger when . . . Stop!" Scott's hand came down again, and this time he winced when it connected.

It was all Riley could do not to run for the doors of the cathedral. He wanted to scream. He wanted to hurt somebody. *Lord, please make it stop! Do something!* His complete and utter helplessness churned at his insides. It was like there was a swarm of bees filling his chest, surrounding his stomach. He squatted to the ground and was surprised to find his .44 magnum in his hand.

"Yes, I understand," Scott said, his voice slightly calmer and his motions more subdued. "I know; I apologize. . . . Of course. Just tell me what you need."

Scott looked to Riley and made a scribbling motion with his hand. Riley quickly felt his pockets, knowing even before he did it that he didn't have a pen. Looking around quickly, he spotted a still-dazed MPDC officer just a few feet away. He stepped over, spun her around, snatched the pen that was sticking out of her chest pocket, and ran it back to Scott.

Scott tucked the phone against his shoulder and poised the pen over his left palm. "Okay, go ahead. . . . Okay . . . Okay . . . That's it? . . . When do you want it? . . . Tomorrow, 1545. Fine . . . Yes, you have my word." Scott shut down the phone.

"How's Khadi?" Riley asked anxiously.

"They smacked her around some," Scott said, anger still evident in his voice.

"But at least we know she's alive."

"Yeah, at least we know she's alive," Scott agreed.

Relief flooded Riley. *Hope. That's all I'm asking for is hope.* "What were you writing on your hand?"

Scott looked at it as if someone else had written it on his hand and now he was trying to make sense of it. "It's a . . . a . . . It's a list—a grocery list. He said they've got supplies to last them tonight and tomorrow morning. This is what they want to have delivered tomorrow and for every day after."

Just then, Skeeter showed up helping along an unsteady Porter. The Homeland Security secretary had a gash on his forehead and was using a handkerchief to dab the streaming blood out of his eye.

"Talk to me," Porter said.

"Just talked with Saifullah," Scott reported. "Got a supply list to be delivered at 1545 tomorrow. I also confirmed our cooperation for tomorrow's Internet feed."

"Do we know when he's going hot tomorrow?" Porter asked.

Scott shook his head. "He just said to keep it open. Listen, Stanley," Scott said. His finger was tapping Porter lightly on the chest, but his head was facing down. "I, uh . . . I'm kind of working on a thought here. I just . . . need . . ." With all the chaos going on around them, the four men stood there silently, waiting while Scott's gears churned.

Then his head popped up, and he gave Porter a look like he hadn't seen him in years. "Stanley! Listen, I need the analysis on that vest device ASAP. Everything they can give me—electronics, materials, origins, everything. And tell them I don't need it all at once—they can feed it to me piecemeal if need be. Pull all the strings you can—get the president involved if you have to. As tragic as this was for that Bryson guy, I think it's very possible that Saifullah may have just handed us our first break."

CHAPTER FORTY-THREE

Khadi wasn't sure how long ago night had fallen. All she knew was that she was cold, hungry, and sore. She lifted her head slightly and tried to look around. Although the lights in the cathedral were still on, without the sunlight streaming through the stained glass, the interior of the structure had taken on a decidedly starker, grayer feel.

After the beating, she had been half led, half carried to the non-Politico group. The chairs had all been moved away previously, and everyone was sitting on the floor. As soon as she was led up, a number of the men slid back to make room for her.

A man who introduced himself as Alan Paine slipped off his jacket and made a pillow for her. He disappeared, but soon he was back with another jacket from someone else and draped it over her as a blanket.

And there she had lain for the past who-knows-how-long, slipping in and out of awareness. At one point, when she opened her eyes she found two pieces of white bread and a Dixie cup full of water.

Alan, seeing that she was awake, had encouraged her to eat the bread, but her mouth was too swollen to even think of trying to put something solid into it. Finally, he had settled for giving her a few sips of water before she had drifted off.

Now it was sometime in the middle of the night. All around her were hushed sounds—small groups of hostages talking softly, others lightly snoring, a sob, a comforting word. Every now and then, one of the terrorists would take issue with one of the hostages. If the hostage were lucky, they would just be berated. If not . . . it was usually the fist they used, but sometimes they went straight for the rifle butt.

And these are your people, Allah. Which means these are my people. I don't understand—I truly don't. How can we both be reading the same book yet come to such divergent conclusions? And then I look at someone like Alan . . . Even now she could see him, jacketless, sitting huddled together with two other men, tucked in a tight ball trying to keep warm; low, soft, unintelligible words wafted through the night air. *They call* him *the infidel. They say* he *is the one who is against you. Yet who was the compassionate one?*

She reached her hand from under the blanket and pinched off a small bit of the bread. But from the feel of it, it had gone stale hours ago, and she left the morsel on the tile without attempting it.

If tomorrow is the day I am to die, I want to make sure my eternal destiny is secure. But even now after a lifetime of following your laws and trying to do the right thing, I have no peace. Why is that? Can't you just grant me that much?

Riley has peace. I knew that from the moment I saw him after his torture in Italy. It's like he has the big picture all figured out, while I can't even figure out where my little piece of the puzzle fits. Why does his God give him that? While you give me . . . what? Tradition? Family harmony? A "maybe's" chance at heaven?

She rolled over, trying to shift the aches and pains to another side. A hand gently touched her shoulder, and Alan said, "Are you okay, Khadi? Can I get you anything?"

"An M4 carbine and a box of loaded magazines?"

Alan laughed. "Now that sounds like the Khadi Faroughi I've read about. You holler if you need anything."

"Wait," she said, placing her hand on his. Without looking back at him, she asked, "Alan, do you believe in God?"

"You think I could be smiling right now if I didn't?"

"What would you think if . . . ? I mean, how would I . . . ?" She closed her eyes and shook her head. "Never mind. Thanks, Alan."

Alan gave her shoulder a squeeze. "Anytime."

His hand left her shoulder, and she heard him slide back across the tile to his little group. The low talking began again, and she found it strangely comforting.

Dear God—whichever one of you is real and is actually listening—help me to get you figured out. I want to follow you, but I just don't know who you are. Don't let me make the wrong choice. I don't think I'm going to have much time to correct it.

She let her eyes close for a moment, fully intending to continue her nocturnal spiritual wrestling. Instead, the next time she opened them color had returned to the cathedral, and by the sound of things, the terrorists were getting restless.

FORTY-FOUR

It had been a night filled with blueprints, debates, and lukewarm coffee. The smell in the truck had taken on the sharp odor of tense perspiration, and the door was now kept open in the futile hopes of allowing some fresh air to mellow the funk. Everyone was on edge.

After seeing the execution of Senator Andrews, the president had finally given the go-ahead for a rescue attempt. "How much of that is because he thinks it's the right thing, how much is that the public is crying out for something to be done, and how much is him trying to keep this from turning into a multinational incident?" Scott wondered aloud to Riley.

"Whatever his motives, at least we're finally going to do something."

The rescue was scheduled for eleven tonight. However, the strategy for the planned attack was in flux again. The initial operation involved four teams of twelve stealthily entering the cathedral through the crypt-level windows on the north and south sides of the building. Once they were in position, helicopters would drop into place above the high-peaked roof. On the go signal, the four teams would ascend the eastern stairway and begin the attack, while from the helicopters, two more assault teams would make their descent on zip lines through the high stained glass windows to the nave below.

Scott wasn't fully comfortable with the plan. There were so many holes and unknowns. His hope was that he could use these next eleven hours to fill some of those holes and answer some of those unknowns.

One of the night's few moments of levity had occurred when an observer from the National Register of Historic Places—part of the National Park Service—had raised a stink about the planned assault. Against everyone's protests, he had been forced into the truck by the secretary of the interior to ensure that the integrity of this national treasure would be maintained. Riley had watched the look on this man's face grow from shock to horror to rage as he grasped the details of the planned assault.

Finally, he could hold his tongue no more. "Objection," he had cried. "Those windows are priceless. Works of art one and all. Why, Rowan LeCompte himself designed more than forty of them! There's even a moon rock embedded in one—a genuine, from-the-moon, moon rock! And you're going to just come crashing through them? No, sir! Not on my watch! I'm afraid I have to veto this plan."

There was a barely controlled silence in the truck while everyone tried to determine whether Stanley Porter was going to verbally assail the man or just pull out his gun and shoot him.

When Porter finally spoke, it was with a calmness that belied the coloring of his face. "I appreciate your input, as ignorant and misguided as it may be. And I, too, think I'll throw my veto into the mix. But rather than vetoing this plan, which truly has significant merit, I think I'll veto you."

He nodded to Scott, who nodded to Skeeter, who lifted the observer off the ground by his belt and collar and launched him out into the night air. Fifteen minutes later, Porter dealt handily with an angry protest call from the secretary of the interior.

The situation had ultimately ended quite unsatisfactorily for all involved in the assault when the vice president himself had called and said that the president hoped that, if at all possible, an alternative entry point could be made into the cathedral. Porter had cursed again, and the helicopter assault had been shelved.

Now Riley shifted with impatience. Scott was on the phone with whoever had taken the lead in the explosives analysis. If he heard the right word, the go light on tonight's assault would turn from yellow to green. If he didn't, it was back to square one.

The whole truck was silent as Scott listened through his recently restored earpiece. "You're sure? . . . Okay, now I'm going to repeat this back to you just for one last confirmation. The devices are electronically based. They are battery operated. They are triggered by remote device. There is most likely a manual trigger. There is most likely a tampering trigger. Any issues with what I've said? . . ." Scott turned to Riley and gave a thumbs-up.

"You guys are awesome," he continued. "Oh yeah, one last thing—did you guys recover the note that Bryson read? . . . Impressive. What did it say? . . . Just 'Boom'? One word; nothing else? . . . Man, that's cold! Hey, again, you guys are awesome. Go take yourselves out to a steak dinner and charge it to Homeland Security." Porter cleared his throat. "Sorry, dude, I meant National Park Service, Department of Interior. . . . Of course, I'll sign the PO. Just send it my way. Later."

"So?" Porter asked as soon as Scott hung up.

"We're go with the HERF. According to these guys, it should take the vests completely out of the equation."

HERF, Riley knew from his research on electromagnetic-pulse weapons, was an acronym for High-Energy Radio Frequency. This still-developing science used high-intensity radio waves to fry electronics on a small scale much the same as an EMP weapon did on a large scale. The nation was still recovering from the EMP that had been detonated over New York just two years earlier. A pulse from a HERF device would be much smaller but still theoretically able to not only take out all the remote devices but disable the bombs themselves.

"So we're go at 2300?" Porter asked, looking at the men surrounding the table.

"Go," FBI Director Castillo said.

"Go," MPDC Chief Sprecker said.

"Go," Secret Service Head LeBlanc said.

Porter looked at Scott, who said, "You're the queen bee; I'm just a worker. It's your call."

Porter shook his head. "I'm looking at you for a reason, Scott. I trust your opinion on this far more than any of the rest of these schmucks because I know that your answer will be the only one that's absolutely, 100 percent free of any politics. So what'll it be?"

"Go."

"Then it's a go. 2300. Let's nail down the final details of the operation; then you can go get your teams ready. The Defense Department already has a HERF on its way here. ETA . . ."

"1400 hours," Scott said. "I really wish we could launch sooner, but sunlight is just too big a risk."

"Agreed," Porter said.

"Signal's gone live," a tech called out.

Oh no, Riley thought with fearful anticipation. *Please don't let it be her!*

As before, Saifullah stood in the center of the screen flanked by his two executioners. Senate Minority Leader Bill Evert knelt in front. Relief flooded Riley's body when he saw who it was, and he hated himself for feeling that way.

"Greetings on this second day of Ramadan," Saifullah said. Then, closing his eyes and lifting his hands to heaven, he prayed, "Allah, on this day, take me closer toward your pleasure, keep me away from your anger and punishment, and grant me the opportunity to recite your verses of the Koran, by your mercy, O most Merciful God."

Turning back to the camera, he said, "Ramadan is a time for purification and a time for commitment. It is a time to examine ourselves and look for where we have allowed sin to have a foothold in our lives. Let me encourage you this day to purge yourself of all that is keeping you from drawing closer to Allah. As the Prophet—peace be upon him—has written in the holy book, 'Indeed, Allah loves those who are constantly repentant and loves those who purify themselves.'

"And as you take the opportunity to purify yourselves, let us take the opportunity to help purify this nation. There is no god but Allah, and Mohammed is his prophet."

Riley watched as Saifullah stepped off screen, and the men in black stepped forward. It all had a nightmarish déjà vu feel to it—second verse, same as the first. But there was one major difference this time, something that was clearly evident to all who watched. Whereas Andrews had been sobbing and begging for mercy, Evert's face was hard and his eyes were steel.

The man on the left grabbed a handful of Evert's hair, and the second man held the paper in front of his face. The senator gritted his teeth at the pain.

"Read it," he commanded.

Evert remained silent.

"Read it," he said again, this time with a blow to the head.

Still Evert kept his mouth closed.

Riley was fascinated by this standoff. How long could he

last? Would he break? He found himself rooting for Evert, even though he was a hopeless underdog.

The second man seemed unsure what to do, and he looked at his partner.

"Read it now," the first one said. He yanked up on Evert's hair and drove his fist repeatedly into the side of the senator's head. The second man joined in.

Watching it was a helplessly surreal feeling for Riley. It was hard to grasp that this was actually taking place no more than a hundred yards from where he stood yet there was absolutely nothing he could do about it.

"Stop it already!" Sprecker shouted out. Riley glanced at him and saw the anguish on his face.

When the first man finally let go of Evert, the senator fell to the ground. Reaching down, the executioner grabbed his hair again and lifted him up. Blood was streaming out of Evert's nose and from a long gash down his right cheek. No longer was there hardness in his face.

"Stay strong," Riley said under his breath. "Finish well, buddy."

"Are you ready to read the statement now?"

Evert nodded, defeated.

The second man held the paper in front of his face.

Evert took a deep breath, then rapidly began singing in a strong, trained tenor voice, "'God bless America, land that I love . . .'"

With quick movements, the first man whipped out his knife.

". . . Stand beside her, and—"

The rest of the song was lost as the blade opened the senator's trachea.

"No," Porter cried out, shouting loudest among the many verbal reactions in the truck. He turned away from the screen and cinched his hands together behind his head. "What is wrong with these people? They're savages, pure and simple!"

Porter's outburst helped to drown out some of the sounds that were coming from the scene in the cathedral. But they couldn't mask the visuals. What Riley saw turned his stomach. Such raw, animal cruelty.

Oh, God, repay these men for what they're doing! Let them feel the full extent of Your wrath! I know You say to love your enemies and pray for those who persecute you . . . Sorry, Lord, I just can't right now. I have absolutely zero love for any of them, and my only prayer is that they burn in hell for eternity.

Finally, the head separated and the body fell. The executioner placed Evert's head in the small of the corpse's back facing the camera. The men in black walked off camera.

Riley turned away. He needed to get outside; it seemed like hours since he'd breathed fresh air. But as he reached the door, a voice stopped him. It was Saifullah's. He was back on the screen.

"Allah is a merciful God, but he is also a just God. Righteousness breeds peace, but sin breeds punishment. And the greatest punishment is reserved for those who commit the greatest sins—like the sins of betrayal of Allah and apostasy.

"The Prophet—peace be upon him—has written, 'O you who have believed, do not betray Allah and the Messenger or betray your trusts while you know the consequence.' Let me show you what the face of betrayal looks like."

Saifullah nodded offscreen, and a man walked in. He was leading Khadi.

"No!" Riley yelled. Khadi barely looked like herself—her face was swollen and one eye had half closed. Her hair was frizzed out in some places and matted down in others. But what frightened Riley most—the thing that sent his heart plummeting—was that the fire was gone from her eyes. The fire, the vibrancy, the sparkle that made her stand out from all the other women he had ever known; they had stolen it from her, beaten it out of her. What stood on that screen was not Khadi; it was simply her shell.

"We've got to go now," Riley demanded. "We can't wait for tonight! We've got to go now!"

"Shut up, you fool," Porter yelled. "He's still talking."

Riley spun to face Porter, but Skeeter quickly moved up behind him and took hold of both his shoulders. He squeezed them tightly, and said calmly, "Just listen, Pach."

". . . this afternoon. Then you will see the just punishment of those who betray Allah."

The screen went black.

"What about Khadi? What did he say?"

The truck was silent.

Riley turned to Scott. "Tell me, Scott! What did he say?"

Through water-filled eyes, Scott said, "Pach, man . . . He said that the punishment for the betrayer is the blade." He pulled a handkerchief from his pocket, wiped his eyes, and blew his nose hard. The handkerchief went back into his pocket, and Scott breathed in deeply and huffed it out. When he lifted his eyes back to Riley, all the sorrow was gone—replaced by pure rage. "It's her turn, Riley. One hour from now, at one o'clock, it's Khadi's turn."

FORTY-FIVE

"We've got to go in now!" Riley said to Scott. He knew he was out of control and desperate, but he couldn't help himself.

"We can't. The HERF is still on its way," Scott replied helplessly. "We launch now, and the whole place will go up."

"Well, we've got to do something!" Riley looked around at the other faces in the truck. "Come on, we've got the heads of every counterterrorist agency in America here short of the CIA, and you can't think of anything? Castillo? LeBlanc? Stanley?"

"Riley, until the HERF gets here, our hands are tied," Stanley Porter said.

"Which will be one hour too late, right?" Riley watched as the eyes of all the others lowered to the ground. "Right? We'll launch an hour after they use a dull knife to hack off Khadi's head. That's what you're telling me? That's your plan?"

"No, Pach," Scott said bitterly. "We'll

maintain our 2300 launch time, because by two o'clock there won't be any need to go in early."

Riley locked stares with Scott. Both men could see the pain in each other's eyes—the soul-crushing helplessness. Riley turned away.

I can't believe it! One hour late? I can't let it happen. I can't just let them kill her—not when I'm standing so close. God, show me what to do! Isn't there some way . . . ?

"Call him," Riley said to Scott, the first inklings of a plan forming in his brain.

"Uh-uh," Edward Castillo said. "He made it clear that we only call during prearranged times. You call now, you're risking lives."

"Listen, Castillo, maybe you can sit here on your thumb while Khadi dies, but I'm not having it!" Riley took his friend by the shoulder. "Scott, he's playing a game now. The whole reason he's picked her out is because of what he knows it will do to you. He's there waiting for your call right now."

"But then we're just playing into his hand," Craig LeBlanc protested. "You give in to his games, then soon he's pulling all the strings."

"He's already pulling all the strings," Riley countered. "What can it hurt, Scott? A little humiliation, some begging and pleading—who knows, maybe, just maybe, it'll help. And if it doesn't . . . if it doesn't, man, at least you know you tried. You can't let her die without at least trying."

Scott's eyes went to Porter, who said, "It's your call."

Scott nodded, looked at Riley, and said, "Start praying."

He pressed a button on his earpiece. Tara, who had shown up at the RoU late last night, answered.

Scott said, "Babe, put me through to Saifullah. . . . Yes, I know; that's why I'm calling—I'm gonna see if I can talk him out of it. . . . Thanks, Tara. Now put me through."

As Riley watched this, instead of praying, he was processing. *Eye on the ball, identify the defenders, pick your moment.*

"Yes, I know I'm not. But you've been expecting my call anyway, haven't you? . . . You know exactly why," Scott said, moving
away from the bolted table. He turned and faced the back corner
of the command center. "I'm asking you to please reconsider
and show mercy to Khadi. . . . Yeah, but aren't you guys always
talking about the merciful Allah, the gracious Allah?"

Skeet's the only one now. Riley chanced a glance at Skeeter and
saw he was looking at the floor, concentrating on Scott's words.

"Yeah, but why now? Wouldn't it be better if you—?"

Riley launched. He drove his body into Scott's back, pinning
him against the wall. The force of the blow drove the air out of
Scott's lungs, and Riley felt his friend's legs buckle. With a swift
move of his hand, he snatched the earpiece and let him drop.

Everyone in the truck seemed to recover all at once from
their momentary shock. Anger flared, and the men rushed Riley.

"Give that to me," Porter yelled, stepping over Scott. "Do
you know what you've done?"

Instead, Riley pulled out his .44 magnum and pointed it
at Porter. In response, Porter and all the others pulled their
weapons and pointed them at Riley.

"Don't come any closer, Stanley. You either, Skeet. Khadi's
life is on the line, so don't test me." With his other hand, Riley
fitted the earpiece into his ear.

"What's going on?" he heard. "Ross, talk to me, or I'll kill
her right now!"

"I'm serious; back off," Riley said to Porter and the rest.
They took a step back.

"Is this the crazy old man from the video?" Riley asked.

"Who is this? How dare you talk to me like . . ." But then
Saifullah paused. When he spoke again, his voice was much
softer and much more pleasant. "Would I have the pleasure to
be speaking to Riley Covington?"

308 // INSIDE THREAT

"It may be a pleasure for you, but it's certainly not for me," Riley said, turning the gun on Skeeter, who was walking toward him.

Skeeter reached out, took the gun from Riley's hand, and said softly, "You're safe. Finish your call." He slipped the gun into his belt, then bent down to help Scott back up. One by one, all the other guns went back into their holsters.

Riley turned toward the wall, secure in the knowledge that Skeeter had his back.

"Well, I'm sorry you feel that way, because it truly is a distinct pleasure for me. How often does one get to speak to Captain America himself? Military hero, football superstar—I had a feeling you might be dropping by. May I ask if you are going to end this call by dropping the phone into a bucket of Gatorade?"

That was an unexpected shot, Riley thought, surprised at the feeling of embarrassment. *Come on, focus. Your job is to knock him off his game, not the other way around.*

"Listen, old man, I didn't just sucker punch my best friend so that I can stand here and banter with you."

"Then why did you come on the line, Riley?"

"Because I wanted to let you know that I'm coming to kill you."

Saifullah grunted. "That doesn't sound very Christian of you, Mr. Covington."

"Cutting someone's head off on live TV isn't very Muslim of you. Oh, wait; I forgot. You practice that special kind of Islam—the kind where you decide who lives and who dies all by yourself and twist the words of your holy book to suit your own pathetic purposes."

The hardness was back in the imam's voice when he said, "You seem to forget that I am the one holding all the cards here. I could put a bullet in your dear little Khadi's head right now."

"Yeah, you could. But then you'd miss the opportunity to do it to me instead."

There was a pause on Saifullah's end of the line. Then he said, "I'm listening."

"Straight up swap—me for her."

Riley heard Scott yell, "No!" but he didn't turn around.

"That's right, old man. You can be the one who finally puts Riley Covington—American hero, destroyer of the Cause, killer of countless Islamic terrorist whacked-out nut jobs like yourself—out of commission. She comes out; I come in—unarmed, hands over my head."

Saifullah seemed to be considering it. Then he laughed. "This has *trap* written all over it. I was not born yesterday."

"No trap. You have my word. We meet at the door. She comes out; I go in. Come on, she's just another woman. Think of the statement my death will make. Can you imagine millions of Americans watching my head come off? How demoralizing would that be?"

"But that's exactly why it has to be a trap. Why else would you do it, knowing you're a dead man?"

"If you have to ask, you wouldn't understand. Now, do we have a deal?"

"How do you know I won't just kill the both of you?"

"Because I believe that, despite all you've done, you're a man of your word."

Silence. "I will have no mercy on you."

"I wouldn't expect any."

"When?"

"Two hours."

"One."

"One and a half."

"One."

"Fine," Riley said.

"You come shirtless with your hands above your head. When I see you coming up the stairs, the woman will show at the door. When you walk in, she will walk out. That is my word."

"I'm still going to find a way to kill you," Riley said.

"I'll see you at 1:30," Saifullah said, then hung up.

Riley turned around and was knocked backward by a fist to his jaw. Skeeter quickly jumped in, holding Scott back.

"You idiot! You shortsighted imbecile! Do you ever think things through, Riley, or do you just act on the first, simple-minded, testosterone-laced impulse that pops into your mind?" Scott yelled. His face was beet red and his eyes were bulging. "Don't you realize that that guy's going to haul you from the door right into Wilson Bay, turn on his camera, and cut your brainless head off?"

"No, he won't," Riley said, rubbing his jaw. "He's going to knock me around a bit first. He's going to savor the kill. He won't kill me right away."

"So what? Whether it's right away or whether he waits an hour, he's still going to kill you!"

"Not if you kill him first," Riley said staring hard at his friend. "My arrival there will be enough of a distraction—and believe me, I'll be causing a scene—for you to get the ops teams into place. The president gave the go-ahead for the operation. This truck is setting the time. So move it up. As soon as the HERF arrives, you launch."

"And what if it's not in time, Riley? What if the thing arrives ten minutes too late? Or what if we can't pull off the positioning?"

Riley held Scott's gaze. "First of all, Scott, I want you to remember that if something goes wrong, *I* made this choice. I know that the odds are low, and I accept it. If I die, it's because of something I did, not because of something you didn't do. Understand?"

Scott didn't answer.

"But second, man—and I want you to think about this— what else could I do? I love that woman. I love her like I love no one else in this world. Think about it; if that was Tara in there, what would you be doing?"

When Scott still remained silent, Riley said, "Exactly! And there's no better way for me to love Khadi than for her to come walking out while I go walking in."

"This is your call, Scott," Porter said from the table. "Riley's not the one running the show here, so don't let him make the decision. If you say go, he'll go. But if you say no, he won't leave this truck."

Scott looked to the ground. Riley could see him wrestling.

"Come on, Scott. Please. I have to do this."

Without looking up, Scott said simply, "Okay." Then he turned and walked out of the truck.

Riley dropped down to a squat. *Thank You, Lord, for having him say yes. Thank You.*

But in that moment the reality of what he'd just signed on for hit him full force. He dropped his head into his hands. *Please, God, save me. Get that HERF here in time. Give Scott and the ops protection and success. I don't . . . I don't want to go through what I saw on that video screen. Oh, God, it terrifies me! I can't . . . I can't imagine . . .*

Skeeter's hand rested on his shoulder. Riley opened his eyes and saw the big man squatting next to him. Everyone else was watching him too.

Riley said, "Skeet, I'm okay. I just need . . . just a little time to process."

Skeeter nodded and stood up. All the others turned back to the table to focus on the upcoming assault.

You know my heart, Lord. I'm willing to do whatever You want me to do. I really don't want to go through this, but . . . but it doesn't really matter what I want, does it? I want Your will to be done—not my will, but Yours. So do it, Lord; do Your will. And no matter what happens to me . . . well, all I ask is that You give me the strength to make You proud all the way to the end, whatever that end may turn out to be.

CHAPTER

FORTY-SIX

"Hey, Riley," one of the line cops said as Riley passed him.

"How's it going?" Riley stopped briefly to shake the man's hand.

"Riley, what's up?" Riley fist-bumped another cop a few more yards down the security line.

"Riley, way to stick it to Bellefeuille," called out a longhaired law enforcement agent who had *US Marshal* written all over him.

"Thanks, buddy," Riley said.

All the greetings and encouragement from the cops was nice. *I guess once you're behind the lines, they just assume you're supposed to be here. And having Skeeter at my shoulder definitely helps cut down on the challenges.*

But as nice as this is, this isn't what I need. I need some quiet, some solitude, so I can process things through. An idea struck him.

He turned back to the US Marshal. "Hey, Deputy . . ."

"Kimmin. Pat Kimmin."

"Deputy Kimmin. How's it going, man? Hey, I've got a huge favor to ask you. Just between you, me, and the wall, I'm about to get pulled into this thing in a pretty major way. I'm looking for a little me-time to try to get my head around this."

Kimmin nodded. "Gotcha. You're looking for a vehicle to crash out in for a time."

"Exactly."

"You've come to the right place, my man. Follow me."

Riley and Skeeter followed Kimmin to an area just inside the cordoned-off zone that had seven or eight cars all parked together. Most looked like your typical government-issue sedans. But there were a few that stood out—a bright-yellow Hummer, a dark-blue early seventies Chevy Nova SS, and a black, late-model Ford Mustang.

Kimmin pulled a key fob out of his pocket and pressed twice. The lights on the Mustang flashed.

"You Marshals get all the cool rides," Riley said.

Kimmin smiled. "Nothing like a good drug seizure to keep you driving in style." He handed the keys to Riley. "Take as much time as you need, and feel free to idle it so you can run the AC—give the press toads behind you a little black lung." Turning to Skeeter, he said, "You, my friend, are going to have to slide that seat way back."

"Don't sweat me, man. I'm good," Skeeter said, putting out his fist.

Kimmin bumped fists with Skeeter, then gave Riley a slap on the back. "As much time as you need," he reminded them as he turned to go.

"Sure you don't want to come in?" Riley asked Skeet.

"Nah, you need the space. I could use the fresh air after that truck."

Riley opened the door of the Mustang and thought, *This car is beautiful! If I'm going to spend the last hour of my life anywhere, it might as well be in here.* Then he caught himself. *Quit thinking that way. Scott's got a plan, and God's got you in his sights.*

Riley eased himself onto the black-and-white rally-striped leather bucket seat and leaned his head back against the embossed Shelby cobra. His hand rested easily on the white ball of the shifter. *Oh, I am so getting one of these.*

He started the engine and listened to the throaty rumble. Suddenly, he had the urge to put the car in gear and tear out of there. He could drive through the afternoon and be three states away by the time it got dark. If anyone caught up with him, he could just claim PTSD, get a little counseling, and all would be well.

Khadi . . . how'd you get yourself caught up in this? This shouldn't be our battle! Why'd you leave CTD to begin with? You could be saving people rather than having to be saved yourself! The whole situation just sucks so bad! I didn't ask for any of this! I was done!

Why me, God? Why do I have to be the one to go in there? Do You know what they're going to do to me? They're going to beat the living crap out of me! Then, unless Scott can pull another miraculous rescue out of his hat, they're going to take a dull knife and cut my head off!

Oh, God, I so don't want to do this! Please, if there is any other way, show me now! The car had cooled down quickly, and Riley turned the air-conditioning to low. Taking his cell phone out of his pocket, he dialed a number.

"Where are you, son?" Grandpa answered on the second ring. "Are you at the cathedral?"

"Yeah, Gramps, I am."

"What's going on? I can hear it in your voice that there's something happening. Is Khadi okay?"

Riley pressed in the clutch and began cycling the Mustang through its six gears. "So far. They're going to kill her, Grandpa."

"I know. I saw the video. Have you and Scott and the rest of the folks there come up with a way to get her out?"

"Well, yeah . . . yeah we have." He dropped the car back into neutral and let out the clutch.

"What is it, son?" Riley could hear the anxiety building in Grandpa's voice. "Talk to me, boy."

"Are you with Mom?"

"Not yet. I'm in the car heading over there now."

Tracing the silver mustang on the middle of the steering wheel, Riley said, "We're doing a swap, Grandpa. Straight up—me for her."

Grandpa said nothing.

"It was the only way I could think of. Any rescue assault couldn't be carried out until at least two. That's an hour too late. So I offered myself—and the whack job jumped at the chance to do a number on Captain America. It buys Scott a little more time, and it buys Khadi's life."

"Does it buy Scott *enough* time?"

"I don't know, Grandpa." Riley leaned his head back and squeezed his eyes shut. "I don't know."

Both men were silent awhile. Finally, Grandpa said, "I won't tell your mother. She's frantic enough about Khadi. And with Jerry's passing, if she knew there was a possibility that you might . . ."

"Actually, Grandpa, she knows. Well, not all the details, but she knows I'm here. Believe it or not, she's the one that told me to come save Khadi."

Grandpa gave a mirthless chuckle. "Oh, I believe it, all right. That sounds very much like your mom. Still, I don't think she planned on you going in there to take Khadi's place."

"No, you're right."

"I have to tell you, Riley—straight up and honest—I don't have a good feeling about this. I really don't."

That wasn't what Riley wanted to hear. But he also didn't want Grandpa to sugarcoat things. "I don't have a good feeling about this either, Grandpa. But what else am I going to do? It's my life for Khadi's life. I have no option."

Riley opened up a storage compartment on the center console. Inside were a .38 special, a pack of Camels, and some Trident. *Either he just got this car, or he's very careful not to smoke in here, because it still smells new.* He stole a piece of the gum and popped it in his mouth.

"Are you sure? There's no other way to buy time? Nothing Scott can do with ops to neutralize the situation? No way to negotiate her release?"

"There's nothing, Grandpa. This guy's sociopathic—absolutely no mercy. Believe me, if there were another way . . ."

"I know, I know. I just had to ask," Grandpa said, the pain in his voice tightening his words. "Oh, Riley . . . Riley, my dear boy . . ."

"Is there any way you could pray for me, Grandpa?" Riley asked, closing the center console and leaning his head forward on the cool leather of the steering wheel.

After a time, Grandpa spoke, his voice low and strong. "Our Father, almighty creator of the universe, everlasting Lord, Holy One of Israel, I . . . I don't even know how to pray to You right now. Protect my grandson. He's all his mom and I have left in this world. You know his heart. You know the kind of man he is. And as much as his mom and I love him, I know that You love him far more.

"You said, 'Greater love has no man than to lay down his life for a friend.' Riley is taking that to heart, Lord. He is living it out. And in the same way we can be saved for eternity through Your perfect sacrifice, we pray that Khadi will take this opportunity to find her salvation in You because of Riley's actions. Riley's eternity is secure; he's at peace with You. Please let Khadi find that same security and peace. If she does, then we can both say that whatever happens to this boy of mine would truly have been worth the price.

"Now, Lord, strengthen this man. Give him the integrity to show Your love to his enemies. Help him to forgive those who desire to cause his death. Let him be a perfect example of who You are—a light in the darkness that's overtaken that cathedral. And, Lord, as we prayed for Khadi, we pray for these men. Let them find You. They are no different than we once were, sinners in need of a Savior. They have been deceived into following a lie—a lie that's about to take them to their deaths. Have mercy on them, O God.

"Precious Savior, I plead with You to please bring this boy back to his mother and me. But if You don't . . . if You don't, then help us to keep trusting You. Your will be done, Lord. Your will be done. . . . Amen."

"Amen," Riley agreed. "Thanks."

"I'm just pulling up in front of your mom's house. Do you want to say anything to her?"

Riley considered a moment. "No, I . . . I think we said it all already. Just tell her how much I love her."

"You got it. I love you, boy."

"I love you, too, Grandpa."

Riley pressed End and stared at the dash controls glowing a faint blue. He looked to the lower left of the console and found a little wheel. He spun it upward, and the blue light got brighter. *That's better,* he thought.

Thanks, God, for Grandpa.

As he prepared to slip his phone into his pocket, he had another thought. Bringing up Keith Simmons's number, he typed, *At cathedral. Don't call, just PRAY! If something happens to me, Parker house goes to your NYC ministry. Love you, bro!*

A few minutes later, his phone chirped. He read, *Put u on chain—EVERYONES PRAYING! Gods got his eyes on u. U already owe me house after burning down my cabin! Love u, bro!*

Riley chuckled and slid the phone into his jacket pocket. He tried to think of anyone else that he needed to connect with but couldn't come up with any names. He checked his watch and saw that time was getting short.

Then, suddenly, a name did pop into his mind. *Duh! How could I possibly have missed that?* He pulled the keys from the ignition, pushed open the door, and spotted Skeeter leaning against the Hummer.

"Come on, buddy," he called out. "I've got one more thing I need to do." And he took off running, with Skeeter close behind.

Khadi lay shivering on the cold stone bench in Wilson Bay. Her head rested on the corner of a long red bench cushion. After the second beating, which had come immediately following Bill Evert's murder and her video appearance—*live and in person*—Alavi apparently had found the last fading spark of compassion left in his cold, dark heart. Although he wouldn't allow her battered body the comfort of actually lying on the cushion, he did provide her with just enough padding to rest her swollen head.

But you will not break me! I don't care what you do to me; I will go out of this life with my head high. And if I find a way to take one of you with me, then you better say your prayers.

Letting her watch the execution of Bill Evert had been the exact wrong thing for Saifullah to do. Watching his strength in the midst of an unspeakable death relit a fire in her soul that had been in danger of going out last night. From the moment the tarp was rolled up, her mind had begun singing "God Bless America," "The Star-Spangled Banner," and strangely enough for her, that hymn from the funeral—"A Mighty Fortress"—and it hadn't stopped.

So despite the fact that her body was rebelling against her and she had lost all feeling in her extremities due to the zip ties, her mind was sharp, and her will was strong. She had no idea when they were going to come for her—when her neck would be offered up to the knife—but she didn't care anymore. Her peace had been made with God, even though she still wasn't sure which God. She had prayed that the one true God would hear her prayers and show her mercy. *There's not really anything else I can do, is there?*

"Come on, old man, what are you waiting for?" she called out. She was ready to die now, but she wasn't convinced that she'd still have this strong of a resolve a few hours from now. *If I'm going to go, I'm going to go in my time and with my head held high! And maybe with one parting shot at whoever gets closest to me.*

"What's wrong, you raggedy-bearded psychopath? You afraid I might bite? Oh, Saifullah . . . come out, come out wherever you are! Here, boy! Come on, boy!"

Majid Alavi came striding in, his face red with anger.

"Oh, the big dog's sent his little lap—"

Her final word was cut off as Alavi pulled the cushion from under her head, letting her skull hit the stone with a *thunk*. Khadi's brain was just beginning to process through the pain when she felt the cushion pressed down tightly on her face. Her zip-tied body flopped like a fish out of water as she tried to find a way to get some air. Finally, when she was just starting to gray out, he lifted the cushion.

Khadi sucked air deep into her lungs. Pain, fear, adrenaline, and relief all rushed through her body, making the world around her spin.

Alavi leaned in close. "Shut . . . your . . . mouth," he hissed.

Khadi spit in his face, and the cushion went back on. This time she knew she was a dead woman and was just making peace with the fact when the darkness finally lifted and the sweet air poured into her starving lungs.

"Have you had enough?" Alavi asked. But this time he stood a little farther back, and the projectile from Khadi's mouth fell short of its mark. Alavi's hand hit the side of Khadi's face once, twice, three times, sandwiching her head against the stone bench. Khadi's world spun again.

"Hey, Alavi," she said, her voice barely above a whisper, "you still beat your wife?"

"Your time is soon."

"Bring it on, little man—lapdog."

Alavi turned to go but stopped short. "Actually," he said with a smile, "I think your time has arrived."

He stepped back, and Saifullah, the cameraman, and the two executioners walked into the bay. Hard as she tried, she couldn't take her eyes off the long blade that hung in the one man's belt.

"I hear you were calling for me," Saifullah said.

"And you came—I'm touched," Khadi replied in a voice that was half mumble, half groan.

"I came because it was time, not because you called."

"Probably an important point for you, but for me—not so much," Khadi said with all the false bravado she could muster. But inside, she was screaming. *I can't imagine that knife on my neck! Please, no! Someone—God, Scott, anyone—please keep me from that blade!*

"Your eyes betray you, little girl," Saifullah said with a smile. "Why do I feel your courage is all talk?"

"Take these cuffs off, and we'll see how much is all talk. Five men in this room, and you still have to keep the little girl tied up." *Come on, rise to the challenge . . . take the bait!*

Instead, Saifullah turned to the executioners. "I'm tired of hearing the ranting of this mongrel whore. Silence her."

Khadi's eyes went wide. *Wait, this isn't the way it's supposed to be! What about the camera? What about Saifullah's speech? Aren't I supposed to have an opportunity to read a false confession? I'm not ready for this! God, help me! Please, God, help me!*

Despite the duplicity of her eyes, Khadi kept a reasonably strong facade. Her face was tight and she pressed her lips closed, not trusting what might come out of them if they parted.

The man not holding the long blade moved quickly toward Khadi. With small wire cutters, he snipped the tie off her ankles. Immediately, blood began flowing back to her feet, causing her to bite back a scream. He grabbed her by her arms and flung her to the ground. She skidded to a landing up against Wilson's tomb.

The man with the blade lifted Khadi by the hair. The pain was excruciating, and she tried to take some of the pressure off by bringing her knees up under her. But she still didn't have any strength in them after being tied up for so long, and they flailed around beneath her.

Saifullah leaned down to Khadi's face. "Prepare to see hell, *gehbah*."

Khadi closed her eyes and heard the long knife slide out from the executioner's belt. The cold, dull blade rested against her tight neck, then pulled across it. She cried out, the executioner released her hair, and she fell hard to the ground.

She lay there gasping and weeping—confused, relieved, angry, hurting. *What happened? What just happened? I'm not dead—I know that because I'm in too much pain.*

A shoe wedged itself under her chest and rolled her over. Her eyes opened, and she saw all five men laughing cruelly at her.

"I think a quick death is a little too good for you," Saifullah said. "I've got something else in mind that will burn like a coal in your heart for the rest of your miserable, traitorous life."

The cuffs on her wrists were cut, and pain again shot

through her body. A cold, wet towel was thrown on the floor in front of her.

"Clean yourself up," said Alavi.

Khadi tried to grasp the towel but found she couldn't control her fingers. Instead she lifted it between her wrists and wiped her face across it. The pain was intense, but with every swipe came renewed hope.

The rest of my life, he said. I think that means I'm going to live! I don't know what just happened, but, God, if that was You—thank You! Thank You so much!

"That's enough; it's time," Alavi said.

He snatched the towel from her hands and lifted her to her feet. She took one last look at Saifullah and was chilled to the bone at the pure evil that was in his smile. He nodded to her, then walked away.

Alavi tightly gripped her upper arm and pulled her forward. Stumbling, she followed him. The footsteps of the other three men echoed behind her. Turning to her right, she could see all the hostages watching her. *Where is he? Where is he? There!*

In the midst of all the bewildered and anguished faces, Alan Paine gave her an encouraging smile and a thumbs-up. Then he pointed to the sky for a moment before reverting back to the thumb. Khadi wished she could say thank-you, wished she could tell him how he had saved her life last night—*I'll say it when I come back to get you,* she promised silently.

She was nearing the front door when one of the terrorists pulled it open. *It's really true. They're letting me go. Oh, thank You, God!*

Alavi released her with a push, and she stumbled into the light of a September afternoon. Reaching out to steady herself, she caught hold of the handrail. *Free! I'm free! I can't believe—*

At the bottom of the stairs was Riley, shirtless, walking her way.

Confused questions flew through her mind. *Did he do this?*

Was Riley the one who negotiated my release? Is he really my knight in shining armor? Why is he looking at me like that? She wanted to run to him, but her legs were still shaky. She took a tentative step, both hands glued to the rail.

Slowly he approached—one step at a time. She couldn't remember the last time she had seen him not take stairs two steps per stride. *Something's wrong! This doesn't feel right! Come on, Riley! Come and get me!*

His hands slowly raised and locked behind his head. Two red dots danced on his chest. *Why are they laser-sighting him? He's unarmed—can't they see that?*

Their eyes locked, and what she saw sent terror into her heart. Nowhere was the joy, the relief that should have been there. Instead, what she saw was trepidation, determination, fear, sorrow.

But then, like a ray of sun cutting through a sky full of clouds, his face slipped into a soft smile, and that smile said it all. It was full of peace and love. The peace she knew was because of his faith in his God; the love was all for her.

It dawned on her what was happening. Her knees buckled, and she steadied herself with the handrail.

"Riley, what are you doing?" She said with a hoarse croak. "No! You can't do this! I refuse! I won't let you do this, Riley."

But Riley just kept walking and held that same smile that said more than any volume of love poems ever could. He was just a few feet away now, and she reached out her hand to him. "No, Riley. Please, no!"

Her fingers landed on his stomach, and she dug her nails in, trying to stop him. But they just left red trails across his flesh until there was no more of him to hold on to. And all the while, his eyes never left hers until he was past.

She spun around in time to see him step into the cathedral. The doors closed.

"No!" she cried out. "Riley, no!"

She tried to pull herself back up the stairs, back in the direction she had come, back to Riley so they could go to their deaths together like some twisted, modern Romeo and Juliet.

Suddenly, hands were on her, lifting her easily. In a brief moment, she was scooped up and held to her rescuer's chest.

It was then she recognized Skeeter and knew the battle was over. Once in his arms, she never considered fighting him—never tried to talk him out of his destination. When Skeeter Dawkins had a plan in mind, it would get done.

Instead she wrapped her arms around Skeeter's neck and began to cry.

FORTY-EIGHT

Gunmen grabbed Riley and roughly shoved him forward as soon as he walked in.

"I'm here, everyone," he called out as he stumbled. "Captain America's come to save the day!"

Something hard hit him squarely between the shoulders, dropping him to his knees. Riley turned to see a man in black holding his assault weapon butt first.

Create as much havoc as possible, he thought. *Anything you can do to get everyone's attention so that Scott and the guys can get into place.*

"Why, Majid Alavi! As I live and breathe," he said to the man who had hit him. Alavi pulled up short on his next blow. "Oh, don't look so surprised. I saw you on the surveillance cameras. I know all about you."

He dropped his voice to a stage whisper. "I hear your dad stunk rocks as a clothes salesman."

Alavi launched at Riley, gun butt first. In a move he hadn't used since his Air Force

Special Ops training, Riley grabbed hold of the gun and pulled hard, yanking Alavi off balance. At the same time, he rocketed himself to his feet, driving his shoulder into Alavi's chest. Just like he'd done against blocking sleds since he was twelve, he pushed the man backward until a pillar stopped their momentum. All of Alavi's air rushed from his lungs.

Riley swung the terrorist in front of him, pulled the pistol that was in the man's belt, and held it to his head.

"Stop where you are," he yelled to the rapidly approaching gunmen. Alavi was gasping for breath, and the back of his head was bleeding. "Come any closer and stinker here gets popped." Then to Alavi, he said, "And you really do stink. Do you guys ever bathe? You smell worse than a hockey goalie's equipment bag."

"Drop the weapon now!" said one of the gunmen.

Recognizing him, too, Riley said, "Forget it, Saliba. By the way, did you tell all your friends here about that girl you knocked up a few years back?"

Saliba made a rush toward Riley and Alavi. Riley fired a shot into the floor. It ricocheted off the tile and embedded itself who knew where. Saliba pulled up, but Alavi took the opportunity to try to pull away.

Riley cinched his hold around Alavi's neck tighter and clocked him hard on the side of the head with the pistol.

"Wait a second, this is Khadi's gun," Riley said, giving him two more hits. Alavi was bleeding from four places on his head now.

As Riley looked around, every eye was on him—hostages and gunmen. Not one terrorist that he could see was watching out the windows or looking at the stairs. *Freaking amateurs!*

"Stop! No more," said a new voice. Riley looked over and saw Saifullah walking toward him. He had an aura of smoldering rage about him, and Riley knew he was no one to underestimate. Walking just behind the imam was another gunman—*Bazzi, I think.* He was calmly leading Senator Lowell Martin, holding a pistol under the taller politician's chin.

"Drop the gun, Mr. Covington, or Mr. Bazzi will kill the senator."

Riley laughed. "What, like that's a threat? Have you seen the crap that's been coming out of Washington lately?"

"The time for joking is over," Saifullah said, and Bazzi cocked the gun.

"Okay, okay," Riley said. "Don't get your ceremonial loin-cloth in a bunch."

He shoved Alavi hard, and the terrorist sprawled out on the floor. "It's just, I've got this thing about being touched," he said, as he slid his gun away, "so if you could please just tell your boy here . . ."

He stopped talking when Saliba pulled a new weapon as he strode toward him. Riley looked down at his bare chest and saw a red dot.

"Not good," Riley said, just before two prongs released from a Taser gun and embedded in his chest. His whole body clenched, and he dropped to the ground. He had been tasered before as part of his Special Ops training, but that had lasted only five seconds. This just rolled on and on as the electricity pulsed through his body.

As soon as the current stopped, the pain stopped. But his muscles were exhausted from the strain. Opening his eyes, he saw Majid Alavi standing over him.

He was holding a long metal rod.

Riley lifted his hands to protect his head. But that left the rest of his body exposed. The first five blows landed across his back, sending shocks of pain from his spine and kidneys. He rolled and tucked himself into a fetal position.

Help me, God! Help me! "*The Lord is my shepherd, I shall not want. . . .*"

The first rod was joined by a second and then a third. Blow

after blow fell on him—bruising ribs until they cracked; crushing the knuckles on his fingers as they tried to protect his head; breaking joints as ankles, knees, elbows, and shoulders were targeted.

"He makes me lie down in green pastures, He leads me beside quiet waters, He restores my soul. . . ."

Riley's battered fingers gave way, and the blows began landing on his unprotected skull. Each crack seemed to knock him momentarily outside himself, before the pain snapped him back into reality.

He walks . . . He walks me beside . . . the valley of shadows. . . . He guides me . . . in my enemies . . . I will not fear . . . I will not fear . . . I will not fear . . .

"Enough!" a voice called out. A stillness like the eye of a hurricane descended on the scene. But even though the rods had stopped landing, phantom blows kept raining down on Riley's body as his nerves and brain danced, trying to process what had just happened.

Eventually, the contortions stopped, but the pain didn't. It was like nothing Riley had ever felt before, and it made him scared to even breathe in. Then fingers grabbed his ear, twisting it and lifting his head up from the tile. Riley fought down a scream.

"My father is a great man," Alavi said.

Riley tried to smile, but his face instead contorted in something that was very much not smile-like. "That's . . . what . . . Saliba's mother . . . said." The semilaughish convulsion his body made sent blood and spit shooting out his nose and mouth.

Alavi threw Riley's head down onto the tile.

"I said enough! We are scheduled to go live in six minutes," Saifullah said. "I don't want to be delayed by having to wait for him to regain consciousness. Bring him."

FORTY-NINE

Scott watched Riley entering the cathedral. The small handheld monitor didn't give the cleanest of pictures, but it was clear enough for Scott to know that his friend was in trouble. Two of the terrorist foot soldiers were stationed on either side of the door, and Majid Alavi was waiting for him. Scott's foot tapped nervously, and his forehead beaded with sweat. The rest of SOG Bravo ops—Skeeter, Gilly Posada, Ted Hummel, Kim Li, Matt Logan, Steve Kasay, and Carlos Guitiérrez—watched on a monitor set into a tech bay in their deployment van.

"Careful, buddy," Li said.

"Get ready, boys. Let's see just how much of a stink Pach can raise," Scott said.

Everything depended on how much of a distraction Riley could make. He was going to have to make a spectacle of himself, and he was going to have to suffer the consequences.

Scott still hated the plan, but Riley had made sure it was a *fait accompli* with

Saifullah—and it did get Khadi out. But the whole premise was just so wrong. The chances of everything falling exactly into place and Riley walking out of that cathedral alive were less than one in ten. In other words, Riley was walking into a death trap.

His anger had still been hot when Riley had shown back up at the command center truck. Now he wished he could have that time back. Riley had hugged him, but he had barely returned the embrace. Instead, he had quickly released him and turned back to the plans laid out on the table. Riley and Skeeter had stepped to a corner of the truck and had a long, low conversation. Scott watched out of the corner of his eye as Riley handed something to Skeeter, embraced him, then walked out of the truck.

Now he was determined to get his friend out of there, even if it was just so he could apologize for being such a jerk.

"Remember, Riley's counting on us. No retreat and no excuses," Scott challenged his team.

SOG Bravo was one of four eight-man ops teams preparing for the rescue attempt. SOG Alpha was deploying behind the low stone wall on the north side of the church. Charlie team, an MPDC SWAT group, had dropped themselves down behind the southern side. The final team, Delta, would be following three minutes behind Bravo. Although Delta—SEALs on loan from Little Creek, Virginia—were primarily trained in amphibious operations, their skills in counterterrorism and unconventional warfare were deemed to be a huge asset to the operation. It was a comfort to Scott knowing they had his back.

"I wish we had audio," Li said as Riley began yelling.

"Ooooh," echoed through the van as Riley went down from a gun butt to the back.

"Tara, get ready to scramble the cell coverage on *go*. I don't want any calls from interested onlookers making it into that building. Carlos, Gilly, get on the doors," Scott said. *Come on, buddy, what are you going to do? It's not enough yet. It's not enough. . . .*

Riley launched himself and drove his attacker back into a pillar.

"Go! Go! Go!" Scott yelled.

The rear van doors flew open, and the eight men sprinted low up the grass on the south side of the cathedral. Just twenty yards ahead lay the crypt-level windows that were their destination. Scott ran with everything he had, launching in the air the last few feet and stopping himself with his back flat against the wall. From here on, the survival of everyone in that church depended on the speed and invisibility of Bravo team . . . and on the HERF.

Word was that the HERF was still five minutes out. That was five minutes no one had to spare. If the HERF was late, Riley was a dead man. And if the HERF didn't live up to its billing, they were all going with him.

The glass on the four-foot-square windows was old, which meant thick and one-paned. As Scott watched impatiently, his team paired up at three separate recesses. The men pulled the backing off of a strong adhesive that had been stretched across pre-sized heavy metal plates. Affixed to each plate were four handles and one thick, round piece of felt.

Two of the sheets were secured in just under a minute. However, Kasay and Guitiérrez were still working on theirs.

"What are you doing?" Scott yelled, more as a chastisement than an actual question.

"It's not going in. We're just a fraction of an inch off," Kasay said.

"Logan," Scott ordered.

Logan slid over. He tried the metal plate. "Not gonna work. Either the window's cut smaller or the plate's cut bigger."

"Let's go with two, then," Scott said. "Skeet!"

Skeeter stepped up with a small battering ram. One hard hit onto the felt muffler and the metal plate fell inward with the glass attached. The team members used the handles to keep them from dropping to the ground below.

As the team slipped one by one through the windows, Tara said to Scott, "Get in there, Bravo. They've started beating him."

Don't think about it! Just keep moving! Scott thought as he tried to put out of his mind what was happening to his best friend. He squeezed himself through the opening, landing his rubber-soled boots quietly on the tile floor below.

"ETA for HERF?" he whispered.

"They're still saying five minutes," Tara replied.

They said that five minutes ago! Come on, people!

They had dropped into a vast corridor. Quite a few rooms and alcoves branched off; Scott tried to identify them to get his bearings—Resurrection Chapel, Chapel of St. Joseph of Arimathea, Center for Prayer and Pilgrimage. Taking point, his silenced Bushmaster ACR leading the way, Scott moved forward slowly until he found what he was looking for—the Good Shepherd Chapel and, next to it, the pathway up.

Silently, they took up positions on either side of the opening. The stairway itself was a beautiful work of art, filled with arches and angles. Unfortunately, the design left them little visibility beyond two short landings.

"Bravo in position. Delta clear."

"Delta, roger," came the reply. Scott knew they should be seeing the members of that team in about a minute's time.

"Scott . . . Scott, it's bad," Tara said, her voice strained with tears. "They're . . . Stop it, already! Oh, Riley . . ."

"Just give me the facts, Tara! I can't handle anything else! Where is he?" Scott asked.

"Still at the back of the nave. Wait, they're lifting him. . . . They're dragging him."

"Where're they taking him?" Scott asked, knowing the answer even as he asked the question.

After a long pause, Tara said, "To Wilson Bay, Scott. They took Riley to Wilson Bay."

FIFTY

FRIDAY, SEPTEMBER 16, 1:38 P.M. EDT

Hands went under Riley's armpits, hefting him up. Riley tried to make himself walk so that he wouldn't just be dragged, but nothing was working like it was supposed to. With every click the toes of his boots made over the tiles, pain rocketed up his legs.

From somewhere off to his left, a voice shouted out, "Hang in there, Riley!"

"Shut up," commanded another voice.

"Stay strong, Riley," called a third.

"Shut up, I said!"

"We love you, Riley!"

"Jesus is with you!"

"Shut up!"

"Hang on, man!"

"God's got you in His hands, Riley!"

"Don't let them break you!"

"God bless you, Riley!"

"Shut up! I said, shut up!"

The calls continued as Riley was carried

through an archway into a small room he recognized from the videos. *Wilson Bay. This is it. Better hurry, Scott.*

Riley was flopped down onto a tarp. He looked up to see a camera at the ready.

Hands grabbed him again, and he was leaned in a sitting position against Woodrow Wilson's tomb. Every part of his body was screaming at him, and the weight resting on his battered hips was almost more than he could take.

Saifullah sat on a stone bench across from him. "So, Riley Covington, any regrets yet?"

Riley slowly shook his head. "No regrets," he said in a voice that sounded like he had been tucked away for the last two days in a seedy bar on a weekend bender.

Saifullah leaned forward, his elbows on his knees. "I must admit, you have me baffled. Your reputation is that of a Mr. Perfect—one of those holier-than-thou Christians—but yet you hurl the most offensive of insults at my warriors."

"Told you . . . don't like being touched."

Saifullah smiled. "Also, you are a marvelous football player, but you throw your career away over foolishness."

"*That* is a long story. . . ." *Drag it out. Keep him talking. Hurry, Scott!* "Ever hear of Rick Bellefeuille?"

"And to top it all, in your last act of irrational contradiction, you, a Christian, trade your life for a Muslim—and a woman, no less."

Riley tried and failed to smile again. "That's seriously . . . one of those you-had-to-be-there stories."

Saifullah shook his head. "Even now, at death's door, you are making jokes. It makes no sense."

Riley could feel his strength fading and his mind starting to clutter. *Keep it together. Finish strong.* "Not to you. . . . To me? Perfect sense. . . . It's hope, man. Right here." He nodded toward his chest. "My body? You can have it. . . . My life? Oh, well. . . . My hope? Sorry, bub. Off-limits."

"Two minutes," said Alavi, who looked down at Riley with intense hatred. Riley noticed that he was now the one with the long blade in his belt.

"Well, Riley, I'm afraid your end is at hand," Saifullah said, standing up.

"Old man . . . one more thing. . . . I forgive you." The imam stared at Riley a moment, then turned away.

Looking up at Alavi, Riley said, "I even forgive you."

Alavi responded by bringing his hand across Riley's face, knocking him back to the tiles. Then he began kicking him, one blow after another to his head, his ribs, his gut. Riley wouldn't have believed he could feel more pain, but with each strike, waves of agony like he had never felt before ripped through his already-battered body.

Oh, Jesus, give me strength! You've been here. How did You keep loving? How did You keep forgiving? Help me, Jesus! Help me to die well!

When the cameraman called thirty seconds to air, Alavi stopped. The pain, however, didn't. It was everything Riley could do to suck in a breath of air. He knew at least one of his lungs was punctured, and there must be bones broken throughout his face.

Saifullah took his place in front of the camera. Alavi took a handful of Riley's hair and lifted him up to his knees. The cameraman counted down.

FRIDAY, SEPTEMBER 16, 1:38 P.M. EDT

"From your time with them, did you get any impressions of their ultimate purpose? Are they really going to release the hostages at the end of Ramadan?"

Khadi shook her head and said bitterly, "No one's getting out of there alive, unless we do something about it. I can guarantee you. They'll string us along, then blow the place at the end. All I can say is this rescue better work."

She stood wearily in the command truck. Skeeter had dropped her off here, given her arm a squeeze, then disappeared. She had been quickly whisked inside, where Stanley Porter had been waiting.

He wrapped her up in his arms—gently, but still hard enough to make her wince.

"Are you okay?" he asked.

"I'm fine," she lied. "Tell me about Riley."

"He's in God's hands now, Khadi. Scott's getting his teams in place. We need to pray they get there in time."

Khadi felt her knees buckle. Porter caught her before she could drop.

"Get her something to sit on," he commanded.

Someone pulled out a stool and set it down.

"Move it to the back."

Porter helped Khadi to the stool and eased her down. The trailer spun for a few moments before her equilibrium returned.

Suddenly she shook Porter's hands off her arms.

"Why'd you let him do it?" Khadi demanded, her anger flaring.

"We didn't have a choice, Khadi. He pulled a gun on us, got on the phone with Saifullah, and taunted him into accepting a trade—him for you."

That news shook her. She had thought this had been a CTD plan.

"Why'd he do it, Stanley? It's crazy! It's a suicide mission!"

Porter squatted down and put his hand on her hand. "We both know why he did it. And that's why we agreed. There's no way we could have stopped him. If we had shut down this way in to you, he would have just found another."

"But . . . but . . ." she sputtered, trying to find another argument. Trouble was, she knew he was right. Tears welled up in her eyes. "I'm sorry, Stanley."

Porter waved her apology off. "Listen, Khadi, I've got a couple people here who're going to give you the postincident grilling—you know the drill. Obviously, it's the absolute wrong time to do it, but I need everything you know. If there's anything that can help us . . ."

"Of course. Just . . . keep me updated on Riley, okay?"

"You got it," Porter said, giving her a fatherly stroke of her head.

The questioning came from two CTD agents she had seen before but whose names she couldn't remember even after they reintroduced themselves. She tried to concentrate on giving thorough answers but had a hard time focusing. Every noise, every exclamation from the front of the trailer where the monitors sat drew her attention away.

"Why do you say they're going to blow the cathedral up?" asked the younger of the two agents.

"That's who they are. They're not out for any cause. They're just a bunch of murdering—"

"The Internet feed is up," a voice called from the front of the truck.

Khadi leaped up from the stool and ran to the crowd that had quickly gathered.

"Move," she said. And seeing who it was, the group parted.

As soon as she saw the monitor, she regretted it. The sight of Riley took her breath away. His face looked like a bad make-up job at a high school haunted house. It was so bloody and swollen that she had to strain to recognize any of his features. A random flash of hope told her that maybe it wasn't him, but she knew the truth. She knew.

A couple of unidentified hands placed themselves on her bruised shoulders, but she barely noticed. She began to feel dizzy and realized she had forgotten to breathe. Slowly, she inhaled.

Oh, Riley, why did you do it? I'm not worth it—I'm not worth this! Why would you sacrifice yourself for me?

Then a phrase Riley used to say to her dredged up from the depths of her memory. *"Greater love has no man than to lay down his life for a friend,"* he'd say with a big smile—a smile she couldn't imagine fitting into the jigsaw-puzzle face now before her eyes. Then often he'd follow up with *"And then Jesus went out and proved His love by doing just that—dying for us."*

And now here you are . . . dying . . .

Saifullah was saying something, but Khadi wasn't paying attention. Tears poured down her cheeks as the sorrow and guilt she felt for Riley blended with rage toward Saifullah and Alavi.

Please, Scott, get there in time. Please, Scott . . . Please, Scott . . . Please, God . . . Please, God . . . Please, God . . .

Scott felt the SEALs before he actually saw them—a push of the air, a hand on his shoulder. Turning, he saw their team leader, Schneeberger—no first name offered. Seconds later, Matt Logan appeared at Scott's shoulder.

Looking at the SEAL who had taken a place next to him and at Logan, Schneeberger said softly, "You saw them setting it up on the video, so no possibility of mistakes. Get yourselves orientated before you disable the device. You don't want *hajji* showing up behind you. Get it done, and get back fast."

Logan and the SEAL, both demolitions experts, nodded and began creeping up the stairs. Kim Li followed Logan, while another SEAL tailed his partner.

Scott nodded at Schneeberger. While still in charge of the operation, Scott had no problem delegating elements to those with more skill or experience. The reputation of this Schneeberger guy was that he was one seriously bad dude who had led combat missions in parts of the world that most people had never even heard of. *It's safe to assume he knows his stuff. Although I wonder if I should let him know that* orientated *is not a real word.*

He glanced at his watch and shifted nervously. *What's taking that HERF so long?*

"Tara, sitrep on Riley," he whispered.

"Don't know. He's out of sight. HERF just arrived. Should be online in minutes."

Schneeberger, who was on the same com line, gave Scott an encouraging thumbs-up.

Come on, Logan! Get that wire disabled. Although the trap that had been laid at the top of the stairs was much more elaborate than a simple trip wire, that's still how Scott conceptualized it. He was no munitions expert. *That's what I keep Logan around for—that and the fact he makes killer guac.*

Two clicks on his earpiece signaled that Logan and the SEAL had completed their mission. Scott gave a sigh of relief. Moments later, the four men reappeared. Scott fist-bumped Logan and Li. The SEALs just retook their places in their squad.

"Tara, I need the HERF now," he whispered urgently.

"Less than . . . The Internet feed just went live," Tara said. "Saifullah's talking. Alavi's holding Riley—he has the knife to his neck. Oh, Scott, how is he even conscious—it doesn't even look like him!"

Scott balled his hands into fists and fought back the rage. *I'm so close! I can't let this happen! I should never have let him go in!*

Tara continued to narrate the action on the screen, but Scott wasn't listening. *Please, God, I may not be one of Your church people, but Riley is! Do something! Save him!*

Tara's voice cut through his prayer. Three words—all he needed to hear: "HERF is online!"

"Fire it! All teams go, go, go!"

FIFTY-THREE

It didn't feel like the knife had cut the skin yet, but the constant pressure of the heavy blade on Riley's Adam's apple was causing his gag reflex to want to kick in. He did his best to swallow down the physical irritant, knowing that any sudden movements could lead to more permanent damage.

Saifullah stood in front of him, his long robe reaching the tarp below. *Help me not to hate this man, Lord. I don't want to leave this world with hate in my heart.*

"Men and women of America," Saifullah said with a self-righteous blend of smugness and pomposity, "today it is with great solemnity that I visit justice upon a war criminal of the first order. Allah, in his great beneficence and mercy, has granted a second chance to the betrayer of the faith, Khadi Faroughi. My sincerest hope is that she will use this undeserved blessing to mend the error of her ways and follow the righteous path back to the true submission."

In the midst of the agonizing pain, Riley couldn't help but smile in his heart. *Khadi—safe. That's all I needed to hear. Thank You, Lord, for rescuing her from this fate. You are so good.*

"But where Allah in his wisdom released a minnow, he has used her as bait in order to capture a shark—Riley Covington."

Alavi pulled hard on Riley's hair and twisted his face toward the camera. Behind that lens, millions of people were watching him right now in horror, wondering what he would do. How would the great Riley Covington show his unbroken spirit?

Riley willed himself to do something defiant—call out a patriotic slogan, sing like that senator, put up a fight to get away—but all he could do was stare at the camera. Because the truth was that he truly was broken, at least physically. They had beaten away every ounce of strength he had left. The only thing even keeping him semiupright was the mass of hair in Alavi's hand.

But he still had his heart. They hadn't broken his will. He stared hard into the camera, praying that the people could still see through his eyes that the terrorists had not won.

"This man you see before you—this man your media calls Captain America, as if he were the epitome of all your nation finds true and virtuous—this man is nothing but a criminal of the worst kind. Beginning with his time in the military while participating in your country's unjust incursion into Afghanistan, through his career in the sinister black operations—the activities your rogue government doesn't want you, the citizens, to know about—this man has raped, tortured, and murdered his way through countless innocents. . . ."

Raped? Tortured? Murdered? Lies! Riley said desperately with his eyes. *All lies! Don't believe him! Please, I would never do those things! Don't let that be your final impression of me! Everything I've done, I've done for the good. . . .*

Then something Grandpa had said cut through his growing anguish. *"You got to make sure you're right with God and with the people who love you. Let Him take care of the rest."*

In that moment, all the fear, all the anxiety, all the wondering what was going to happen and how he would be remembered—all of it disappeared. Replacing it was faith—the complete and unquestioning belief that God is on His throne and that Riley was in His hands.

He felt the hardness in his eyes soften. *Lord, do with me what you will. Make this about You and not me. Let me decrease and You increase. Let me fade away, so they can see You—Your love, Your forgiveness, Your salvation.*

Another jerk of his hair brought Riley back into the here and now. Saifullah was still speaking: ". . . and today justice will be carried out. The Prophet—peace be upon him—has written, 'If anyone killed a person not in retaliation of murder, or to spread mischief in the land—it would be as if he killed all mankind.' This man is a murderer of mankind. Today, he receives his retribution."

Saifullah stepped to the side. The blade lifted from Riley's neck.

Father, I am Yours.

The first cut was like fire burning so hot that all the other pain in Riley's body seemed to coalesce itself in that one spot. Then the knife sawed back, taking the agony to a new level.

Please, Lord, let it end quickly! Take me into Your hands!

The blade began its cut back down again—muscle ripped and cartilage tore.

Then the lights went out.

Scott was moving even before the HERF took the power down. *This better work or they're gonna blow the roof of this place down on us!* The stairway went dark.

Scott flattened himself against a stone wall as the sound of breaking glass echoed from above, quickly followed by the ear-splitting staccato of twenty stun grenades detonating.

Immediately, he was back up and running. Fifteen steps later, Scott burst through an arch into a colorful gloom—the only light in the shadowy grey building coming from the stained glass windows above.

Movement caught his eye—he recognized Ubaida Saliba on the ground, pushing a button on a remote control device, once, twice. A round from Scott's Bushmaster stopped him from trying a third time.

Bravo and Delta teams spread out quickly, and the gunfire began. Off in the distant back of the sanctuary, the sound of doors shattering resounded through the cathedral. Scott glanced over to see Alpha and Charlie teams swarming into the nave.

Continuing at full sprint, Scott beelined for Wilson Bay. All around, bullets flew and men dropped to the ground—but whether good guy, bad guy, or hostage, he didn't stop to find out.

To his left, a gunman stepped from behind a pillar, his AK-103 leveled at Scott.

He was pegged, and it was too late for him to do anything about it. *Skeeter, be there! Skeeter, be there!*

A shot from behind Scott caved the gunman's chest in, and he crumpled to the ground. *Skeeter, my man!*

Spotting the arched passage into Wilson Bay, Scott slid to a stop against the pillared entry. Not knowing where Riley was, he fired two rounds high, then ducked back. A volley of bullets flew past him. Then three precise, evenly spaced shots sounded from his right.

Scott dove in and found Saifullah, Majid Alavi, and a third man behind a video camera dead on the ground. Skeeter, who had fired the three shots from the opening to the nave, jumped through, slid over Wilson's tomb, and landed next to Scott.

"Where is he?" Scott yelled.

Skeeter dropped to the ground in response. He threw the dead cameraman out of the way, the body bouncing off Wilson's final resting place.

Now Scott saw him too. Riley had been shoved under a stone bench, a long red cushion placed in front to conceal him. Skeeter already had hold of his shoulders and was gently easing him out.

Scott fell to his knees. "Is he . . . ?" He couldn't bring himself to say the word.

Skeeter's eyes said it all.

"No!" Scott took hold of Riley and pulled him to his chest. The blood from the gaping wound in his neck had slowed to a trickle, but his friend's entire upper body was soaked with it. "Riley, no! No! No! No!"

The gunfire outside was slowing down, but Scott hardly noticed. Skeeter, too, seemed to be in a world of his own—squatting down, his head in his hands.

In his ear, Tara's voice was saying, "What? Scott, what is it?"

He pulled the earpiece and threw it across the bay. "How could this happen, Pach?" Scott asked through his tears. "You're invincible, man. You're Captain America."

A couple of minutes passed while both men grieved in their own ways, until a hand rested on Scott's shoulder. He looked up and saw Gilly Posada.

"We're clear," Posada said softly, the sorrow evident on his face. "Schneeberger needs to talk with you."

Scott nodded. Gently, he laid the body on the tarp and stood up. He was about to tell Skeeter to stay with Riley, but he realized he didn't need to. Reaching around to the back of the big man's neck, Scott pressed his brow to the top of his friend's bald head, then walked out.

FRIDAY, SEPTEMBER 16, 6:10 P.M. EDT

Khadi endured the endless questioning for the next four hours—telling her story over and over again. Finally she pleaded exhaustion and was allowed to go with a sworn promise to be at Homeland Security headquarters at 8:00 sharp tomorrow morning.

As she left the trailer, she spotted a man about ten yards away squatting in the grass. He had a cigarette in one hand and a cell phone in the other.

When he saw her, he said into the phone, "Oh, gotta go." Standing up, he addressed Khadi. "Didn't expect you out quite so soon."

"Yeah, I said I was exhausted, and they let me go until tomorrow morning."

"They're going to be pretty pissed when you don't show," he said.

"They'll get over it," she said with a tired smile.

"I'm Pat Kimmin, US Marshal. Your

friend Skeeter asked me to wait for you. He thought you might be looking to get away for a while."

Khadi eyed the man for a moment, then said, "My friend Skeeter was right."

"Then follow me," Kimmin said, extending his arm, which Khadi took.

They didn't say anything while they wound through the trailers. Finally, they came to a black Mustang.

Kimmin dropped a set of keys into her hand.

"You take care," Kimmin said, opening the door for her. "Just bring her back sometime, or else I'm going to have a boatload of paperwork to fill out."

He gave her a hug, and the smell of tobacco clung to her for a long while after. Slowly, she eased herself through the scurrying foot traffic, found a path out to the road, and pointed the car in the direction of her parents' house in Arlington.

Riley would have loved this car, she thought sadly as she drove down the freeway. *The sound, the colors, the cool white shifter knob. He would have been all over this.*

She burst into tears. The sobs poured out of her so violently that she pulled to the shoulder and parked.

When she first got word of Riley, she was still at the monitors, which had all gone blank when the HERF fired. There was nothing to see, but she stared blankly at the screens anyway, hoping to somehow catch a glimpse of him from the cathedral's security cameras. Then Stanley Porter came over and gently pulled her back a few steps.

Looking in his face, she knew what he was going to say, even before he said it. "Scott and Skeeter found Riley. I'm sorry, Khadi. He's gone."

She had nodded her understanding, then walked to the stool at the back of the trailer. There she had sat, emotionally numb, feeling like she should be crying—wailing—but unable to shed a tear. It was all just so unreal.

After a time, Porter came to tell her that she was needed to complete her debriefing. Again she nodded and let him lead her to another trailer, where the same two CTD agents were waiting for her.

The emotional anesthetization helped her remain business-like throughout the four hours of questioning. But all the while, she knew that her sorrow was just a Dutch boy's finger away from bursting through.

And now, on the side of the freeway, her emotional dike had finally ruptured. It was a full fifteen minutes before she could finally force herself to merge back into traffic. She probably could have stayed there all night, but the overwhelming desire to be with her family pushed her forward.

Her mom answered the door, and soon the whole house rose into an uproar. Most of her extended family were there praying for her and waiting on news. When she simply appeared out of the blue, it was almost as if someone had stepped out of the grave.

This is what I need. Family. Oh, Riley, I wish you'd had time to get to know them all. They would have loved you.

Dad, a physician, tended to her wounds. Mom jumped to her every need. Her brothers swore oaths against the criminals who had done this to her.

After the initial flurry of loving and doting, she realized just how tired she was. Mom turned down the covers on the bed she had slept in until going to college, and her sisters-in-law promised to take turns sitting by her as she slept.

She didn't open her eyes again until morning.

Morning—that was when things started to go wrong. From years of habit, her internal alarm clock stirred her early. Her eyes cracked just in time to see one of her sisters-in-law slipping from her bedroom. *What's going on?* she wondered, still in a half sleep. Part of her felt like she was in a movie, compelled to follow the mysterious apparition.

The aches and pain from her many cuts and bruises made it difficult to pull herself out of bed, but eventually her feet reached the floor. Finding one of her old robes in her closet, she wrapped herself tightly and stepped out of her upstairs room.

Gently, she inched her way down the hallway. Her mind was still foggy, and she wondered if maybe the beatings of the last two days had damaged her more than she realized.

The sound of the morning Ramadan prayers reached her first. An anxious, jittery feeling took hold of her body. Slowly, she peeked around the corner. Down below her in the great room, all the furniture had been pushed to the side, and her entire family were on their knees in prayer—the men in front and the women behind.

Her stomach retched as visions of her captors doing the same thing only yesterday flashed through her head. Stumbling to the bathroom, she vomited noisily. Footsteps echoed up the stairway, and Khadi dove to close and lock the bathroom door before anyone arrived.

The door slammed, and immediately she heard knocking.

"Khadi, are you okay, honey?" her mother called.

"Sweetheart, this is Dad; open the door. I want to make sure you're all right."

"I'm fine," Khadi called out. *Go away! Leave me alone!*

"You may have a concussion. Sometimes the symptoms don't appear until the next day."

"I know that, Dad. Please, everyone, I'm okay. I'm feeling better already."

But she wasn't okay. The vision of her quiet, good, loving, sane Muslim family on their rugs praying to Allah kept intermingling in her head with the evil, radical, violent, terroristic Islamic kooks on their rugs praying to Allah. And as much as she tried to keep the two categories distinct, she couldn't. The lines between moderate and radical danced and twisted and blurred until finally it all coalesced into five words: *I've got to get out!*

She waited until she heard all movement behind the door fade and the prayers begin again below. Slipping out the door, she stealthily made her way back to her bedroom, knowing from her childhood which areas of the carpet were safe to step on and which ones were creaky danger zones.

Once in her room, she changed as quickly as she could into some of her old clothes that still remained in the dresser. Then, spotting the purse her sister-in-law Zanita had left by the bed, she rifled through it. She found a Visa card and slipped it into her pocket.

Phone, phone, she's got to have a phone . . . there! She checked the cell phone but saw that it had only half a charge. *Not worth it,* she thought and left it behind.

After quickly scribbling a note—*Sorry, Zani! I'll pay you back! Khadi*—she slid open her bedroom window, stepped out onto the garage overhang, then dropped painfully into the grass below. The starting of the Mustang's deep-throated engine was to her like the sound a cell door being slid open would be to a prisoner who had just received his walking papers.

As she pulled away, out of the corner of her eye she could see the front door open and her father come running out. *Don't look back! You can't look back!*

Her first stop was to a Verizon store to replace her phone. As soon as she got back to her car, she texted her dad. *Just need some time to work things out. I'll call later in the week. I love you all so much!*

Sending out the text must have activated something in her phone, because all of a sudden voice message after voice message and text after text began coming through.

Ignoring them, she inputted Scott's number and typed, *I'm fine. Just need to process. Please let everyone know. I'll call later.* As soon as the *Message Sent* icon appeared on the phone, she shut it down.

She began driving north and eventually found herself out

on Cape Cod. There, she found a quiet bed-and-breakfast and for the next few days alternated between walking the beaches and crying in her room. Sorrow mixed together with guilt—*I am the reason Riley is dead*—and formed a cocktail of self-loathing that she found bitter but all too easy to drink.

Then, on the third morning, as she was on her way out to the beach, the owner of the B&B—an older woman who had pretty much left her alone until now—said in a low whisper, "I know who you are, Khadi."

Khadi had just nodded, thinking that when she got back from her walk she'd find a new place to stay.

"You know they're all looking for you," the proprietor had said.

"Who?"

"All of them—everybody."

"I'm sure they are," Khadi replied, turning the front door-knob.

"They all say you're a hero."

This stopped Khadi. She turned. "I'm sorry, Mrs. . . ."

"Milholland. But my friends call me Juanita."

"I'm sorry, Juanita, but I'm no hero."

"That's not what everyone's saying."

"'Everyone' is wrong. 'Everyone' wasn't there." Khadi again turned to go.

"Well, some of them were. There's that old lady who was in the church. Then there was another man who was in the church too. Then there was that funny-looking policeman with the goatee—I don't think I care for him much."

"Scott Ross?"

"Oh, honey, I don't know. I'm so bad with names. That's why I didn't recognize yours until this morning."

Khadi stood there processing. *I certainly don't feel like a hero. But maybe—just maybe—Scott and everyone else don't blame me after all. Maybe . . . maybe they still . . .*

"You look like you could use a cup of tea, dear. Why don't you go to the sitting room, and I'll bring you a cup of this new honey vanilla chamomile I found. It's simply scrumptious."

Later that afternoon, Khadi drove back to DC. It took her another day before she summoned the courage to show up at 9:00 p.m., unannounced, at Scott and Tara's front door. But the exuberant reunion she experienced assured her that no matter her own doubts, she was home and she was with family.

EPILOGUE

It's definitely a full house, Khadi thought as she took in the packed House of Representatives chambers. From her place in one of the VIP sections of the gallery, she was able to see the entire House floor—every seat taken except for twelve that were conspicuously draped with American flags. To her left and right were other VIP areas blocked off for the families of the slain.

All told, seven senators and five congressmen had lost their lives, whether by direct assassination or during the rescue attempt. Also lost were two MPDC officers, one SEAL, three Homeland Security ops agents . . . and one superhero. *Riley, I still can't believe you're gone.*

Khadi sighed deeply, picturing a shirtless Riley walking toward her with red dots dancing on his chest—the last time she had seen him. This vision seemed to be with her constantly now—*his eyes, so much love, so much sacrifice.* Khadi knew that with each mental viewing, Riley was becoming more and more perfect. *Soon he'll be floating towards me with wings on his back and a halo around his head . . . which is fine, as long as I can see his face, his eyes.*

Empathetic hands squeezed hers. Gladys Cook followed up her grasp of Khadi's right hand with a gentle pat and a rub. Winnie Covington, however, just kept holding tightly to her left in an apparent attempt to draw out as much strength as she was trying to pour in.

Khadi leaned over and let her head rest on Winnie's shoulder, awkwardly shifting the sunglasses that were partially hiding her healing face. She hadn't seen Riley's mother until earlier this morning, and it had been a bittersweet reunion. Few words were spoken; there would be plenty of time for conversation later.

A couple of days ago, when they had that first tearful conversation on the phone, they had decided that after the service they would take a week together slowly driving back to Wyoming, where friends and family would be gathering for a private memorial. As the two women in the world who had loved Riley most, they looked to each other to help begin their slow healing processes.

Sitting on the other side of Winnie were Riley's grandfather, Skeeter, Scott, and Tara. Behind her were the guys from SOG Bravo minus Ted Hummel, who was still in the hospital recovering from bullet wounds to his forearm and thigh. The RoU analysts were back there, too, as was Keith Simmons.

The only other person Khadi had asked to join her up in the balcony was Alan Paine, who was now seated on the other side of Gladys. That reunion, held just about ten minutes ago, had brought back so many painful memories for Khadi that she had to quickly break off their tearful embrace and walk away.

The ceremony began with a prayer from the House chaplain. Then families of the slain were recognized, including

Winnie Covington and, strangely, Khadi herself. From there, it was a long procession of obituaries, recognitions, stories—some funny and some tearful—and promises to end these kinds of attacks. Khadi listened whenever Riley was spoken of but mostly tuned out the rest. The speeches came from senators, congressmen, several cabinet members including Stanley Porter, and finally, President Donald Lloyd.

Lloyd ended up focusing on Riley more than anyone else, telling the story of their first meeting in the Oval Office. Riley was wearing a smelly, torn T-shirt, shorts, and rubber boots that were caked with mud, having just been snatched away from a clamming expedition in Alaska. Khadi remembered how mortified Riley had been. *But he rose to the occasion—he always did.*

He also told a story that Khadi hadn't heard before—a story of receiving a desperate phone call last week. Riley was asking for a favor, but his reasoning had been so vague that Lloyd had suspected he wasn't receiving the whole truth.

"But with Riley," the president said, "I knew there had to be a good reason. So I politely informed one of our proud Marines that he would be guarding one of our secret military installations down in the Antarctic if he didn't let Riley through his checkpoint."

The crowd laughed.

"So I'd like to offer my heartfelt apologies to that Marine, and my even more heartfelt assurances to the attending press that no, we do not really have any secret military installations down in the Antarctic."

More laughter.

But Khadi's mind had already drifted away again. *He wanted to get to me so badly that he pulled in a favor from the president?* Winnie must have been thinking the same thing because she turned to Khadi and smiled. But Khadi didn't return the smile; her mind was too troubled.

Why did you do it, Riley? I wasn't worth your life. Really! I know myself; I know how messed up I am inside.

But you . . . you've touched so many people, done so much good. You should be sitting here listening to stories about me, not the other way around. You were worth any ten of me. It should have been me, not you! It should have been me!

Mercifully, the service ended. It took a while to clear everybody out, and Khadi made small talk with the RoU analysts while she waited.

Finally their turn to exit came, and they all filed out into the open air. Khadi gave hugs to all the ops men and the kids from the RoU. There were still a lot of unanswered questions surrounding the ties between Saifullah's group and all the other attacks that had taken place a week ago, which meant that taking the time for this memorial service was a luxury they would have to pay for with many extra hours at their workstations.

Next she said good-bye to Alan Paine and Gladys Cook. Suddenly, the whirr of cameras sounded around her. The media, her constant companion since getting back to DC, absolutely ate up stories of her with Alan and Gladys. These pictures would probably soon be at supermarket checkout lines across America.

"Sorry about them," Khadi said as she held Gladys.

"Oh, don't worry about that," she replied. "At my age, it's about time I got my fifteen minutes of fame."

Next Khadi turned to Alan. "Thank you. I couldn't have survived without you,"

"You've got it wrong. You were the inspiration to all of us," Alan said.

Khadi stepped back, surprised.

"It's true, Khadi. Seeing your strength—well, we just held on to it. Honestly, what I kept telling the other guys was, 'If that little girl can take what she's taken and keep the fire burning, what excuse do we have?' I wanted to tell you that before the service, but I didn't get the chance. So thank you . . . from all of us." He kissed her cheek and turned away.

Tears formed in Khadi's eyes as she watched Gladys and Alan disappear into the crowds.

I gave them strength? Really? If that's true, then maybe . . . I don't know. Just thank you, Alan. I think maybe that's twice now you've given me my life back.

When she turned around, Scott, Tara, and Skeeter were looking at her. Grandpa and Winnie were in deep conversation with Keith Simmons about fifteen feet away.

"Walk with us," Scott said as he put his arm around her shoulder and led her to the many steps leading down from the Capitol building.

"But what about . . . ?" Khadi said, looking toward Grandpa, Winnie, and Keith.

"They'll catch up."

They walked the steps in silence, and when they reached the bottom, Scott led her around to a fountain that stood at the base of the Capitol grounds.

He sat her down on a low stone wall opposite the fountain and squatted in front of her. Tara sat next to her, while Skeeter glared the paparazzi back to a safe distance.

"So what's going on?" Khadi asked warily. "I kind of feel like I'm having an intervention."

When Scott didn't smile at her little joke, it just raised Khadi's concern level that much more.

He reached into his jacket pocket but kept his hand there. "Before Riley went into the cathedral, he said there was one more thing he had to do. He took my iPhone, disappeared for a few minutes, and then came back saying that he had recorded something on it—for you. He said that if he survived, I was to delete it without watching it. But if he . . ." Scott's voice cracked, and he stopped. Then he pulled out his iPhone. "He wanted you to see this."

Khadi took the phone in her hands. She didn't know how to feel—excited, afraid, nervous. "Did he record any others?"

"No," Scott said, shaking his head. "Just to you."

"Do you want us to leave you alone?" Tara asked.

"No . . . I—I think I'd rather you stayed."

Tara put her arm around Khadi's shoulders; Scott placed his hand on her knee.

Riley's face was frozen as if he were in the middle of a word. His hair was sticking up a bit, like he either hadn't combed it or he had been sweating and running his fingers through it. He was wearing a hoodie jacket, and she could see an MPDC SWAT truck behind him. Her finger hovered over the phone. Taking a deep breath, she touched the screen, and his face suddenly animated.

". . . hope that I'm working this thing right."

The phone spun and Khadi saw all the police and military that were surrounding the cathedral. Then it spun back around. "Looks good, I think. Khadi . . . Khadi, what do I say? I had all this stuff in my head when I went to get Scott's phone. Now it just seems like so many words."

The shot was shaky and his face wasn't always centered. But Khadi soon picked up the rhythm of the picture and was able just to focus on Riley's words.

"I guess . . . I guess if there were two things that I want you to know more than anything, the first would be that I love you—always have, always will. From the moment you told me that you Persians serve your coffee with toothpicks, I was hooked. I love everything about you—your huge heart, your amazing smile, your sense of humor, your inner strength, your . . . your . . . I don't know. There're a lot of other *yours*, but the situation here is kind of forcing a blank on my mind. I think we really could have had an amazing life together if it weren't for that whole Christian/Muslim thing."

Riley's face took on a grave look, and Khadi could hear frustration in his voice.

"Ah, Khadi, that whole Christian/Muslim thing . . . I don't know why God gave me such an amazingly deep love for someone that I could never have. I've asked Him, yelled at Him, begged Him. But as much as I tried to argue with God, I never could seem to convince Him that my way was best. Maybe that's why He's God and I'm not."

Riley looked offscreen, and the shot slipped down to his chest. After a moment he said, "Just two more minutes. Just two."

Looking back at the camera, he said, "Sorry, I really don't want to rush this, but . . . Listen, I know you're probably struggling with the fact that you're alive and I'm . . . not. Please don't. Please, please, Khadi, you gotta know that I would do it again a thousand times over for you. I love you, Khadi, and it feels so good to finally say those words to you, and I'm so sorry that I've never said them before. I truly, truly love you."

He stopped now and seemed to be thinking over his next words.

"But the second thing you need to know—and please hear me out on this—is that I'm not the only one who loves you. And I'm not the only who has died for you. Jesus loves you more than I ever could. He died for you, Khadi, and an eternity with Him is only a relationship away.

"Khadi, I left my Bible on the kitchen table this morning. I want you to have it. Truly, it's the most precious thing I own. My whole life is written up in the pages of that book.

"But more than that, eternal life is written up in that book. Promise me you'll read it. Start with the book of John. All you need to know about Jesus, his sacrifice, and his amazing gift of salvation is in that Gospel—John 1:12; John 3:16; 14:6; 15:13— ah, Khadi, it's got everything! Please, Khadi. I promise you . . . I promise you that once you really look into the Bible—really read it and study it—everything I've been saying to you will make sense. And whatever doesn't make sense, just ask Mom about. You know there's nothing that would please her more than to be able to guide you along.

"I know I'm raving. It's just . . . you know how you always talked about me not being afraid of dying and how I can always seem so peaceful in any situation? It's because I know, I absolutely know, that when I close my eyes for the last time here in this life and open them for the first time beyond, I will see my Savior's face. And if you're watching this, that's where I am right now, with my Savior experiencing some pretty freaking amazing things. You throw your lot in with Jesus, you'll never, ever have to be afraid of death again!

"Khadi, I so desperately want to see you there too. Sure, partly for my sake, but mostly for yours. Eternity's just a prayer away, my love. Jesus is holding out that free gift of grace, of mercy, of salvation. I'd give my life a hundred times over for you to take that gift.

"Ah, man, I'm babbling now. I . . . Please get my Bible. Promise me you'll read it. That's all I ask. I just really want to see you there."

Again, Riley looked offscreen. "Okay, Skeet; thanks."

"Listen, I've got to run. I truly hope you never have to watch this, but if you do, just know that everything's okay for me. Jesus loves you so much, Khadi, and I . . . I love you more than I could ever say." Riley stared at the camera like he had one more thing to say, but then his finger went to the screen and the picture froze.

Winnie, who had arrived while Khadi was watching the video, sat down, and Khadi buried herself in her arms and cried. She cried for their wasted past. She cried for their absent future. She cried because she missed Riley so unbelievably much. And she cried because for the first time since he had died she truly believed that one day she would see him again.

JASON ELAM spent 17 years as a placekicker in the NFL before recently retiring. He was born in Fort Walton Beach, Florida, and grew up in Atlanta, Georgia. In 1988, Jason received a full football scholarship to the University of Hawaii, where he played for four years, earning academic All-America and Kodak All-America honors. He graduated in 1992 with a bachelor's degree in communications and was drafted in the third round of the 1993 NFL draft by the Denver Broncos, where he played for 15 years.

In 1997 and 1998, Jason won back-to-back world championships with the Broncos and was selected to the Pro Bowl in 1995, 1998, and 2001. He is currently working on a master's degree in global apologetics at Liberty Theological Seminary and has an abiding interest in Middle East affairs, the study of Scripture, and defending the Christian faith. Jason is also a licensed commercial airplane pilot. He and his wife, Tamy, have five children and live in Alaska.

STEVE YOHN grew up as a pastor's kid in Fresno, California, and both of those facts contributed significantly to his slightly warped perspective on life. Steve graduated from Multnomah Bible College with a bachelor's degree in biblical studies and barely survived a stint as a youth pastor.

While studying at Denver Seminary, Steve worked as a videographer for Youth for Christ International, traveling throughout the world to capture the ministry's global impact. Most recently, he has stepped into the position of senior pastor of Strasburg Community Church in Strasburg, Colorado. With more than two decades of ministry experience, both inside and outside the church, Steve has discovered his greatest satisfactions lie in writing, speaking, and one-on-one mentoring.

Surprisingly, although his hobbies are reading classic literature, translating the New Testament from the Greek, and maintaining a list of political leaders of every country of the world over the last 25 years, he still occasionally gets invited to parties and has a few friends. His wife, Nancy, and their daughter are the joys of his life.

2003
OPERATION ENDURING FREEDOM
BAGRAM VALLEY
HELMAND PROVINCE, AFGHANISTAN

His count was off. Second Lieutenant Riley Covington of the United States Air Force Special Operations Command was on watch at a perimeter security post. He had been lying at the top of a low rise, watching his sector, for four hours, and each time he had counted the boulders on the hill across the small valley, he had come up with thirty-six. This time, however, the count reached thirty-seven. *Keep it together, buddy*, Riley thought as he rubbed his eyes. He shifted slightly to try to allow the point of a rock that had been boring into his left leg to begin a new hole. *I have no doubt these guys scattered these rocks out here 'cause they knew we were coming.*

"You seeing anything, Taps?" Riley whispered into his comm. At the other security post, located on the opposite side of the harbor site, Airman First Class Armando Tapia was stretched out behind a small, hastily constructed rock wall.

"Everything's good to go," came the reply.

On this sixth night of their mission, Riley had chosen a less-than-ideal position to set up their camp. He didn't feel too bad, however; there were probably fewer than a half dozen ideal sites in this whole desolate valley. He was positioned on a low hill to the east of his Operational Detachment Alpha, and Tapia was planted to the north of the team. Rising on the south and west of the ODA camp were steep cliffs. If anyone wanted to approach their bivouac, they would have to come through one of the two security posts.

Typically, AFSOC missions were carried out singly or in pairs. The special-ops personnel were dropped in from high altitude to take meteorologic and geographic measurements, then silently evacuated. Very clean, very quiet. But Riley's team had lost three members in this area during the last two weeks. So it was on to plan B—take in a group and protect everyone's backside.

The moon exposed the barren landscape, eliminating the need for vision enhancement. Riley shifted again and flexed his fingers to keep the cool night air from cramping them. A scorpion skittered up to check out the rustle. Riley's number-two man, Staff Sergeant Scott Ross, said these creatures were called *orthochirus afghanus Kovarik*; Riley preferred to call them the "nasty little black ones." A well-placed flick sent the arachnid careering down the front side of the hill. *Time to start counting boulders again.*

Riley Covington knew that if he could survive this tour in Afghanistan, chances were good that by this time next year, the scenery around him would look a whole lot better. He was two years out of the Air Force Academy, where he had been a three-time WAC/MWC Defensive Player of the Year and, as a senior, had won the Butkus Award as the nation's top linebacker. He was six-two, rock hard, and lightning fast. His nickname at the Academy had been Apache—later shortened to "Pach"—after the AH-64 attack helicopter. *Hit 'em low, hit 'em hard, hit 'em fast!* Riley had sent more opposing players staggering to the sidelines than he could count. Once, a writer for the *Rocky Mountain News* had compared his hitting ability to Mike Singletary's, the infamous linebacker who had broken sixteen helmets during his college days at Baylor. He still felt proud when he thought about that comparison.

Two years earlier, Riley had been selected by the Colorado Mustangs in the third round of the Pro Football League draft, and commentators believed Riley had the possibility of a promising PFL career ahead of him. However, his post-Academy commitment meant putting that opportunity off for a couple of years. In the meantime, he had spent his last two thirty-day leaves in Mustangs training camps before rushing back out to wherever AFSOC wanted him next.

Riley's insides tensed as he came to the end of his count. *Thirty-four, thirty-five, thirty-six . . . thirty-seven . . . thirty-eight! Something is definitely happening here,* he thought.

WHOOMPF! The unmistakable sound of a mortar tube echoed through the valley below.

"Incoming!" Riley yelled as he opened fire with his M4 carbine at "boulders" thirty-seven and thirty-eight, causing one to stumble back down the hill and the other to remain permanently where it was.

A flare lit up the night sky as heavy machine-gun fire, rocket-propelled grenades, and small arms rounds targeted Riley's ODA. Riley looked to his left and saw an anticoalition militia approaching from the north, right over Tapia's position. Riley, seeing the size of the enemy force, let off a few more three-shot bursts, then bolted back down to the harbor site.

He took cover in a low ditch and scanned the camp. What he saw was not encouraging. Four of his ODA members were down—two with what looked like some pretty major shrapnel wounds. There was no sign of Tapia anywhere. The rest of his squad was scattered around the camp, pinned under the heavy barrage. One of their patrol Humvees had been hit with an RPG, and the large quantity of ammunition inside was cooking off. This situation was spiraling downward fast.

Movement caught his eye. It was Scott Ross, lying flat behind some empty petrol cans and waving to catch Riley's attention. Using hand signals, Ross indicated that his com was down and pointed back toward the second patrol vehicle.

Riley looked in the direction Ross was pointing and saw their salvation. Off to his left, about fifteen meters away, an MK19 automatic grenade launcher was mounted on its low tripod. Riley quickly signaled back to Ross to provide full-automatic cover fire, then rocketed out from safety and across the dirt. He almost made it. Something hit him in the hip, spinning him counterclockwise in midair.

He landed hard, gasping for air. As he tried to get up, a mixture of stinging and deep, throbbing pain dropped him down flat. He knew his men desperately needed him, but he couldn't move. Helplessness quickly overwhelmed him. *Lord, I can't stay down, but I don't know if I can get up! Give me what I need! Please, give me what I need!*

Ross was shouting at him, but the surrounding noise made it impossible for Riley to make out the words. Without the Mark 19, their chances were bleak.

Mustering all the strength he had left, Riley began pulling himself the rest of the way to the weapon. Bullets danced all around him, kicking up puffs of dirt into his face and clanging against the nearby Humvee. With each grab of the rocky ground, his adrenaline increased. Finally, the endorphins began to get the best of the pain, and Riley was able to get his feet under him. He stumbled forward, launched himself behind the Mark 19, and let loose.

It took him just under a minute and a half to empty the ammunition can of sixty grenades. The sound was deafening, and the explosions from the shells hitting the enemy positions lit up the night. Riley knew from experience that there was nothing to do but fall back in the face of that kind of fire, which was exactly what the enemy militia did. But RPGs and mortar rounds kept dropping into the camp.

Riley signaled for Ross to come and load another can of ammo on the Mark 19. Then he half ran, half staggered over to what remained of his ODA. The rest of his team huddled around him and he took a quick head count. Besides Ross, there were Dawkins, Logan, Murphy, Posada, and Li. *Not good.* They would be outnumbered if a second wave came.

"Posada, contact the command-and-control nodes in the rear and request immediate close air support and a medical-evacuation flight."

"Yes, sir!"

Riley drew his team close. "Okay, men, we have two options. We dig in here and try to hold off another attack, or we surprise them while they're regrouping."

"Tell ya what, Pach," said Kim "Tommy" Li, a man with an itchy trigger finger and way too many tattoos, "if there's gonna be target practice going on here, I'd rather be the shooter than the bull's-eye."

Riley laid out his plan. "Okay, then, here's how it's going to work: I'm guessing they'll feint another attack from the north, but their main force will come from the east, because that's where the Mark 19 is. They know that if they don't take the Mark out, they're toast. So, Murphy and Li, I want you to belly out to those boulders twenty meters north to meet their feint. Logan, you and Ross remount the Mark on the Humvee and get her ready to go head-to-head with their onrush. Dawkins, you and I'll hit the east security post. When you all hear us start firing, circle the Humvee around east; then everyone open up with everything and blow the snot out of these desert rats. Got it?"

An excited mixture of "Yes, sir" and "Yeah, boy" was heard from the men.

"Excellent! Posada, sweeten up our coordinates with command."

"You got it, Pach," Posada said as he pounded away on his Toughbook—a nearly indestructible laptop computer perfect for use in combat.

"We've got five of our guys down, with at least one probably out—that's unacceptable. Let's make 'em pay." Riley locked eyes with each member of his team and tried to draw from them the same courage he was attempting to instill. "Dawkins, don't wait for me to hit that security post with you! Ready . . . go, go, go!!"

Skeeter Dawkins was a good old boy from Mississippi. Fiercely loyal to Riley, there were several times when he had to be pulled off of fellow team members who he thought had disrespected their lieutenant. He was big, strong, fast, and knew only two words when under fire: *Yes* and *sir*.

Dawkins ran out ahead and was already in position by the time Riley got there and dropped next to him with a grunt of pain. Sixty meters out, Riley could see between forty and fifty well-armed enemy militia members prepping for another attack. "I'm guessing they're not done with us yet, Skeet."

"Yes, sir." It sounded more like *Yeah, zir.*

"Looks like they'll be feinting inside while rolling a flank around left. Must be boring being so predictable."

"Yes, sir."

The two men lay silently for a minute, watching the preparations of their enemies. Riley turned to look at the empty sky behind them. "Sure would like to see that air support come in right about now."

"Mmm."

"Skeet, anyone ever tell you that you ain't much of a conversationalist?" It was hard not to slip into a Mississippi drawl when talking with Skeeter.

Skeeter grinned. "Yes, sir."

The random actions of the enemy force suddenly coalesced into an organized forward movement.

"Looks like the Afghani welcome wagon's rolling again."

"Yes, sir."

"Skeeter Dawkins, you gonna let any of those boys through here?"

Skeeter turned to Riley. He looked genuinely hurt at his lieutenant's attempt to force an expansion of his vocabulary.

Riley laughed. Nothing like feigned confidence to hide what you're really feeling. "Don't you worry, airman. Just make sure you give them a gen-u-ine Mississippi welcome."

Skeeter smiled. "Yes, sir!"

Riley could hear the muffled sound of the Humvee starting up as he and Skeeter readied their M4s. Red dots from each of their M68 Close Combat Optics landed nose level on the first two attackers. Their fingers hugged the triggers.

The sudden whine of two Apache helicopters halted Riley's counterattack. The 30 mm cannons mounted on either side of the choppers strafed the enemy force. The ensuing carnage was hard to watch. One life after another was snuffed out in rapid succession.

When the last bad guy stopped moving, the Apaches turned and headed back to where they'd come from. Skeeter pulled Riley to his feet and helped him down the hill. Pain crashed through Riley's hip, and his left leg buckled. Kim Li rushed over and slipped himself under Riley's other arm.

"Well, Pach, it was a good plan," Li laughed. "Guess I'll have to take my target practice elsewhere."

Riley knew it was just Li's adrenaline talking, but he still had a hard time not laying into him. Too much blood had been spilled and too many screams filled the night air to be joking about killing just now.

Back at the harbor site, an MH-53 Pave Low was just dropping in to evacuate the team. Riley was eased onto a stretcher and carried the rest of the way. As he was lifted onto the helicopter with the two dead and five injured, football was the furthest thing from his mind.

Riley Covington's hand shot out, clicking the alarm to Off just before the numbers shifted to 5:30 a.m. This was a game Riley played against the clock every morning, trying to wake up as close as he could to his alarm time without having to hear the obnoxious chirp. He was pretty good at it too. His days at the United States Air Force Academy had ingrained in him a sense of time that most people would find borderline compulsive.

He tossed his down comforter off and slowly swung his body out of bed, feeling the cold hardwood floor under his feet. The firmness of his mattress could be manually adjusted, and for the two days after each game, his bumps and bruises forced him to put the setting at "way soft."

Moving to the window, he pulled the drapes back, and instantly the room filled with white light. The sun wasn't up yet, but the reflection of the moon on the fresh snow made Riley squint. *Why would anyone want to live anywhere else?* he mused. He had always loved the Colorado winter—the frost on the windows, the muted sounds caused by a blanket of snow, the feel of a cold house in the morning while you're still warm under the blankets.

Feeling invigorated, he padded into the kitchen, flicked on Fox News, and began to assemble the ingredients for his daily breakfast shake—a simple concoction of protein powder, soy milk, whey, and frozen berries. As the blender whirred to life, Riley read the crawl at the bottom of the television screen.

HOMICIDE BOMBER IN NETANYA, ISRAEL, KILLS FOUR AND WOUNDS SEVENTEEN.

Riley's anger flashed. This was the fifth bombing in the past two weeks. What was the matter with these people? Didn't they care whom they killed? Didn't they know that these women and children had nothing to do with their war?

As he stewed on this, his mind drifted back to a conversation he'd had with Tim Clayton, the senior pastor of Parker Hills Community Church, his home church when he could attend.

"I'm sick and tired of hearing people say we need to have compassion for these murderers and understand their belief system," Riley had said the day a Palestinian bomber had killed fourteen people on a bus in Haifa.

"No one can make you love anyone, Riley," Pastor Tim countered. "But keep in mind that these people are caught up in one of the greatest lies ever perpetrated on mankind—the lie that it is worth killing others for your beliefs. These people need our prayers, they need our pity, and they need the power of our nation to try to stop them before they throw their lives away like this."

"I'm with you on your last point," Riley responded. "They need to feel a serious U.S. smackdown. But, Tim, you haven't seen what I've seen. You haven't seen your buddies lying in pieces in front of you. You haven't seen the children mangled by the screws and ball bearings from some terrorist wacko's bomb. I'm sorry, but pity's something I really have a hard time with right now."

"I understand," Tim had said gently. "Maybe because I haven't seen it, I can keep more of an objective viewpoint. I just know that the moment after these men—and women now—detonate their bombs, they've got a huge surprise waiting for them."

Riley's brain knew Tim was right. Convincing his heart was a different matter. *I gotta mull this over a different time. I've got work to do.*

He chugged the purple liquid right out of the blender—no use dirtying a glass—then moved back through the bedroom and into the bathroom, where he cranked the shower to full blast. Fifteen minutes steaming up the glass stall would work out the kinks in his body and leave him ready to start another day.

Riley felt great, especially for fourteen weeks into a PFL season as a starting linebacker. He had always taken care of himself physically—even as a cadet at the Academy—and it paid off this late in the season. While other guys' bodies were starting to break down, he was still at the top of his game. He knew that he was living an American dream—a dream that could disappear with one good hit or one wrong step—so he did everything he could to make the best of it.

///////////////////////

After his role in Operation Enduring Freedom, Riley had been unsure what would be next for him. He could have had a very promising career as an officer in AFSOC. He knew how to lead men and was able to garner their respect through his example. Besides that, the military was in his blood. His father had been a navy man in Vietnam, and his grandfather had flown an F-86 in Korea, chalking up seven MiGs to his credit. Riley's choice to try for the Air Force Academy in Colorado Springs rather than the Naval Academy in Annapolis had led to all sorts of good-natured ribbing of his dad by his grandpa. Holidays with the family had never been the same again.

Although he knew the military was an honorable profession, Riley still had that Pro Football League dream. He'd been on leave on draft day, and he could still feel the incredible tension he experienced while sitting in his parents' living room. The talk on ESPN was whether any team would pick this year's Butkus Award winner, since, like all Academy graduates, he had a five-year military commitment hanging over his head. As the picks progressed, it was hard for him not to get disheartened.

All the pundits said Riley had the skills to be a first rounder, but he'd begun to wonder if the specter of mandatory military service was just too much for most PFL teams. Riley's dad kept feeding him words of encouragement, and his mom kept feeding him lemon pound cake. Half a day and three-quarters of a cake later, he finally heard his name called in the third round. The cheers in the Draft Central auditorium could only be matched by the screams in that little house. To be chosen in the PFL draft and to be chosen by the Colorado Mustangs—what could be better than that?

The selection had been a definite risk for the organization, but they felt it was worth it if they could bag someone with Riley's playing potential. Of course, both Riley and the team would have to wait. Riley had no problem with serving out his commitment. He was more than willing to fight for his country—die for it if necessary.

And he had come fairly close to doing just that. The bullet he had taken during the firefight back in the Bagram Valley in Afghanistan had entered just above his hip. It had chipped a bone and caused a lot of bleeding, but thanks to the quick medical evacuation and the incredible medical team at Ramstein Air Base in Germany, the only lingering issue he had was a dull ache when the weather turned.

After returning from Germany, Riley had been called to his commanding officer's desk. The CO had looked up directly at Riley. "Covington, I brought you in here to make you an offer I hope you won't take. The higher-ups want me to give you the ludicrous choice of opting out of the rest of your full-time service commitment to the United States Air Force so you can go play in the Pro Football League. You'd stay in the reserves, and we'd have you in the off-season until your time's up. Now, I've seen you lead men, and I've seen you save lives. I think it would be a shame for you to give up the chance to make a lasting difference for this country so that you could go play some kids' game. But, hey, that's the choice I'm told I have to offer you. You've got twenty-four hours. Dismissed."

Riley had struggled with the choice as he walked back down the willow-lined street to his quarters. A lot of what his CO had said was right. Would choosing the PFL be taking the easier and less meaningful way out? But he could still make a difference in many people's lives playing football, right? And he certainly wouldn't be the first guy to follow such a path.

The precedent for a professional athlete opting out of military obligations had been set after the first Gulf War. Chad Hennings had returned a war hero after having flown A-10 Warthogs during the liberation of Kuwait. Although he had a long commitment still awaiting him, the Air Force believed he would serve them better in a public-relations role. It turned out to be a great decision; Chad had taken the opportunity to help lead his football team to three championships during the nineties.

Once the door was opened, others had stepped through. Steve Russ and Chris Gizzi both served full-time for a couple of years after the Academy, then completed the bulk of their service in the reserves during the summers while spending most of the year playing professional ball.

Riley wrestled with the decision through the night. He had made a commitment to the Air Force, and he did not take that lightly. The guys of his squad depended on his leadership, yet to a man they told him he would be a complete idiot not to jump at this opportunity. Still, he held back.

Finally, early the next morning, a three-way call had come from his dad and grandpa.

"God has given you the abilities and the opportunity to do something that few people have a chance to do," Grandpa Covington had said. "Obviously, He's got something special in mind for you."

"Riles," his dad said, "you know that whatever decision you make, we'll be proud of you. We're much more concerned about who you are than what you do."

By the time Riley hung up the phone, it was like a weight had been lifted from his shoulders. He finally felt free to pursue his dream. Why it was so important to get the go-ahead from these two men, he couldn't say. Maybe he wanted their affirmation, maybe he wanted their wisdom, or maybe it was just plain old respect for their opinion. All he knew was that their words were the key that opened the door to his PFL career. Six months later, he said his final good-byes to full-time Air Force life.

Riley chuckled to himself as he thought about the final party his squad had thrown for him before he left AFSOC. He had never seen so much alcohol in his life. While he nursed his Diet Coke, his guys gave speeches that became more syrupy and less coherent as the night wore on. Skeeter Dawkins gave him a tribute that stretched out for a record eighteen words, and Kim Li actually cried during his fourth toast of the evening. The party had officially ended with last call at 2 a.m., but Riley had spent until four thirty driving his men home.

Two weeks after that, he was running onto the Mustangs' practice field at the Inverness Training Center.

DON'T MISS ONE THRILLING MOMENT.

Look for all four Riley Covington thrillers,
available now in bookstores and online.